Zebras Crossing

Rebecca Gregson is a freelance journalist and former radio presenter for BBC Radio Cornwall. She lives with her husband and two young children in Cornwall, where she is currently working on her third novel.

Zebras Crossing

Rebecca Gregson

LONDON · SYDNEY · NEW YORK · TOKYO · SINGAPORE · TORONTO

First published in Great Britain by Pocket Books, 2000
An Imprint of Simon & Schuster UK Ltd
A Viacom Company

1 3 5 7 9 10 8 6 4 2

Simon & Schuster UK Ltd
Africa House
64-78 Kingsway
London WC2B 6AH

Simon & Schuster Australia
Sydney

A CIP catalogue record for this book is available from the British Library

ISBN 0-671-01594-X

Typeset in Sabon by SX Composing DTP, Rayleigh, Essex
Printed and bound in Great Britain by
Caledonian International Book Manufacturing Ltd, Glasgow

For Sloey, brave, vulnerable and still smiling.
My love always.

*Acknowledgements*

I could not have written this book without the total support of my sister, Debbie Nevins-Pickford. Special thanks are also due to Liz Luck, Matthew, Sharon Thomas and Leigh Chambers at the British Agencies for Adoption and Fostering, and to Jilly Luck for sharing with me some of her vast professional knowledge of neo-natal care.

Author's Note

When I was three, my parents adopted my little sister Debs. She is black, I am white, and so we are obviously different creatures. But at the same time, we share enough to be similar. I grew up thinking she had everything she wanted, she grew up knowing there was something missing. On one level, everything about this story is fiction, but it would be nice if it wasn't. The truth is not only stranger, it is more painful. The good thing though is that we still know each other, we still love each other, and we still laugh our heads off at things that no one else finds in the slightest bit funny.

Rebecca Gregson

Author's Note

[illegible]

[illegible]

Chapter 1

April 1968: The Rev Dr Martin Luther King Jr, assassinated a week ago as he leaned over a balcony at a Memphis Hotel, is to be buried in Atlanta today. The charismatic son of a prominent Negro preacher will be taken to his final resting place in a simple coffin on a wooden farm cart drawn by two mules. More than 15,000 people are expected to follow. Among the mourners who, at his widow's request, will hear the tape of his last sermon, will be Mrs Jacqueline Kennedy and the Vice-President, Hubert Humphrey.

If her subconscious was anything to go by, Honor Lovell knew she had a battle on her hands from day one. It was hardly a surprise that she slept badly given her natural disposition towards insomnia, but in the few fitful hours that her body did succumb she dreamed (of all the crazy things for someone usually too scared to even go out of her depth) that she was a cross-Channel swimmer.

The sandman was in a ruthless mood that night. He was only passing, but he still made her forsake the soft haven of her quilted mattress for the muddy and barren sands of the cold Norfolk beach a mile away. No matter that any foray from such windswept shores would have led to Skegness or Siberia, Honor knew exactly where she had to go. Her slight body shivered beneath the warmed blankets of her marital bed and, under their lids, her eyes searched the horizon for France.

As she slapped on the layers of thick white grease scooped from a tub on the shore, her trainer – a hybrid of her mother-in-law and Billie Jean King – kept telling her to go steady. 'Too much of that stuff and you'll sink,' the crossbreed said, tapping with a pen on the instructions for use. 'But I'm only skinny,' Honor murmured in her sleep as her voice was carried away by the sea breeze, 'and besides, I need all the help I can get.'

In the big wide nightmare of the ocean, the rollers came thick and fast. Every single time they engulfed her she thought she hadn't got the breath left to re-surface, but then she caught the distant cheer of a small voice and she somehow managed to keep her head above water.

By the time she finally woke in a tangle of bedclothes, only two fragments had survived the journey into her conscious mind – the size of the waves and the persistence of the voice. It didn't matter that she couldn't remember the rest because she knew she had found the courage of her convictions at last.

It was a massive metaphor of a dream. When she told John – there was never any *if* with them – he would undoubtedly add a cautious footnote to remind her that the real challenge still lay ahead. But for her, this was the moment of victory. Every last vestige of self-doubt had finally been drowned. If her body couldn't provide the second child she craved, an adoption agency certainly could. And why should a black baby be any different from a white? They could do it now, she *knew* they could.

Honor sat up, bent her knees to make a tent with the vast patchwork quilt she'd poured her soul and God knows how much midnight oil into over the last few bewildering years, and picked up her bedside diary. In small capital letters at the top of the space for that day's date, being careful to leave plenty more room for what was to come, she wrote DREAMT I SWAM THE CHANNEL. WOKE FEELING INVINCIBLE. Then she looked around her bedroom, expecting to see everything in a new light.

The powder-blue mini-skirt still in its polythene cover was hanging on the wardrobe door. Oh God. It looked limp, like *it* couldn't bear the weight of so many hopes being pinned on it either, and for a split second, she was back treading water again. Could they really do this? *Should* they do this? Would they ultimately be *allowed* to do this?

She forced herself to think of something else – her local dry cleaners for instance, who had come up with a headline-grabbing ploy to charge for skirts by the inch rather than the garment. The same photograph of a leggy model passing the poster in the launderette window had been syndicated to all the newspapers and, without conferring, every sub-editor from the *Mirror* to *The Times* had used captions along the lines of *The shorter it is, the cheaper it gets*. Anything that 'captured the spirit of the age', as editorials continually phrased it.

So, if her skirt had cost her three shillings and fourpence at twopence an inch – the cogs of her overwound brain turned slowly – it must be twenty inches long. She heaped the quilt, sheet and blankets on to John's comatose body, and with her fingers she walked twenty small steps from her waist down her narrow bare thigh.

There, the diversion lost its effectiveness. Was that a suitable length for someone offering herself up as a mother? Would it be better if she wore the matching jacket, or was that too stiff for what had been described as an informal visit? What was the ideal mother supposed to look like anyway? Most people would assume she already knew.

She ran through a panicky inventory of her wardrobe for alternatives. Hipsters? Kaftan? What did people expect from a twenty-eight-year-old woman nowadays? The previous guidelines were all to pot, so to speak.

'Adoption is a huge step, and I advise you to leave no stone unturned,' Father Michael had cautioned when she'd chosen the local priest as their only confidant at the beginning. John had accused her of taking his pastoral exhortations too far. Boulders – even pebbles – were fair enough, but according to her husband, she'd been kicking up the merest chipping. That was just looking for trouble, he said.

If only he would wake up, she could tell him she wouldn't be doing, didn't *need* to do that any more. She let her knees fall apart and her right one hit his back almost on purpose, but the sudden contact made no difference. He'd have to wake soon anyway, if they were going to stick to the timetable they'd drawn up for the day.

It amazed her that sleep should come so easily to John when she had to practically snake-charm it. If ever she should have fallen asleep quickly, it was last night. She had feared that the removal of her quenched and redundant womb would make her feel less like a woman, not more, so the return of her seductive powers post-hysterectomy had been a happy surprise for both of them. Spontaneous sex was now actually playing a part in their marriage again, after nearly two years of merely going through the motions, and it was such a relief.

Yesterday evening, high on nothing more than anticipation, they'd made love in the kitchen with the lights on and the blinds up, and then again later, in bed. Just before John's breathing had moved down a peg, he'd murmured something she thought she should write down somewhere, for posterity. He was good like that. He couldn't always be relied upon to speak when required, but every now and then when the pressure was off, he'd come out with a gem.

'You could say that was like a sort of conception.'

'Mmm?'

'The consummation of an idea.'

'I love that.'

The suggestion that Frances, the child they'd not yet met but who in their minds was already kissed and tucked up in a bed just along the landing, had in one way actually been *conceived* by them swamped her with excitement. But she could tell her husband was already sliding into sleep and in that minute she'd resigned herself to insomnia. Somehow, it was always more inevitable on the nights that oblivion came to John so effortlessly. His creation analogy had hit a rich stream of thought to keep her occupied, although to be pedantic, he was only half right. The conception of their intent had happened not last night but (coincidentally) exactly nine months ago. *That* was when the first seeds of the idea had been sown. Then there had been the gestation – months and months of forms and appointments and questions. And now labour was imminent. No wonder she couldn't sleep. Every mother-to-be she'd ever known worried about a safe delivery, herself included, the previous and the only time round.

She wondered not for the first time how many of their close circle would celebrate this new arrival with them. How many teddies would they get this time? How many cards? How many cold shoulders? At least Morgan and Brian would embrace the idea – once they knew, obviously.

Their warts-and-all friendship thrived on its unconventional beginning. In 1955, John had been a young art teacher at a private boys' school and Brian Hanlon had easily been his most talented pupil. With only seven years between them they were really contemporaries, but institution protocol ruled and they had never found a good enough excuse to speak outside the art department. When Brian's final Speech Day came, however, and John had to shake his hand on the rickety wooden stage in the marquee, he didn't say, 'Well done,' like he'd said to all the others, he said, 'Come for a drink after all this. I've got something to show you.' This of course had become Brian's favourite story, which he embellished with fictional extras such as how in that split second he'd seen John as a convincing predator of young boys. Actually, what John *had* wanted to show him was a Newlyn School sketch he'd just bought in a junk shop for three shillings, something Brian now joked was enough to arouse him anyway.

After that, they'd kept in touch in the sporadic way men do but it wasn't until their women later came along that the pattern of enduring friendship was established.

It was odd that Honor and John had so far chosen to tell them nothing – but then again, maybe it wasn't. Playing devil's advocate was something they all did to each other. If any one of them dared moot a half-baked opinion or ill-considered plan, the other three felt it their moral duty to shoot it down in flames. Even with two against two, Morgan and Brian would have provided too formidable a sounding board before now.

But – thank God – this plan was no longer half-baked or

ill-considered. And anyway, Honor's soulmate wouldn't be shocked. Morgan never was. She might, if she was being completely honest, be a little peeved – not because she wanted a family too, but because, as an idea, it was *so* bloody up-to-date.

Oh, that was a thought. If anyone ever accused Honor of doing it for effect, saw their decision as just another gimmick that 'captured the spirit of the age', she'd . . . *uuh!* Every time she tried to blank off one thought process, another would begin. She banged her head back on her pillow in protest at her one-track mind.

At least now, though, she could justify it as the racing of an excited brain rather than the sort of displacement anxiety she'd so regularly propped herself up with over the last few months. She had been that busy worrying about the fine print, she hadn't had time to take in the big. Well, it was different now. She felt as if she'd read the whole contract, start to finish.

John rolled on to his back, returning the heavy jumble of bedclothes to his wife and leaving himself covered only by a crumpled corner of sheet and a blue satin-edged blanket. As Honor reached across him to check the time on his wristwatch on the bedside table, her bottom ribs hit his bare shoulder. They were two bags of bone, with not a spare pound between them. How very un-pregnant I look, Honor thought, but at least it's fashionable. Good old Twiggy.

It was six-thirty. There was little point in staying horizontal any longer so she got up, pulled on a ghastly towelling house-coat that her mother had given her for one of her miserable hospital stays and crept along the landing to Judith's room.

The light was still on, but superfluous now. Honor pinched the switch tightly and pulled it up without a click then soft-footed it over to the bed to watch the gentle rise and fall of her four-year-old daughter's ribs and rounded tummy through her brushed cotton nightdress. There was something so fundamentally reassuring about the oblivion of child-sleep, probably only because it was so entirely different from its elusive adult relative.

Last summer, drained but permanently awake after three miscarriages in twenty months, when insomnia was the one thing she did right, Honor used to steal into the nursery almost every night to study the undeniable evidence of her only successful pregnancy. But even as she stood there contemplating its amazing product, studying the downy skin of her daughter's arms or the untroubled smooth brow, the blemish-free features and the tiny hands, she would wonder why it wasn't enough. She couldn't love Judith more. She was everything. So why, *why*, wasn't she enough?

One morning, John had woken to the increasingly familiar empty space next to him, and found his wife in there on the floor, head on a folded cellular blanket, body curled in that psychological cliché, the foetal position.

'We could adopt,' he'd said tentatively, crouching in his striped pyjama bottoms next to her. He never wore a pyjama jacket, but equally, he never slept naked. Honor used to tease him about it in their first year of marriage, especially when they would lie post-coitally depleted for no more than five minutes before he would sneak his trousers on. He felt the cold, which she never did. Years later, when boxer shorts were the norm, he'd complain about the gaps. 'We could take a child from the bottom of the pile, couldn't we?' he'd said. 'Because let's face it, we've already got one from the top.'

Potent words and still true, she thought now, a whole winter and spring wiser. Judith was barely visible under a heap of bedclothes and knitted animals, but her mother knew exactly what was under there. Healthy, bright, and cherished by socially privileged parents, it was hard to think of an advantage she didn't have.

The child murmured and turned over, her expression cautious even in sleep. The cheek she'd been lying on was red with warmth and several wisps of light brown hair were plastered to it with perspiration or dribble. Honor felt the forehead but there was no temperature, just over-cosiness. She pulled a beige knitted donkey away from her daughter's face and crept out.

If only we could bottle the effect she has on us, Honor thought. Love is all we need to make this work.

Down the open wooden stairs and into the kitchen, she turned on the little blue wireless and was reminded of the day's other major event. Today was not just the day she was going to meet the feisty little face of the much-thumbed photograph in her handbag for the first time – it was also the day Martin Luther King was to be buried in Atlanta. Half the world was awash with grief. Even the normally stiff upper lips of the BBC were quivering their way through the tribute programmes.

'King's career in black civil rights began in 1956 in Alabama when, as a Baptist minister, he organised a successful boycott of the city's buses after one of his flock was arrested for refusing to give up a Whites Only seat. He based his reform movement, which resulted in segregation laws being declared illegal and equal voting rights for blacks, on non-violent disobedience. As a consequence, he was awarded the Nobel Peace Prize in 1964, just before the rise of a more militant black movement under the leadership of activists such as Malcolm X.'

Honor blew the air, still hardly believing that such an inspiration could be wiped out just like that, but as she heaped ground coffee into the percolator, she was shamefully thankful for the distraction. As far as everyone else was aware, this had to be just another ordinary Tuesday. Judith was going to play with a neighbour while she and John went to London to see the current Pop Art exhibition of repetitious silk-screen reproductions featuring the high priest himself, Andy Warhol. Art teachers did that sort of thing in the holidays.

It was such a convincing cover story, she would almost believe it herself if she could. But today already felt like her wedding day, her labour day, Judith's first day at nursery, exam day, graduation day, interview day, all her red-letter days ever rolled into one. In terms of what was resting on her performance in the next few hours, it was the most important day of her life. Not that she could forget – there were a trillion tiny bubbles of hope coursing round her bloodstream to remind her.

Her first priority was not to raise suspicion until everything was more certain. Judith already had worry off to a fine art, particularly over things she didn't fully understand. John was exasperatingly confident that she wouldn't be a problem, but all the same it was essential they made this shift in their family a smooth one. The number of books on their shelves about sibling rivalry had almost overtaken the ones about rearing a first child, although Benjamin Spock's *Commonsense Book of Baby and Child Care* was still the most thumbed. Its radical proposition that a mother's instincts were just as good as any expert's left Honor alternately bold and bewildered, depending on the definition of 'mother'.

In her head, she had written a list. Judith and Frances – an as-yet unknown quantity – were at the top, underlined and level pegging. She and John came next, and then, even though they still had no idea about anything, she'd pencilled in Morgan and Brian. On paper, they weren't key players when it came to the complexities of the extended family, but she knew they would feature strongly in the whole commitment somehow. After that, everyone would have to jockey for their own position. She wondered where her own parents would place themselves. She hoped they would respond reasonably, or at least better than John's; his father was a model of intolerance and his mother simply a sponge.

The radio distracted her again. *'In 1963, on the steps of the Lincoln Memorial in Washington, DC, King delivered his famous "I have a dream" speech to an audience of more than 250,000. That dream was one of racial tolerance, hope for a future in which blacks and whites lived together in an equal society, in a world powered by love . . .'*

Well, she had dreamt too, in a much smaller way. Suddenly, she was exhausted. For two pins, she could have joined the mourners lining the road in Atlanta in their weeping, but it was no good letting the enormity of it get the better of her now. She was a cross-Channel swimmer, remember. And anyway, another twenty minutes and Judith would be up and about.

She went to her handbag and pulled out the photograph from the front pocket. Little runny-nosed Frances. She deserved a more intriguing name. The photographer could have given the nose a wipe – although maybe he'd left it like that on purpose, to make her seem even more in need of a mother than she already was. When she looked more closely though, something behind the child's eyes made her suspect that being needy was not really Frances's thing.

The picture had been given to her by the assigned caseworker, Marjory Roger, a softly spoken Scottish Highlander, on her last visit. On her first, she had produced a whole catalogue full of portraits showing wide-eyed children with puzzled faces.

'We're not supposed to choose from this, are we?' Honor had asked, horrified, as she browsed through the ringbinder file.

'No, no, no, goodness me, no,' Miss Roger had clucked reassuringly. 'It's just my way of helping us to see the children as individuals. Sorry, no, you can't order them by model number, I'm afraid.' And all three of them had laughed then, very nervously, in admission of the fact that it was actually about as far from funny as you could get.

Miss Roger had 'popped back' three times since then, unannounced, as she had said she would. 'I'm often in the area, I'll just call when I'm passing. Don't make any extra effort just in case now. You've got your work cut out for you with wee Judith here, haven't you?'

Her patent court heels were barely on the pedals of her well-kept car before Judith's questions began.

'Who is she?' the child asked accusingly.

'Um, well . . . she's called Miss Roger.' Honor's voice was false and light, hoping her thin reply might be enough.

'But who *is* she?'

'She's . . . oh well, she's a friend of mine. She loves children.'

'Does she love me?'

'I expect so.'

'Then does she want to take me away?'

'No! Of course not.' Honor felt herself trip over the first tip of a landmine poking above the surface of what used to be a bomb-free field. 'You belong to me and Daddy.'

'But she said children needed new families.' Judith's ears may have been small but they were well-tuned, especially to conversations carried on at a level intended to go over her head. Her eyes were keen too. Miss Roger had been given a cup and saucer and not a mug like Morgan and other friends drank out of when they came.

'Ah, well, she didn't mean you, she meant children who don't have Mummies and Daddies.'

'How do they get born then?'

'Oh, they have Mummies and Daddies when they're born, but then they get separated. And some grown-ups don't have children, and some Mummies and Daddies would like more, so people like Miss Roger go round matching them all up.'

'Like the child-catcher in *Chitty Chitty Bang Bang*?' asked Judith, who had to be taken out of the cinema screaming when John had misguidedly taken her to see the new Disney release.

'Er, no, not at all,' said Honor, 'the complete opposite, in fact. Right, what were we doing? Biscuit-making?' This was some minefield, even if it was one they'd chosen to cross voluntarily.

On the fourth and last visit, when Miss Roger had left Frances's photograph and arranged the first visit to Hoarewood Children's Home, she'd said, 'The staff will know she is the recommended child, you will know she's the recommended child, but Frances herself will not. You will not be anything more than Mr and Mrs Lovell who are just visiting for the day. There's no point in raising hopes, is there? Just in case.'

Miss Roger liked the phrase 'just in case' almost as much as she liked reminding them, in her gently assertive Highland way, that 'nothing was certain in this business'. And what an odd business this was when you thought about it.

Better not to think, Honor decided, and went back upstairs to start getting ready. The mini-skirt would be fine. She'd chosen it with Frances in mind anyway, on the basis that it was

Judith's favourite. Who cared what some official for whom this really was just another ordinary Tuesday thought? It was Frances who mattered. It was Frances who this was all about. Wasn't it?

Not long ago, Honor had asked John if he thought their actions could be seen as selfish. 'Of course they could,' he'd replied. Better not to think, she thought again, slipping through the bedroom door.

She managed the grand total of forty-five minutes of not thinking before she succumbed again, by which time Judith had gone unsuspectingly off with the family from the neighbouring farm, clutching the remainder of an Easter egg and a packet of Spangles. John was outside checking the car and Honor stood around like a lost soul in her powder-blue miniskirt and pale pink lipstick, looking for all the world like every orphan's dream mother. The fact that she felt she had much more in common with the orphan made her pick up the phone and finally call Morgan. She was just about to put it down when her friend answered.

'It's me. Sorry it's so early. Did I wake you?'

'Just as well you did – we're supposed to be at an art auction at nine.'

'Anyone special?'

'Another impoverished painter trying to make some studio space. Brian thinks he's quite good though. Is everything OK? You sound a bit strangled.'

'Do I? God, Morgan, you know me too well.'

Twenty miles away in another Norfolk village, Morgan sat down. She knew better than to shriek, 'You're pregnant!' She'd said that too many times over the last few years for it to be a cause for celebration, and anyway, there was no womb there any more.

'Go on.'

'We haven't said anything before because, well, just because, but, well, OK . . .'

'Oh, just tell me!'

'OK. John and I have decided to adopt . . .' Honor's sentence was cut short by her friend's whoop of pure delight.

'That's wonderful news! I knew you'd get there eventually, I just *knew* you would! Do you know, I very nearly said something last time we saw you because you seemed so much more positive, but . . . oh, we can do all this later, but that's such good news, Honor, it really is. So do you know how to go about it? Is it a local authority thing or an adoption agency or what?'

'Well, we do now. We would have told you sooner, but it's all been so uncertain.'

There was a very brief silence as Morgan realised she was being brought in at the end, not the beginning. She scratched around to retrieve the feeling of euphoria but it had already gone, deflated by hurt.

'So what's the score then? Is it all sorted?'

'No, far from it, but we're going to a children's home in Oxford today to meet a little girl called Frances.'

'With a view to actual adoption?'

'That's the idea.'

'Really? So it's a big day then. How have you managed to keep it so quiet? Are you nervous?'

'I'm trying not to be. I had this dream . . .'

'Oh, that's just, it's just . . .' Morgan was suffering from shock, but mainly as a result of having to re-assess her position in the pecking order. She needed to know who else had been told. 'So, if it all goes according to plan, can you just bring her home? How does it work? How long have you known about her?'

'Hardly any time at all really, so I shouldn't even be saying anything now, should I? I just suddenly wanted you to know – before everyone else. Look, I'll ring you tomorrow.'

'Oh no, don't go, I need more! How old is she?' The words 'before everyone else' were music to Morgan's ears.

'Nearly two.'

'What does she look like?'

Honor wavered for a moment. 'Very sweet, but how can you tell from a photo?'

She couldn't bring herself to say 'black', not even to her best friend. It didn't matter whether Frances was pink, black, yellow or purple with green spots. If Honor was beyond doubt that the race issue needn't come into it, then as Frances's mother – if God or fate or the authorities were good enough to smile on her – she would have to lead by example.

Chapter 2

Honor flipped down the sun-visor and looked at herself in the mirror. 'I don't look old enough, do I?'

'With bags under your eyes like the ones you've got this morning, you look nigh on grandmother material,' John lied as he changed down the final gear and crawled the last few yards up the poplar-lined drive towards the Hoarewood Children's Home. 'Anyway, you're hardly going to be judged on your appearance, are you?'

'What else have they got to go on?'

When she thought she had nothing to prove, Honor let her straw-coloured shoulder-length hair hang the way it fell, but now she quickly redefined the parting and tucked the bulk of it behind her left ear. She re-applied some pale, almost white, lipstick and opened her eyes wide out of habit, wondering how on earth she could prove she was twenty-eight if anyone challenged her.

Sometimes, when she was in queues or crowds in a strange town with Judith, she found herself over-using the title 'Mummy' for fear of being mistaken for the big sister. Had she sought any kind of post-miscarriage therapy, a psychologist would have told her such behaviour indicated a lack of maternal confidence, that maybe she thought of herself as a mother by accident rather than design. The truth, as always, was veering more towards the simple – she really could still look eighteen sometimes.

The wide potholed drive curved to the right to reveal a large mishmash of buildings, set around what would once have been an imposing if small Georgian Manor house. Now though, with clusters of long low extensions on either side, and metal bars at its windows, it was, as John commented merely to relieve the tension, 'architecturally annihilated'.

He pulled the Zephyr up next to the only other car, an Austin A30, stuck its nose in a humdrum evergreen bush opposite the main entrance and got out. Pure bravado. Five years ago, when they had both been in an aeroplane for the first time, flying to Sweden for their honeymoon, he'd been the same. Honor's nails had dug deep into his thigh on both take-off and landing but he – the brave new all-singing all-dancing husband – had appeared entirely relaxed. Only after they'd touched down on their return trip did he vow he'd only ever fly again under the influence of mind-altering substances. Both of them had fake courage off to a fine art.

He intended to stroll casually around the large square boot to open her door but a swarm of boys beat him to it, tapping on the passenger window and grinning. One of them even had the boldness to pull on the handle and escort Honor out. She was pleased. In her imagination, the place had been full of plaintive expressions and outstretched hands. This was like a piece of cheeky street theatre – more Artful Dodger than Oliver Twist.

'If you've come for 'im, you've got to 'ave me too,' the leader shouted to a chorus of laughter.

'Ged out Donny,' said a boy who had to be the other's twin, bringing his foot down hard on his brother's toes. They had red hair, matching T-shirts in faded green stripes, and wire-framed spectacles. One of them sported an ointment-pink eye-patch and the other had the purple stain of iodine crusting up around the corner of his mouth. A cold sore, presumably. Honor laughed encouragingly although she was almost repulsed by the sight of them. She despised herself for being so easily turned off and forced herself to ruffle her delicate fingers through their rough hair despite the strong image of swarming lice. The gesture did nothing to help the guilt since she then immediately wanted to wipe her hands on her skirt. What kind of a heart have I? she asked silently. Not big enough, obviously.

As she walked through them, smiling non-committally at their impertinent questions and trying not to trip over any of their sandalled feet, she hung on to the difference between ten-year-old boys and baby girls the world over. Slugs and snails, sugar and spice.

'D'you want a sambo or an 'onky?' asked a black boy with a flesh-coloured hearing aid – except not the colour of his flesh, of course – clamped to his right ear.

'Hey, hold on, we've only come for lunch! Watch your fingers!' John said. Think father, not teacher, Honor tried to signal with her eyes. No, maybe not yet, maybe teacher now, then father later. Oh, whatever. She'd forgotten how to react normally to anything.

'Perhaps we're not taking from the bottom of the pile after all,' she said quietly, remembering John's maiden speech nine months previously, when he had made the act of adoption sound so generous and giving and so entirely removed from what she was feeling now.

'Oh, I'm sure we're not.' His short answer made her feel shallow for even thinking they might have been in the first place.

'Boys, boys, boys. Let Mr and Mrs Lovell through. It is Mr and Mrs Lovell, isn't it?' boomed a hearty woman standing at the pillared entrance. She extended a plump arm with a pelican's bill of hanging flesh waving unreservedly around under her short-sleeved floral dress, the belt of which was all but concealed under a hefty bosom.

'Edith Cooke, Matron,' she confirmed, crushing the bones in John's puny but artistic fingers and holding out her hand to Honor for the same torture, noticing the young woman's bitten nails as she did. 'Off you go boys, shoo, go on! Or if you haven't got anything better to do, you can come in here and tidy your dormitories!'

That got rid of them. Honor and John followed her into the cavernous hall painted in thin cream emulsion that consumed even the most robust voice. A creak from a hulking radiator echoed round the space, and Honor almost expected a prefect to come along and order her back outside until the bell went.

'We're draining the heating system. Takes for ever in these big places,' trumpeted Miss Cooke, already stomping off into the bowels of the house down a corridor devoid of warmth that had nothing to do with a lack of heating. It could have been any institution from a hospital to a prison – children didn't seem to come into it.

When they were safely in her office with the door shut, she picked up a thin file open on her desk and waved it in the air, ploughing straight in. There was no small talk.

'Frances is a tough little thing, not that it says anything quite as useful as that in here. She's created a considerable shell for herself really for someone still under two years old, but then as children in her position know only too well, it's a matter of survival of the fittest. You know her history, don't you? Sorry, would you like a cup of tea?'

'Well . . .' said John, momentarily taken by surprise, 'yes, to both.'

'You tell me what you know and I will see if there's anything I can add.'

'Are we allowed to look at the file?'

'By all means, although don't expect to learn a great deal. They're very dry, these official forms.' She put the file on the desk with a slight slap.

'We were told she was here because her mother couldn't cope,' Honor said rather feebly. It was all feeling a bit too much like a sales transaction. She wanted empathy, a meeting of minds.

Edith Cooke recognised the deficit and her tone softened. She remembered a colleague once telling her she came over as too strident sometimes, but she could never feel entirely in debt to these parents. She knew and they knew that adoption was never strictly and entirely altruistic, not when it came to healthy children anyway. She liked and admired most of those who took the step, but she just couldn't bring herself to build their gesture up too much. In the great scheme of things, it wasn't enough. There was a scrapheap of children out there that never got any smaller.

'That's more or less it. Frances's mother was seventeen years old and already had two other children. It's a familiar tale. Mercifully, there was a grandmother to take over for a short while, but obviously, the longterm answer had to be adoption.'

'For all three?' Honor asked. She and John had already decided they wouldn't remove a child from its siblings.

'The eldest girl stayed with her grandmother, and the boy sadly has a severe handicap. He's a special case and already with foster-parents.' Miss Cooke was reading from the notes.

'What's wrong with him?' John jumped in almost accusingly. It wasn't sympathetically put but Matron understood his immediacy. He meant, was the handicap genetic? Did it affect Frances in any way? They had to know these things.

'I believe he was deprived of oxygen at birth. He was in care almost immediately because of his condition. Let me see.' She looked at another piece of paper on her desk. 'Frances's caseworker has written here that there seems to be little or no recollection of either her brother or her mother but she does sometimes talk about her sister and grandmother.' Edith Cooke paused before looking back up.

'You sound dubious,' John said.

Don't make it sound too much like we're buying a used car, Honor willed silently.

'Well, Frances has been with us for ten months, so she was just over one when she came. I'm not sure she actually remembers anything about her home, such as it was, but you know, we have a whole team of very well-meaning counsellors and social workers here who've tried to keep some things alive for her.'

'And you're not sure how useful all that is?'

'The child is twenty-two months old. She can barely repeat nursery rhymes so I find it hard to believe she can communicate on that kind of level.' Edith Cooke stopped talking abruptly and sniffed quietly. They all knew she had spoken out of turn.

'So where is Frances's mother now?' Honor wanted to move the conversation on. She'd read the arguments about keeping an adopted child's sense of identity alive, although nobody ever said to what extent. Constantly drawing attention to the difference seemed reckless, maybe even cruel. A fresh start had its own merits.

'No doubt we'll find out when she next needs us.'

The three of them sat quietly for a few seconds until Matron suddenly clasped her hands together and let out a short little puff of air. Under the capable frock and the heavy-duty bra lay a featherbed heart. It was hard for her, letting her children go, but that was what she was here for.

'Most parents want white children, you know.'

Neither Honor nor John spoke, taken aback by her abruptness, so she carried on.

'It's quite unusual for people like you to actually request a black child.'

'It's not an issue for us,' Honor finally said, offended by what she wrongly interpreted as a shock example of veiled racism.

'That is to say, we routinely place children in families of a different race, so I don't suppose it can be that rare nowadays to hear a black child call a white adult Mummy or Daddy but very often these families are social workers or adoption workers anyway. Most couples who are referred to us through other channels usually want a child that looks like them – you know, blonde hair or tall or short. They often have a wish list–'

'Do-gooders, do you mean?' Honor interrupted.

'No, I merely mean that the big wide world out there is still essentially racist, regardless of what the social commentators insist on telling us.'

'Are you trying to dissuade us?' John asked gently. It dawned on Honor then that if Edith Cooke was prejudiced against anything, it was society.

'No. I suppose I just want to know why.'

It was hardly the interview they had both imagined, more a disguised attack on some people's motives, although for some reason John found he liked the spiky Edith Cooke enormously. It was just as well, considering the spin on her next question.

'Tell me, did you think your way would bring quicker results?'

'What is our way?'

'Specifying a black child.'

'Not for a minute. I don't think that advantage has ever occurred to us, has it?' John looked at Honor for confirmation.

'Never.'

He spoke assuredly. 'I accept that adoption is ultimately all about wanting something for yourselves, but I'd like to think – well, no, I *know* that our motive wasn't entirely selfish. We just wanted to take from the bottom of the pile.' John latched on to the phrase again, forgetting his earlier dismissal of it. He wanted to believe there was at least a little altruism in their intent, that they were prepared to take a child other couples might feel inclined to leave behind. That for him made it a risk worth taking.

'Frances is by no means the bottom of the pile,' Edith Cooke said shortly.

Both of them felt momentarily squashed, like earnest students on hearing their flimsy essays ripped to shreds.

'We didn't feel we could dig as deep as the handicapped.'

'John!' Honor gasped with reproach. 'He's not normally so insensitive.'

'Not at all,' Edith Cooke nodded. 'I understand. That is something different again, much more bottom of the pile. Now, shall I show you the day room?'

As soon as they had all passed through the fire door at the end of the corridor, it was as if a demarcation line had been drawn right through the middle of not only their conversation, but the entire house. Children were allowed here but not there. Opinion was allowed there, but not here. Matron now kept strictly to her lines.

'Why did you make a point of it?' Honor hissed to her husband under her breath as they were guided from room to room.

'Of what?'

'The colour thing. I won't have it flagged up, I–'

'I thought that was what she wanted, what she was getting at.'

'Please don't mention it again,' Honor begged him.

John squeezed his wife's hand. 'Relax. You're looking for trouble again. It's fine.'

Matron turned to face them, looking more welcoming than she had done previously. Her little walk had been time enough to decide she liked them.

'This is where the children spend out-of-school hours, rainy days, quiet times. We only allow ten in at a time or it gets too rowdy. Board games, books, cards – nothing too lively. We have a rumpus room where they can let off steam if the weather is bad. I'll show you in a minute.'

The day room was trying hard to look jolly. Someone with better intentions than talent had painted a floor-to-ceiling Mickey Mouse on the wall to the right of the door with other Disney characters, smaller but no less misshapen, on the other three. Honor hated herself for needing to grade the effort, she wasn't marking coursework now, and it flashed across her mind that maybe being a teacher came more easily to her than being a mother. Not exactly the best time to start feeling unworthy.

Elegant French windows were propped open with green vinyl easy chairs and the generously proportioned fire surround had been given a lick of ugly brown gloss paint. Its brick-effect linoleum grate was being used as a place to stack faded yellow plastic potties, and the mantelpiece was home to a line of scruffy books, but a sense of former grandeur still somehow hung about the room. Out of the windows, she could see a terrace scattered with tricyles and a large lawn that sloped gently away towards woodland.

She scanned the little faces for one that might be Frances but most of the children were running around too fast to properly observe, no doubt aware of the need to build up an appetite for the gravy smell she had detected in the corridor.

A solid baby no more than a year old was on the floor, playing a peep-po game with a bit of old blanket and a nursery nurse, and a young girl maybe Judith's age stood close by, not exactly joining in but enjoying the spray from the waves of laughter. Her hand-knitted short-sleeved Fair Isle sweater rose up her back in a curve and made her arms hang awkwardly. Both its pattern and its colour clashed with her tartan kilt, and Honor thought of all the co-ordinated clothes in Judith's wardrobe that were perfectly decent but never got worn. She tried to engage the girl in a smile, but the child slunk into a chair and turned her face away.

'She's only here short-term,' Miss Cooke whispered as she took a tea tray from a woman in white overalls and set it down on a chipboard cupboard built beneath a sash window. 'Her mother is currently being detained at Her Majesty's Pleasure.'

Honor bit her lip.

'You can't take them all, my dear.'

A flash of a child with pigtails at right angles to her head shot across the open windows. She had the unmistakable gait of a child who ran before it could walk and Honor braced herself for an inevitable scream that never came. When Judith was learning to use her legs at speed, there had always been at least one or other parent there – sometimes even a posse of grandparents – to hold out a steadying hand.

'Was that . . .?'

Matron nodded at once. 'I know this is what you're here for, but try to remember to hang on to the fact that the object of your interest has no idea.' Her eyes moved deliberately towards another child. 'What was it they said in the war? Careless whispers cost lives?' She drank her tea in three impatient gulps. 'Shall we stretch our legs?'

They stepped on to the terrace where the air was clean and fresh. Neither Honor nor John strained to look for the one thing they had come all this way to see. Instead, their gazes remained firmly and falsely on the rural view.

John could hear his wife taking unusually regular breaths and he put a calming hand on her arm, but whether it was this or the fact that she was visibly shaking anyway that upset the precarious business of her cardigan draped round her slight shoulders, he didn't know. Maybe it was fate.

The cardigan slid to the floor and Honor, relieved to be able to do something other than just stand there, bent down to pick it up. As she did, she caught another glimpse of pigtail, this time in close-up.

After weeks of trying to conjure this pivotal moment from one small photograph, of considering what to say and how to smile, whether to try and touch or to hold back, how to predict her emotions or spin from it something to hang on to for ever more, here it was. Mother and, please God, daughter were breathing the same air.

Frances was so much smaller in the flesh. From her head and shoulders mug-shot, she'd seemed chunky. Now, her beautiful brown cheeks seemed less round, her jaw less solid, her nose less splayed. If Honor hadn't known for sure, she would have aged her at sixteen months, not nearly two years.

'Hello,' she said, feeling the brush of a warm hand as Frances, encouraged by Matron's waggling finger, lifted the cardigan and offered it up. The child's eyes were big and bold but her runny nose was still trickling over her lips.

Something warm and fizzy coursed round Honor's body, as if she'd just taken a few swigs of fermenting cider that had been left in the sun. She had to steady herself with one hand on the paving slab but even that slight movement made Frances back off. Her diminutive legs took her off again down a grassy bank. She ran as if she was made of rubber, not in the cautious way that Judith did, but as if she would bounce back up again, unharmed, if she fell.

So that was it, that was our beginning, Honor thought as she rose with a wobble to her feet. A psychic certainty that told her there was so much more to come bolstered her enough to give John a sideways glance. He winked back.

She tried not to be consumed by the same post-natal rush of love that she'd experienced after Judith, telling herself that was jumping the gun. Four years ago, when she'd looked into the puffy pink slits that passed for her newborn daughter's eyes, she'd been struck by the ready-made wisdom she'd seen looking back at her. This was its match. Frances was already very definitely somebody. But she wasn't hers yet.

'There you are,' said Matron smiling. 'I'll make myself

scarce for a while. The children find it easier without me. Have a walk around the grounds and see if you can find who you are looking for. Come and join me in the office when you're ready. No hurry.'

As soon as she had turned her back to the garden and started to head towards the house, the swarm of boys reappeared by John's side as if by magic.

'Can you be goalie?'

'Will you be all right on your own?' he asked his wife as he was dragged towards two discarded sweaters on the lawn.

'I won't *be* on my own,' she told him.

Frances was standing by a rusty swing, waiting her turn. The ground around the frame was bare from constant trampling and damp from an early shower. One child – it could have been a boy or a girl – was drawing in it with a stick.

'That's a big face,' Honor commented as she wandered up. She waited for the child to do the mouth, intrigued in an amateur psychologist's kind of way, to see if it would be a happy or a sad one. Really, it was just something to say while she plucked up the courage to speak to Frances again. The child glared and dropped the stick.

'Oh, but you haven't finished. What about a mouth?' Honor asked.

The child – on closer inspection Honor guessed she was a girl – shook her head.

'Not even a little one?'

The girl shook her head again.

'You're wastin' your breff,' said the older girl on the swing. 'She don't say nuffink. She can't speak.'

Honor picked up the stick and drew a dash of a smile which got some semblance of a response. The silent child put her head on one side and then the other, looked a little less anxious and took the stick back to carry on.

Much as she would have liked to stay drawing mouths in the mud with this flawed stray, Honor wanted, needed, to speak to Frances. It was just a question of turning forty-five degrees.

'Thank you for picking up my cardigan,' she said, bending down to her level once again.

'Go,' said Frances, her eyes clouded with suspicion and her mouth turned down at the sides.

Honor's heart shrank. She twiddled with the tiny beads around her neck and put her palm to the dirty ground. Of all the possible outcomes, she hadn't contemplated child rejection. She'd thought about not fulfilling official requirements, or being left cold by things herself, but she hadn't even considered outright refusal from someone not yet two years old. Fundamental mistake. It was Frances who all this was about – wasn't it?

'Fankie go,' Frances said a little more forcefully, pointing.

Honor just squatted there blankly, trying to think of something to say.

'FANKIE GO!!' the tiny child shouted, and ran at the swing, putting her hand out and grabbing the chain, sending the present incumbent jolting and swaying, forcing her to put her eight-year-old feet to the floor and bring herself to a stop by scuffing the ground with the toes of her shoes.

'Oh, you want a *go*!' The relief of understanding unbalanced Honor and she twisted over on her kitten heels, scraping her ankle on the grit.

'*Frankeeee*,' the girl on the swing shouted angrily. 'You should wait your bleedin' turn.'

The fierce little toddler took no notice, because she had got what she had set out to get. She clambered on without a second's expectation that someone might help her, and Honor noticed the impression of tight elastic on her chubby thighs where her rompers were cutting in.

There was a nappy underneath for sure, although Judith had been dry by this age. It seemed incongruous, jarring with all the other gestures that signalled such ferocious independence, but Honor loved to see it. It told her that the little girl hadn't really done any growing up at all.

Frances dangled her short legs impatiently. Her white ankle socks and red leather shoes were impressively clean, much more so than the other children's Honor had seen so far. She thought of the way her own shoes had been polished, her skirt dry-cleaned and her hair cut, ready to impress. Nobody really knew who was selling what here, did they?

'Puss!' Frances ordered impatiently. 'Puss!'

'Say please.'

'Peese.'

Honor pushed as requested, and as her palms pressed gently but firmly against the soft back of this living tyke of a child, she realised with a quick thrill that the parenting had already begun.

Chapter 3

There was more hands-on parenting to be done when they got home. Bush telegraphs and grapevines were to be avoided at all costs, so telling Judith was their first major challenge. Their minds had been full of Frances for days, but as soon as they pulled back into their drive, it was Judith who took up that pole position once again Get this right, they reassured each other, and the rest will follow. How to do it had been discussed to the point of exhaustion and yet, at the last minute, there was hesitation.

'I think *you* should do it.'

'No, it would be better coming from you.'

'You start, and I'll join in.'

'We'll do it together.'

Telling their daughter turned out to be the easy bit. A compulsive people-pleaser even at that age, Judith would do and say whatever she thought would make her mother happy. She radiated continual subliminal messages – Whatever you want, Mummy, I want, Whoever you love, Mummy, I love, Wherever you go, Mummy, I go.

Honor often worried that Judith displayed too much selflessness in too little a heart. Sometimes, when she wasn't feeling worthy of such filial devotion, she wanted to scream, 'Say something selfish or ungrateful like other children do!' but she never did. Self-indulgence just didn't live in the little girl's body.

To reject such devotion would have been heartless, so Honor learned to live with it – and by learning to live with it, of course, she unintentionally gave it her backing. Not only that, but she then covered her guilt at feeling annoyed in the first place by over-endorsement. The signals she gave out – gratitude and praise for obedience and consideration – made Judith's young spirit soar. The child was on a mission.

It didn't occur to Honor that she might be laying a seriously rocky foundation for her daughter to build on, but then how could anyone have predicted at such an early stage that making her mother happy would become Judith's life's work? If any parent could see from their initial groundwork what the final structure of their children's lives would be, how many of them would ever get past the architect's plans?

The little girl sat quietly on her father's lap that tea-time, sucking her thumb and playing with her hair. She was tired and pleased to be home. Her parents had been gone all day and she had kept a piece of Mrs Hardy's chewy meat in her cheek all through the rice pudding, which she'd spat out in the field later when no one was looking. She'd been more worried about offending Mrs Hardy's culinary sensibilities than being told off for not finishing.

'Well, Joo,' John started in his familiar 'A.A. Milne reads *Now We Are Six*' sort of voice, 'how are you?'

'Very well – et tu?'

They said the same thing to each other every night as soon as John gave her his after-work cuddle. It must have come from a story book, or a film or a poem or something – no one could remember any more – but its origins were not important. It was the tradition that counted.

After the greeting, he would usually lapse into an accepted silence while he read his post or the newspaper. This time though, he said, 'Jolly good,' and didn't shuffle her off, which made her realise something was about to happen.

As soon as he opened his mouth, he knew he'd never find the right conversational tone. There was no easy way to say it. It didn't really matter what words he chose – whatever they were, they would be sufficiently clumsy for his four-year-old to detect the imminence of a Big Speech anyway, but the task had fallen to him so he had to get on with it. Honor just didn't think she could do it.

'Er . . . now listen carefully a minute, small child, because Mummy and Daddy have got something to ask you. Stop wriggling.'

John stopped.

'Are you sitting comfortably?'

'Uh huh.'

'Then I'll begin.'

Judith smiled. It was like story-time on the radio. She hoped it was going to have a happy ending.

'Well, we've had an idea which we think is a good one, so we want to know if you like the sound of it too.'

That's heavily loaded, Honor thought, as Judith nodded and moved her hand from twiddling her hair to twiddling his. The whole foreplay thing was pointless really, since all three of them knew she had already decided to agree with whatever they had to say.

'Do you remember when Mummy had to keep going into hospital last year? We were trying to have another baby, a brother or a sister for you, weren't we, but it kept going wrong. Do you remember all that?'

Judith did, but she'd have preferred not to. She nodded again glumly. Watching anxiously, Honor started heaping too much intellectualism on to her, forgetting that she was still only four years old. The child always used her own criteria for trying to understand other people's motivations, so anything her parents did, or tried to do, Judith probably assumed must have been done to please her – or at least someone other than themselves. Whatever she said, it wouldn't be the whole truth. Her response only confirmed this for Honor.

'I don't want a baby any more, Daddy,' Judith told her father quickly, before the idea could run away with him. Honor clenched her fists and smiled bravely.

'But do you know what?' he said, flicking her thin bunches and using one to brush her nose, 'Mummy needs one, and I need one, not just for you, but for ourselves too. We love you so much, you make us so happy and we are so proud of you that we want to do it all over again, to make it four of us, not three.'

'Oh. Has Mummy got another baby in her tummy then?' Judith may have only been four but she *did* know what usually happened to any babies in Mummy's tummy. They didn't turn out to be babies after all, and her mummy got red eyes and spent lots of time in bed or in hospital, and she wasn't allowed to climb on her lap afterwards.

'Nope, because babies can't grow in her tummy any more, can they?'

'There's nowhere for them to make a bed any more, is there?'

'That's right. So we could look after a baby that has already been born instead, couldn't we? Bring her home and love her, just like we love you.'

'Yes. Can I choose it? One with curly hair.'

Honor realised with relief that Judith was thinking about dolls, not babies.

'Well, you can't really choose babies like you can dolls.'

'Oh.'

'And anyway, one has already been chosen for us.'

'Who by?'

Honor and John looked at each other and laughed.

'There's no answer to that, unless we want to get spiritual about it,' John said quickly to his wife.

'Who borned it?'

'Someone else.'

Was it all right for someone else to born your baby? Judith looked at Honor for endorsement which she got through some kind of amniotic seventh sense. Her mother's expression barely changed, except for an imperceptible raise of the mouth and eyebrows.

Then after a pause, their daughter said, 'Did she say you could have it?'

During bath-time, once Judith had ascertained that the plan really was something to look forward to and not anything else in disguise, she was like a child obsessed. She wanted to know what orphans looked like, what orphans wore, what they ate, if they wore glasses, if they had ever tasted chocolate. It was all part of some innocent fascination with adversity, but by bedtime Honor was orphaned out.

'Let's not call the baby an orphan, darling. She's still got another mummy, you know, but she can't live with her, that's all. Her parents aren't dead.'

'Well, I wish they were,' Judith said, feeling her little face go hot at such a terrible thought.

'Oh, why's that?'

''Cos then they wouldn't be able to come looking for her and we could keep her for ever and not have to share her.'

'We'll be able to do all that anyway.'

'Who says?'

'A piece of paper will say.'

'Paper can't talk,' Judith giggled, but she was satisfied. Her mother looked more certain about this baby's arrival than she had about all the others put together. Maybe this one really was going to happen.

Both Honor and John heard the eight and nine o'clock clattering and shuffling that night, but by then they were so emotionally beat they shrugged it off and allowed their daughter a rare freedom. It had been a big day for her and she was probably restless. When they poked their heads round her bedroom door at midnight, it was like seeing a mind in cross-section.

The heap of stuff on her floor was very obviously a bed for someone. Under the window at right angles to her own mattress, Judith had taken pains to spread out her bottom sheet, her pillow and her eiderdown. Peeping just over the top of the covers was Gooby, her beige knitted donkey, his limp sucked ears hanging tantalisingly over the edge of the paisley silk. Her floral sprig nightdress, a Christmas present from John's parents, lay as folded as a four-year-old could manage on the pillow, and her bedtime drink and biscuit were untouched and close by.

Judith was fast asleep on her bare mattress on a towel, using a teddy bear for a pillow and a dressing gown for her blanket.

She was holding a naked pink plastic doll covered in biro scribbles and was in a pair of shorts from her dressing-up cupboard and a T-shirt two years too small that she sometimes put Gooby in.

'What *has* she been doing?' John asked, puzzled and amused at the disruption.

'Can you really not tell?'

'Tell what?'

'She's getting her bedroom ready for Frances.'

Honor wanted so much to be right, although the deduction worried her. Judith's charity, or her largesse, or whatever it was that had made her want to heap so many favours on to so unknown a cause, smacked of the kind of guilt trip she thought only she went on. Was it that the child had concluded that her own privilege of birth should now carry some sort of penalty? I've got parents so I can't have toys, I've never been hungry or cold so I'd better not have biscuits or blankets?

'Or maybe she's just been playing a game,' John felt the need to say.

Whatever was going on in her daughter's young head, Honor went to bed that night feeling as warm as toast. She knew with a mother's instinct that Judith wanted Frances in their family too.

The only chill factor came, as expected, from the East. Icy blasts of disapproval came from John's parents in Lowestoft – first down the telephone and then in a frosty letter in which they extended an unprecedented supper invitation. John refused to go, saying that if he wanted to go to Siberia, he would prefer to fly Aeroflot. A browbeating from his close-minded father and the occasional back-up murmur from his mother was not exactly his idea of a fun-packed evening, he said.

Such immediate and rigid parental objection didn't surprise him in the least. He had always joked privately to Honor that he hoped he had been either swapped at birth or that his mother had enjoyed a brief fling with a stranger, but this time he lost his sense of humour entirely.

When his father delivered the most offensive blow of all in a telephone lecture about 'black blood', John chose to cut the loose thread of relationship hanging on between him and his parents completely.

With one eye on the future, Honor spent a few half-hearted days appealing to him to try and work things through, but when it came to stubbornness, it was a question of like father, like son.

'What *is* this?' her normally placid husband asked, snorting with disbelief. 'A battle? Support can either come naturally or not at all. People can take it or leave it, simple as that.'

Actually, most people not only took it but embraced it. The more one set of grandparents withdrew, the more the other set advanced. It was like a strange primitive dance, watching where everyone stepped in relation to the person next to them. Honor's parents wallowed like pigs in muck in the new idea that they were – comparatively speaking anyway – the more open-minded and impartial elders. It was a role they continued to play for the rest of their lives.

In the run-up to bringing Frances home, the phone rang frequently, just as it might have done, Honor thought a little wistfully, had one of her pregnancies worked out. Admittedly there were a few notable silences, but John's parents were the only significant casualties and, fortunately, they licked their wounds in public far too often to retain even any vestigial sympathy.

The day before Frances came for good, Honor posted them a last-ditch attempt at reconciliation. *The longer you pick at the scab, the deeper the scar will get,* she wrote without John's blessing. *Just leave it to heal on its own for a while, please, for Judith's sake.*

Don't talk to me about Judith's sake, John's father wrote back in furious ink. *And when you weep over* her *scar, which Marjory and I both believe will permanently disfigure her, then we hope you will both remember who it was that inflicted the injury in the first place.*

That was the last communication the four of them ever

shared, other than the cold exchange of greeting cards. That first Christmas, Honor got Judith to sign it, so in large sloping letters the five-year-old wrote, *To Grane an Granpr with luv from Judith and Funjessica.*

'Francesca' was an abridgement of Frances Catherine, the name on the adoption certificate, and Honor had been rather proud of her inspired compromise up until then, even if it was rather a mouthful for small people. But Judith's new phonetic version seemed to sum up the effervescence in their new family so perfectly that she and John tried to encourage it to catch on.

It didn't. What the Lovells' youngest daughter eventually ended up being called was Chess, a name that had well and truly stuck by the time its awful aptness dawned on anyone.

'Well, you *are* both black and white, aren't you?'

'Here's to a chequered life ahead of you.'

'Let's see your white bits.'

Insensitive banter only ever came from outside the close circle of family and friends and it started in her teens, when people presumably thought she was old enough to get the so-called joke. Inside the circle, it was the ultimate crime for anyone to draw attention to the colour of Chess's skin, in jest or otherwise. To draw attention to it was to mark the difference, and Honor felt sure that to mark the difference was to spell the danger.

'We're all the same underneath,' she chanted like a mantra throughout her girls' childhood. 'It's what's inside that counts.'

She constantly referred to them as 'my girls' as if they were indistinguishable parts of the same unit, and when Morgan picked her up on her tendency to clone two such obvious individuals, Honor would say she was only taking the lead from the children themselves. She supported her argument with an example from their very first afternoon together.

From the moment all four members of the new Lovell family lived under one roof, Chess – or Frances, or Francesca, or Frankie, or Funjessica, or whatever it was she was supposed to be answering to then – laid the first stone.

Speech was still a precious commodity for such a young

child, and she had been more than a little overwhelmed at being carted off in such a big shiny car to go and live with what Matron called 'her new Mummy and Daddy', so she let her actions speak louder than her words. It was indisputable from the start which one of the three she had decided to put her faith in, and Judith didn't seem to mind.

In the car on that historic journey home, Chess sat so close to her new sister on the cracked leather seat that Honor could see their tiny faces both at once in the rearview mirror. The picture remained at the front of her memory for ever more. She couldn't look at a school photograph or a posed hug without seeing that leather car seat somewhere in the backdrop, not even when they were grown women with children of their own.

Chess's homecoming had been carefully planned, if not contrived. Even after ploughing into the pile of presents in the sitting room and the rabbit-shaped jelly in the fridge, the child would still only reply to questions with nods and shakes. She was shown her bedroom where they hung up her clothes, she was taken round the garden where they found her a trike, she was given a tour of the mantelpiece photographs where her own portrait had been attentively placed, but all the while, she maintained a wide-eyed face of suspicion.

Her older sister kept holding her hand and smiling right into her, but then the urge to pee took over and Judith freed herself from the toddler's vice-like grip, sprang to her feet and disappeared without explanation through an unfamiliar door. As yet unaccustomed to such freedom from supervision, Chess felt sure her only ally was absconding for good, and the scream she let out was heard by the neighbours. Things from then were clearer. Where Judith went, she followed – for years.

That night, she refused point blank to go into the specially prepared cot in Honor and John's room. She slept instead with Judith, like teaspoons in a canteen of cutlery, curled in a single bed between the beige knitted donkey and the dark brown bear she had been given by Edith Cooke as a goodbye present.

She slept there the next night too, and the next and the next. Neither girl ever fell prey to nocturnal wanderings and this had a welcome knock-on effect for Honor's sleep pattern too. It suited everyone for the two girls to continue to sleep either next to each other or to top and tail until they were treated to bunk beds at the ages of seven and five. Even then, their parents would invariably find them together, usually on the top bunk when they came to tuck them up. In the morning, they would learn that Chess had had her nightmare again about the gorilla with the big stick who lived in a tree outside her bedroom window.

Judith soon caught on that she was less cute than her new sister. Right from the start, old ladies would speak to Chess in the street and not her. They made a striking pair – one pale and shy, the other dark and boisterous – but Judith got used to being the more dispensable of the two and she quickly gave up even hoping to be noticed first. (Happily, she grew up the better for it, working on the premise that if her face wasn't enough to draw the crowds, then what shone through it would have to.)

They were each other's favourite plaything. The jigsaw boxes on the playroom shelves remained neatly stacked and the dolls in prams sat rigid for days while Judith and Chess reinvented a world entirely from their heads. Their games were populated with all manner of characters, but orphans had a habit of cropping up more than most.

'I know, pretend I'm an orphan and you find me in the woods.'

'And I become your mummy, and look after you.'

Honor, who quickly reduced her teaching work to one still-life class a week, relished overhearing their uninhibited conversations. She often wrote them down, although if she had taken off her rose-tinted glasses for a moment, maybe, just maybe, she might have seen a few more shadows dancing between the lines. John saw them sometimes, fleetingly, but the light in his wife's eyes made any darkness disappear as quickly as it had come.

An ominous silence coming from upstairs one rainy half-term day lured Honor to the bathroom, or rather just outside it, from where her radar picked up an intriguing mix of childish chatter and the rummaging of small hands in her make-up tray.

There was a faintly self-conscious twinge to Judith's first question.

'Do I look like Mummy?'

'Yes, now do me,' Chess said, paying lip service.

More rummaging.

'It doesn't show up.'

'Press harder.'

'Doesn't make any difference.'

'Use another one then.'

'Ow.'

Honor pretended not to notice the talcum powder all over the bathroom floor or the white dust over Chess's face and in her hair later that night. She could see no harm in a little experimentation in changing the tone of one's skin. Judith could well be at the cocoa tin tomorrow.

Morgan didn't subscribe to her friend's colour blindness and she pulled her up on it from time to time.

'Don't you see though that while Chess might try and turn herself white, Judith will *never* raid the cocoa tin?'

'Why shouldn't she? That's just as likely on the face of it.'

'Because Judith knows that white is the majority. Chess just wants to be like everyone else around her.'

'Oh, come on, Morgan. That's just an adult getting in the way of kids' games.'

Once, when Chess was about nine and Judith eleven, a fat boy in a village playing field made the fatal mistake of hurling racial taunts in the sisters' direction. Every time he launched his overfed body a few inches off the ground in an attempt to hang casually from a climbing frame, his T-shirt rode up to show off rolls of pink flesh.

'Oy, Sambo! Do you taste of chocolate? Give us a lick! Nigger girl! Blackie! Go back to your own country and eat bananas!'

Chess flicked him the V-sign with considerable aplomb,

considering she had only recently learnt it, but Judith, who must have been half his size, jumped off her swing and went over to him.

'Do people ever call you fat?' she shouted up.

'What?'

'I said, do people ever call you fat? Because you are, aren't you?'

'Shut your face.'

'Then you shut yours.'

Much to Judith's amazement and pride, he slunk off and children around them cheered, but the episode came back to Chess later that night. Did some people think being black was as embarrassing as being fat then? Was that why Mum thought it was rude if anyone mentioned it? Was it like being smelly or having a Dad in prison or something?

It was the first inkling that she might be at a disadvantage and it kept her awake for weeks. Honor had so successfully pummelled in the race taboo that Chess had never questioned it before. In just the same way that being encouraged to say please and thank you now came naturally, or how she never asked for the last biscuit on a plate at someone else's house, so she had never queried why being black should be such an unmentionable thing. It was something she was free to deal with only by making it a part of her games, where all rules were suspended.

One of their favourite flights of fantasy was to be grown women with children of their own. They played it in bed after lights out – a talking game which could go on for hours until one of them became too sleepy to reply and the other too sleepy to challenge the silence. In it, Judith had an imaginary husband called Cliff, as in Richard, and Chess had one called Johnny.

'Is that after Daddy?' Honor dared to ask when she'd sneaked a listen one night.

'No,' Chess said, looking at her mother as if she were mad. 'It's after Johnny Mathis.'

Her answer should have made the alarm bells clang noisily throughout the house, but instead it made Honor bite the inside of her cheek until the desire to smile passed. The singer was the only black male the child had access to and only then because his face stared out at her from her parents' LP collection. Rural Norfolk didn't exactly have a healthy ethnic mix to choose from in the 1970s, but because Honor's mantra – 'it's what's inside that counts' – echoed round and round the home, no one ever wanted to believe it mattered. If the golden rule not to mention skin colour *was* ever broken, it was made light of.

'Who do I look like, Mummy?' Chess asked once, when she'd been listening to Honor pore over a newborn child and pick out all the various inherited genetic features.

'You look like you, silly.'

'Yes, but whose nose do I have?'

'Well, I hope it's your own, otherwise someone somewhere isn't going to be able to sneeze very well.'

It was so much easier to make a joke, and anyway, Honor could always claim she was taking the lead from the children again, since Chess and Judith had made the best joke of all.

The Zebra Crossing gag was a snapshot of their childhood more vivid than any cinefilm footage could ever capture. It was a comedy act the girls stuck to for many years, and it became as much a part of family life as John allowing them to ride on the car bonnet on the lane down to their farmhouse in summer or Honor treating them to sweets from the next shop they saw after passing a flashing ambulance. It *had* actually been committed to camera once but the moment was staged, filmed on the third attempt, and therefore too self-conscious to count.

The tradition was originally born on an out-of-season holiday in North Devon. Their caravan parked up in a farmer's field had become infested with a late batch of flies, so they had blasted it with Vapona, shut all the windows and abandoned it for the day.

It was drizzling, none of the small town shops were open, the cinema didn't have a matinée and Honor and John were feeling as if luck was conspiring against them. Not that the girls minded two hoots. They were off school when they shouldn't have been, and they were going to have fish and chips for lunch. Life was a laugh.

As they rounded a corner, Chess saw a pedestrian crossing and ran over without looking. She wanted to see if the two-bedroomed tent was still in the window of the camping shop. It was what she was going to buy as soon as she got a job as a zookeeper on the other side of the estuary.

'Chess, come back!' Judith shouted. 'You'll get told off!'

'See this! It's even got a loo!'

'No, I'm waiting for Mummy and Daddy. You come back this side.'

'Come on, wimp!'

'We're not allowed to cross the road without–'

'Chicken!'

As they shouted to each other from either end of the zebra crossing, Chess got an idea. She leapt into the air and landed in a start position on the first white strip.

'Now you see me!' she shouted.

'What?'

Then she jumped again, this time on to the black.

'Now you don't!'

Judith laughed despite herself, and suddenly wanting her parents to see that she could be brave and funny too, she took her sister's mischievous cue and launched herself rather more cautiously on to a black strip.

'Now *you* see *me*!'

Hop.

'Now you don't!'

They kept it going on purpose until their parents caught them up, by which time they had the alternate timing off to a fine art. Honor and John were oblivious of any enticement and the scene became one of those perfect parable moments which from then on passed into family folk law. Years later, only Chess knew why the tradition had suddenly stopped. It wasn't because they had simply grown out of it, it was because she no longer found it funny.

The older she got, the more she got teased. Often, she couldn't care less what other people thought, so she would usually let them get away with it, but there was one memorable exception at a family wedding when a particularly repugnant male guest tried to grope her on the dance floor. At twelve, Chess could sometimes look sixteen.

'Wanna be my black queen, do you, darling?' the alcohol-fuelled reptile had bellowed in her ear, spits of whisky splashing her bare neck. His tie was undone, there were big patches of perspiration circling his underarms, and in his mind he was a gorgeous twenty-five-year-old, not a ruddy-faced has-been two years away from his pension.

'Why don't you just fuck off, you dirty old man?' she yelled back over the disco, much to the secret admiration of an adolescent Judith jiggling nearby without timing or confidence.

At that time, Chess had the breasts and Judith had the brace – but the older girl also had the brains, and therein lay their eternal difference. Even in the unlikely event of her being fumbled by a wedding guest, Judith would never had been reckless enough to tell anyone to fuck off. Someone had to be the sensible one, for her parents' sake. Not that her little sister was out of control or anything – she just had difficulty understanding cause and effect.

For the formative years of her life, Chess was more or less happy to do whatever other people thought best – not specifically to please them in the way Judith wanted to but just because it saved hassle. The adoption agency had chosen her parents, her parents had chosen her school and her school had chosen her subjects. It wasn't that she didn't know her own mind, it was just that she couldn't see anything to get excited about between the options. It was only when the options seemed to dry up that the log jam of sensibilities began to take effect.

Chapter 4

September 1984: Fourteen people have died and hundreds more wounded in violent riots around five black townships in Johannesburg, South Africa. The fighting was triggered by yesterday's inauguration of a new constitution and with the appointment of P.W. Botha as President. The new rules allow limited government participation by Indians and those of mixed racial descent, but blacks are still excluded. All those killed were black, ten of them by police counter-attack.

From the moment the envelope containing Chess's A-level results dropped its inevitable bomb, there was trouble.

'Take them again,' John advised.

'No point.'

'Take just one again,' Honor almost begged.

'What good is one?'

'Walton College runs a secretarial course . . .'

'Do I *look* like a secretary?'

'Well then, what *are* you going to do with the rest of your life, Chess?'

'Become a brain surgeon, drive a bus, travel the world – *I don't bloody know*.'

Mother and (sometimes) daughter ended up crying secretly in their own locked bedrooms but John stuck to a repertoire of two expressions throughout – disapproval and disappointment. The thing was, it was disappointment and disapproval with *himself*. The female triumvirate that had ruled his household for more than sixteen years had slowly stripped him of the only role he'd ever really craved. He still wanted to be the best father Chess ever had, but somewhere along the way she had ceased to need him, so he had ceased to offer himself. Now, he sometimes thought, she didn't even seem to like him very much.

The gap between them had widened imperceptibly, and by the time he'd realised how big it was, he thought it was too late to make amends. The moment of truth hurt him so much it featured silently in their relationship for ever more.

A few years previously, Judith and Honor had gone away for a weekend to select college accommodation and he had been left in charge of Chess (not that she needed a lot of looking after at fifteen, Honor reassured him). Great bonding plans had gone on in his head for their time alone. *Amadeus* was on at the cinema, a new Italian pizza place had opened in Norwich, they could decorate her bedroom.

But when it came to Saturday evening and she still hadn't materialised from a day in town with her friends, he'd lurched from appreciation into resentment. By the time she eventually phoned, at half-past eight, he had drunk too much wine to drive anywhere anyway.

'Why don't you just stay over?' he'd said coldly, thinking that perhaps she would respond to a more relaxed approach, that it would make her feel adult.

'What about you?'

'What about me?'

'Won't you be lonely?' She'd wanted him to say yes, so she could tell her friend, 'Sorry, Dad needs me.'

'What? With the coven out of the way? I might even have a bath. See you tomorrow, no hurry.'

And they'd both put their receivers down feeling superfluous – again.

When John thought back, as he did more often than anyone knew, to how determined he had once been, it made him sad. In the beginning, Chess had been *his* idea, one that had even cost him his relationship with his own parents, but over the years people had chosen to award the credit to Honor. Maybe now, some might even look at him and conclude he had just kind of gone along with it, for the ride. And who could blame them?

The painful daily arguments about her future made him seek refuge in his study, where he sat for hours feeling dead inside while his second daughter lay on her bed wondering why life was cruel enough to provide her with fathers who rejected her. Should she apologise for not being the perfect child he'd imagined she would be, for not entirely filling the void of the baby they'd really wanted, for not managing to be anything like Judith at all? Where she got the creeping idea from that she wasn't as good as the real thing, she didn't know, but it was there like a throbbing malignancy in the pit of her stomach every time she failed.

It took the return of Judith from Durham University to put it into words.

'Can't you see? She has absolutely no self-esteem,' Judith told both her parents in mitigation after another mealtime row.

'But why not? She's funny, beautiful, brave, different,' Honor pleaded.

'Because she's not clever and that's what she thinks you want.'

But Judith was fresh from a graduation in which she had picked up an effortless first and so she wasn't the best person in Chess's book to make that particular point.

'Keep out of it, Judith,' her younger sister spat. 'You've been away for three years, you don't understand.'

'I still live here, I can still see what's going on.'

'All you can see is your own future.'

'And strangely, that involves your happiness too.'

Chess lifted the corner of her top lip in reply.

'Smile,' Judith said. 'If you can remember how to do it.'

'Maybe I haven't got anything to smile *about*.'

'You never used to need a reason.'

Mostly, the tears belonged to Honor and Judith – Chess would just retreat into angry silence, which would never win her the sympathy vote. Judith was often tempted to remind her sister what her alternative life might have been, but she always stopped short, aware that it could be the one thing to put a stop to their perpetual reconciliations.

They usually made friends again in their own tiny bathroom under the eaves of their bedrooms. No matter how bad the argument, all it took was a couple of knocks on the unlockable door to put an end to hostilities. If both sisters were in the house, it was almost unheard of for one of them to have a soak without the other sitting against the radiator or on the loo. It was the place where they compared cellulite and sexual conquests, although Judith had more first-hand experience of both.

'You didn't!'

'I did!'

'What was it like?'

'I need more practice.'

Perhaps Chess's unsettled mood would have passed if she had spent the summer working on the lavender farm again, or if Judith hadn't then disappeared without trace into Turkey for three months, or if Honor and John hadn't unexpectedly been invited to New England on an art teachers' exchange. Maybe then, if it had been business in the Lovell family as usual, she would have eventually succumbed to the dripfeed suggestion that she re-sit her exams at the local college.

But it wasn't, and she didn't, which meant that by mid-August, for the first time since her beleaguered Jamaican grandmother had reluctantly handed her over to the adoption agency seventeen years previously, Chess was surplus to requirements. This time though, she was old enough to feel the fear.

And then, out of the blue, just when life was beginning to be absolutely no fun at all, Morgan Hanlon, like a conveniently passing mother bird plucking someone else's young from a nest under attack, picked up the phone and offered her a job.

The Hanlons had never been merely friends of her parents. They had been the first people to be told about Chess's adoption, they had been the first to see her, to hold her, and to look after her – and, of course, they were her godparents too, just as they were Judith's. Chess knew them better than anyone outside her immediate family. In fact, as far as she was concerned, they *were* family. She didn't need blood-ties to work out people's hierarchical worth.

Brian was an eccentric artist in that he admitted he got a bigger kick out of selling his pictures than he did painting them, which meant he was unconventional for another reason too – he was awash with money. Not having planned for such wealth, he had just continued paying the stream of cheques into the bank until one day, without being asked, he was assigned to his own financial adviser.

Threatened with a lifetime trying to understand the sedentary world of prudent investment, he and Morgan decided the only solution was to toss all their savings into the air and see where they landed, so they hot-footed it to an estate agent and took out a wildly exorbitant lease on a Chelsea interiors shop just before prices went through the roof.

They pulled down the swagged pelmets, replaced the chandeliers with halogen bulbs, stripped the duck-egg blue Regency Stripe wallpaper and painted everything white. Then they removed the wooden flooring, poured down a tanker full of ready mixed concrete and swapped the finely turned wooden stair rail with steel tubing. Finally, with a ladder and a paintbrush, Brian daubed the words *The Wall Space* across the top of the window.

Despite taking a minimalist's – or cheapskate's as Brian preferred to call it – approach to the re-haul, they had nothing left over to pay anything remotely like an average London wage to staff it, which was exactly where Chess came in.

'Chess, how do you feel about coming to live with us for a few months, as a kind of Girl Friday?' Morgan asked on the phone to Norfolk one night. 'I've been late picking Dan up from school twice this week, and if Brian is made to eat one more take-away pizza . . .'

Their son Dan was an only child, conceived by his parents in their early forties just when they had been lulled into a false sense of security over contraception because of their increasing age. At six years old, it never even occurred to him to give a damn that his mum was older than all his friends' mums, but Morgan felt it and worried about it. And then the answer occurred to her. Chess, drifting helplessly in the country, was the perfect solution. She could come to London, be a big sister to Dan and help bridge the age-gap. Maybe she could even listen to the incessant childish chatter about inter-galactic wars and magic space dust without wanting to tell him to shut up and let her read the newspaper. Pre-menopausal parenting was not easy, as Morgan was finding out. The only thing she could find to say in favour of late motherhood was that at least her most turbulent hormones should have settled down by the time Dan hit adolescence.

'There'll be some pocket money in it for you,' Morgan added down the line. 'I'm sure I could clear it with your mum and dad.'

Honor and John – who had been on the brink of turning down the trip to New England on the basis that their directionless daughter needed them around – agreed to the proposition alarmingly quickly. Honor worried about whether Chess was really mature enough to be suitable childminding material, being practically a child herself, but John stopped her just in time.

'The responsibility will do her good,' he said. 'She's got to start feeling that people need her.' People like me for instance, he thought, but didn't say.

'*Start*?' Honor cried. 'God *knows* how I need that child.' And bingo, his wife had claimed the emotional high ground once again.

Chess had been to London only twice before, once on a school trip, and once to see *The King And I* with Honor and Judith as a birthday treat. On the second trip, she'd purchased a laminated Harrods bag and a Carnaby Street T-shirt, and she packed them both that August. It took the whole two weeks to decide on exactly which clothes to take to make the right impression, but it never even occurred to her that most people would initially identify her by the colour of her skin.

It occurred to Morgan though, but only because the gallery's first exhibition was *Big, Black and Beautiful – a Celebration of Caribbean Art*. Then it was her turn to worry. Would anyone think she was using Chess for commercial gain, as a kind of appropriate display of an equal opportunities employment policy? Brian mocked her gently and said if anything showed the void in her middle-class political correctness, that did.

A red-wine punch had originally been planned for the private view – invitations only went out to people Morgan and Brian knew for a fact had money to burn – but at the eleventh hour, when the sun was still unseasonally strong for a late summer evening, Morgan shouted, 'We need Pimms!', forcing Chess into a dash around the supermarkets for mint leaves and cucumber.

A thunderstorm was brewing, and the only spare air in the long, brightly lit showroom came courtesy of two huge electric fans that whirred discreetly but ominously at each end. Only a few of the fifty guests remained inside – everyone else opted for the elegant Chelsea pavement instead, where they slugged back their Pimms as if it was shandy. Not surprisingly, they were the ones to flourish their cheque books first. 'So?' Morgan whispered triumphantly. 'I'm not stupid.'

Of the four black artists whose work was being shown, three wore coloured vests. The fourth wore a linen jacket and shorts, but had dispensed with the formalities of shirt and shoes. They looked deeply hip, making everyone else – especially Brian in his trademark denim – look just as deeply conventional. Would-be buyers who stood in front of a particular painting for long enough would find themselves being personally introduced to one of them by an enthusiastic Morgan.

'Leroy, have you got a minute? This is Felix and Lydia Ames. They're interested in your series of Fiesta pictures.'

There then followed a succession of self-conscious questions about inspiration or light or brush technique, which the artist somehow had to find answers to if he was to strike the likely deal. Chess noticed that three of them – two vests and the linen suit – were much more rehearsed than the fourth, Poncho, who made his replies sound as if the customer had no right to ask. He was noticeably younger and the least scrubbed, but she couldn't help admiring him. He didn't seem to care if anyone bought his stuff or not.

After catching her glances for the third time, he wandered over to where she was standing, behind a table of upturned glasses and two and a half jugs of freshly mixed drink.

'Wha's dat stuff in dere, den, eh?' he asked, shaking a dirty nailed hand at one of the jugs.

'Pimms. Do you want some?'

'Me nah need vegetation in mah cup, man!'

'Go on, there's nothing else.' She wasn't exactly sure what he had said, but she could tell by his tone it wasn't complimentary.

'You comin' out from yuh lickle cage to have some wid me, yeh?'

Well, Brian *had* told her to keep the artists happy. Without the security of the table, she felt both gauche and nervous in her pristine white brushed cotton skirt and bright green crew neck sweater when he had obviously been in his clothes for days. Standing closer to him, he smelt sweet and seedy and there was a tiny diamond in the centre of one of his front teeth. It made her momentarily wonder what it would feel like on her tongue. She'd never kissed black lips before – only her own, in the mirror.

A bizarre idea came to her from nowhere. What if he was her brother or cousin or some other member of her birth family? How would she know? They shared the same skin tone, they were more or less the same age. She had been born in London – it was just as possible as it was ridiculous. Her mind wandered around this mad notion while he spoke.

'I hate myself for all dis, yeh?' he said above the dooby dooby doos of the jazz quartet.

'Sorry?'

'For sellin' us out, you t'ink dat, yeh? I c'n see it in yuh face, man. All dis heritage crap. Fat black mamas singin' de gospel, old boy playin' de blues. I did 'em a year ago but I'm workin' on street culture now, innit? Puttin' in a bit more about the real fight, yeh?'

He was shifting from foot to foot, jutting his head almost aggressively as he spoke. He held a battered dark red tobacco tin on the flat palm of his left hand, and used the open lid as a work surface to roll a cigarette. Chess could see Rizla packets, pieces of ripped cardboard and something in a twist of cling film inside. She was having enough trouble just holding a couple of glasses.

'Right,' she nodded, as if she had at least some idea what he meant. 'Selling who out, exactly?'

'*Us*, man,' Poncho repeated.

'I work here,' she said, just for something to say. 'I'm sort of related to the owners.'

'Yeh, right, sort of,' he smiled, his jewel flashing. 'You Jamaican?'

'My mum was,' she answered with confidence, since it was one of the few facts she did know about her gene pool. As to what difference that made, she had no idea. 'Are you?'

''Course, man. Comin' outside for a lickle smoke?' He put the tin back into the deep pocket of his baggies.

'You can smoke in here. Honest, Brian does it all the time.'

'Me nah t'ink so,' he laughed. 'Come wid me, yeh?'

'OK,' she smiled, 'just for a minute,' and she followed him not through the front door and on to the pavement with the rest of them, but across the showroom and into the storeroom at the back, where Poncho, in a borrowed car without insurance, had dropped off his work the day before.

The fire door, leading straight on to a quieter side street where the sun couldn't reach, was unlocked, and she followed him through that too, letting it slam behind her. As soon as they were outside, Poncho leant against the wall, lit his cigarette and took a deep drag, holding the smoke in his mouth before sucking it into his lungs. Then, resting his head against the brickwork, he handed it to Chess without looking at her. Slowly, he exhaled and said, 'Dat's better.'

She tried not to take it too gingerly. There was no question about sampling it, she just wanted to make sure it didn't look like her first time. She'd been pretending she'd tried it for the last six months anyway, just to keep up with her schoolfriends, so she put her novice lips around the cardboard end, and pulled gently on it. The mellow sweet smoke escaped into the air as she pretended to inhale.

'Thanks,' she said, only a very slight swimming sensation going on in her head. Then it was gone, and everything was exactly the same as it had been before. She obviously hadn't drawn in enough.

'You want for me to buil' you one?' Poncho asked.

'No, it's OK. I'm supposed to be working.'

'You c'n work 'pon dis, it won' hurt.'

'Can I share yours?' As far as she knew, joints *were* shared, puff by puff. For Poncho, it was more usually one each.

This time she took in more, forgetting there was no spongy filter to drag the smoke through first. The seeds popped and burned and the hot fog came so much more easily than it did when she had a Silk Cut. It *was* a fog too this time, and it swirled happily around her head, behind her eyes, through the labyrinth of her brain, and then, like a blanket, it wrapped itself warmly around her.

The private view going on inside was suddenly something entirely to do with other people. The jug of Pimms sitting on the table was not her responsibility, no more was she, leaning against the wall out here on the pavement, anyone else's business. She tried to assemble something to say but she could no longer deal in words. She had deliberated after the first abortive drag how best to react, and wondered what, if anything, would happen to her body. Now, she didn't care.

'Y'alright?' Poncho asked.

'Oh, yeh, I'm great,' she said, inhaling right the way in again. She always went the whole hog with a new experience. No caution, John said, which she had always taken as a criticism but he had always laced with a sneaking admiration.

When she'd passed it back and he'd taken one final pull, he

dropped it on the ground, twisted his trainer on the butt to put it out and scuffed it away. In one movement, he sprang his body forward, turned on his foot to face her, and pinned his glossy bare arms either side of her body, showing off a glorious definition of young muscle. He stared into her eyes, and gave her another flash of the jewel.

'Hey, wha's up?' he smiled, slightly maniacally.

Would she feel the diamond if she kissed him? There was only one way to find out. She put her own arms up, clasped them to the back of his head where her fingers wormed their way into his wiry henna-ed hair, and put the tip of her tongue against his teeth. There it was, tiny and rough against the filmed enamel. He tasted of late nights and dark clubs, of bedrooms where the curtains remain shut during the day. Even the bourgeois tang of Pimms had transmuted in his mouth to something shady.

His tongue, rigid and curled, pushed hers to one side, and then he was the one in control. His kiss was hard, like it was going places, and if she hadn't been cushioned by mild hallucination, she sensed she would have been frightened. It made the fumblings of the school disco and the exhibitionist snogs with the boyfriend in the pub car park seem embarrassingly tame.

He took one hand off the wall and lifted the hem of her jumper to find the curve of her left breast, heavy but supported in a seamless sports bra. He tried to pull the bra up so he could feel her properly, but the tight elasticated stitching dug into her skin and wouldn't move, so he ran his hand over and over the smooth cotton surface instead, expecting to find her nipple hardening. He kept it going for a little longer but her body had become tense and defensive, and eventually he came up for air.

'You still all right?' he asked, and smiled.

'Yeh,' she said, 'but I'd better go back inside.' She felt woolly and a bit sick.

'No man, you're safe wid me. Stay, yeh? I wan' a feel you.'

'I'm supposed to be working.'

'I could paint yuh pretty lips no trouble,' he said quietly in her ear, trying to kiss her again. He liked her soapy smell and her substantial bra, which felt to him like the harness of a virgin. She laughed shyly, and hurriedly pecked him on the cheek. Then she put her own hand up her jumper and re-positioned her bra with a twang.

'I thought I was only coming out for a breath of fresh air.'

'Nah, you never did,' Poncho said before he saw the genuine alarm on her face. 'Y'did? Ah, no worries. Next time, yeh?'

'I've locked us out,' she said, pushing on the fire door.

'It's only a lickle walk round de front, innit? C'mon, I don't make woman do t'ings she nah want fe do, yeh?'

He took her hand and escorted her back, dropping his grasp just as the gallery crowd came into sight. She yearned for a second to know him better than she did, although the fleeting fantasy that they were related had been usurped by another. Now that she felt safe again, in the earshot of people she knew, she could indulge in it further. His body and hers, together.

Later, after the guests and musicians had gone and Morgan had left to pick Dan up from friends, Brian insisted the artists join him in one last drink.

'People must have bigger walls than I thought,' he said, handing Poncho a scribbled note to confirm that all but one of his vast canvases had been sold. 'You went down well.'

'I wish, man,' Poncho replied, flashing a look across at Chess, who found herself flashing one back.

'No, you did, you did,' said Brian, missing the double entendre.

Poncho sniggered at the misplaced reassurance, looked at the note, raised his eyebrows but spoke directly to Chess, who was packing boxes of dirty glasses.

'It don't make me feel dat great, y'nah?'

'What's that?'

'Takin' money for dis stuff.'

Brian looked mildly offended, but then Chess batted back.

'Don't knock it. My dad's an artist and he can't sell diddly squat.' (If Brian hadn't been there, she would have said 'fuck all'.) 'He has to hang most of his stuff in our garage.'

Poncho sniffed and drew on a Camel he'd bummed off a customer.

'I'll tell you what, yeh? My next work'll tell everyone de truth about bein' black. And I'll tell you wha' else. I bet de same people dat t'ink I was so fuckin' good tonight don't even buy one of 'em.'

'Any time you need me to make you rich, just shout,' said Brian, and he walked into the stockroom, where he added, 'Jumped-up little shit.'

That night, Chess experienced a delayed reaction to her tentative foray into a world she didn't know. The more she thought about the way Poncho had held her against the wall, and how she'd noticed his strong but not unpleasantly smelly fuzz of armpit hair no more than a couple of inches away from her face, the more she wished she'd made more of it. She thought about his malleable wet lips and the urgency of his kiss, and then, inevitably, she wondered about him naked.

Lying on her quilt – she was too hot to lie under it – she ran her hands over her own body, around her big liberated breasts, over her slightly protruding but taut tummy, and around her narrow hips to what she thought of as her big bottom. She imagined him doing the same, black limbs against black limbs, and an isolated surge of intense energy happened somewhere in her groin which she recognised as her first ever real shot of sexual desire. Up until now, she'd been happy to be motivated by sexual curiosity. The difference was extraordinary.

She turned on the light, got off her bed and went to stand in front of the large dressing-table mirror. As she cast her eyes over her shoulders and breasts, she realised for the first time how much she liked her own colour, deep and rich.

Then she thought about Simon, the only boy she had ever seen erect, and remembered how put off she had been when she'd first seen his anaemic pubic hair. Black fuzz suddenly seemed so much more erotic, even the little line that ran down from her navel and that Judith had once offered to wax.

She pouted her lips and scooped up her breasts, but the pose made her look ludicrously titillating. Then she tried stretching her arms above her head and standing with her legs astride, which made her look like some terrifying Amazonian warrior. Poncho was quite small, he'd probably worry about being crushed to death if he saw her like that.

Next, she crossed her arms demurely over her breasts, with her palms resting on opposite shoulders, and pulled a few come-and-get-me faces. None of them was even remotely convincing and she laughed derisively at her reflection. Then she tried – one of her favourite tricks – to pretend she was looking objectively at a magazine photograph. What conclusions would she draw from her own appearance?

Her build was much chunkier than either Honor's or Judith's, she didn't have much of a waist like they did, her tummy stuck out and her thighs were more muscular. Not that she'd swap. She liked her own loose rhythmic way of moving better.

She looked deep into her own face, staring at her eyes and their knowing expression, studying the shape of her nose and the way her lips moved when she smiled. For a split second, a different person was looking back at her, someone who knew something she didn't. Then the moment passed and she was herself again.

She had developed a strange private game since she had been in London. If she walked behind someone the same colour and build, she would send her eyes into a detached kind of focus and imagine she was following herself. The walk might be dissimilar, and the clothes, but she could usually, after a minute or so, manage a ring of truth somewhere. It made her feel more secure, like she *was* someone, not just a figment of her own imagination. At least, that was the only reason she could think of for doing it.

It was suddenly cold, and as she reached over to pull a baggy T-shirt off a wicker chair by the window, she realised she hadn't drawn the curtain. Diving to the floor, her hand fumbled with the rope tie-back. As she pulled the single canvas drape across by its padded cotton hem, she tried to work out if anyone could possibly have seen her. Her bedroom was on the third floor, so only those neighbours in a similar height room would have been able to look directly at her. She turned off the light and had a tentative peer out. There was a lit bathroom opposite – she could see shapes through the frosted glass.

Crawling back into bed, embarrassed and amused, she imagined a knock on the door from someone complaining to the Hanlons that their new nanny exposed herself at night. Comforted by the fact that both Morgan and Brian would find something like that enormously funny, she lay back and began contemplating the evening's other puzzle.

Poncho had said his next work would tell everyone what it was really like to be black. He obviously thought she already knew. Well, she was black too, wasn't she? But the truth was, as far as her peers were concerned, she had always been 'coloured' – and worse than that, she could see now that if she had thought of herself as anything, she had thought of herself as white. Or another Judith anyway.

In Norfolk she had been a novelty. Friends used to stick their fingers and pencils in their hair and try to extract a tight curl, or play noughts and crosses with their fingernails on her legs. That wasn't what it was like to be black, that was what it was like to be popular.

Poncho didn't look as if he would let anyone put their fingers in his hair, ever – except of course, that was exactly what she had just done. And then it dawned on her. He was *her* novelty, her bit of black. There was something very wrong somewhere.

Chapter 5

Years later, when anyone asked Chess how she came to do it, she would say it all just kind of happened. There was never really any one moment when she could have said 'I made the choice', but then she always was a girl who had to wait for options to fall into her lap before she realised they even existed. Once they had, she often took them without stopping to think. Amazingly, this particular choice really did fall into her lap, or at her feet, or out of the sky. Actually, it fell out of a Filofax, but she still saw it as fate knocking on her door.

That morning's timetable was hardly thrilling – taking Dan to school on the bus, and then on to the gallery to sort out the aftermath of the private view. Morgan had dumped everything – wine glasses stained with grainy red deposits, forgotten cardigans and full ashtrays – in the stockroom, and was now up to her eyes in the showroom, working out the sales figures and sorting a long list of fresh commissions.

Chess looked at the pile of abandoned possessions without curiosity. The small room smelt of a hangover and she opened the back fire door to let in some air. It was difficult, in the sharp morning light and without the bonus of alcohol or drugs, to believe what had happened out there just a few hours previously. To be sure she hadn't dreamt it, she scanned the pavement to see if the butt of Poncho's herbal cigarette was still lying there.

It was – well and truly flattened and hiding with a few less intoxicating filter tips against the wall. Seeing it brought back the special details, the exact way he'd snuffed it out with his foot and then moved in on her with such expert carnal coordination, the gentle massaging of her breast, the taste of his saliva. It seemed unromantic to leave it lying there and she almost put it into her pocket for keeps, but instead she rolled it under her flat pump and then separated it from the others with her toe.

Her eyebrows arched as her groin echoed with a faint surge of the same desire that had kept her awake for so long last night. There was the chill of early autumn in the air and all she had on was a thin T-shirt but she propped the door open anyway so the roach could continue to distract her while she cleared up. It embodied something she knew she wanted to explore further. Not drugs but something else, something to do with other people's disapproval – or did she mean approval? That depended on who the people were.

She began to tackle the heap of possessions with a heavier than necessary sigh. A wad of identical business cards were crammed into the slots at the back of the unnamed bulging Filofax so she began by ringing the number in bold type. A voice reeled off a company name so robotically that Chess didn't catch any of it.

'Er . . . is that the *Daily Mail*?'

'Advertising or editorial?'

'Sorry?'

'Which department do you want?'

'Um, I want to speak to someone called Clare Davies, because she's left her–'

But before she could finish her story, the operator interrupted with another number. At last, after three failed attempts, Chess got another inaudible bark down the receiver.

'Is that Clare Davies?'

'Yeah.' There was a lot of background noise – traffic and wind. 'Who's this?'

'I'm phoning from The Wall Space Gallery. Have you lost anything?'

'Yes, my bloody Filofax! Is it there?'

'What's it like?'

'Liberty material, blob of red felt pen on bottom left.'

'We've got it safely here for you. What do you want me to do with it?'

'I'll come round and pick it up after this job – say, an hour?'

'OK.'

'Cheers.'

The line crackled and cleared. The girl had been barely civil, so as Chess put the business card back she had no qualms about taking a sneaky flick through the overcrowded book to see if there was anything interesting in it. As she did, a sealed letter addressed to Office of Population Census and Surveys fell to the floor. It lay there unnoticed until well after Clare Davies had been and gone, and it was Morgan who eventually picked it up.

'Is this yours?' she asked Chess, ignoring the whispered counsel she had had with Brian. He had advised her to post it, no questions, that if it was something to do with Chess and she wanted to talk about it, then she would. But even Brian had been lost for an answer when Morgan had asked him what evidence he had to support the theory that Chess ever shared her thoughts with anyone.

'What is it?' Chess asked.

'Have a look.'

The girl gave a blank stare at the address and shrugged. 'No.'

Morgan looked relieved. 'Oh, I thought it might be. I found it on the stockroom floor and because this is where you write to get your birth cert–'

'Morgan,' said Brian, purposely interrupting, 'have you got the final sales figures for last night yet?'

'I know it's not your writing but I just thought–'

'Morgan!' Brian almost shouted. 'The figures!'

Chess took the envelope from Morgan's waving hand and looked at it. 'I've got a feeling it might have fallen out of that Filofax. I'll go and call that journalist again and ask her if she wants me to post it.'

'Tell her she doesn't need to keep finding excuses to come back and see me, she's welcome any time,' Brian joked emptily.

All women, attractive or otherwise, received the same treatment.

'Desperate, was she?'

'She'd have to be.'

Only when Chess had walked back into the stockroom did she appreciate that Clare Davies's number was in the Filofax and the Filofax was now back with Clare Davies. She looked at the letter again. The Office of Population Census and Surveys didn't sound too thrilling to her. Why had Morgan thought it was hers?

The answer smacked her in the face like a crude wake-up call as soon as she opened it up. It was an application form for access to birth records, signed and dated the previous day and the word *adoption* – even though it was in an identical font to the rest – leapt from the page.

Chess slapped the paper face down on the table and kept her hand over it while she waited for the ripple of shock to subside, her skin burning with embarrassment.

'Oh shit.'

When she felt able to take a more controlled look, she shut the stockroom door and pulled a telephone directory from the shelf to use as a cover should anyone come in. This was weird. She was being presented with a golden opportunity for information that wouldn't come her way a second time. It was a moment of stolen chance and the thought of anyone stealing it back made her speed-read like she had never been able to before.

Clare Davies had given her full name, the names of her *adoptive* parents (a term new to Chess's previously uninquisitive ears) and her date of birth, but she had left the space for the date of *adoption* blank. The empty rectangular box was small but Chess's eyes locked on to its nothingness. It meant the journalist had chosen not to consult her parents – her *adoptive* parents – to get this piece of information. Chosen? *Was* there a choice? What was Clare Davies thinking of? Why was she doing this?

Up until now, Chess had decided not to like Clare very

much. She was a weasly-looking woman in her early twenties with big red glasses, lank mousy hair and badly capped teeth. She'd been verging on the rude on the phone and not shown a great deal more gratitude when she'd turned up at the gallery in person. But if she was adopted . . . well, that was different. Allowances would have to be made.

Chess continued to pore over the detail. At the bottom of the confidential form, in the box which asked where she would like to receive counselling, Clare Davies had Tipp-Exed out a tick against the General Register Office at St Catherine's House, London, and then gone over it again in ballpoint. It was the only mistake on the whole application, which had otherwise been filled in with great care – fountain pen ink, immaculate lettering, a signature that looked practised. Chess suddenly and inexplicably felt close to tears.

She had been entitled to get hold of her own birth certificate for four months, since her eighteenth birthday in May. Until now, the option had hovered somewhere near the back of her mind, but it had been there nonetheless, first planted by her parents during a celebratory restaurant meal in a way that had made her visibly cringe at the time, and made her feel no less self-conscious now.

Pudding had been and gone. Judith and her innocuous college boyfriend had adjourned to the restaurant lounge to plot how they would get to sleep together that night and Chess's platonic friend Paul, who would have quite liked *not* to have been platonic, but hadn't a hope in hell, had 'nipped outside for a fag'. Suddenly there was just her, Honor and John. She'd started wincing as soon as John had looked at her and raised his eyebrows in the way he did whenever anything inevitable was on the horizon.

'Well, Francesca Kate . . .'

'Oh no, Dad, scrap the speech.'

'Go on, humour an old man . . .'

'As long as you don't say anything too sloppy.'

John reached across the table and squeezed her hand. She remembered the gesture so well because it was so unlike him and yet the pressure of his clasp felt so genuine.

'OK – but it's been a privilege to watch you grow up.'

Somewhere between her brain and her fingers, the message to return the squeeze, to let him know that she loved him too, got lost. It was always the way.

'You said it was high time I *did* grow up the other day.'

'Darling, a moment please.' Honor was earnest and the room went quiet as she said, 'We want you to know that we will always be here for you, whatever you choose to do.'

'What can I do at eighteen that I can't already do?'

'You can get hold of your birth certificate for a start.'

'Why should I want to do that?'

The emptiness of such a premature reassurance had echoed all around the long low restaurant like the howl of wind caught in a concrete tunnel, but her mother had looked madly grateful all the same.

Reading Clare Davies's private correspondence now seemed a serious invasion of privacy and Chess folded the document hurriedly, trying with too many fingers and thumbs to put it back into the ripped envelope. On the other hand, she thought, mitigating furiously, maybe it wasn't so confidential – a journalist would surely appreciate that once such a letter reached its destination, any number of complete strangers would soon see it. Perhaps invasion of privacy wasn't such a big thing for a *Daily Mail* hack.

She felt an urgent obligation to get the letter in the post, and ran into the showroom to whip a clean envelope from the desk drawer.

'What's the matter?' Morgan asked, alarmed at the sudden rush.

'She wants me to post it for her. She didn't say what it was, but she was keen for it to go off.'

Chess copied out the address in block capitals and casually slid the old envelope in her back pocket.

'Could you take these for me too?' Morgan handed her a five-pound note and a pile of identical white envelopes addressed in bottle green fountain pen. 'You should think about going to get Dan too, because if the traffic's bad . . .' She was peering over her glasses.

'Sure,' Chess said, suddenly re-opening the desk drawer and filching a writing pad and another envelope. She put everything quickly in her bag. Morgan was too busy with a calculator to pay any attention. 'I'll see you at home then,' she said as casually as she could.

'Bye, sugar.'

At the post office, she stood edgily in the queue thinking about Clare's letter in her hand and the blank sheet of paper in her bag. She was filled with an obscure sense of shame, that she was doing something that would dismay her family, that she was already letting people down. But how? By having thoughts? But then something else, something stronger, got the better of her, and she left her place to go to the only empty writing shelf.

Using the black chained pen, she began a letter of her own. *Dear Sir/Madam, Please send me an application form to apply for my birth certificate. I am eighteen. Yours sincerely, Francesca Lovell.*

She looked at her immature script and at the words which lacked authority, like the letter she'd written as a child to the Queen or one of her fake sick notes, and she screwed it up. Then she wrote another but the result was exactly the same.

If time hadn't been of the essence, she might have had another few goes to perfect it, but she sealed the second attempt before she had a chance to change her mind. She pulled Clare's ripped envelope out of her back pocket, copied out the address, slotted the secret letter into the middle of her pile of post and put the whole lot in the box marked First Class.

Waves of panic, regret and excitement washed over her as she sat on the bus on the way to Dan's school. Was that a turning point back there? she asked herself. How big a decision have I just made? Significant or not? What if I get some information I don't really want? What would the postman think if I stood there and waited for him to empty the box?

Would he give it back?

I don't have to do anything with it, she reassured herself as the bus swayed on. When the certificate arrives, I'll put it in the zipped leather case I keep my private letters in and no one need ever know. But what if Mum went through my things? What if Morgan opened it by mistake? What would I say?

In fact, her questions subsided almost as quickly as her plan had been hatched in the first place, and she soon took to staring into shop windows from her bus seat without thinking too much more about it. After all, the deed was done. Chess always had been good at shrugging her shoulders when thinking got too much like hard work.

By the time she became aware, three weeks later, that her one hasty action had catapulted her on to a professionally sensitive, well-oiled and ever-moving social services conveyor belt, it felt too late to get off.

The application form duly arrived and she completed it without ceremony at the kitchen table one morning when the house was quiet. Normally form-filling fazed her and under more usual circumstances she would have waited until someone was available to talk her through it. Now though, she was utterly on her own and it thrilled her a little.

When another envelope arrived shortly afterwards, she was so convinced it would be the certificate itself that she didn't open it all day, not until Dan was in bed and Morgan and Brian were out. It seemed more than a mere coincidence that she was alone in the house every time a significant piece of post dropped through the letterbox, like it really was meant to be her secret.

To her disappointment, and if she was honest, a small amount of horror, it wasn't the certificate at all but a notification of an appointment to meet an assigned counsellor. At that point, she and her previously detached behaviour parted company. The waiting *had* begun to feel a little like expecting to receive a driving licence or a passport, something mildly exciting but hardly worth worrying about. Now though, the episode had a distinction all of its own. Counselling? The prospect of actually having to talk to someone about it was terrifying and she could soon think of nothing else, not even Poncho.

A small glossy handbook was enclosed with the appointment letter. Chess had to re-read it a few times to grasp the official language, but after a few repeated paragraphs it was clear she was going to have to try harder – she could hardly ask anyone else to translate it for her. Little by little, it started to make sense.

People adopted before November 1975 are required by law to see a counsellor before they can be given access to their records. By law? What law? What if she refused? Would she be arrested?

The Registrar General will have sent your counsellor most of the information from your adoption order. This includes your original name, the name of your birth mother, possibly but not certainly, the name of your birth father, and the name of the court where the order was made. The counsellor will not have a copy of your original birth record at the interview but will be able to give you the necessary application form. You can use the information which the counsellor will give you and the application form to apply for a copy of your original birth record at any time if you decide you want one. There is a statutory fee for this birth certificate. You will understand that it is very important that precautions are taken against information about you being given to an unauthorised person. To avoid this, you must take with you some means of identification, such as a bank card, a passport/identity card or a driving licence.

Chess thought she would try pretending she had never posted the letter in the first place and see how long it took for it to go away, but ignoring it was impossible. For the next three days, the handbook sat in the back pocket of her jeans, from where she would pull it out and re-read it whenever she was alone. The entire week passed in a quandary.

'So what do you think I should do, Dan?' she asked her

gangly little friend in the park after school on Friday, even though she had spoken to no one about it.

'Take me to McDonald's for supper?' he replied. 'Or Pizzaland, obviously.'

She tried the same arbitrary approach on Morgan later that evening, as they were cooking.

'What do you think I should do?' she asked, with reference to apparently nothing. 'Just say yes or no.'

'If it's drugs, no. If it's sex, make sure you're sensible. Anything else, yes,' Morgan declared, throwing her a bag of salad. 'In the meantime, wash this.'

Morgan related the incident to Brian later, when she'd had time to feel a dereliction of duty in not pushing Chess further.

'What do you think she meant?'

'Why didn't you ask her?'

'She's so *private*.'

'Maybe she's just shy.'

But Morgan sensed it wasn't that at all, and that Chess was being purposely clinical about her emotional involvement with people around her. She thought how ironic it was that Honor had been afraid that in her absence Chess would transfer her daughterly affections, that Morgan would be a better 'mother', that she would come back from America to find herself usurped. Unlikely, Morgan could report back to her friend now, since Chess seemed to reject *any* offer of closeness.

That much was true. Chess's thoughts might have been too raw to share but that didn't stop her wanting answers. Hypothetical throwaway questions were as much as she could manage. If only, she kept thinking, if only she could answer the big one herself. Should she go along with it or not?

What was stopping her? The thought of Honor's face when she told her? The prospect of having to open up to a complete stranger? The risk of getting in too deep? None of it really mattered if she stuck to her original plan to keep it as her own very private piece of classified information.

Eventually, for no one particular reason but after a hundred changes of mind and heart, she knew she didn't really have a choice. On the day of the appointment with the counsellor, she told Morgan she was going to the doctor for some advice about irregular periods.

'You are old enough to go on the pill for whatever reason you like,' Morgan said lightly, imagining she was so laid back she was practically horizontal. That approach didn't work either.

'You think that's what I'm going for?'

'Of course.'

'Confident . . . but wrong,' Chess laughed, pleased to have pulled some wool. She put her cheque book, cheque card, driver's licence and the letter in her bag and headed for St Catherine's House, wherever that was. The cab driver knew. Her empty stomach growled without wanting to be fed and her eyelids felt heavy through erratic sleep, but she kept up an impressive front.

It felt uncannily like being at the doctor's, actually. There were three other 'patients' waiting on the vinyl bench with her. One by one, they were plucked off by smiling social workers who called them through an internal fire door to a corridor of more doors, but none of them, she observed with a certain amount of relief, looked as if they were exactly at crisis point.

Chess was relieved that her counsellor, who introduced herself with an outstretched hand and a non-committal smile as 'Jeeva', was the one with the thick straight black hair held back with a metal hairslide shaped like a lizard. She was about thirty and stylishly large, wearing an oversized purple silk shirt with buttons that went all the way down one side, and voluminous black silk trousers that fell in billowy folds until just above her ankles, when they narrowed dramatically.

'I like your top,' Chess said, following her into a counselling room with bare cream walls apart from two small insipid woodland scenes in flimsy steel frames.

She heard in her own words Honor's favourite opening gambit – praise for a new hairstyle, clothes, car, kids, anything. Not always genuine but said with the best of intentions. Being liberal with compliments was a family trait. Judith was almost worse than Honor now. It suddenly seemed an age since they'd all been together under one roof, and she had a flash of something akin to homesickness, quickly followed by an uncomfortable pang of remorse.

She had told herself time and time again that the guilt was unnecessary. Her parents had given her their permission, they'd even brought the subject up first. But then, she was doing this behind their back, wasn't she? Surely they never intended that.

'Sari silk,' Jeeva said, giving the cloth a tug. 'I made it myself, and the trousers, for a tenner.'

'Bargain.'

Her counsellor smiled a sort of cut-off smile. She only had twenty minutes. 'Take a seat, Francesca.'

'Everyone calls me Chess.'

'OK, Chess. Let's sit down.'

A silence fell upon the room and Chess wondered what she was supposed to do next. Eventually, Jeeva spoke.

'Well, a good place to start is to ask what prompted you to apply for your birth records in the first place.'

'Oh. Does there have to be a reason?'

'No.'

'It was just a spur-of-the-moment thing.'

'Uh huh. Sometimes, it's for purely medical reasons. Lots of adoptees start their search when they're facing parenthood for the first time, for example.'

'I'm not pregnant,' Chess said quickly. A cubed box of tissues was sitting on the table with the top one pulled invitingly out. The very thought of needing to use it embarrassed her.

'No, no.' It was Jeeva's turn to smile. 'I'm just giving you an instance. Some people do it because they feel a need to know their origins, or because they've never felt they really belonged in their adoptive family, especially where trans-racial adoptions like yours are concerned.'

'What do you mean?'

'Some children, if they've grown up in a family of a different race, need to understand more about their roots, about their place in the world.' An earnest encouragement swept across her round face and she paused for a reaction. The first few minutes were always the most stilted. 'They're confused, in search of an identity, a little displaced.'

Chess nodded to show she understood Jeeva meant well. 'But I'm none of those.'

'Lucky you – there doesn't have to be a reason, as you said. Now, I don't have a copy of the original birth certificate here, you can apply for that later, but what I do have are a few details you may or may not already know. There's no rush if you don't want them.'

'Sure. I mean, I'm fine.'

Jeeva had seen too much to believe totally in this girl's persistent display of self-assurance. Nothing that happened within these walls was entirely inconsequential.

'So,' she said, putting down her papers to play for time, 'do you understand why we ask to see people at this stage to talk things through?'

'Er, not really. To be honest, I never expected to have to see anyone, so I was a bit taken aback when the appointment came through.'

'You came though.'

'Yes.'

'And are you glad you did?'

'Um . . .' Chess hedged apologetically with a small dismissive laugh. She wasn't sure what a truthful answer would be. On the one hand all this advice was a bit of a pain, but on the other, well, who else could she talk to? She shrugged.

'You see, searching for and maybe even confronting your birth mother takes a lot of courage, even if you don't think that at the moment. It forces people to face all sorts of hitherto unknown facts about themselves.'

'But I don't want to search for or confront anyone.'

'Uh huh?'

'I just want my birth certificate. Or at least, I thought I did.'

'Have you changed your mind?'

'Well, it's just that I didn't know it would be this involved. Nobody knows I'm here. I haven't told anyone.'

'Who do you mean by anyone – your adoptive parents?'

'I don't really like you calling them that. They're my *parents*. They're on holiday in America and I'm staying with friends.'

'It's just a phrase used for clarity, it doesn't mean anything. But you haven't discussed anything like this with them previously?'

'It was their idea, on my eighteenth birthday. They brought it up first.'

'Great. And how do they feel now?'

'Well, sorry, no, I'm being confusing. They suggested I do it, and now I have. It's just that they don't know I have. I didn't think there would be much to discuss. I just thought the certificate would arrive in the post, and I could keep it somewhere safe.' She began to feel naive and wondered if it was too late to make her excuses and leave.

'Why don't you want anyone to know?'

'I wouldn't like Mum or Dad to think I'm not satisfied with what I have, because I am.'

'It's a very common and understandable reaction on both parts. But let's go back to my first question for a moment. Do you understand *why* we should talk things through?'

'Not entirely, no.'

'OK, Chess – well, not so long ago, people really believed it was best for all concerned if an adopted child's break with his or her birth family was total. That means your birth mother would have been told that you would *not* have any access to your birth records in the future, but society has moved on and that's obviously not the case any more, or you wouldn't be here.'

'Sorry? Could you just repeat that?' Chess was struggling to get back into her body after leaving it for a moment and staring down on the scene from somewhere near the ceiling.

'We have a greater understanding of the needs of adopted children now, so the law has to be changed to allow you information that would previously have been denied to you. Do you see what I'm saying?'

'Yes.' Chess felt fraudulent, as if Jeeva thought she was a

genuinely needy case. 'No. Well, sort of.' A picture of Judith was now filling her head to the point that she could think of nothing else. What would she say if she could see her now?

'I'm suggesting that there are things you might like to consider before you set off down this road. You know, your mother might not be alive, she might be mentally ill, or possibly worst of all, she may not even want to see you. Have you thought about any of these possibilities?'

'I only want my birth certificate,' Chess repeated. 'I don't actually want to *meet* anyone.'

'So you've said, but I'm here to help you in case you change your mind. You might want your mother – should you find her – to know that you're all right, that she did the right thing, that you're glad she had you. Or you might want to tell her how angry you are with her, that she had no right to have you. I don't know. *You* probably don't know yet. That's why it's important we talk.'

'OK.' It made her uncomfortable the way Jeeva used the word 'mother' as if it applied to someone other than Honor, but the counsellor was obviously contractually obliged to say her bit, so Chess thought she might as well try and listen. It was difficult though. It sounded like a spiel intended for someone else.

'In many cases, adoptees who deny any real need to know about their birth family often hurtle into very intense emotional relationships with them once contact is made. Now I'm not saying this is what will happen with you, but it is something to bear in mind. It's not easy, that's all I'm saying.'

'But there won't *be* any contact.'

'Not if you don't want there to be, no. Would you like me to read through these notes?'

'Sure.'

Jeeva was relieved that her latest client was noticeably less tense after learning nothing new from the details she was given. Her natural mother's name was Christine George and there was no information available at all on her father. Her birth name was Frances Catherine just as she'd been told it was, although it still didn't sound to her like the kind of name a young girl would give to her illegitimate baby.

'Why bother giving a child a middle name at all if you're not going to keep it? Or *was* she going to keep me, once upon a time?' Chess asked, thinking she was merely making conversation.

'You see?' Jeeva said. 'There *are* questions you want answered. It might be worth asking yourself if you do actually care *something* about all this – or why else would you be making an effort to find out more? I don't mean to suggest that you want your birth mother in your life, or that you're looking for her to claim you or anything, but you have made a big decision just by coming this far, and you should bear in mind that you're probably searching for something, even if it is just a missing jigsaw piece.'

'Well, yes, but it's closer to curiosity than need.'

'I'm happy with that. Have a think about how much you really *do* want to find out, and if you want to take anything further, come back and we'll talk some more. Here's the application form for your original birth record which you can use at any time. This is my direct line. If I'm not in, you can always leave a message.' Jeeva stood up and checked her watch. 'I'm busy, but always here, in the wider sense, OK? It's been good to meet you, Chess.'

'And you, thanks.'

They'd been talking for exactly nineteen minutes.

Chess let the television wash over her that night. Morgan was hooked on a sex and shopping mini-series and Brian had his nose in a book, so the only talk was in her head. She wanted to work out – or actually, for someone to tell her since she never gave credit to her own deliberations – exactly what she had done. Had she made the big decision yet or not? Was she following an inevitable path, well trodden by coming-of-age adoptees the world over, or was it unusual to take such impetuous action so soon? Maybe it was an expression of a need in her she hadn't yet recognised. Maybe Jeeva was right.

She already felt changed in some way. Being adopted used to

be just another insignificant label that other people put on her, but tonight it felt almost glamorous in a wounded kind of way. It was a bit like the dope – one drag and she wanted more.

For a reason she couldn't quite identify, she badly wanted to talk to Judith. Not that she intended to reveal anything, but there would be something reassuring in the sound of her sister's kind and attentive voice. It was the first time Chess had properly missed her since she had upped and gone to Turkey, and she realised that the secret resentment and hurt she'd been harbouring at not being asked to go too had completely gone. She also felt quite excited at the thought that they were beginning to lead separate lives. The sands were shifting under both their feet and she was no longer purely frightened by the way it made her feel. But talking to Judith was academic anyway – she was well and truly out of contact – so instead, her insecurities latched on to Honor and John.

'Would it be OK if I tried to call Mum and Dad?' she asked casually during the adverts.

'Of course,' said Morgan anxiously. 'Are you missing them?' Maybe that was what it was all about, a simple case of Chess feeling like a stranger in someone else's home.

'Only kind of.'

But Chess couldn't reach them, not even in her thoughts.

In the twenty-four hours that followed, she felt as if she was on a roller-coaster ride. On the highs, she was bewitched by the possibilities, but on the lows she felt truly alone, terrified that she might be counselled and guided so much that one day she might not know her own mind.

By the time she entered Jeeva's office on impulse again three days later, she hardly knew her own mind any more anyway. She had made the appointment with the intention of taking her enquiries one step further, but the moment she walked into the counselling room again, she exacted the perfect U-turn.

'Put me down as a time-waster,' she back-pedalled straight away. 'I've decided to stick with the information I already have. That's all I intended to do in the first place so . . .'

'Is that what you came to say?'

'Yes. Well, no, but it's best all round if I–'

'You don't sound too convinced to me.'

'It's really hard. One minute I want to know more and the next . . .'

Jeeva interrupted her flow by standing up and holding out a brown envelope. 'Maybe you should decide after you've read this.'

'What is it?'

A noise somewhere stopped, or the air conditioning kicked in, or the clock struck or something. In any case, Jeeva's office became a completely different place all of a sudden – much, much stiller.

'Don't look so alarmed. It's something rather special – a seventeen-year-old letter.'

'Uh?'

Chess's world went on pause.

'It was with your file which I received yesterday. Would you like to sit down and have a look?'

'What . . . what does it say?'

'I'll get us a coffee and then we'll talk.'

'No, no, I'm fine, honestly, I'd rather talk now. Could you tell me more?'

'Sure, when you stop looking so terrified.'

Chess smiled feebly.

'That's marginally better,' Jeeva smiled back. 'OK, well, sometimes, by the late 1960s, the adoption services were enlightened enough to suggest to birth parents and relatives of babies being put up for adoption that they leave a little something on file, just in case the law ever changed, so that if and when the child grew up and wanted more information, there would be at least something to go on – you know, to keep the avenues open – a message or something to let the child know he or she was loved despite being given away.'

'Yes?' asked Chess. I'd like that, she thought. The cubed box of tissues was now staring her in the face with a 'Use Me' label slapped across them.

'And in your case, the suggestion worked.'

'That's a letter from my real mother, isn't it?' Something in her head and stomach contracted at the same time.

'It's actually a letter from your *grand*mother, the woman who put you up for adoption, who handed you over.'

'My *grandmother*?'

'That's right.'

Chess's blood, warmer than usual and being pumped top speed by a heart on overdrive, swirled around inside her. No wonder Jeeva had suggested she sat down. She tipped her head forward for a few seconds. Discovering a mother, or even a brother or sister had occurred to her, but a grandmother? It was like a message from the dead.

'*Really*? When . . . when did she write it?'

'In 1968, at the point of your adoption. Would you like to read it?'

'No!' Chess yelped before she could stop herself. 'Yes, no, you read it to me . . . Oh no, sorry, I don't mean that, of course. I mean, yes, well, I can't not, really, can I?'

'Not really,' her counsellor smiled.

Chess took the envelope from Jeeva's dry hand and noticed how clammy her own had become. The front was blank apart from a reference number in ink in the top right-hand corner. Something smaller had obviously been sitting on top of it for a long time because the brown paper was two-tone, faded to a buff colour around its edges with its original colour forming a square in the middle. The glue on the unsealed flap had cracked.

Almost in a stupor, Chess took out and unfolded a single piece of decorated writing paper, bordered with a cartoon puppy. In a mix of capitals and lower case, adorned with curious curves, unpunctuated and written in diminished fountain pen ink, she read:

To Frankie You been loved and cherished sleepin in my bed since you was born and I will surely miss the sweet smell of your baby breath on my face The Lord knows it make my heart cry to give you away but there is no good life for you here so I pray that He will find good people to keep you safe and happy I keep you in my heart always I am forever your lovin grandmother Minnie George.

The blood that had been swishing round her head now turned to salt and water, filling her eyes. Her swallowing reflex stopped working and she gagged and spluttered on a mouthful of saliva as her lips began wavering uncontrollably. I'm crying, she thought. I'm crying and I never thought I would.

So I am not Frances Catherine or Francesca or even really Chess. I am Frankie, a sweet-smelling baby with a pet name who used to sleep with my grandmother.

She somehow knew that was the truth, like she'd always known it. After reading the words again, she held the paper crisp with age against her lips as Jeeva came back into focus.

'Are you OK?'

Chess shook her head, and the counsellor moved closer to put out a comforting hand. 'It's a lovely letter to have though, isn't it?'

The movement of Chess's nodding head caused the pool of water in her eyes to spill two or three drips down her face. One of them splashed on the seventeen-year-old ink, smudging a few words. Jeeva pushed the box of tissues towards her, but Chess used her knuckles instead, grinding them into the corner of her eyes.

'We'll talk, when you're ready.'

'I'm ready,' she managed to say. 'Sorry. It's so . . . it's sad . . . the letter. It hurts to think of anyone having to write something like that.'

'Giving a baby away must be a very difficult thing. But it was written a long time ago, remember.'

'Does that make a difference?'

'Well, it means Minnie might not be alive, she might not want to know, she might be mentally ill – there could be hundreds of other reasons why this letter won't be able to help you further.'

'Oh,' Chess said in a voice she didn't recognise. 'Minnie might be dead. That's her name, is it? My grandmother's name? Minnie?' She stroked the signature. 'Minnie . . .' and finally, a groan from deep inside her made itself heard.

Jeeva – a veteran of such episodes – stayed quiet. When the tears stopped, Chess was only glad Honor and Judith weren't there to comfort her. Minnie, whoever she was and whatever she looked like, was still no more than a shadow, but at that moment she felt more real than the rest of her known family put together. A picture of Honor and Judith holding on to each other, united in their shock and genetic connection, gazing at her as if she were an exhibit in a freak show, invaded her head. It was wrong, she knew that, but they felt momentarily hostile. In a funny way, she would have found her father's comfort easier to accept, because she saw briefly the truth that he was on the outside too.

'It's not really fair,' she murmured.

Jeeva waited.

'It's just not fair that children should be taken away if there is someone in their family who wants to keep them . . .'

'You weren't taken away, Chess. You were put up for adoption.'

'But my grandmother wanted to keep me.'

'She did, but she couldn't.'

'It's not fair!'

'What isn't?'

'Being me, being given away. It means I haven't got anyone, doesn't it? I'm the only one in my family who doesn't have anyone special. Everyone else has got someone special . . . Judith's got Mum, Mum's got Dad, who've I got? I'm just tagged on the end like a . . . like a . . .'

'You've got everyone you've always had.'

'But who have I *really* got? Which one of them *really* needs me?' Chess asked. As she said it, she knew deep down that they all did, even John. The question she had really meant to ask found its way out next.

'Do you think Minnie needs me?'

Jeeva's neutral shrug made Chess start crying again, shaking uncontrollably this time. She put her head on the desk as her counsellor pressed an intercom button and asked for all calls to be held until further notice.

Chapter 6

It took just nine nail-biting days to establish that Minnie George was neither dead, missing, mentally ill or even mildly reluctant but in fact alive and kicking at the same address she had given in 1968, in a third-floor flat in Ladbroke Grove in West London.

The concrete tower block that was now so much more her home than the beaches and farms of her beloved Jamaica missed the whiff of gentrification from Notting Hill by less than a quarter of a mile, but it still smelt firmly of Skid Row nonetheless, even to her resolutely positive nostrils. Not that moaning about things she couldn't change was something Minnie George allowed herself to do, not even when she and her fellow settlers at the Emmanuel Baptist Church got locked, as they often did, into reminiscence.

'Jus' what are we doin' here?' Dudley Amos would cry when another mugging or drugs story broke in the neighbourhood.

'We makin' de mos' of a bad job!' Minnie always replied, without dwelling on just how bad a job that was.

The post that brought her the miraculous news of Frankie arrived during her second cup of tea of the morning. Her ears were well-tuned to the sound of the letterbox flapping in the part-glazed door to her council accommodation because she and the Royal Mail had enjoyed a close relationship over the years.

In her younger days, it'd had the power to make her heart soar and dive but nowadays it merely flirted with her. Somehow though, despite the fact that the postman had long ceased bringing her those secretly adoring letters, a tiny part of her still half-expected that bolt from the blue to arrive and for her life to start again.

She picked up the envelope from her floral coir mat and turned it over and over in her hands, trying to guess its contents. The smudged mark made by a franking machine suggested some sort of official correspondence, yet the address was written in ink and in her limited experience the two things didn't usually go hand in hand. Her curious fingers burrowed their way under the sealed flap and pulled out the single sheet of Local Authority notepaper before she had time to come up with any possibility at all.

Its contents were a bolt from the blue all right – maybe an entirely different shade of blue from the one she so often imagined, but they were a bolt nonetheless.

'I ca'an believe it, I ca'an believe it, I ca'an believe it,' Minnie murmured over and over again as she read the short, carefully drafted letter. An involuntary reaction took her to her aching knees on the cracked vinyl floor in the doorway.

'T'ank You Father for answerin' my prayer in Yuh time, not mine. Forgive me for t'inkin' it would never happen, for not puttin' all my trust in You. I ask You to be wid us now as we journey together at las', Lord . . . Yuh love shine true, in Jesu's name, Lord, Aaamen.

Her husband Gladstone, in his habitual vest, saw her down there and didn't care whether she was worshipping her God or washing the floor; he only cared that she was in his way and she hadn't poured him *his* second cup yet.

'Get up, woman,' he snarled, but Minnie was used to his unpleasantness and chose to get up because *she* wanted to, not because he had ordered her to. When she told him a woman from St Catherine's House had written to say Frankie was trying to trace them, it was as much as he could do to look up from his racing newspaper and say, 'Who de hell is Frankie?'

Two hours later, she found herself in the reception area of St Catherine's House in her best coat and a fluster of misunderstanding. She realised she was jumping the gun but the alternative was to sit at home surrounded by people who had forgotten, and she'd had enough of that to last two lifetimes. Her faltering nerves as she approached the woman behind the glass screen worked in her favour as her voice, braced with false courage, boomed around the spartan space.

'It say here my granddaughter has applied for *access to her file*. So . . .'

'Yes?' asked the receptionist, thinking it was going to be one of those days.

'So I come to see her,' Minnie said, as if it was obvious.

The council clerk took the letter patiently from her and gave it a cursory glance. 'Um, no, Mrs George, that's not what it says. It says . . .'

'I know what it say. Ca'an I speak wi' dis person here?' Minnie demanded, pointing to Jeeva's name.

'I'm not sure she's–'

'Or her boss?' Minnie insisted. She wasn't used to insisting, but they didn't know that.

Jeeva, who was paged and extracted from a meeting, found her perched on the same black vinyl bench that her granddaughter had been sitting on ten days earlier, her tweed coat tightly buttoned over her solid frame.

'I should explain properly about not rushing things,' the counsellor said gently. 'We advise people in this situation to establish a relationship by mail or phone first.'

'Not rushin' t'ings?' Minnie said in disbelief. 'Seventeen years I bin waitin' for dis.'

As Minnie George perched on one bench, so Honor and John Lovell perched on another, in Baggage Return at Heathrow Airport. Their flight from New England had been delayed for six weary hours, and the taxi they had booked in advance to take them to Battersea had long given up the waiting game, so while John watched for their suitcases to show, Honor went in search of a phone. She braced herself to hear tales of death and destruction, not at all confident of John's assurances that the two of them could remove themselves for this long *and* return to a life intact. Her girls were barely adults. They still needed her overview, surely.

'Morgan? We've just landed. How are things?' Tell me quickly, she urged silently. Get it over with. The worst first. My girls. Are they alive? In hospital? Missing?

'Fine, absolutely fine. Judith has only just this second telephoned from Izmir to see if you were home. She's going to phone again tonight if she can but you're not to worry if she can't.'

'Is everything all right?'

'She's fine, we're fine, everyone is fine,' Morgan purred indulgently.

'And Chess?'

'Of course. Why shouldn't she be? Chess is just . . . well, you know, *Chess*.'

But Honor saw the inaccuracy of that throwaway comment the moment she wrapped her arms around her. Chess's welcome hug was too deliberate, a little bony and dutiful and lacking that shot of relief that, in all Honor's previous experiences, was so tangible after a stint of parental absence. And her face, which usually (if you ignored the hiccup over her exams) sat on the edge of laughter, looked like a giant question mark. There was something palpably wrong.

As the spoils of the holiday were tipped on to the table and Dan scrabbled noisily through the cellophane twists of chocolate and packets of biscuits while the adults talked animatedly over him, Honor watched her daughter from the corner of her eye.

Even if Chess had been able to barge her way into the activity, she wouldn't have known what to say once she got there, so she just hung quietly around the edges, hoping no one would notice her disquiet. The gifts – a jar of the same authentic maple syrup which she'd had a passion for as a child, a soft and expensive sweater and a bag full of autumnal leaves Honor had swept up from the roadside the day before – made no helpful impact. It wasn't that she behaved ungratefully in any way, it was just that she didn't feel *there*. It was as if she were on the other side of a transparent screen. Her mother felt it so intensely she could almost have tapped on the glass. John on the other hand was used to it. He had felt on the other side of the glass for years.

Thank God for Dan's excitement over the bendy ET doll John had insisted on buying him.

'The neck stretches up to twice its length.'

'Oh cool!'

'And its feet are suctions strong enough to stick him to the wall.'

'Yeah!'

But even that noisy diversion didn't cover the gaps for long enough, and in the next lull Honor spoke.

'You look a bit peeky, love. Are you OK?' Damn, she chided herself, why did it come out like an accusation?

'Course she is,' Morgan reassured her, recognising maternal panic when she heard it. 'As far as I know, she's neither a junkie nor a mother yet.'

'Can you confirm that?' Honor tried to joke but Chess managed only a thinly disguised frown. Her parents had become strangers to her, set apart by her secret. What would they say if they knew? How could she say it? Why was her mother's forced concern so grating? Why did she feel so damn guilty? She reminded herself again that they had started the ball rolling, on her birthday. It felt like clutching at straws.

Dan started using ET's pointed fingers to flick the pile of red and yellow leaves on to the floor. 'They *do* look better on the ground, I think,' John said, attempting to keep any lightness going.

'You do realise by stealing these, you've cut the winter food supply off for a whole generation of American worms, don't you?' Brian teased. 'I'm phoning the RSPCW.'

'They're gorgeous. We could frame them,' Morgan said, fingering one lightly and pretending not to have noticed any tension.

'They won't sell.'

'Not for the gallery, you imbecile.'

Chess stayed silent. She started to tidy up the table, moving the Duty Free carrier bags already ransacked for the wine into a corner by the fridge and binning the rubbish. She just couldn't whip up any enthusiasm for her parents' return – not after a mere seven weeks. She wasn't even sure if she was pleased to see them. As reunions went, this one was hardly historic, not compared to another one that could be lurking just around the corner.

Then, a harsh noise cut through the babble and a sixth sense told her it was about to become more memorable. The phone was ringing at top volume, sounding discordant and urgent.

Dan raced to it and answered it clumsily, knocking it off its African drum table. He hung on to it by the receiver, letting the bottom-heavy rest of it dangle and clonk against the ethnic tribal instrument in a peculiarly satisfying rhythm.

'Hello . . . who? what? . . . Chess, it's someone called Gina, or Jesus or something.'

Honor caught the wake of panic surge across her daughter's face.

'I'll take it upstairs if that's OK?'

'It would be if I hadn't taken the extension into the gallery yesterday. The one in the storeroom is on the blink.'

'We won't listen,' Honor said readily, but the way Chess looked so gratefully back made her think that perhaps it would be useful if she did.

Brian and John were exchanging loud comments about Dan's secretarial skills as the boy tapped out a frantic tune with ET's head on the drum.

'OK, what's this one?'

'Sshh, Dan! Chess won't be able to hear what Jesus wants.'

'Me for a sunbeam,' snorted Brian. 'Good bit of gospel beat you got going there, son!'

Honor grabbed the first prop she could find – a gallery brochure – and pretended to flick through it, leaning over the table with her back to Chess and turning her solicitous ears into the cautious one-sided conversation coming from behind. The child had looked about as uncomfortable as she had ever seen her. Who was she speaking to? Not a friend, certainly not a contemporary, someone in authority and yet . . .

'Um, well, my parents have just arrived back from their holiday . . . No, not yet. I haven't had a chance . . .'

The sounds around Chess became distorted and Jeeva's voice, amplified and resonant, was the only clear signal reaching her. Her counsellor reiterated calmly from the echoing solitude of her office that her grandmother Minnie George had turned up, in person, at St Catherine's House earlier that day. The intonation was the same as ever – light, calm and in control – but to Chess, it echoed round the room like the soundtrack in a cinema.

'Sorry – could you just tell me the first bit again?'

Honor, with only half the script to go on, was gripped with a sense that she had been gone far, far too long.

'Are you sure? I mean, are you sure it was her? . . . What . . . how . . . what . . .? Is she coming back?'

Chess backed further towards the wall and tucked her head so far into the receiver it looked like she would have preferred to climb down it and disappear for ever. Honor concentrated harder on looking casually interested in what she was reading. She had been staring at three framed prints of nude men without even recognising what it was she was looking at.

'But you didn't say for definite, did you? I mean, if she came straight to see you, it must mean she wants . . . I wouldn't want her to think . . . Look, I can't really talk now.'

Dan looked up from his drum and his high-pitched chirping cut through the fuzzy air between mother and daughter enough to bring Chess back to reality.

'Can't talk? Can't talk?' he quipped in the way annoying six-year-old clever clogs do. 'What do you think you're doing now then?'

'That's enough, Dan,' Morgan shouted unnecessarily harshly, steering him away and suddenly grasping a vague idea of what might be going on. That stray envelope for the Office of Population Census and Surveys came back to her, as did Chess's hesitant requests for answers without questions.

From her office, Jeeva heard the commotion and suggested finding a more convenient time, but the prospect of being left hanging was more than Chess could bear.

'No! Don't go! I don't even know what she's like.'

She needed to know everything – what Minnie looked like, what she had said, if she seemed happy, shocked, kind, confused, cross – whether she was on her own, whether she was old, or ill, or . . . anything. *'What* is *she like?'*

'Well,' said Jeeva with a smile in her capable voice, 'I have to say I thought she was lovely . . .'

It would have been so much easier for Chess to just stay where she was, facing the wall and running back over Jeeva's words until the room cleared, but she knew she couldn't. There were four adults and a gawping child behind her who weren't going to let her get away with it. She had to brave her audience sooner or later so she took a deep breath and turned round. Honor, who had straightened up, could see her daughter rubbing her scalp around the temples in the way she did around exam time.

'What was all that about?' John asked. His wife felt the knot of anxiety tighten as she detected concern in his face too. He tried to sound merely curious, but the heaviness in his voice made his question sound more like a reproach.

'Um . . .' She could almost touch the ripples of distress in the air.

'Who *was* that, Chess?'

'No one you know.'

'What did they want?'

'Nothing.'

Brian and Morgan stopped pretending to be busy. Chess felt the walls beginning to close in.

'What's *who* like?' Honor asked, against her better judgement.

'*What?*' Chess made a snap decision to play angry.

'You asked on the phone what she was like.'

'For God's sake – it was supposed to be a private call.'

'Who's Jesus?'

'Chess?'

'What? Just drop it.' It was easier to lash out than tell the truth.

'It's great to be back,' John said sarcastically, jet lag suddenly hitting him head on. 'I see things haven't moved on any–' It was about the most useless thing he could have said and he regretted it instantly, not that anyone else would have realised. His face remained expressionless.

'Let's not fall out,' Honor pleaded. 'Look, Chess darling, something unhappy is written all over your face. Wouldn't it be easier just to tell us?'

'I'm not guilty of anything!'

'Who said you were?'

'Because if you're in some kind of trouble . . .'

'God! You've only been back five minutes and you're already getting at me. Leave me alone!' and she ran from the room as fast as she could, hitting her left thigh on the corner of the table as she went.

'Shit, shit, shit, shit, shit!' she spat as her feet pounded the stairs up to her room, but it was OK. Honor was right behind her.

Not far away, Minnie sat in her armchair thinking. The sofa bed had been folded up, which meant that Gladstone would not be back tonight, and the way things were going lately, if he wasn't back for one night, he wasn't back for two or three. His presence at home was entirely dependent on the long-distance lorry-driving shifts his fancy woman's husband worked. Huh! She was welcome to him!

Her eyes stared somewhere beyond the television. The hard face of her own daughter Christine kept reaching her – a face she hadn't seen for a decade and still had no particular desire for. Such irresponsibility! Seventeen years old and three babies, none of whom she had ever showed the slightest interest in. But it wasn't Christine's face (which was the spitting image of her father's) that she needed right now.

Even as a baby, Frankie had been a Clarke, not a George. No, Frankie would look more like . . . she hesitated to indulge in such a frivolous thought . . . more like herself, maybe. A little bit softer around the eyes, a little bit chubbier around the chin, a little bit warmer round the heart. As she conjured it, something in her resolve gave way and she indulged in a short cry.

All three of Christine's illegitimate babies had been a secret source of delight to Minnie – even the middle boy who had never even focused his eyes on the world before going to be with Jesus. She'd tried hard to conceal her joy each time her wayward daughter Christine delivered, because such sexual looseness was to be admonished – but the babies, the babies were a lifeline, something to pull her out of the relentlessly grey sea in which she seemed to swim permanently back then. And of course she knew that if she hung on to them tight enough it would mean that Christine would let go altogether and then they would be hers.

The first grandchild, Della, became more her own *than* her own. Minnie had been present at her birth, had bottle-fed, weaned and potty-trained her and had been to every parents' evening since. Much good it had done in the end. Whenever she tried pinpoint exactly when and where the rot had set in, it seemed as if it had been in the girl always. And yet Minnie still preferred to blame peer pressure than the George gene. Who else could she pour all her love into?

It was comforting to remember how hard she had hung on to Frankie. The three of them – she and Della and the baby – had been a close-knit little unit for nearly a year, which was far longer than the authorities had first suggested. But then Gladstone had lost his job and she had been forced to find work in a toothpaste factory and everything had fallen apart in a matter of weeks. Saying goodbye had been the hardest thing she had ever done.

In her mind's eye, she had Frankie's unknown childhood well-documented. The child wore dresses with ribbons and had a pony and a bedroom of her own. She played the piano, had big birthday parties thrown for her and her doting childless parents gave her everything she wanted. Now that obvious fantasy bore scrutiny, Minnie hated it for what it was – a romantic invention cooked up to get her through the bad days.

What if the child had been neglected or unloved? What if she had been punished for being different? Who would stick up for her then? Who would *understand*? How sweet the reassurance of Frankie's health and happiness would be now. How quickly would it come her way?

Della shouted something rude and angry out of a window and Minnie winced as a door slammed. Maybe adoption, with all its sense of failure and unfairness, had been the best route after all. It would have had to try pretty hard to be worse.

The flat was unusually empty and she felt taken over with a need for some physical evidence that Frankie was really once here and hers. As she shifted her tired large body from the sitting room to the bedroom, she felt sure the child would still be in the flat somewhere – a ribbon, a shoe, a photograph or a toy perhaps. Anything to associate a memory with the brief but bewildering letter she still held in her hand – anything. The first place she always looked for comfort was under her bed.

Chess knew it was a bit of a cliché, the way she sat on the bed with her arms around her knees and her head hidden in her lap so Honor couldn't find a way in, but she didn't know how else to be. She couldn't bring herself to look into her mother's face and see all that hurt. She was glad her mother had followed her up though. It would have been awful if she'd been stuck up here on her own when everyone else was downstairs discussing her – or worse still, *not* discussing her. Part of her felt lonely, another part felt worried, but the rest, the big rest, was dying to tell someone what she had just learned.

Honor didn't see any cliché at all in the foetal rocking form of her baby. She saw someone who needed her and it gave her the courage to take the first step to discovery. She thought she probably already knew where the road led, but she had to hear it from Chess first. Then she could work out how to deal with it. She put her freckled dry arm out to try and ease the clamped arms from around her daughter's knees but Chess just gave a little squeak and held on tighter.

'Hey, come on.'

'I can't.'

'Yes, you can. It doesn't matter what it is, we'll cope.'

'We won't.'

'Yes, we will. Come on, you can tell me.'

'No I can't.'

'If you can't tell your mother, Chess, who can you tell?'

'But you're not . . . not really, are you? Which is why I can't . . .'

The latch was up and the gate was creaking open. Honor didn't want to step into the landscape beyond one little bit because it was too big and too remote and it went on for ever and ever, but if Chess was already there, exploring it on her own, then she had to follow.

'Is this about being adopted?' It was a clumsy question, but there was no time to search for a better one.

'Sort of.'

'I can't help if you won't tell me.'

'I *can't* tell you.'

'Why don't you start with who was on the phone?'

Chess freed her knees and looked up. Her eyes had dried and Honor saw both the woman and the child in them.

'You won't be cross with me?'

'Promise.'

'OK, then, it looks like I might have – well, that is, I *have* traced my real family.' It came out not as a confession or an apology or even a challenge, but as a bald statement of fact. Honor couldn't speak for a moment. The only thing she wanted to hear was the ending, but there was a long way to go before any of them got to that, so instead she just nodded slowly, as if she was thinking. Eventually, she moved her lips and smiled, although her mouth felt as unconnected to the rest of her as if she had been to the dentist and had every tooth filled under local anaesthetic.

'Have you met your . . . ?' The word 'mother' just wouldn't come.

'I haven't met anyone yet.'

'Do you want to?'

'I don't know. I don't know anything any more.'

'It's all right.' Honor soothed Chess's hair the way she did when she was calming her after a nightmare. 'It's all right, it's all right.'

It might be all right for *you*, her daughter wanted to say but didn't.

The next twenty-four hours weren't too bad, considering. John joined them eventually and the three of them spent the time talking and crying and hugging and shouting and sleeping, only to wake and start all over again. Judith and Minnie floated like invisible spirits above and between them, hardly mentioned but silently invoked. Other than that, it was as though nothing else was going on anywhere in the world outside those four walls. Morgan made meals which were half-eaten and Brian made jokes which fell flat, and somehow they all just kept going. The atmosphere in the house took on something of a Blitz spirit, much like a household might behave if one of its members had just been involved in a major road traffic accident and was pinned up in hospital coming to terms with life on only one leg, or if a long-lost son had returned from a war in which he'd been missing presumed dead. Time didn't matter. Meals at midnight, baths at midday, brandy at brunch. But just when it looked as though real life might kick in again soon, John made a fatal mistake.

'You should think about starting to get your things together,' he said to Chess the moment he thought it was safe to talk practicalities. 'If you're anything like your mother, you'll have twice as much now than you arrived with.'

'I'll just throw a few clothes in a roll bag. The rest can stay here, can't it, Morgan?'

'Sure, if . . .'

'Well, we're back now. There's no need.'

'I'm not coming back for long,' Chess warned him. 'My job

is here, looking after Dan. Morgan relies on me. She–'

'And what about the small matter of college?' John dared to ask. He had to, he owed it to her.

'What about it?'

'Can we please move on from this?' Honor screamed. 'I can't take it any more.' And because she really looked as if she couldn't, the matter was dropped.

So Chess returned to Norfolk the next morning in the back of her parents' car, trying not to feel like a naughty little schoolgirl who'd been found out in mid-misdemeanour. She wished Judith was going to be there when they got back, but her sister hadn't even telephoned a second time from Izmir like she had said she would. If Judith could somehow have seen the last ghastly few days, she would have flown home for sure, but for once in her life, she had been miles from the crisis. Now she would never know, not fully.

Chess had agreed to go with her parents on the understanding that it was a temporary arrangement to give everyone time to talk and that she would return to London as soon as possible. It had been a difficult negotiation, well handled by Brian, and at least the three occupants of the car that morning all thought they knew where they stood. Honor blamed jet-lag for the lack of journey chit-chat but she needn't have bothered. They all had reasons for their individual silences.

Within minutes of pulling into the gravel drive of their farmhouse, John took the keys to his MG off a hook in the lobby and disappeared without comment. The family home, deprived of human company for seven weeks, felt cold and a little damp. Everything was as Honor had left it, and yet it looked emptier, cleaner, less cosy, like it did the first day after the Christmas tree was abandoned to the compost heap.

Chess shook her head at her father's receding figure in contempt.

'It's his way of dealing with it,' Honor defended him.

'And what's yours?' Chess asked.

'Me? I've been expecting it all your life,' her mother lied.

'I wish you'd told me that.'

'I should have done, I'm sorry.'

'Well, in that case, will you come with me when I meet my grandmother next week?'

Chapter 7

Minnie George pushed a shoe-box full of yellowing airmail letters from Jamaica back under her bed and heaved herself up by sliding her hand under the mattress and pushing down. She had spent a whole morning purporting to sort out the accumulated nonsense that found its way under her bed, but really, she'd spent it dreaming about the past. About Frankie and then, inevitably, about Reuben Fisher.

We can be a family, Reuben had written all those years ago. *I will be a good father to your children and a fine and loving husband to you. Say yes and one day we can be grandparents too. Say yes, my love.*

She had two shoe-boxes full of pleas from Reuben Fisher like that. His first letter – more of a declaration than a plea – had been written in the summer of 1948, and his last was dated ten years later. To her though, it was the long gap since that had really confirmed her love for him. Even now, in the 'empty years' as she called the drudgery of the decades they'd been lost to each other, she wrote to him. She hadn't posted these outpourings but she couldn't bring herself to throw them away either so they were kept, along with the others under the bed, unsealed and unsent. In her fantasy, she showed them to him one day when they were reunited. He would know then the strength of her lasting affection. If he was still alive, of course.

Reuben's letters were the most precious things she owned. If her husband Gladstone ever found them, he would surely take delight in destroying every single one, which was why she always made sure the bed was against the wall and the box was shoved as far back as her arms would reach. Anything that took that much effort to hide would be way beyond Gladstone's reach.

It was the grandparent bit she was longing to find this morning. If only she could just run her fingers over those few words. Her whole body was boiling over with excitement about news of Frankie and she hadn't yet found a soul to share it with. Gladstone was worse than indifferent. He was being callously silent, other than to throw in the occasional ungenerous suspicion that the child might be 'on de make' as he put it.

'What *are* you talkin' 'bout?' Minnie had snapped after his third unpleasant comment. 'She want *love* not money, not dat you know how to give either, eh?'

Della was no better.

'You stayin' in to meet yuh sistah today, Della?'

'Nah, Granny, I got t'ings goin' on . . .'

'For pity's sake, de girl *needs* us!'

'From wha' you bin tellin' me, she got everyt'ing she need already.'

Reuben Fisher would rejoice with her if he could, she knew he would. She muttered his ancient cry quietly to herself. *We can be a family. One day we can be grandparents too.* Too much water though and too long a bridge for them ever to cross it at this late stage. But what conviction, and what a waste it had all turned to dust.

They had now been out of each other's touch and sight for a quarter of a century, but not once had he crept out of her mind. What *he* now thought about *her* – if he ever did, of course – was a truth Minnie could only imagine since she had long given up the right to know his heart.

Willimina Clarke and Reuben Fisher had managed to grow up in neighbouring villages in Jamaica for twenty years without so much as a glance of admiration between them. Harvest after harvest, their mothers had shelled pimento under the same trees, and shoot after shoot, their fathers had divided out the wild pigs and pigeons, but Minnie and Reuben had gone to different schools with different friends.

The closest they ever got to each other as children was at a Baptist Church by a beach one Christmas Day when the best voices from the local school choirs had been pulled together for a seasonal concert. The two of them sang together, just one kid apart, and Minnie had glowered at Reuben for chewing on a chunk of coconut during a reading. Neither of them ever recalled the exchange.

Anyway, even if the flame of their love *had* flickered in those days, Reuben's rickety bicycle would never have made it up the lush green hill between their two homes.

It was a mutual sense of adventure that finally led them to meet. At twenty-four years old, Reuben had returned from the war to a state of economic decline in Jamaica. Banana cultivation on the island had been knocked sideways by a terrible hurricane and coconut trees were hit by a rampaging disease. Plenty of land was available for any farmer who wanted to start again, but no one had any spare money to invest in re-planting. It was hardly the homecoming Reuben had dreamt of during his darkest nights listening to the rain on the corrugated ceilings of British Army camps all over Northern England.

He couldn't so much as sniff a prosperous future. Not even the thriving plantations were taking on men at the level he wanted to be employed, and his frustration was compounded by a sudden determination not to waste his life. Some of his old soldier friends, the ones who would be forever young, no longer had the choice.

It was no surprise to his family that when he read in the *Daily Gleaner* about the troopship *Empire Windrush* offering limited accommodation when it sailed from Jamaica to England on 24 May, 1948, he was one of the first in the queue for tickets.

One of the last in the queue was a young man with hooded eyes called Gladstone George. He hadn't managed to find work after the war either, but then, he hadn't really tried. England seemed worth a shot, and so his father had willingly put up the twenty-eight pounds and ten shillings ticket money, if only to save himself from the shame of hearing other people call his only son a lazy good-for-nothing scrounger.

Unhappily as it turned out for Minnie, Gladstone – heavy-lidded eyes and all – also happened to be extremely handsome, so when he offered to take her with him to 'the mother country', she agreed on a teenage impulse. After all, the whole island, 150 miles long by 50 miles wide, was talking about the voyage as if it were a once-in-a-lifetime opportunity. It seemed worth marrying a good-looking man in return for such promise. Her hardworking mother, with nine younger children to look after, hardly had time to argue between looking after the babies, the chickens and the goats.

Three weeks later, the animals were left to fend for themselves for a day as the rest of Minnie's loving entourage insisted on travelling the sixty hot and uncomfortable miles to Kingston to bid her a tearful farewell. Four hundred and ninety-two other Jamaicans boarded the *Windrush* with her that May day. Only one of them was to turn out to be the love of her life.

At nineteen, Minnie was the youngest of only twenty women on board, and to Reuben Fisher's eye, she was by far the prettiest. He noticed her as soon as she stepped on, and she held his attention for the entire passage. The other women laid desirability – and lipstick – on with a trowel whenever they could, but Minnie, at Gladstone's jurisdiction, wasn't even allowed to attend the on-board cinema or the organised dances.

Reuben took as many risks as he dared with her during the month-long voyage, but Minnie's new husband was big as well as handsome, so by the time the huge ship docked on the Thames on a chilly June dawn, the two of them had only communicated with their eyes.

As they said goodbye and he whispered in her ear about his aching heart, Minnie knew with a horrible conviction that she'd married the wrong man, but she resigned herself to her fate as Mrs Gladstone George and forced herself to forget the sweet things Reuben Fisher had just murmured.

It took him four months to find out what had happened to her after disembarkation. By the time he tracked her down he knew he was hopelessly in love, but Minnie was pregnant, bruised, and no better off than she would have been in Jamaica.

Her bullying husband had quickly set about beating her into accepting that her only tasks were to look after him and as many of his children as she could manage. She'd tried to stand up to him at first, but because the noisy world of inner London was such a frightening contrast to the vibrant isle she had taken for granted, Minnie was almost grateful to him for making her a prisoner in her own home (if you could call the grimy terraced house she had swapped her tropical farmstead for, a home).

The gentle and frequent affirmations of Reuben's love – usually in writing but twice, much to her consternation, on her doorstep when Gladstone was at work – were all that kept her going in those first alienating years. He said he'd take her, baby and all. Then, when she got pregnant again, he said he'd take her, *babies* and all. In 1950, Minnie had her third child, Christine, and Reuben finally decided he was wasting not only his breath but probably what prospect of happiness he had left.

Shortly after Christine's birth, Minnie found a letter from him lying on her doormat. Just seeing his handwriting made breathing worth while, and she quickly stuffed it into her patterned overall pocket before questions were asked. There it stayed all day, warming her floppy post-natal belly like the kiss of the Jamaican sun.

Ten long hours later, with Gladstone out of the house and the children asleep, she opened it up hungrily only to read the awful news that Reuben, her forever-there Reuben, had gone and married a woman called Ivy, a sister of another *Windrush* settler. He wrote that he was going to try and love his new wife as he would have loved Minnie, and he hoped she would understand. She'd put the letter back in her pocket but it had felt like a block of ice melting into her stretchmarks.

The few people close enough to her to notice her

permanently swollen eyes over the next few months – her two neighbours and a well-meaning church minister – put her lack of sparkle down to post-natal depression. Gladstone either didn't notice or didn't care.

With her safety belt gone, she tried to throw herself wholeheartedly into bringing up her children, but they had inherited their father's heavy eyelids which Minnie suspected betrayed his hard heart gene too. She never really entirely loved any of them, not in the way she would love her grandchildren one day.

In 1958, a few Christmas cards and one disastrous *Windrush* reunion down the line, Reuben wrote out of the blue to say that he, Ivy and their three children were leaving Portsmouth to return to Jamaica to take over his father's village shop. It was the nearest thing to a love letter she'd received from him in eight years. *I plan to stock everything you could ever need,* he wrote, *but, as we know, money don't buy you everything.*

Every time over the next three decades that Minnie had felt the rough side of Gladstone's hand or the pinch of his selfish purse, she comforted herself with the dream that somewhere, Reuben was comforting himself with thoughts of her. It still went some way to helping her get through, despite her acceptance that the whole thing had long since sailed into the seas of pure escapism.

She was on that very boat now, the only place she wanted to be until that knock from Frankie came at the door. Her morning had started before dawn and she had tidied as much of the flat as she could, but with two o'clock sitting like some distant temporal threshold to a better life, she couldn't really do much more than wait and hope.

There was a rat-a-tat-tat and she pulled herself hurriedly up from her chair, shuffling in barely controlled panic along the hall. Two figures were beyond the glass. Her tight deep brown fingers, like perfectly cooked plump sausages, fumbled hastily with the lock.

'Trick or treat?' asked the children from next door in plastic witch's hats from the market.

'Oh, you makin' me jump!' Minnie roared with a bucketful of relieved tension. 'You makin' me really jump!'

Chess's 'leaving home' suitcase had been sitting in the hall since the night before, making its undeniable statement echo through a house that was already fraught with tension. Even the easy bits, like choosing what to wear, were brimming with insecurity.

Chess found fault with Honor's entire wardrobe – the navy blazer was too formal, the rainbow sweater too homespun, the pink silk two-piece made her look too, well, pink. Then Honor chose the last minute to tell Chess her loafers needed a polish and that she should have put her denim jacket through the wash if she'd known she was going to wear it. The argument that had been brewing for days finally found its raison d'etre when Honor wouldn't let Chess drive to Norwich railway station.

'You're not in the right frame of mind.'

'I am.'

'Well *I'm* not,' Honor snapped. 'I'd like us to get there in one piece.'

'I passed my test, didn't I?'

'And as your examiner said, that doesn't mean you're no longer a learner.'

'So how am I supposed to improve if you never let me practise?'

'What are you talking about, never? You can drive another time, just not today.' Honor threw a thick foam pad on to the driving seat. She couldn't see over the steering wheel without it.

'Like when? You've already told Morgan and Brian not to put me on their insurance.'

'I'm not having you taking their car out in the city traffic. It's too dangerous, and you're not experienced enough.'

'No, and I never *would* be if you had your way.'

Falling out about clothes and cars was an excellent buffer against the real core of unrest between them. Each time something truly harmful was nearly said, it somehow managed not to be. It was the so-far happy story of their life. There had been ample opportunity on both sides in the recent past to give vent to their terrible thoughts – 'sometimes I wonder just who you really are' and 'if you were my *real* mother, you'd understand . . .' But they had each refrained, frightening themselves half to death by just giving space in their heads to aberrations like that.

They got to the station early, but the platform was already heaving with teenagers in neon orange masks armed with an inexhaustible supply of party poppers and spray cans of fun foam. Hallowe'en usually meant John pretending he'd seen a ghost outside when he went to get the logs in or some tedious school disco in a pumpkin-strewn hall, so the commercially fabricated hysteria going on around them now made them feel even less connected to the everyday world than ever. Anyway, Chess was very obviously living in her own little bubble, and Honor was trying her absolute best not to pop it.

The small waiting room had been taken over as base camp by the revellers, so the two of them stamped their feet outside and watched their breath freeze in the air as the wind whipped along the line of the tracks. When ribbons of yellow paper were fired from a nearby cardboard capsule into Chess's hair, Honor went to pick them out with exaggerated care.

'Mum! If you're going to do it, then do it! Don't just faff around!'

'I was trying not to pull.'

'That's never bothered you before.'

'Oh, I can't win, can I?'

Chess took an Afro comb from her bag and flicked it through her bushy mound of hair. She had never had it professionally cut. Honor would clip it for her in much the same way as she clipped the box hedge in their herb garden, and say things like, 'I wish I had your hair, it stays exactly where it's put,' but lately, Chess longed for the straight glossy hair of Diana Ross. Only since living in London had she realised 'box' was not her only option. Her hair had gone from being perfectly acceptable to an acute embarrassment. As soon as she could, she was going to have it plaited, or straightened, or somethinged. Anything but boxed.

The train pulled in and the neon masks barged disrespectfully on, leaving a huddle of indignant pensioners and puzzled children in their wake.

'Excuse me!' Honor said aggressively to a boy twice her size. 'Will you please wait?'

Then she ejected two inappropriately erotic skeletons from her reserved seats and the way they scurried off made them look as if they feared a detention was in store. Chess could have happily crawled under the seats and not re-surfaced until London.

As the journey progressed, the noise level became the source of much complaint from other passengers, but the two of them just sat back and watched the chaos since it saved them from searching for conversation of their own. When the ringleaders were thrown off after two station stops and the mob slunk back to their seats, Honor closed her eyes to let the shake, rattle and roll of the train take over and Chess pulled all her hang nails off until she bled. Eventually, the storm cloud in her head began to pass and she found her voice again.

'Mum?'

'Mmm?'

'Just wondered if you were awake.'

Honor recognised her cue and kicked off her shoes beneath the table, then stuck her feet on to the edge of Chess's seat opposite. Her legs were slender enough for it to be an easy gesture and her daughter was glad of it. A blob of copper nail varnish had bonded with the nylon toe of her tights and Chess started to pull at it gently.

'You didn't let it dry properly before you got dressed, did you?'

'I was in a bit of a flap.'

They swapped weak smiles and Honor let her daughter continue to pick, despite running the risk of a ladder.

A question kept sticking in Chess's throat. She wanted to ask how Honor thought Judith was taking all this, but she felt too self-conscious about needing to know. She had spoken to her sister twice, once straight after Honor had broken the news, and once on her own, when no one else had been around. The conversations had been brittle, shrill, too lighthearted somehow, sticking to the safe areas of London and Dan and boyfriends. After that, Chess had successfully avoided answering the phone at all just in case, but Judith hadn't phoned again. It suddenly mattered a lot what Judith had said or would say to her mother in private. The prospect of any disapproval, or worse still denunciation, confused Chess.

On the one hand she was desperate for Judith's support, and on the other she considered it none of her business. The fear of rejection loomed large.

'So what does Judith think?' she finally managed to ask her mother.

Honor was momentarily thrown. 'Well, you've spoken to her, haven't you?'

'Do you think she hates me?'

'No! Would she ever? Why do you say that?'

'Because she didn't sound normal, like she was putting on a brave voice.'

'She was calling from Turkey, love. It's a long way and the lines haven't been good.'

'Are you making excuses? What has she said to you?'

'Nothing that she hasn't said to you, I'm sure – just that she finds it–'

Chess broke into the sentence. 'Don't tell me if it's bad, I don't want to know,' she rushed, putting up her hand. It was all very well for them.

'Hold on, hold on. I was going to say she doesn't fully understand why you haven't spoken properly to her about it. She's a bit hurt. I think she feels you're avoiding the subject with her.'

'It's hard.'

'Oh, you know your sister as well as I do. She's just being Judith, isn't she?' Honor said it as if the confidence existed between her and Chess, not her and Judith, and it felt good. Chess was able to smile widely back.

'In what way?'

'Like offering to come straight home, and be with us all and play her part – that kind of thing.'

'Why didn't she?'

'Because I told her not to make a drama out of a crisis.'

'Was she upset?'

'A bit.'

The two of them raised their eyebrows knowingly at each other and that was all it took for their loyalty to find its rightful home again. When Chess went in search of coffee, she sat back down in the seat next to Honor rather than opposite, and rested her head on her mother's slight shoulder. Honor's left hand automatically reached across to rest on her daughter's right cheek and they stayed in that awkward but cosy position until their muscles ached.

At Liverpool Street, they got straight into a cab. Chess pulled out a letter from Jeeva giving her grandmother's address and directions and read it verbatim to the driver.

'Tell you what,' said the cabbie jovially, 'you drive and I'll sit in the back and keep your friend company.'

'She's not my friend, she's my mum,' Chess retorted.

'And I'm the rightful heir to the throne, darlin'. Right, where was it again?'

Honor laughed nervously, keeping a strange rictus-like smile on her face for the rest of the ride. Only when they pulled up in a side street off a wide busy road flanked with huge red-brick towers of council flats on one side and shabby shops with grimy windows on the other, did her fake vigour waver.

'Oh,' she said. 'Is this it?'

'What was you expecting? Buckingham bleedin' Palace? Call it four quid, love.'

Mother and daughter – or something else if you were being biologically strict about it – stood on the pavement watching the back of the cab indicate left and re-join the traffic. The bewilderment of having absolutely no idea where they were dispelled the last dregs of the morning's antagonism and they were suddenly, without anything being said or done, cohorts again. In this together, a team of sorts.

Chess pulled out Jeeva's notes from her canvas bag. Block A, St Paul's Building, was on the main road, set back from a row of telephone kiosks next to a curved concrete ramp for wheelchair access.

'We have to cross over.' She grabbed hold of Honor's hand.

'Then let's find a pedestrian crossing.'

'We'll be OK. Come on, be brave. You'll only get run over if you hang around.'

Showing off, because even with her limited experience of London she was more conversant with the city than Honor ever would be, Chess dodged between three lanes of stationary traffic to a central island. As she pulled her mother off the safety of the kerb to tackle the next three, the lights changed to green and cars started coming at them from all directions.

'For God's sake, Chess!' Honor shouted, hanging on for dear life.

'Oops,' Chess laughed, putting her hand up in apology to a motorcycle courier.

'Well, that's one way to get yourself killed, I suppose,' said Honor back on the pavement, but it had worked. The adrenaline necessary for their next leap of faith was now pumping plentifully round both their hearts and they were suddenly on a shared adventure.

Block A was no flagship for council accommodation. The lifts didn't work, the stairs smelt, and a trickle of water, or something, ran down one flight, but neither of them wanted to acknowledge that they recognised the stench as pee. At the top of one section, four bin bags had spilled their contents, mainly beer cans and wine bottles.

'Someone's had a party,' Honor puffed unnecessarily as they wound their way up.

A heavy swing door with *Level 3* stamped on it, just discernible through some scratched graffiti, led them out on to a concrete corridor. Only the peeling black railings prevented them plummeting to the feeble patch of communal grass below. A picture flashed into Honor's mind of Chess as a child, plummeting from a tree-house in the turkey oak tree at the bottom of their garden, somehow managing to land on her feet and race up the lawn as if she'd never even fallen. What compensation was a tree-house for this kind of emotional tangle? But then at least she'd had a tree-house to fall *from*, and not just some rank concrete balcony like this one.

'It's a bit . . .' Chess said quietly.

'Yes,' Honor agreed.

The door to Minnie George's flat was a fading Burgundy with one panel of reinforced glass and a number 238 painted in unskilled small black figures above a Yale lock that didn't look man enough to keep anything desirable out. Honor's stomach was churning bile.

'OK?' she asked her daughter before she knocked. 'Ready?'

Chess nodded, trying hard not to look like she wished now she had come on her own. Jeeva had tried to persuade both parties to slow down, to make more use of the telephone or postal service before arranging a face-to-face meeting, but one brief exchange of letters and an incomprehensible phone call had been enough. And what had happened to the advice about arranging their reunion in a neutral place?

Honor rapped her knuckles positively on the door. Chess's own fist was curled tight, her nails making indents on the fleshy part of her palm.

'I feel sick.'

'You're just nervous,' her mother said, squeezing her hand.

There was a shout inside, and then footsteps. The door was opened by a young woman with her hair scraped off her face. She was wearing a tight red leather skirt that hovered just below her knees and black heeled ankle boots with an admirable but tarty stretch of bare leg between the two. On top, she wore a loose shirt in a black silky fabric and a black leather cropped jacket with padded shoulders and panels of gold-printed black suede. It was not even midday, but she looked dressed for the night.

'Dey here, Granny!' the girl yelled, pushing past them and giving a display of her delinquent brown almond-shaped eyes. Chess felt as if she were looking into a slightly distorted but quite flattering mirror and she wanted to keep on looking.

'Hello,' she said self-consciously, but whoever the girl was, she wasn't going to stop and make more of it, that much was obvious.

From the darkness of the hall came Minnie, emitting a sound somewhere between laughter and tears as she made her slow approach to the door. Her heart was thumping so loud inside her brown cardigan she didn't hear her granddaughter's first tentative greeting. When she got closer, Chess could see she wasn't as old as her walk suggested. It was her large fluffy slippers, worn over beige nylon ankle socks, that made her shuffle.

'See my baby here, my baby here, you here, you here, my baby . . .' she kept repeating, putting her woolly arms out in front of her like a lifeline for Chess to grab hold of. Not knowing what else to do, Chess took them and was pulled slowly into Minnie's bosom. She was almost suffocated by the alien smells and the raw emotion, but somehow, deep down in her consciousness, she could feel that they had shared the same bed once upon a time. Something somewhere was familiar.

Minnie pushed Chess away to take a look at her face, and then pulled her back into her again. The more Chess was hugged, the more she wanted to be. The sudden need for physical closeness was almost overwhelming, as if between the two of them they could make up for all that lost time.

Honor knew she had been temporarily forgotten. As she stood like some dispensable childminder on the doorstep watching the ebb and flow of her daughter's back, a few lines of a poem came to her, something she had come across and given, years ago, to a colleague who had lost a child to leukaemia. It had a simple sentimentality and she hated herself for remembering it. Even more, she hated thinking of it as faintly relevant to her situation now.

'I'll lend you for a little while this child of mine,' God said.
'For you to love the while she lives and mourn for when she's dead.
'It may be six or seven years or forty-two or three
'But will you, till I call her back, take care of her for me?'

She banished it. Chess was not dead, or dying, she was just starting to live, for God's sake. This was as fundamental a moment in the journey of adoption as taking the baby home in the first place. She had always known that, and she had to deal with it, like a loving mother should. God help me, it hurts! she cried inwardly.

Minnie spotted her and scuffled towards her, ushering her in. The way she pulled on her skinny freckled arm and glanced almost fearfully up the corridor made Honor think the old woman was about to harbour the enemy in wartime.

'Hello, come in, come in,' Minnie muttered without really looking at her.

Chess turned round and grinned at Honor as if there was a joke to be had somewhere, but she could see from her mother's face that there wasn't. The two of them followed the old woman back down the brown carpeted hall and into the kitchen, trying not to feel oppressed by the heat and the heavy smell of cooking meat. Actually, Minnie George was still only fifty-six years old, but the greying hair around her temples, the shuffle of the slippers and the way life had burdened her expression made her look ten years older.

She sat down with a heavy flop at a small square table covered in a plastic cloth of giant pink and orange flowers which clashed bravely with the red and brown striped curtains and the broken green and cream lino. She motioned to Chess and Honor to do the same but she was too busy taking deep breaths and wiping her eyes to speak. One side of the table was against the wall, and the third chair was heaped with magazines and newspapers.

'Go on, you sit,' Honor urged quietly, ushering Chess into the only empty place.

'No, it's OK, you . . .' Chess took backward steps like a frightened horse being pushed into a horse box.

'Aah, dey don't tidy a t'ing for me,' Minnie laughed, getting to her feet again and shovelling the papers up. She dumped them by the fridge, then opened the door and took out two jugs.

Who's 'dey'? Chess wanted to ask, but didn't. The girl who answered the door? Who else was there? Daughters, sons, grandchildren? Honor and John had tried to tell her everything they knew, but they had kept it deliberately vague – a brother with a serious birth defect, maybe an older half-sister.

The sound of a television drifted in from another room, and Chess wondered if anyone was in there watching it. A few weeks on from now, she would know that its continual burble was by no means an indication that someone was even in the flat, although it could have been any one of the four adults and two children who lived there.

'You wan' to take some Guinness punch? Or dis Ribena-lookin' t'ing is sorrel juice,' Minnie said, clearing a heap of cassette tapes with one hand and putting three glasses on the table with the other. 'You had a good journey?'

Honor poured herself a small glass of dark milky liquid. It was ice cold with a hint of nutmeg, but incredibly creamy. 'Mmm, delicious,' she said, not taking another sip fast enough to convince Chess.

'Wha' about you?' Minnie asked.

'Sorrel juice, please,' Chess replied shyly.

'I like to hear yuh manners!'

Honor took the compliment for herself and smiled gratefully. 'You see, Chess? I told you all my nagging would pay off one day.'

'Wha' you call her den?' Minnie asked, sounding confused.

'Chess,' said Chess. 'It's short for Francesca.'

'Fran . . . wha'?'

'Francesca.'

'Oh, my lips don't get round dat one! We call you Frankie when you a baby.'

'I know, you put it in the letter.'

'Ah,' sighed Minnie. 'You know, I forget all about de letter until de other day.'

'Well, a lot must have happened since,' said Honor, 'to all of us.'

'Did you mind me getting in touch?' Chess asked.

'Mind? *Mind*? Darlin', I prayed for it!'

'Do I look anything like I did when you last saw me?'

Minnie broke into a laugh. 'You a bit bigger now, darlin'.'

'But would you have recognised me if you'd passed me in the street?'

Minnie laughed again and saw Chess glance at a torn poster pinned above the cooker that proclaimed in naive irony *The family that stays together prays together*.

'You here now, aren't you?' she said.

Honor looked on bravely, but it was time for her to sit back. She could see how her daughter's eyes were locked into Minnie's. The staring was on both sides as the two women, separated by so much more than a couple of short generations, searched for their physical similarity.

'I bin turnin' out some photos for you, darlin',' Minnie said, pulling a handful of snaps from her cardigan pocket. 'I always keep one of you as a baby in my Bible – you been fallin' out at me from de Good Book ever since you gone.'

'Have I?'

On the top of the pile was a copy of the very first photograph of Chess Honor had ever seen, the one handed to her by Miss Roger, the Scottish case-worker, before their first visit to Hoarewood in the spring of 1968, the one she had carried round in her handbag for so many fretful weeks as the only available image of the child she and John hoped to adopt. No, Honor realised slowly, no, this one here isn't the copy, it's the original – I'm the one with the copy, aren't I?

Chess recognised it too. 'Hey, we've got that one too, haven't we, Mum?'

'So we have.'

Most of the photos Minnie had sorted out were of other

members of the family, invariably in smart clothes and standing in formal but dishevelled lines, smiling with a sense of occasion. The throwaway snaps that populated the kitchen drawers at home, of water fights in the back garden, children in wheelbarrows and baths, the backs of adults on wintery walks, were missing. Chess knew somewhere at the back of her mind that they'd probably never even been taken. Families in highrise flats didn't need wheelbarrows.

She found herself looking at one in particular. It was a colour snap taken, judging by the clothes, in the mid-1970s and everyone was in it – except her.

'Dis one de only one I have of yuh mudda, before she disappear for de secon' time,' Minnie said. 'We had a party for someone, but I forget who.'

It wasn't seeing the blurred figure of Christine that pinched at the edge of Chess's heart but her own absence. She could almost see the blacked-out silhouette where she should have been. She put her finger over a gap and pretended she was underneath.

'Who's that?' she asked, pointing to a girl of about ten.

'Let me see . . . now, is dat Della? Yes, I t'ink it is.'

'Who's Della?'

'She no say who she is when she answer de door? She one naughty girl. Della is Christine's eldest daughter, yuh sistah.'

'My sister?'

'Yuh sistah. Well, yuh half-sistah.'

Chess looked confused and helpless. She wanted Minnie to hold her again but they were sitting too awkwardly at the table for that now.

'You tell me when you findin' all dis stuff too difficult for you, eh? Dere's so much to tell you, an' you don' want to hear it all at once, do you?'

'Uh huh. I'm OK, honestly. How old is Della?'

'I t'ink she twenty.'

'Remember we thought you might have an older sister, Chess?' Honor said carefully.

'I've always had an older sister, Mum – she's called Judith, remember?' Chess gave a special secret smile in her mother's direction but her voice was quiet. It had been said for Honor's benefit alone.

'Yes, I t'ink – 1964, so she is, dat's right, twenty.'

'Why wasn't she adopted too?' The question just popped out without prior warning.

'I could cope wid one extra, you know? But when yuh brudder was born so sick and den you come along . . .'

'The disabled one?'

'Uh?'

'Was he very ill?'

'Too ill, darlin', so we pray for de Lord to take him. He died when he was jus' t'ree.'

'Was Christine – my, um, my mother – was she still here then?'

'No, she was never here! Not even after she have her babies. Each time she produce a chile, she go off somewhere, and leave me to deal wid it.'

Chess put her top teeth over her bottom lip and waited for more.

'Not to worry 'bout dat,' Minnie added wistfully.

'Does Della live here?'

'When she chooses. Tch! Don' follow Della 'cos Della have no use!'

Honor scrabbled back to the subject of Christine, the contender to her throne. She had mistakenly assumed that Chess's hidden agenda was to find out about her natural mother, but in fact her daughter had no immediate desire for any more details. She was happy enough just watching the way Minnie's lips pulled together in the same kind of end-of-sentence pucker that hers did sometimes too.

'Christine don't know de meanin' of de word responsibility,' Minnie said sharply. 'She have t'ree babies in t'ree years, and den she goes off to America and we don' hear another t'ing for years. She come home ten years ago and den she go again. I don't know.'

'Do I have any other brothers and sisters?'

Minnie shrugged. 'By now, maybe, but God knows who de daddies are, darlin'.'

Chess found the reply curiously funny, but as she laughed, Honor's grip on reality started to reel and the events and the emotions of the last week began swirling around her head as if she was succumbing to a heavy anaesthetic. She realised suddenly how relieved she was that Chess was sitting here with her grandmother, not her mother, and that Christine George was not and never would have been as good a mother as herself. At the same time, she saw Chess as Della, dressed in the cheap rags of a girl on the make and the whole picture of what her daughter could have been made her sick and unsteady. To retrieve herself, she asked a question that had already been answered.

'Just tell us who all these other people are again?'

Minnie took them through the group photograph slowly, embellishing her descriptions this time with details of where they lived, what they did, how many children they had.

'Wesley an' his secon' wife gone back to Jamaica now.'

Then she got up, put her hand on Chess's springy head of hair as if blessing her, and shuffled towards the fridge again with the Guinness punch. She came back with a chopping board full of meat, which she started to hack away at while they continued to talk about people Chess had never even dreamed of. It looked like hard work, slicing through the lines of fat and gristle.

Chess spoke of Judith and John, Norfolk, exams, Morgan and Brian and Dan, but none of it sounded real, not even to Honor. After two hours, which felt less than half that to Chess and more than double to Honor, it was time to go.

'Mum's got a train to catch.'

'You no want to stay to see Della?' Minnie said. 'She say she come home for her dinner but, tcha! I don't promise.'

'Oh,' said Chess. 'Should I?'

'Next time,' Minnie said, remembering the girl's less than pleasant comments.

Chess realised then that it was distrust she'd seen as well as defiance in those doorstep eyes.

'Next time,' Minnie repeated, smoothing the child's upper arm and singing for joy just because she was, after all this time, touching her again.

'OK, next time.'

Honor tried to melt into the air, as if she wasn't there, in the same way she did when two French friends of hers started talking in their native tongue.

'You stayin' in London now, or you goin' back to de country?'

'Staying in London. I live here now.'

'Dat's good.'

'Yeah.' Chess's lips almost reached her ears. 'It is, isn't it?'

Back in Battersea, Morgan had been expecting her best friend and daughter to come back any minute. She had already decided that the three of them, all girls together, would eat out at the Thai restaurant near the gallery and leave Brian to babysit, but when Honor phoned her from the station to say she'd much rather just get home, Morgan realised she hadn't been expecting them at all.

'No grieving,' she told her friend. 'It's not a death.'

'I know, but it feels like one at the moment,' Honor whispered back. She emerged from the kiosk looking as white as a sheet. The little knot of nausea that had been developing in her stomach all day was now making her feel properly sick and the taste of the rich Guinness punch kept coming back to jeer at her.

'Did Morgan mind?' Chess asked.

'Not at all. Do you?'

'No.'

They sat in tired silence on a metal bench, willing the train to arrive so they could escape into their own separate thoughts.

'I'm going to miss you.' Honor's shaking utterance vibrated under the cavernous roof space.

'But I'll come home loads, like Judith does. And I'll phone.'

'The house is going to seem empty.'

'Don't re-decorate my room, will you?'

'As if!'

The agitated quietness between them returned and neither of them had ever heard a sweeter voice than the one announcing that the 4.50 train to Norwich had arrived on time on Platform Two. They hugged dutifully by the open door to carriage C where Honor had reserved a single seat.

''Bye, darling, and thank you for making me so proud of you today,' Chess heard her mother say through the springy mound of hair that Minnie had pressed down so lovingly an hour ago.

'That's OK. Thanks for coming with me.'

Honor climbed up the metal step and the estrangement seemed complete. 'Be good.'

They held hands at arm's length through the window.

'I will.'

'Help Morgan all you can.'

'Yes.'

'Bye, darling.'

'Bye, Mum.'

'I love you,' Honor mouthed as the gentle pull of the train separated their hands.

'Me you,' Chess signed back.

Then both of them pushed back a retch of emotion that could so easily have spewed all over the platform but instead settled somewhere in the back of their throats.

The first thing Honor did when the train was safely out of the station was to throw up in the sink of the claustrophobic British Rail loo and poke the bits down the plughole with her nail file. She chose the sink because the thought of her lips and nostrils being within splashing distance of the germ-laden steel lavatory bowl was an indignity too far, and anyway, she was far too wobbly to kneel on the damp floor. She dabbed her mouth, rinsed the bowl and sprayed the tiny room with her perfume, then she promptly upgraded to first class and hid herself away again.

Cushioned by more space, fewer people and laundered head supports, Honor rubbed her forehead and closed her eyes.

She'd lied through her teeth when she told Chess she'd 'been expecting this all her life'. The reality was, she had shelved the entire issue, from start to finish. The moment the adoption papers were signed, sealed and settled, Chess had been her baby. Not black, not white, not from the top or the bottom of the pile, but just her baby, her second child, her youngest daughter. Never had she allowed herself to think that somewhere, someone might be using a matching photograph of the one she so treasured as a bookmark for a Bible.

All the manuals she and John had read, all the advice she'd been given from counsellors, and officials and other parents – it meant nothing once she'd had Chess in her arms. If Chess was happy, she was happy – and since Chess had nearly always been happy, there had never been good enough reason to think the child needed anything more. Chess got what Judith got, and vice versa.

Big mistake, the continuing knot of nausea in her stomach told her now. Swamped by the startling knowledge of her own inadequacies, she started to list the derelictions of her duty to Chess.

Did we ever teach her about her own culture? No. Did we ever make any effort to seek out black friends for her? No. Could we have scraped enough money together to take us all to Jamaica one year and would she be better off now if I had? Yes. And where was John in all of this? How had he become so sidelined? Was that his choice? Did he mean to be so neutral?

What Honor was suffering from was not sickness or tiredness or shock, but loss – although she would have needed a trained therapist to untangle all the different categories of it. A good one would have been able to explain that the very act of adoption is created through loss. Without Honor's own early losses – the babies that would have been born to her if her womb had allowed them to be – there would have been no adoption. Had she mourned those losses yet? Enough to find room for the mourning she now wanted to do for Chess? It wasn't her fault if she hadn't, no more than society's anyway.

Adoptive parents are expected to be happy in just the same way that adoptees are expected to be grateful.

Well, Chess *had* made her happy – too happy maybe – which meant that woven into all those complicated feelings of loss was the equally complex fear of rejection. Could her style of parenting be seen as overprotective, oppressive even? Maybe Chess now needed something less overbearing. Maybe she was the fourth baby she was destined to lose after all.

The only other first-class traveller, a cream-suited middle-aged male *Daily Telegraph* journalist, played a guessing game with his fellow passenger and decided this slight and stylish woman was sleeping off the effects of an illicit afternoon love-in with her husband's best friend in a Mayfair hotel. It was the way she kept shaking her well-cut grey bobbed head that suggested the subterfuge. If he'd known how much that same head throbbed with guilt, he'd have opted for something of more consequence than a mere peccadillo.

Chess on the other hand felt as if her head would explode if she hid her elation any longer. She'd seen the train pull out of the station with transparent relief, then she'd dragged her suitcase back down to the Tube and returned to Notting Hill, with absolutely no idea what she was going to do when she got there.

What she ended up doing was simple. She wandered up and down the roads near Minnie's tower block people-watching. Just about everyone was black. Some of them could even be the same people she'd seen in the photographs. Some of them could be Minnie's friends. One of them could be Gladstone. None of them would be Christine.

The only thing that separated her from the crowds was her suitcase. She wished she'd left it at Liverpool Street. She was in the mood, just for now, to merge with this world and leave her own in some left luggage lock-up to pick up at another time.

If she had been able to find the confidence, she would have gone straight back up to her grandmother's flat to talk and touch some more. The similarity between the intense passion of her reunion and the early stages of a love affair failed to strike her, but only because she hadn't yet been in love. If she had, maybe she would have recognised that she was entering something Jeeva would have called 'the honeymoon period'.

Chess didn't see Della leaning on a battered car watching her with eyes now spiked with jealousy as well as distrust. Her half-sister had waited until Chess and Honor were in a cab before going back up, three stairs at a time, to reclaim her place in Minnie's affections, but when she'd got there, her grandmother was different. She was singing and crying and laughing all at the same time and when Della asked her if she was OK, she'd thrown her arms around her and said she was off to church to give thanks to God. And the stew wasn't even ready.

Della was thinking what she would do if this 'Frankie' staked too big a claim. Minnie was *her* grandmother, not anyone else's, and especially not some half-stranger from the country who'd long ago lost her right to belong here.

'Yeah, dat's it, piss off!' she hissed as Chess finally headed for the Tube station.

They almost touched shoulders, but Della kept her face to the pavement and Chess was too deep in thought to recognise the clothes. She was wondering what she would say back in Morgan's spacious basement kitchen with its scrubbed pine table, real terracotta floor and bottled water in the fridge. It couldn't be her base for much longer, she knew that. Not if she was finally going to grow up.

Chapter 8

Nine o'clock in the morning still seemed like the crack of dawn to Della George, mainly because the *actual* crack of dawn was her more usual cue for bed. She hadn't seen anything much before midday for months, other than the underside of her black and red duvet cover and the drawn curtains of her bedroom. She'd learnt to party into the small hours so well, she was almost nocturnal.

But then, she had been offered a job. Not just any job, but a job working for the legendary Dora Martin, self-crowned Queen of Kensington Market. As one of her mates said, when Dora Martin makes you a proposition, you take it, sleep or no sleep. 'She don't ask again, man. You got one chance. Respect.'

Dora had first spotted Della on Carnival day, standing on a street corner with a rail full of hand-painted crop tops on her left and a bin full of hoops of twisted material on her right. Because Dora had an eye for business, she'd noticed the one thing everyone else had missed – that the twisted hoops were actually just the lopped off hems of the once much longer tops. On a waste-not want-not basis, Della had stitched the off-cuts into tubes and was now selling them with impressive bravado as anything anyone wanted them to be – a low-slung belt or a crazy turban, tied from the back of the head, crossed at the front and then secured at the nape of the neck.

The following week, Dora took the unprecedented step of actually bringing down the metal shutters on her lucrative market stall for a whole hour one day to go looking for her. She'd found Della in her usual lunchtime place – asleep under her duvet in Minnie's flat.

'You wan' us to make money, child? Put in de hours, bide by my rules, an' we talkin', eh?'

The rules were this. Shoplift to order between ten and twelve. Deliver cloth between twelve and two. Return at five to pick up pocket-money and unsold goods. Dora didn't like hot stuff hanging around, which was more a marketing strategy than a fear of the law. If word got round that she had some top bits on offer, then buyers came straight away. She often cleared her haul by the end of each day.

Dora's 'front' was the perfectly respectable and even mildly profitable sideline of period clothes and jewellery. She dealt with this on a sale or return basis too, except she gave it a little more time to sell and it all came from legitimate sources.

The indoor market attracted every manner of browser from the yuppie to the down-and-out, so all in all her busy unit opposite the coffee bar was highly convincing, even if it did have more visitors than any of the others put together.

At forty-six, Dora had never been the object of any man's roving eye unless he was on the lookout for a good grafter, so consequently she took no pains with her appearance. The hat she wore – a brown trilby with a shabby artificial pink rose shoved through the greasy band – was more of a trademark than a fashion statement. 'Look for de hat,' people would say if anyone asked where to find her. She was as much a part of the inner city market scene as the Indian saris, the cheap sunglasses, the second-hand records and the cramped hairdresser's salon.

Della thought Dora was 'de business'. She overlooked the emptiness in the older woman's yellow eyes when she locked up her shack and went home alone every night to count her money, stroke her cats and smoke her weed. As far as Dora's new twenty-year-old recruit was concerned, her employer was at least queen of *something*, even if it was a crooked little market stall.

Della would imagine it was hers sometimes. She'd paint it in one block of bright colour, purple maybe, with clothes in all the same pastel palette hanging in staggered rows down the sides. Or drape rich-coloured muslin from the ceiling like a Bedouin's tent, leave incense sticks burning and sell scarves, bags, cushions and bed throws. Or just black and gold. She knew plenty of women who would buy black and gold until it came out of their ears.

Her normally agile body was adjusting badly to her new work regime. Her eyes looked permanently puffy and her legs dragged behind her, but it was her mind that was in the true state of collapse.

She had been living on the edge of a foul temper for days – not with Dora, of course, or with any of her new 'contacts' but with anyone who crossed her at home. Particularly with Frankie, or Chess or whatever it was she was called. *Chess*. What a silly name dat was, eh? But not as stupid as all the shit Minnie was coming out with about the girl 'comin' home' and stuff. Della had barely spoken to Minnie since Chess had moved in. What was her grandmother thinking of? The flat was jammed up enough. There was already her step-cousin Jax and her two kids camping out in the back bedroom until their own flat was made safe again by the council, and no one was going to share her room, no way.

'So jus' where you gonna put her?' she screamed at Minnie when she first learnt of the plan.

'She can sleep in my bed. It's big enough.'

'*Wha*'? You gotta be jokin'.'

'Family's family, Della. She's yuh sistah so dat's dat.'

It wasn't really the lack of space that Della objected to, it was Chess's arrival on the scene per se. One minute, she was just some kid in a photograph that Minnie had probably only ever shown her twice in her entire life, and the next, she was the long-lost bloody prodigal granddaughter. That was going some in six weeks.

Della's anger and resentment just made sure she worked harder than ever for Dora, the perfect excuse to get out of the house and leave Minnie and her smug bloody 'baby' to it. It was a punishing schedule getting up at nine every day but it was amazing what a body could get used to if money was involved. And it was good money, although not even a fortune would have been enough to sweeten the pill of the ever-present imposter in the flat.

Minnie was ignoring her sullenness and drawing instead on the compensation of her more functional hours.

'You turnin' over a new leaf at last?' she'd asked her this morning, the third time running that Della had appeared for breakfast.

'Yeh, a gold one, innit?' Della had laughed in Chess's hopeful face as Minnie's heart sank.

She was recounting her clever retort to Dora at the market as they discussed orders for that day. Dora was slipping a small plastic re-sealable envelope of white powder into the back pocket of a pair of fake Armani jeans, and handing them carefully to a thin stubbled student.

'You got a bargain there,' Dora winked as she took some folded notes from him.

'Yeah, I always find the jeans here to my liking,' he said, and walked off down the dark corridor towards the light.

'Granny t'ink I find some other kinda shop work,' Della scoffed. 'She t'ink I operate on de other side of de till. She got some hope, eh?'

'Dat don't sound like you to be bad-mouthin' yuh grandmother,' Dora said, who knew Minnie and liked her.

'She need some bad-mouthin' lately.' Della fiddled with the band that pulled her hair back. She'd done it up so tightly it was giving her a headache.

'What's yuh problem, child?'

'My sistah from de country come to live wid us. She chat like posh white girl and she dress like a 'ippy, man. I caan't understand her. She's not like me and you, y'know, she's diff'rent.'

'Choh! No one is ever like anyone, Della. Every man for himself, you know dat.' Dora hung a few strings of jet beads on a brass hook before changing her tone. 'Now, today, I need silk and wool. Not rough stuff – you bring me cashmere and mohair, y'hear? Find some posh bits and dere's gonna be a lickle change in it for you.'

'But she's in my face, man.'

'An' you in mine! Get goin' – it's ten t'irty already.'

Chess knew it was disloyal to be embarrassed by the mere sight of Honor's middle-class handwriting on the envelope lying on Minnie's doormat, but she couldn't help it. The way Honor wrote – fluently, in fountain pen with loops and correct punctuation – was the way she spoke. Now that she was fighting hard to find a way – any way – to fit into this neighbourhood of under-privilege and lawlessness, her mother's genteel voice even in print was too much. It over emphasised the culture gap, if that was possible. She used to be proud of Honor's easy graciousness, but now she was ashamed of it. It made her want to bury her childhood for being an advantage too far.

Chess also knew she was overreacting in imagining that the dusty print of trainer sole on the letter was meant to be some sort of comment from Della. Her sister had made it quite plain that she considered white people her enemy, and she'd made it plainer still that some whites were less acceptable than others, particularly any that Chess might think she could bring home.

Home. That was a concept she was much less sure of lately. Once upon a time it had been the farmhouse she'd grown up in, plain and simple. But at the moment, nowhere seemed to earn the privilege, not Battersea, not Norfolk, not even here if she was honest, even though this was now the basket in which she kept all her eggs.

Things had started to go wrong at Morgan and Brian's almost as soon as she returned from her disjointed week back in Norfolk. It wasn't helped by the suspicion that her parents were at the bottom of it. Morgan had started to question her too heavily about where she was going and who she was seeing, and when Dan let the secret out that she had taken him to Minnie's without anyone's permission, Brian decided it was time Honor and John were summoned 'for a chat'.

The whole thing was an adult conspiracy and Chess knew it. The 'chat' turned out to be more of a gentle sacking in which both parties agreed that the arrangement was no longer 'really working'.

'You're welcome to stay, but you'll have to find other work, and pay a little towards the rent,' Morgan said, having rehearsed her lines with Honor beforehand.

'I think the best thing is for you to come back with us and get on with your re-takes,' John said, as if there was now no choice. 'It's not as if you've got anything better to do.'

'But I *have* got something better to do,' Chess told them. 'I've got to get to know my grandmother.'

'And how will you pay Morgan and Brian their rent?'

'I won't have to, because I won't be living here. Minnie says I can move in with her.'

'No!' Honor blurted out before she could stop herself. This wasn't in the master plan.

'Mum, I'm eighteen, you can't stop me.'

'You'll still need money.'

'Then I'll do what everyone else does and go on the dole.'

The fact that no one tried to drag her kicking and screaming back to Norfolk made her more inclined to try and explain.

'I can't just leave it at this,' she told Judith, who in turn told her parents.

'We understand,' Honor said, but they didn't really.

Chess had hoped to avoid mentioning anything as precise as sleeping arrangements to them but then Honor had insisted on helping her move. Once they'd started unloading her belongings and carrying them in the lift up to Minnie's flat, the lack of space was all too painfully apparent. Chess had even been forced to ask her mother to take some things back with her.

Honor, tactful to the last, hadn't said a word, not even as she tripped up over the pile of skateboards and mountain bikes in the hall, or had to move a pile of comics from a kitchen chair before she sat down. To make conversation, and to cover up her alienation, she'd asked who they belonged to, and Minnie had given her a potted history of the current occupants.

'Dere's Jax an' her two piccanees, Lloyd an' Connor. Jax is Wesley's – dat's my fus' boy's – step-daughter but he live in Jamaica now an' Jax don't like to stay wid her mother 'cos cat hair make Connor's lungs sick see, so she stay here, 'cos Wesley like it like dat, and we have Della, and now we have Frankie, eh?' She'd beamed broadly at the last bit. It made her so happy to welcome her child home.

'Oh, and dere's Gladstone.' Her voice dipped noticeably whenever she mentioned his name.

Honor had lost the plot from Jax on and she nodded stupidly in the wrong places. Minnie's patois was not strong but it took some getting used to, although what she did understand was that she wouldn't have to try too hard. The desperate handing-over ceremony was nearly complete.

'It's what I want,' Chess tried to explain when they said another goodbye on the concrete path outside.

'Well, it's great to know what you want,' Honor had said bravely. 'But I'll leave you to tell Dad the whole picture, if you feel he really needs to know.' Meaning of course, that he didn't.

Desperate for a sympathy of sorts, Chess had written a long letter to Judith, the longest one she had written for ages, about why she was there. *Please try not to see it as disloyal or ungrateful or rash. I need to be here, to live here and not just visit. I want to know as much as I can about this life, what they eat, what music they listen to, how they speak. I'll never be accepted here if I don't, apart from by Minnie who would accept me even if I had two heads, which I sometimes feel as if I do. At the moment, I can see people wondering who the hell I am. I stick out like a sore thumb, I really do. It's not an experiment or anything. I really do have to be here. Mum says she understands but then she says something and I can tell she doesn't, and Dad just keeps his mouth shut. Will you tell them from me how important it is for me to do this? And anyway, what do you think? Let me know, love Chess.*

But so far Judith hadn't let her know. She'd sent a card with kisses, a photo of herself in Turkey and a bag of jelly beans, but she hadn't written one single word. When Judith kept her own counsel, it usually meant she was also biting her tongue.

Chess picked up Honor's envelope, tried to wipe the dusty trainer print on to her trousers, and took it into her bedroom – or rather Minnie's bedroom, because she and her grandmother really *were* sharing a bed again after all these years. Gladstone, her grandfather who had shown no interest in her at all and even less in Minnie, always slept on the sofa when he wasn't elsewhere.

The huge bed dominated the small space. She hadn't yet got round to asking Minnie why she needed two mattresses, or ten blankets for that matter. It seemed ungrateful, to question her accommodation when it was so patently obvious that her presence had only added to the already pressing problem of where to swing a cat.

The cuddling hadn't stopped yet. Jeeva was right when she had said they would be 'physically hungry' for each other, and Chess loved the way her grandmother still insisted on calling her Frankie. She hadn't noticed that Minnie rarely hugged Della, or that Della turned her nose up when she caught sight of any of the intimate contact. It was beyond analysis, this blessed feeling of belonging.

Between the cuddling came the frequent requests for stories, like the one about the day Minnie brought her home from hospital and put her to sleep in a bottom drawer.

'Dat bottom drawer,' Minnie was able to say, touching it with her slippered foot.

'What? I actually slept in this?'

'Uh huh, an' mos' peacefully too.'

The portable television in the corner of the tiny bedroom was covered in a film of dust, its top used as a shelf for old medicine bottles. Black bin liners full of clothes were piled in corners, and at the end of the bed, leaving just enough space to squeeze through, were two huge cardboard barrels.

'What are these for?' Chess asked, having rummaged in one to find a brand new iron, some saucepans and a cellophane pack of green towels. The other had an assortment of clothes, from underwear to coats. Some had been worn, others still had price tickets on.

'Dat's for me to bill a label.'

'Bill a what?'

'Bill a label, to send to family back home,' Minnie explained. 'My sistah, yuh auntie, she have boys an' no man to support her, so we get wha' we can. You come wid me next week to de export office and we can bill a label, eh? For Christmas? Dey come and pick it up and ship it to Jamaica for me. Choh! Such generosity!'

'But some of this stuff you haven't even got yourself.'

'Ah, me no need it, darlin'. Della, well, she t'ink she need it. She keep takin' t'ings out as I put dem in,' Minnie chuckled. 'I jus go in her room and take dem back. We have some runnin' battle, y'know?'

Chess sat on the edge of the unmade bed, waiting for an appetite to read what Honor had written. Minnie had been up, as usual, at dawn, and she was now at the fruit and vegetable market for the third time since Chess had moved in a fortnight ago. The amount of food that got consumed in this flat was awesome, not just by its occupants, but by the constant flow of visitors that trooped in and out around the clock.

Her grandmother would soon be home with her plastic woven basket full of yams, plantain, okra, dasheen, and baby chilli peppers which she would unload into a wooden bowl and put on top of the fridge until they joined one of her juicy but unspecific meat stews later in the day. Chess hung to snippets of her grandmother's routines and habits like a lifeline, because it made her feel like she knew, just for a little while, where she was.

She began to give her mother's letter a cursory glance and imagined Honor writing it at the kitchen table in Norfolk, surrounded by quality newspapers and the day's mail. *Her* wooden bowl would be full of apples and oranges from Marks and Spencer, all clean and round and individually stickered. The two worlds were so far apart.

The four sides of cream crinkle-edged writing paper were

full of 'family news' as Honor put it. *Judith came back from Turkey two days ago, with her new boyfriend in tow. He's called Tim, he's six feet five and ties his hair back with a shoelace! I can't see it lasting as he now has to start a job in Bristol and she's already back in Durham, studying for her M.A. She sends you lots of love and says she'll catch up with you properly at Christmas. Daddy thought a goose would be nice this year for a change. What do you think?*

'I don't know what I'm doing for Christmas yet,' Chess muttered crossly out loud. There was a telephone in the flat but she would go down and use the kiosk later. That way, if Honor heard the pips, she wouldn't think to ask for the number. Handwriting on the doormat was bad enough, without the voice to go with it. Quite how Della would respond if she heard Honor's telephone voice was anyone's guess.

The sound of the key turning in the front door made her jump. She pushed the letter into the back pocket of her blue and cream striped jeans and went out to help Minnie unpack. But it wasn't Minnie, it was Della, wearing a tightly zipped flap-fronted denim jacket that was obviously concealing something.

'It's not raining, is it?' Chess asked.

'Nah man, it's a beautiful day, innit?' Della opened up her stonewashed jacket and flicked out the black bundle. With one shake, it unfurled into a knee-length raglan-sleeved dress. 'Look at dis cloth, man! Caa-asshmeee-re!'

'That's fantastic,' Chess said.

'Dat's money fantastic!' Della bragged, waving the soft wool aggressively in Chess's face. 'Dat cost a hundred quid.'

'Did it? Where did you get it?'

'Dora gave it me, for doin' a bit of stuff for her.'

'God, she's generous.'

'Shit man, I earn it.'

Della dumped the dress in a heap on the kitchen table and took a can of beer from the fridge even though she had not yet had breakfast. She sipped at it quickly, lit a cigarette and disappeared through the sitting room into her bedroom, taking the dress with her. Two minutes later she was back out, wearing it with a pair of high black suede ankle boots which emphasised her athletic, almost masculine, calf muscles.

'What d'ya t'ink?'

Chess had already sussed one thing about her half-sister. She was never more alive than when she was in possession of something new. So far this week it had been a car radio, a little red leather waistcoat and now the dress, each one passed off as a gift or – and Chess hadn't swallowed it as she knew she was supposed to – the world's best bargain. Minnie always walked out of the room when Della started showing off her spoils.

She obediently admired this latest acquisition. It *was* rather special, and she felt jealous. She also decided it was exactly what she needed for the party Morgan and Brian were having. Morgan had been trying to persuade her to come to what she called an 'end of exhibition bash' at the gallery for ages, but because Chess suspected Morgan wanted her to go just so she could report back to Norfolk, she had stubbornly decided to give it a miss. The second invitation, though, made her change her mind.

We haven't heard if you're coming or not yet. Poncho has now put in a request for you to be there twice! Do phone us, Chess, the restaurant need to know numbers. Hugs, Morgan. PS Dan says Hi and would love to see you sometime.

Chess had developed an almost obsessive fantasy around Poncho which had more to do with teenage lust than everlasting love, and the prospect of seeing him again was even more intriguing now that she had just a little more knowledge of his world. Eighteen seemed old enough not to be a virgin any more, even if it did turn out to be only in her dreams. A black boyfriend? Now that might make Della sit up and take some notice of her.

Her sister catwalked through the flat.

'Maybe I could borrow it for a party?' Chess said feebly after her.

'Nah! You get yuh own!' Della spat nastily and waltzed out.

It was advice that, ten days later, Chess dearly wished she'd taken. On the morning of the gallery party, the flat was unusually empty. Minnie was at her day club where she and other people of her creed and colour played bingo and cards and supported each other in the march of time. There was a strong sense of community among the elders. They worshipped together, shopped together, sometimes they ate together. If Chess had been a pensioner, a way to belong would have been handed to her on a plate.

She presumed that Jax had taken her children Lloyd and Connor to school, but in fact the kids were urban sporting, messing with danger on the Underground, and their mother was down at the Job Centre hoping for news of a cleaning contract. Such commonplace information was the kind of detail Chess longed for but would never get because Minnie was the only one who really spoke to her.

Della had been out all night, and judging by her previous form, this meant she would be out for the rest of the day as well, sleeping it off somewhere. Chess still hadn't figured out where. Communication was not their strong point.

So, what shall I wear for Poncho? she thought, knowing she was merely going through the motions. She owned nothing even remotely seductive. Black, she kept thinking, I want to look black. And this time, no bra.

She crept along the hall and across the sitting room and, her heart thumping with caution, she eased down the door handle to Della's private world. She'd only caught glimpses of her sister's room before, but even from those snatched clues she could tell it looked as if a small discount electrical appliance business was run from in there.

Stacked up one wall were stereos, video recorders and car phones. A clothes rail along another was crammed with designer label padded shoulder jackets and leather skirts. To disguise it, Della had built some kind of wooden construction around it which she had draped with old silk curtains, somehow artistically at odds with the rest.

Next to the double mattress on the floor was a folded pile of black Levi jeans, a bundle of shrink-wrapped video cassettes and a huge basket tray of more lipsticks, eye liners and mascaras than one girl could ever use. The sweet smell of Della's heavy perfume hung stickily in the air.

A full-length mirror took up the only free wall space and a huge television towered over the proceedings. Above the head of the mattress was a vast monochrome montage of photographs of black men and women. Chess had no idea where you could buy a poster that big, nor where you'd find such an enormous and original black and white tiled mosaic frame to put it in. She didn't consider the possibility that Della had made them both.

She pushed back the silk curtains across the rail to see if there was an alternative outfit to the cashmere dress – which, after all, was supposed to be out of bounds – but most of what she saw suggested more sexual experience than she could ever hope for. She had a rifle through the piles on the floor, fast coming to the disappointing conclusion that Della had worn the dress herself last night and was probably still in it. Then, at last, she spotted it, rolled up under a huge fluffy red mohair sweater. The mohair had left its mark all over the dress, which looked shabbier than it had a few days earlier, but Chess pulled it out all the same and held it against her.

She imagined Poncho wanting to feel her curves in it. She and Judith were always borrowing each other's clothes and it was easy to tell herself that Della wouldn't really mind. Before she could admit how far from the truth she knew that was, she was out of the room and back in her own.

Pulling her clothes off, discarding the old virginal Chess on the floor in a heap of comfortable underwear, denim and cotton, she tugged on the cashmere dress like there was no time to waste. The wool stank of sweet smoke and perfume but it only made her feel more powerful. I want to smell like Della too, she thought. I want Poncho to smell me, to take in the taste of sex, to know I want him.

'Yes!' she hissed to herself out loud, feeling her free breasts under the softness. 'Yes!' And then she ran from the flat all the way to the Tube station before Della could catch her and spoil her fun. In the bath at Morgan's, she placed both hands on her pelvis and pressed slightly. Tomorrow, I'll be changed for ever, she thought. Or at least, I hope I will be.

The fact that the basement restaurant the Hanlons had taken over for the night was dark and ever so slightly scruffy helped Chess relax into her seduction. It was easier to flirt in the casual surroundings of a room where people put cigarette butts out on the wooden floorboards. The place was trendy by default. Kensington wasn't used to candles being shoved in Mateus Rosé bottles or exposed walls and green painted furniture, so word quickly got out that the Italian owners took their food much more seriously than their décor. Not that food was high on either Poncho or Chess's agenda. From the moment their bodies were within feeling distance again, sex was at the top, the bottom, and at every level in between. Chess drank and drank. With every mouthful of red wine, her body rose a little stronger to its challenge. I want him to be the one, she thought. If I could choose anyone in the world to show me, it would still be him. I want him to know I want him.

By pudding, they still hadn't touched. He was on her left, and she could smell him and feel the heat from his body in the air around him. She was the one to kick off her shoes and find his leg under the table first. Not that anyone watching them would have known their game. She continued to hold a conversation with someone opposite, and he remained talking to a woman on his other side.

Her feet felt ineffective against his heavy duty boots so she explored further to find his ankle, the hem of his trousers, the top of his sock. To her surprise, she knew how to trace her toes around his calf and push the sock down to find his bony ankle, which she curled the tip of her own foot around and around. A bearded man diagonally opposite asked her a simple question but she barely knew how to reply.

When Poncho, still looking and nodding in the other direction, leant down as if to scratch behind his knee and grabbed her foot, she let out a little involuntary gasp. The breathy squeak made him weak with desire, reminding him again of the way she had let him feel her breasts through her firm bra. He put his hand across the back of her chair and then ran it down her spine. There was nothing between her skin and the soft wool of her dress. She knew he knew and they turned to lock eyes.

'You told me the last time that you don't make women do things they don't want to do,' Chess said in a deep whisper.

'Dat's right,' he said, taking the lobe of her right ear between his thumb and forefinger and applying a little pressure before whipping his hand away.

'So what about the things they *do* want to do?'

'Dey got to show me first.' He spent a long time letting the word 'show' leave his mouth, which meant that his lips were formed in a small 'o' long enough for Chess to study them and feel the imprint of them tightening somewhere behind the horizontal line of her pubic hair.

'I'm going to say my goodbyes,' she said quickly, sliding out of her chair and letting the swing of her breasts brush the air around him. 'And then in a minute, when we're somewhere else, I'd love to show you.'

Am I really doing this? she wondered as she walked calmly up the stairs with her handbag. And if I am, shouldn't I be just a little frightened? She saw Poncho rise from the corner of her eye and her heart contracted. He was coming to join her.

Outside, twenty feet above Morgan and Brian and the rest of the party, they came together with a clash of bodies, as if some magnetic force had pulled them up and out of the building and was now joining them regardless of will or judgement. Their first kiss was hungry – starving even – and when Chess pulled away, confusion swept across Poncho's face.

'Our fire exit,' she said, as if that explained it. 'Let's go back to our fire exit. It's just down there.'

He laughed. 'I c'n offer you somet'ing better dan a pavement an' a wall, Chess. I c'n even stretch to a bed, y'nah?'

'No, I want it to be the fire exit. That's where it has already happened, in my head.'

'Wha' you tellin' me, eh?' Poncho's tooth diamond caught

the flash of a passing car's headlights. 'You bin plannin' for dis?' he asked, reaching for both her hands.

'Only since about half past ten this evening,' she lied.

'You a reckless woman.'

'I am tonight.'

'You seducin' me?' He ran his palms up and down the sumptuous sleeves of her dress and crooked his neck to look into her eyes.

'Yeah,' she smiled shyly.

'An' are you sayin' wha' I t'ink you sayin' here now? Dat you wan' me to make love wid you against a *wall*?'

'Come with me,' Chess said, and she started to pull him along the pavement until they were soon running together at full pelt. The tiny fibres of cashmere were tickling her perspiring cleavage and spine by the time they both stopped at the gallery door, and the smell of the dress's previous nights seeped through to her nostrils as she got her breath back.

'Inside,' she puffed. Suddenly, she wanted the dress off. She wanted him naked, her naked, she wanted as much skin touching as possible. 'I've got the key. We can go inside. We have to go through the showroom, round the front.'

Poncho held her still, and put his mouth to hers, moving his lips to her hot neck, licking the rim of her ear.

'Come on,' she said. Even her words felt like caresses. They held hands tightly as they walked around the building.

'Dis place mus' be alarmed, Chess. You gonna set somet'ing off,' he said as she fumbled for the key in her bag.

'Don't tell anyone, but it isn't. I'm sure Morgan has forgotten I've still got this.'

'Den you're gonna set me off if we don' get inside quick.'

The door opened, and she pulled him in. It was no longer a purely sexual adventure she was on. She was just breaking all the rules, all over the place, and it felt so wild, like the most exciting moment of her life so far. I'm going to do it, she repeated to herself, I am actually going to do it. Then I'll be a bit more valid, won't I?

In the cold quiet space of the showroom, with the door shut

behind them, Poncho went down on his knees and buried his face in her stomach, his hands on her hips, shifting the wool of her dress around her flushed body, still clammy with the speed of their sprint.

'Come with me,' she said, holding the sides of his head and giving them a gentle lift.

'God, wha' you doin' to me?' he moaned, kissing her torso.

She led him by the hand into the stockroom, leaving the door open so the street lights could shine through and she let go. Then she took off the dress over her head, and with her arms stretched above her and her legs a little astride, she was the same Amazonian princess warrior that had looked back at her from her bedroom mirror after their first meeting. She knew this time that Poncho would find her ravishing, not terrifying. The dress lay in a black heap on the floor, and she slid off her pants to show herself naked.

'This is my body,' she heard herself say. 'And you're the first man to ever see it like this.'

Poncho couldn't speak. He remembered feeling the sports bra again and how much it had turned him on to know she was untouched, and now here she was, unclothed and offering herself to him.

'Y' beautiful,' he whispered, moving to touch her. 'Y'beautiful, y' nah? Jus' so fine.'

'Can I see your body too?' He felt her breath in his ear. 'Like this? Undressed?'

And so slowly, in the dark tiny room with only a few square feet of floor space, he took off his clothes one by one. First his boots, unlaced and eased off at the heel. Then he began to unbutton the flies on his jeans and peel them back to expose a glimpse of stretched cotton, taut over his straight hard penis. He left himself like that while he shed his jacket, letting it drop to the floor, and then reached up, echoing Chess's own movement, to pull off his black T-shirt. His chest was strong and smooth, his stomach flat.

'And your jeans,' she said, leaning backwards against the small table and looking at the triangle of his underpants, wondering exactly what lay underneath. 'If you take them off, we'll both be the same.' Well, we already *are* the same, she thought. That's why I want you.

'You do it,' he said, bringing her hands to the denim. 'You do it, an' den I know you doin' wha' you wan' fe do, eh? You show me wha' you wan', Chess.'

And so she did. Realising she was tipping the cup of virginity and pouring its precious but outgrown contents on to the floor with their discarded clothes, she put her hands on his hips and slid his trousers down.

'I really don't know what I'm doing here,' she admitted as she took the cotton of his briefs in her fingers and eased them down. He was bigger and harder and more beautiful than she had ever imagined.

'An' dat's why I'm feelin' so special,' Poncho almost groaned. 'I gonna be so gentle, yeh? We jus' do wha' you wan', OK?'

And as they sank to the hard floor together, Chess knew she had at last got one thing right about what she wanted out of life.

You don't use a hot iron on cashmere, especially not directly on to its surface, but at eighteen, Chess didn't know that. Della's dress had been slept *in* as well as *on*, and before it could be secretly returned to its rightful place, Chess felt she had to restore it to at least some of its former glory. She and Poncho had stayed in the stockroom till dawn. It got so cold around three that they had dressed each other and huddled up, but neither of them had suggested leaving for somewhere more comfortable. They both knew it was a one-off, that even if they did see each other again (and both hoped they would) it would never be as thrilling and as new a second time. These moments only came by once. When light came, they left. Chess could have taken the early trains or buses home, but she chose instead to walk, taking twice as long as she needed, stopping for coffee and window shopping on the way.

'I'm not a virgin any more, I'm not a virgin any more,' she kept chanting as she rigged up a makeshift ironing board with towels and a sheet on the kitchen table. No one was in, so it didn't matter how loud she said it. I must let Judith know, she thought elatedly. She'll love the details!

She was back in her jeans and rugby shirt although she hadn't washed Poncho's sweat from her own body on purpose. He could stay there all day. Her mind leapt backwards and forwards, from the restaurant to the stockroom, from their pavement race to the moment she saw him erect after pulling down his pants. It was hard to think of anything else.

She was just wondering why the bottom of the iron kept catching on the downy black wool when she heard the front door click. Before she could think of what to do, Della burst in. 'What's dat stink, man?'

Chess leapt out of her skin. She hadn't even thought of the possibility that Della would catch her out *after* the event.

'I was just going to try on your dress. I wasn't going to borrow it. I–'

'What de bomba claat you a do?' Della shouted an inch away from her face. 'What de fuck you a doin?'

Della whipped the dress away and held it up. The scorch-mark was the burnt orange of the henna Jax had just put in her hair.

'Dat's my fuckin' dress! Wha' you doin', eh? Wha' you doin', you weird bitch!'

And without waiting for a response, she flew. Spitting and raging like a feral cat defending its patch, she flicked her sharpened talons and slashed the dress across Chess's body three or four times. Then she reached for the iron and yanked it from the plug on the wall. For a very bad moment, Chess thought she was about to be hit with it and she held her arms across her face until she heard the iron being flung to the floor. It hit the fridge and left a serious dent.

'I'm sorry,' Chess yelled. 'Stop it. I wasn't going to – I'm sorry.'

But Della hadn't finished. She lunged crazily towards her, grabbing Chess's face with her fingers and drawing her claws down the smooth skin of her left cheek.

'You scratch the black and dere's white underneet!' she screamed, as the brilliant red blood trickled down Chess's chin. It barely hurt. She was desensitised with fear.

'You get me anudder one,' Della ordered, pushing her against the cooker. 'You don't touch Della's t'ings, never. You get me anudder one, you bring it to me, then you get out of dis house for ever or you can consider yuhself one dead woman.'

Chess was shaking and she also thought she was crying, but when she put her hand up to her face, the only moisture was the blood coming from her wound. She went to pick up the iron by its flex but Della, breathing demonically down her neck, kicked her arm as it went down. She stood back up and Della imprisoned her, standing so close to her she couldn't move a limb. Then, just when she thought she was going to lose her sanity, she was rescued.

'Jus' WHAT you t'ink yuh doin'?' Minnie yelled from the doorway. 'Jus' WHAT you t'ink yuh doin'?'

'Granny, she burn up ma dress.' Della snivelled like a bully challenged by authority.

'An' you gonna *kill* her for dat?' Minnie asked, walking towards Della now. Della stopped speaking and shook her head. It was her turn to be frightened.

'I'll get you another one,' Chess promised.

'You will *not*,' Minnie said, raising her voice even louder. '*Della* will get out of dis house now. OUT! OUT!'

She picked up a broom and pushed it against her granddaughter's bottom.

'Get yuh batty out of dis house NOW! I don't want to see yuh face till it's too dark to see de shame in it. OUT!'

Della resisted a little but then Minnie shoved harder. 'OUT!'

'You get me anudder one, or you dead!' Della shouted back at Chess, slamming the front door and running for her life.

It took a long time for Chess to stop shaking. First, she thought she was going to pass out, then she felt sick, and finally she came over so cold that Minnie had to drag the blankets off her bed to wrap round her.

'It's shock, darlin', jus' shock.'

'It was my fault though. I took her dress when she told me not to,' Chess blubbered. 'I wore it to a party.'

'An' you t'ink she never does t'ings she told not to do? Eh?'

'No, but–'

'And you t'ink attackin' you like dat is OK?'

'No.'

'I tell you, don' follow Della 'cos she have no use!' Minnie thrust a mug of sweet tea on the table but her hands were shaking and it slopped on to a newspaper. Chess had never seen her so angry before and it made her frightened for what was to come next.

'What will you do to her?'

Minnie shook her head. She knew there was nothing much she *could* do against a temper like that. Chess followed her with begging eyes.

'Don't make her hate me even more, will you? I don't want to make this even harder. I want us to be friends, I–'

'I won' have de word *hate* in dis house, Frankie. Dere's lots said I can't do not'ing about, but hatred in yuh own family – no! She's jealous of you, see?'

'But I want her to like me. I *really* want her to like me.' Chess began to cry again. They were tears of frustration, defeat and shame. Even making love with Poncho felt dirty now. The tiredness of a whole night awake hit her.

'She's jus' seein it all wrong. She's good at seein' t'ings all wrong.'

'She'll hate me now.'

Her grandmother pulled up a chair and sat down heavily next to her, burrowing her plump warm fingers into Chess's blanket cocoon and finding her hand to hold. Her voice was soft and calm.

'Darlin', tomorrow she won' even remember wha' you fell out about.'

'She won't?'

'I'm tellin' you, all it goin' a take is anudder new piece of cloth an' she'll forget all about it.'

'D'you really think so?'

'I really t'ink so,' Minnie said, soaking a flannel in a bowl of warm water and TCP. 'Now, hol' still while I clean you up.'

By the time Chess was in a fit state to leave the flat, it was no longer the beautiful day that she had celebrated at dawn. A gloom had moved in, not just into her spirit, but into the whole huge London sky above her. As she walked to the Tube station, her left cheek tight with the forming scab, rain started to fall.

She opened her rucksack and took out the folded laminated Harrods carrier bag she had bought with such pride two years ago, and she used it to cover her head as she ran to the Tube station. Her hair was no longer box hedge. It was still a mound, but now it was straight and sprung from her crown like an umbrella. She had been taking secret blow-drying and heating-tong lessons from Della and Jax, who both styled their hair daily in the sitting room, but she still hadn't quite got the hang of it. An inspection of the hair relaxants and coconut oil on the bathroom shelf had helped and she had since added her own concoctions to the array. But hair was the last thing on her mind. She needed to make immediate amends with Della because until she did, she would live in fear of her return. Her big moment with Poncho had gone, as if it had happened to someone else.

'All it goin' a take is anudder new piece of cloth an' she'll forget all about it,' Minnie had said quite emphatically.

So another new piece of cloth was what she would get . . . but buying a new cashmere dress was out of the question. Money of that sort was simply not available on social security. And although she was pretending to herself that she was just off for a walk to clear her head, Chess knew deep down that it would turn out to be no ordinary walk.

Della did this kind of thing as easily as falling out of bed. So did hundreds of others, every minute of every retailing day. And why should she be caught anyway? No one was ever caught on the first time, surely. How difficult could it be? There would be a double bonus attached too – not only would Della get a dress back but she might even look twice at the criminal bravado.

Knightsbridge was just as wet as Minnie's neighbourhood but somehow not as bleak. Honor's comment about the Christmas goose came back to her when she saw the famously showy Harrods ablaze with festive lights. Pantomime figures moved mechanically up and down, across and around the huge window displays. Shoppers pushed their way in and heaved their way out, laden with goods. Goods in bags. Goods in marked bags, with receipts.

She wasn't yet ready to go in, so she walked down the side of the world-famous store, and along Basil Street at the back. Then she came back up Hans Road and found herself back on Brompton Road, taking in the road names as she went.

A uniformed commissionaire in the green livery that exactly matched the colour of her bag was busy welcoming an excited gaggle of old women. As they passed on in, he took an umbrella from a nearby stand and went to the door. Opening it out in a theatrical flourish, he accompanied a tiny glossy woman with feet that looked barely big enough to keep her upright to a waiting taxi. Chess smiled at him as she entered, but he looked right through her. She was neither rich nor old, so presumably she didn't count.

There was a security guard just inside the door, giving directions to a Japanese couple who wanted the food hall. His much less showy white shirt and black tie and his quasi-Services peaked cap told Chess precisely why he was there. These were the guys she had to avoid. She thought about smiling at him too, but then thought that might draw attention to herself unnecessarily, so instead, she studied the floor plan, clutching her old Harrods bag as if it gave her a certain legitimate right to be there, and tried not to think about the wound on her cheek. Had Della really expected to find white skin underneath? Did she really think of her as some sort of alien in a B-movie whose human face could be ripped off to reveal a maze of oozing green veins and only one central eye?

The stupid thing is, thought Chess as she waited for the lift to take her to Ladies Fashions on the first floor, I want to make it up to her, I want to be able to give her something to make her eyes sparkle, I want her to forgive me. And *I'm* the bloody victim, literally.

She'd done her best to look like a shopper rather than a shop*lifter*. Her charcoal-grey cowl-neck sweater with the bold cream V plunging down her front had been a present from Honor and John from the States. It was not exactly her taste but it was good quality, she knew that much. And her button-through straight skirt in grey and black pinstripe looked respectable, or had done until she entered this world of riches. The bored looks she was getting from the harshly coiffured lady assistants made her feel like she had no business here. But she did. That was the whole point.

Every time she went to touch one of the clothes on the rails, she caught a small static shock. No one else seemed to be getting it. She imagined her whole body wired up, crackling with tension, letting off invisible sparks of fear. If she was picked up on one of the in-store security cameras, she would probably show up with a flurry of electrical activity around her, then the peaked caps would home in on her and escort her off the premises in a discreet show of efficiency. A big part of her wished they would. At least she could have said she'd tried.

The place was a designer label junkie's dream. Big names blared at her from every corner, but she couldn't find one measly jumper dress on the whole floor that she thought good enough for Della. They were all too safe, too Naval wife, too *white*. She returned to the information board. There were seven floors to choose from, and she picked the fourth.

Way-In, the mecca of all young Sloanes everywhere, was full of affluent schoolgirls and their matching mothers, their invariably blonde bobbed hair pulled back by velvet bands, their empty minds on the one task of spending money. Chess was aghast to hear the amount of derision in the daughters' voices, and even more surprised at the way their mothers still bought them what they wanted to accompany them back to their rural boarding schools regardless.

There was a whole rail given entirely to black wool, and when she found what she was looking for, she checked the label not for the price but for the content of cashmere. One hundred per cent. You could feel that just by touching it. Then she took a glance at the size. Twelve. Then the cost. Ninety-nine pounds. Here we go then, she thought, as she took it into the private changing room with another three items.

No one stopped her, or gave her a ticket, or counted her hangers or even seemed to notice her going in. She pulled the curtain across and took the dress off the hanger. She rolled it up as tight as it would go and pushed it to the bottom of her Harrods wipe clean bag, throwing in half the contents of her rucksack on top. Then she waited for exactly three minutes by her watch, and walked out, handing the three red herring garments to the assistant.

'No good?' the girl asked pleasantly.

'No,' said Chess. 'Not quite me.'

She had forgotten how to walk casually. It was a physical effort just to lift her feet to take each step. Every time she did so was an achievement. With every sinking of the heel of her low court shoe into the deep carpet, she expected to hear a shout.

Amazed to get as far as the lift, she pressed the button to go down, and waited. The longer she stood there, the more she expected to feel that heavy hand on her shoulder, that firm male voice asking her to step this way. She waited a while longer but the hand never came. Two other girls, younger than her but more poised, decided to take the stairs, and she followed on the premise that there was safety in numbers.

The rolled-up dress at the bottom of the Harrods bag started to get heavier; it began to radiate and flash and bleep and eat its way through the plastic-coated cotton, or so it felt. She started to sense eyes burning into her from other shoppers, and when she passed a security guard at the bottom of an up elevator issuing instructions into his walkie-talkie, her legs buckled momentarily.

She turned round to see if he was following her, but he was

still at his billet, legs astride, hands now behind his back, like part of a waxwork exhibition. He saw her though.

Her body temperature was sky high, and a damp film was sitting on her skin. The cowl neck of her American sweater began to itch and she started to panic about fainting. They might search her bags for medicine or identification, and then they would discover that she wasn't a customer at all, but a thief.

The more she thought about fainting, the more she thought it a possibility. Her heart pounded in her ears as she made her way round and round and down and down until she was on the ground floor. Having no idea which one of the ten entrances would take her out on to familiar territory, she quickened her pace and took the nearest.

It wasn't until she had crossed the threshold that the security tag made its presence known. She had never heard the sound before and yet she knew exactly what it was. It was her wake-up call to run like hell. The lobby was clamorous and confused and she barged through, apologising to people as her shoulders hit theirs.

The sound of heavy steps came thumping up behind her, and she swung her bag up and across someone's face without looking to see who it was. Suddenly she was out on the street. Faces from the safe insides of the rush-hour traffic studied her with dispassionate curiosity, their headlights beaming down on her like a hundred searchlights through the steady drizzle.

This wasn't the main facade. Her bearings had gone and she needed to get to the Tube station to lose herself in the crowd. All she could do was run, so she did – straight into a wall of uniform.

'Oof!'

'Going somewhere, are we?' Her captor, for he now had her upper arm in an unnecessarily brutal grip, was a man with a grey moustache and a curl to one side of his lips. He loved his job, especially when it took him outside. This was even better, because it was a blackie.

'OK Dave, I've got her,' he spoke into his favourite gadget.

He pulled her forcefully back inside the nearest entrance and hustled her, much to her acute shame, across the shop floor.

'Come on, Dolores,' he said. 'We want to see what you've got in your bag.'

'My name's not Dolores. It's Francesca,' Chess said. For a hopeful second, she thought they might have confused her with someone else, an habitual offender who deserved this rough handling.

'You can be Minnie Mouse for all I care,' he said.

An unexpected calm came over her in the police car. It was the first time since Della's attack that morning that she hadn't had to think for herself. One of the policemen who sat in the back with her tried to explain the procedure. She would go back to the station, answer a few questions, and then she would be released with or without charge. Then he asked her what had happened to her face.

'Um, it's a long story.'

He looked only mildly interested. 'Did it happen in the store?'

'No, this morning. It's OK, it isn't anything you need to know about.'

'You don't come from London, do you?' he said.

'No.' Her eyes filled with tears. *Don't be nice to me,* she wanted to say. *I can hold it back if you're horrible.*

'So where do you come from then?'

'I don't really know,' Chess wanted to reply. Instead, she said, 'Norfolk.'

At the station, he asked a stocky policewoman to look at Chess's arm which she was holding limply by her side. The security man with the walkie-talkie had dug his nails right into the muscle and it hurt her to move it.

'Here?' asked the WPC, squeezing.

'Ow,' Chess winced. 'Yes.'

'You'll live,' she mocked, pushing her in the direction of a windowless corridor that reverberated with the clanging and banging of metal doors.

Is this what Poncho meant, she wondered, lying in the cell and crying for Honor, or Minnie, or *someone* to sweep her up and take her home. Is this what it is really like to be black? No dress, no love lost and no point in sticking with this thing any longer.

Three days later, with the terror of a shoplifting charge hanging over her and an overwhelming sense of failure at everything coursing through her veins, she was still wondering the same thing – this time lying on a green checked duvet in her eaves bedroom in Norfolk.

No one had dragged her back against her own volition this time. She had come running of her own accord as a gut reaction to crisis. The stupid thing was, the moment she had got into her mother's car, before they had even driven to the end of the London street, she had known it was a mistake. Her head had turned involuntarily upwards, to the flat's kitchen window, and she had stared at it until it was just a blur, hoping for a last glimpse of her grandmother. But Minnie, as Chess feared, was in a heap in her armchair, weak with sadness.

And then there had been Honor – relieved, grateful, frightened Honor – sitting at the wheel of the car trying hard not to look as if she had found the top of the world once more. Everyone had cried too hard and too long for it all to be for nothing. Chess had decided she must be the most selfish person alive. How could she ask for love and then discard it? Or reject a life and then expect to have it back again when it suited her?

She'd felt like a child being both kidnapped and rescued, that she was leaving the life she had only just begun to understand, to return to one she no longer felt a part of, and it was as early as that first car journey that she decided the easiest thing was probably not to feel at all.

Little by little though, day by day, Chess found comfort in staring at her ludicrous collection of fluffy toys and the out-of-date poster of Michael Jackson in red leather. She knew these things, she had chosen them, they were hers. And there was nobody around who might judge her by them because her face, her clothes, her habits and her possessions were so familiar to this corner of the world that she was one of them, on the inside looking out. She retreated into a world that may have had little to do with who she really was, but almost everything to do with who she had become.

Her parents had a quick gloat (or at least that's how their chastisement had sounded to Chess) and then they carried on as if nothing had ever changed. 'If you *will* insist on going at things headfirst like you always do, then what do you expect? You *must* start thinking things through! When *will* you learn?' and that was it. They were drawing a line under it, and they expected her to as well.

But she couldn't. She missed everything – the smell of Minnie's stews, the permanent burble of Minnie's television, the rolling timetable of different mealtimes. She missed Poncho and their brief union. She missed feeling his tooth diamond on her tongue, seeing his skin against hers, hearing his language that she sometimes only half-understood. And she had forgotten how Honor served salad with a wooden fork and spoon and always suggested a game of Scrabble instead of television.

'No! This is not me any more!' she wanted to scream, but she didn't, if only because it begged the question, 'Then what is?'

If only Judith had been there to tell her that Honor was waiting for her to say exactly that, that her mother was longing to redress the balance of her childhood, that she was ready to acknowledge her mistakes and start to make up the difference. But no one was there to push either woman into such new territory and so they remained rooted to the spot.

Chess's mind traipsed in ever-decreasing circles until, eventually, she decided she had found the centre of her existence once again. Her life was here, where it almost always had been, in rural England, where she had parents to bail her out, a sister who gave her the benefit of any doubt and a whole community who thought they knew who she was. It was the well-trodden path to an easy life so she took it, preserving the part of herself that had been awoken by Minnie in an imaginary aspic which she naively expected to keep labelled but untouched for ever.

Chess Lovell became once more the girl who waited for choices to be made for her. Well, for fifteen years anyway.

Chapter 9

June 1999: A government survey released today shows a sharp increase in the rise of reported racial attacks in Britain since 1992, the year black teenager Stephen Lawrence was stabbed to death as he waited for a bus. The report, which includes last month's nail-bomb attacks at Brixton market and Brick Lane in London, has been given a widespread welcome. A spokesman for the Commission for Racial Equality said it was 'encouraging that the police and government are at last taking racial attacks more seriously.'

Kezia Jacoby nudged the front door shut with her rounded little bottom and dropped all the envelopes in the dusty square where the doormat would eventually go. The postman hadn't said a word to her. He hadn't even given her a smile. In Norfolk, George sometimes used to give her and Sam Polos. That was another reason she could write in her diary why she didn't like London as much as her old home. Still, at least he had given her a parcel. In her experience, envelopes were for grown-ups but recycled Jiffy bags like the one she had in her hand were definitely for children.

'Oh,' she said, charging back into the kitchen and looking with disappointment at the address. 'Mummy, it's for you.' She skimmed the big brown padded envelope across the cluttered table and it clipped the rim of a cereal bowl.

'Careful!' Chess lunged forward to protect a cup of coffee and then, pulling the package from a stream of milk, she recognised the handwriting as Judith's and the flicker of excitement left her too. She sat the wet parcel on a tea towel without inspecting it further and carried on packing two coloured back-packs with books and bananas.

'Aren't you going to open it?' her eight-year-old daughter asked in disbelief.

'It's from Auntie Judith.'

Kezia tried to understand how that could possibly be an adequate answer to her question. 'Does that mean it will be something to do with Granny?'

'Everything is to do with Granny at the moment as far as Auntie Judith is concerned,' Chess sighed, the layers of pity and frustration and jealousy well hidden under the shell of irritation.

'Granny's dead,' said Sam. 'Up there,' and he pointed to the ceiling.

'Stop saying that,' his sister shouted. 'You're only five, you don't know anything.'

'What's that then?' Nick walked in, tightening the knot on a lime green and purple silk tie that Chess hadn't seen before. So far, she'd resisted ribbing her husband about the sartorial make-over he'd undergone since they'd all moved to London. In Norfolk, Marks and Spencer had done the job. Now it was all much more serious stuff – double cuff shirts and bird's-eye check from Savile Row.

'Just some parcel from Judith.'

'Aren't you going to open it?'

'Not you as well,' she growled, but then smiled. She knew it wasn't fair to take her inhibition out on Nick. Not that he wouldn't understand. He understood everything, always, even her silences.

She pulled the tea towel out from under the envelope and it flipped over. On the back, Judith had written *Save for a quiet moment*. Some chance. Besides, she knew more or less what it would contain anyway. Memories, grief, pain, desolation.

Honor's death seven weeks ago had all but finished her sister. Poor Judith had shrunk to almost nothing – not in size because, as bad timing would have it, she was pregnant with her fourth baby – but most certainly in variety of moods. Every single thing she did or said lately sprang from a craving to keep their dead mother centre-stage.

It wasn't as if they hadn't had a dummy run at parental bereavement. When John had died five years previously, Honor had very definitely been the main mourner and Chess and Judith had propped each other up equally. In the morning he'd been gardening in his old threadbare cords and by the evening he – or his corpse – had been in the Chapel of Rest. It had knocked all of them for six, but they had got over it, kind of, and that's why Chess had come to treat his death as a practice run for the big one. But losing Honor had been more traumatic for Judith than anyone had ever imagined. Chess was trying her best to be sympathetic but it was difficult when her sister was hell-bent on behaving as if she and she alone had the ultimate right to be the most unhappy. No one had expected to lose their parents, not even when they were old, and Honor and John had been relatively young, not even pensionable. It hurt for everyone, and Judith should see that.

'That was a big sigh,' Nick said, coming over to his wife and putting his hand on her cheek. 'What were you thinking?'

'About Dad, actually.'

'Yeah?'

'Yeah.' Chess smiled at her husband shyly. Nick knew some of the difficulty she had gone through after John's heart attack because, for once, she had actually shared it with him. He told her it wasn't her fault she hadn't recognised the 'wonderful father' the vicar spoke of at the funeral, that it was just the way the world went sometimes. But even now, she still couldn't shake Brian Hanlon's words from her mind.

'God, he loved you,' Brian had slurred, pink with grief and brandy after John's burial.

'Sure,' Chess had replied. 'We just weren't very good at showing it.'

'I'll give you that. I'll never forget the silly bastard turning up on our doorstep stinking of whisky one night because of you. He always wanted to be closer to you than he was, you see.

Your mother and sister had gone away and he'd seen it as your big chance to bond or something, but then you stayed over with a friend and he was left on his own again, so he got pissed and came to us. How the old bugger wasn't stopped I'll never know.'

'I thought he'd be relieved.'

'*Relieved*? Bloody hell, girl, you two just kept on missing each other, didn't you?'

His comments had branded her with the truth, failed father, failed daughter, and she had hidden in a bedroom for the rest of the funeral pretending to feed her newborn son. In reality, Sam had slept like a drunk for a full two hours and she had stared at the walls next to him, the first seed of realisation growing inside her that her entire life had never really been what it seemed. It was a lethal little seed too, because from time to time it sprouted shoots that could make her doubt almost everything else.

'Come here,' Nick pressed, seeing her struggle with the memory. He put out his arms to clamp her.

'I'm fine.' Chess wriggled away and busied herself with the breakfast things. 'I just worry that Judith might be worse than me because . . .'

Nick knew what his wife was going to say. She had tried the same theory out on him before – that the extent of Judith's misery had something to do with the extent of her genetic relationship with Honor.

'No,' he interrupted before she could go there. 'She's just not handling it as well as you. It's got nothing to do with how much either of you loved her.'

'Then why do my tears never feel quite good enough?' she whispered. The children didn't need to hear this stuff.

He put his other hand on her cheek. 'Because, Chess,' he held her face straight, 'that is you all over.'

The affectionate display suddenly embarrassed her. His careful surveillance of her grieving process made her self-conscious. She made light of it by turning to Kezia, who was watching them carefully, and tossing her the package.

'Here you are Kez, you do it.'

'What? Can I open it?'

'Yep.'

The bubble wrap gave a few satisfying pops as Kezia tore hopefully into it, but the odds of it being anything at all exciting faded to nothing as she pulled out something shabby and orange. Despite a thirty-year estrangement, Chess identified it instantly.

'Oh, my old bag!' she cried as her daughter held it at arm's length and made a face.

'Er . . . Mummy, you mean you actually used to *use* this?'

'Your mother's never had any taste,' Nick teased.

'Tell me, did you pay good money for that tie?' Chess retaliated. Phew, she thought, that's better – familiar territory again.

Their mutual taunting, only a few short steps away from the modus operandi of the love games played in senior school playground was an easy way of letting each other know that the flame continued to flicker even after ten years of marriage. Chess much preferred playful derision to any kind of romantic gesture, a choice she had developed mainly as an antidote to the nauseating slush Judith and her husband Tim used to come out with. At one time, Nick would still have kissed her any place, any time, at the drop of a hat but he'd been cold-shouldered enough times now not to bother. The physical side of their relationship was alive and well, but carried out entirely in private.

Twelve years ago, he had noticed her long before she had noticed him. Given that she was the only black girl in town at that time, it was hardly surprising, but that had nothing to do with his lasting attention. Most girls he'd come across until then wore their achievements on their power suits like shining badges, just below their padded shoulders and to the centre of their financially motivated hearts. Their phenomenal salaries meant they were placed on an aspirational ladder that they then had to scrabble all over each other to climb. They talked up their jobs, their holidays and their backgrounds as if they would be judged on these things alone, and they were careful to litter their conversation with the right dates from the social calendar. Chess in contrast was like a breath of fresh air, happy with her job as a secretary in a small publishing company and content with the occasional game of pool at the local pub.

'Have you ever wanted to go to Henley or Glyndebourne?' Nick had asked his future wife after their first evening together as a little test.

'Where?' she'd answered.

That was it. Nick Jacoby was in love! He had no idea how on earth he had managed to attract such a rare bird when he was nothing special at all, just a newly qualified solicitor working his way up a small country practice for an unimpressive wage, but the day he asked Chess to marry him was the day she finally and truly felt her decision to stay put in Norfolk had been the right one.

'You mean you really want me?'

'I do. I really want you.'

'Then I really want you too,' she'd told him in her parents' back garden in the rain, hoping he would accept that reason alone as good enough. It had been, so far.

Kezia sniffed the orange bag and screwed up her nose. 'Phaw! It stinks.'

'Nice rope detail,' Nick teased.

'That's enough!' Chess shouted, snatching it protectively. 'I used to keep all my favourite things in this when I was little. Judith must have found it at Mum's.'

She ran her fingers over the intricate beading, remembering how she used to nibble at the thread until the little bobbles of plastic broke free and popped into her mouth. Honor must have kept it somewhere safe all these years in the vague hope that there would one day be a moment like this. It was good to realise that some things, like your own childhood, were still and always would be there. She should probably start putting Kezia and Sam's outgrown things away. Judith no doubt had an attic full of her children's already.

It was a comforting thought, but as she slid back the tinny zip, her nose caught the smell of uncontrollable grief as well, and she pulled it quickly shut again. It would have been OK if it had been her own grief seeping out, but it wasn't, it was Judith's and she was at saturation point with that as it was.

'What's inside?' Nick asked as he saw his wife tugging hurriedly to close the zip.

'Just photos.'

Judith had phoned her rather mysteriously two days ago to say that some pictures had been found next to Honor's body and that she thought Honor must have meant Chess to have them.

'You OK?'

'Stop looking at me, Nick, you make me feel nervous. I'm not about to break down as well.' She couldn't possibly match her sister's grief anyway, so it was better all round if she only ever let herself go when she was alone. 'I'm sorry.'

It wasn't Nick's fault that Honor had died and he had been offered a new job in the space of a week, but she couldn't help holding him just a little bit responsible for the subsequent upheaval all the same. Moving to London was dragging up far more confusion than she was able to let on.

'No problem,' he soothed. 'What photos?'

'Some stuff Judith must want me to sort through, but I haven't got time now. Why they've only just come to light, I don't know.'

'We'll do it later, together.'

'Just let me be.'

Putting her bare foot on a kitchen chair, she started to ease the knot on the soggy friendship bracelet around her ankle. It had survived three showers, although the colours had now run into each other and it was also feeling a bit on the slimy side.

'Mummy, don't – it's not supposed to come off!' Kezia shouted.

'Not even to look smart for my first day at work? I could put it back on tonight.'

'Don't worry. You don't have to look *that* smart. Daddy

told me it's not a real job, it's just Auntie Morgan being nice to you because of Granny dying.

'Thanks, Kez,' Nick winced, giving his daughter's wiry bunches a yank. 'Come on, we're late. Where's Sam gone?'

Chess tried to decide if it was worth being cross or not. Probably not. 'You're out of the bloody Ark sometimes, Jacoby,' she said.

Kezia took her cereal bowl over to the sink, and put her head against her mother's chest. 'You're supposed to make a friendship bracelet for me now, and then we wear each other's for ever. Yours is the colours of the Jamaican flag, did you notice?'

'So it is. OK, so it can come off when it falls off.' Chess put her foot back on the dusty floor. 'These boards need sealing, Nick.'

'Get on with it then,' he teased, although she heard a sting to his banter. His time was completely taken up, and hers wasn't, or didn't have to be. It had been her choice to take Morgan up on the delivery job at the gallery. Now she *was* cross. She waved her hand vaguely at the back-packs.

'Don't forget Sam's PE kit. And Kezia needs a cheque for the trip. I've got to get going,' she said. 'Bye, children. I'll pick you up later.'

Disappearing up the stairs, she was relieved it wasn't her morning to do the run. The smell of so much polished wood at the private preparatory school she and Nick had so carefully chosen for their children made her hanker for the good old state school stink they'd left behind in Norfolk. In London, it just seemed too much of a risk to stick with the system they had once been determined to support. Life in the city was just as dangerous as she remembered it.

When they had first flicked through the glossy prospectus, they'd had a good laugh at the models posing as parents before it dawned on them. Professional parents in London really did look like that. If ever Chess felt a fish out of water, it was at the school gates.

'I don't feel I belong here,' she admitted to Nick, who always escaped the small talk by seeing the children safely in the playground and then leaving immediately. It was a man thing, he claimed.

'But you've never felt you belong *anywhere*.'

The letterbox flapped and made her jump. Being alone in their new house felt so different to being alone in their old one. Here, it was as if it was only quiet because someone was lurking. Still, it had been a joint decision to move, possibly even more hers than Nick's. A six-figure salary in a City law firm specialising in commercial work was not exactly his big dream, and he'd only taken the job because it meant added security for his family. Once or twice, she'd suspected he'd tried to encourage her to protest, just so he could justify turning such ridiculous money down.

During one 'should we, shouldn't we?' discussion, he'd unwisely tried to make a point out of Chess's previous brush with London life.

'I just want to be sure you're up for it,' he'd said. 'You know from experience it's easier being coloured in the country than it is in the city. At least you're a novelty in the sticks.'

'Black,' she'd told him testily. 'I'm black, not coloured. And how you can *really* think it's easier to always be the odd one out beats me. Anyway, I was eighteen, for God's sake, and you didn't even know me then. You're making a mountain out of a molehill.'

'A criminal conviction is hardly a molehill, Chess.'

'Well, a hillock then. I got a conditional discharge. And it had nothing to do with the colour of my skin, so how dare you?'

Now she was here though, life in the multi-coloured city was turning out to be both so familiar and so alien, she didn't know whether to embrace it or run like hell from it. It was interesting being invisible in a sea of so many different skins after years of sticking out like a sore thumb, but interesting wasn't enough.

She looked around the ransacked kitchen. Its emptiness made the whiff of grief coming from the orange bag seem even stronger, and she looked at the clock to see if she had time to take a look. Not really. She should err on the side of caution and leave forty minutes to get from Clapham to Chelsea at this time, even though she knew it wouldn't really matter if she didn't turn up at all.

Kezia was right – helping out at Morgan and Brian Hanlon's art gallery wasn't a *real* job, it was a position conjured up out of thin air by Morgan for all sorts of reasons, none of them economic. The most likely one was that Morgan was being motherly. She had always been just one tiny step down from Honor in the roll-call of significant older females as far as Chess was concerned, so now it seemed quite natural for her to take over the top job completely. Judith had reacted badly because she couldn't bear to see Chess accept maternal favours from anyone other than Honor.

'Mum is just NOT replaceable.'

'I'm not replacing her. I'm just adding to my collection.' Flippancies like that, said with the best of intentions, always had and always would backfire as far as Judith was concerned.

Morgan still held herself partly responsible for dragging the eighteen-year-old Chess to London in the first place, so by asking her back to work at the same gallery, delivering paintings and – ha ha – babysitting the now twenty-one-year-old Dan who'd just been made a partner, she was trying to atone for what she considered her original 'sin'.

Anyway, whatever the motive, Chess was happy. Part-time unskilled work was exactly what she liked. She grabbed the orange bag, stuffed it as best she could in her black leather satchel, put the milk back in the fridge and left.

It was sunny outside, and she felt a little rush of pleasure when she saw that her potted tulips arranged either side of the original black and white tiled path were still going strong. As she double-locked the part-glazed front door and ran her eyes over the larger floral green tiles around its frame, she half-hoped someone was watching her. It was secretly a surprise to her that she lived in the kind of house most London-dwellers would kill for. Seeing herself through other people's eyes was one way she used of placing herself, of trying to work out where it was she fitted best. How many people *did* know where to pitch themselves, she wondered.

Walking down the straight arterial road towards the common, she tried to build on her flurry of positive thinking. Lack of identity or not, this was *their* neighbourhood now, and she had to learn to like it.

If you ignored the whiff of social climbing, the air smelt good. White-barked trees lined the pavement every tenth house or so, the kerbs were clean and the paint colours were vibrant, but she had been walking for at least five minutes before she started finding the uniformity unsettling.

She started counting the number of huge unframed canvases she could see on the sitting-room walls until she realised it would be quicker to count how many there *weren't*. Then she started noticing similar light shades, pot plants, sofa styles. Perhaps there was some unwritten rule about conformity. Perhaps, as she'd read on a barrier screening a huge new development in Chelsea the other day, it wasn't just 'a place to live, but a way of life'.

The west side of the Common, the side they lived on, was – according to property prices anyway – the most desirable, although she had yet to fathom why. When the vendors of their new home had decided to go on the market, the estate agent didn't even bother to call round to value it because he had sold an identical one in the same street the week before. All he had to do for his three per cent commission was to phone Nick in Norfolk and fix up a viewing. They bought it the following weekend, putting in an offer of the full asking price. Printed details never even made it as far as the office photocopier.

There was barely anything to choose between the two-storey Victorian terraced houses, give or take minor discrepancies in the level of maintenance. The neat red brickwork with the ornate white cornicing above the bay windows and the efficiently allocated on-street parking glowed with the care and attention of modest wealth.

There was no access from front to back so she could only assume that the gardens were as long and narrow as their own. She tried to identify from the snatches of curtain material or books in the window which ones were hiding swings and slides and sand pits, and which ones stuck to barbecues, courtyards, or cats.

During the day, people carriers were parked almost bumper to bumper, but just now it was as if the entire fleet had left the depot. She walked down another street interchangeable with her own, but as she crossed over towards the mile of flat green grass, she entered different territory.

If she and Nick had just paid more than a quarter of a million for a relatively modest four-bedroomed terrace house, then what any one of the tall gated Georgian mansions lining the Common would cost didn't bear thinking about. Most of them had been split into three-floor apartments, snapped up as soon as they came on to the market. Intimidating and aloof, they were just like the people Chess imagined coming out of them.

A number 137 bus was already at her stop on the Common, with the queue moving steadily. The 137 was a good one to get because not only did it use a bus lane all the way, but it was the only one to go over Chelsea Bridge, so she ran the last hundred yards as if her life depended on it.

Only when she puffed to a stop behind a large elderly black woman wearing a torn tweed coat and flip flops did she realise that other people were still sauntering up. She felt silly and provincial and her folksy wrapover red cotton skirt reinforced it. Nick had re-vamped his wardrobe, so maybe she should do the same and dress only in charcoal separates.

In her heaving effort to get on, the woman left a flip flop on the second step, the grubby white sole worn through to the red. Chess could tell it was in its death throes by the way the rubber had cracked around the thong. Was it accepted behaviour to pick it up?

The conductor said something unpleasantly sarcastic, so she bent down to grab it, flashed her new bus pass at him without comment, and followed the large tweed coat up the stairs. Taking an adjacent aisle seat, she handed the flip flop back to its owner, hoping for but not getting some kind of pleasant exchange.

The woman took it with a silent nod, and the bus rocked its way into town, allowing Chess to study her neighbour's clothes, her callouses, and her leathery hands without staring. She looked weary but indestructible, as if she was resigned to being outnumbered. Chess bet she lived her life according to a Lord of fixed principles, even when everyone else around her had long since stopped bothering. She was another Minnie, right down to the plastic woven basket at her feet.

Her grandmother had been shelved at the back of her mind for fifteen years, but lately, Chess had dug out the memories almost daily. For the first few years, she had promised herself it was just a temporary measure, that she would renew contact next month, or at Christmas, Easter, some time soon when it felt right, when she felt stronger. Then, when too many excuses had been made, she tried not to think about it at all. Their lack of communication shamed her, made her hate herself, sometimes even made her punch pillows and snap at the children. What confused her now was the way she felt obliged to keep such thoughts hidden from view. Why should she?

It had hurt her that Minnie hadn't kept in touch with her either, but that had been Chess's own shabby fault. Or was it a chicken and egg situation? Who had withdrawn first? Would Minnie have any idea *how* much it hurt to stay silent? How could she? She had nothing to go on.

Chess wondered whether she would ever have enough courage to redress it, but even the thought made her lose heart. The whole episode of the shoplifting and the court case had been so shameful. Even now, she couldn't untangle the separate strands of her experience. London had been a failed episode, everyone agreed.

After the unthinkable horrors of the police station, she'd gone straight to Morgan and Brian's, where she had sat in a weeping heap on their doorstep for an hour until they'd appeared excited and laden with goodies from a late-night Christmas shopping trip.

'Hello,' she'd said feebly, huddling her knees and not having the strength to stand.

'Hello, love,' Brian had replied, reaching down to pick her up. The love and concern in his voice had snapped her resolve in pieces and although neither of them had asked about the mark on her cheek, she'd told them anyway. Della's attack had been and always would be the ordeal, not what had unfolded as a result.

The next day, too confused and ashamed to face either Minnie or Della alone, Morgan had driven her round to her grandmother's flat where they had spent an awkward hour packing the same belongings that had been unpacked just a few weeks previously.

Minnie had been almost delirious with pleasure to see her back and had started a lecture like she knew a good grandmother should. The scolding had been soft though, and fair.

'I tell you not to follow Della 'cos Della is no good, so wha' you go an' do, uh?'

'I'm sorry, I know, I'm sorry.'

'Sorry sometime jus' not good enough.' But the old woman had stopped mid-stream. 'You goin' somewhere?'

'I've got to.'

'Why? No, no, no. You can stay. Della can go.' She'd grabbed Chess's forearm and squeezed it.

'It's OK. I've got a job back home I have to start.'

'You don', do you?'

Chess could remember now the dead weight of her sinking heart as she'd watched Minnie wander slowly back into the dim bowels of her flat. She'd found her bending over a pile of magazines, sorting through them while she'd wept and prayed. 'I believe in You Lord even when You is silent,' she'd been crying.

Chess could recall even now the long rambling letter she'd written to her grandmother after running back home to Norfolk with her tail between her legs. But why hadn't she posted that one instead of those few brief lines of apology scrawled on a card? *I'm sorry I let you down, but I've learnt my lesson, and I won't do it again.* She'd been frightened to write any more in case it made Della even angrier with her than she already was.

Why had she left the longer one in her diary for a whole year? And why, when she finally *had* plucked up the courage to contact Minnie again, did she just send a feeble Christmas greeting? The three letters Minnie had written her, all in the first three months, were still in a box of old school reports and photographs in the attic in Clapham. She had caught a glimpse of them when they'd packed up to move, but she hadn't dared to open and read them again. Maybe she would.

Where was Minnie now? A mile away? Back in Jamaica? In heaven? She should know these things.

The bus swung precariously round a bend and her speculations went with it. There was nothing to stop her finding out now that Honor was so utterly out of the equation. In that sense, Honor's death had freed her – maybe that was why she was dealing with it better than Judith, because it had opened something up rather than shut something down. Not that when Honor had been alive, anyone had ever actively discouraged her. The pact had been unspoken.

Chess unzipped the orange bag and pulled out two black and white photographs paper-clipped together inside a scribbled note in Judith's handwriting. She folded the note back up without reading it because she knew it would be more of the same, and looked at the photos.

The corner of the first one had been nibbled by something, but the people were still intact, or their images were anyway. A four-year-old Judith, in a stiff sleeveless dress, had complied with the usual request to smile, and Chess, in rompers a few sizes too small, hadn't. Only Honor, in a pair of trousers and a fitted poplin blouse, looked really relaxed. She was so thin though, probably not much heavier than she was when she died.

On the back, in faint quick pencil, Honor had written *Our first day together, April 1968* which automatically made Chess think of their *last* day together. The recent past clouded everything. Cancer ate into good memories just like it chomped up healthy cells, but Chess, unlike Judith, could see a time when it would spit them all back out again one day. She put the nibbled photograph back in the bag and concentrated on the other one.

It was the famous beach picture – one of those snapshots that had never been on display or put away in an album, but that had cropped up in different drawers and desks all over her childhood.

It had been taken on the seaweed day, the running away and falling off the swing day, their first trip out as a family day. She had no idea if she really did remember it in such prolific detail or whether she'd been told about it so often she just remembered imagining it. The latter was more likely, given that she couldn't have been two years old at the time.

In Chess's baby mind, a beach had been just a sort of sandpit, but with nicer buckets and spades. No wonder she had freaked out when she'd been confronted with that vast expanse of East Coast grit, and the churning grey of the boundless ocean.

John, desperate to get the solemn toddler laughing, had started a seaweed fight, and a filmy tendril had broken off and landed on her bare baby foot like a slimy toad, sending her running off into a cave before anyone could catch her, and Judith had been sent in with ice creams to coax her out. Later, in a park, John had been pushing her high on a swing and she'd scrambled to her feet and thrown her arms out wide, roaring with excitement until she'd fallen off and grazed her knees, shins, palms and chin.

The farcical image of Honor and John having to take their prospective daughter back to the children's home covered in plasters and Germolene after only two hours in their sole care still raised a smile, even if the family joke that she had evidently started exactly as she'd meant to go on had worn thin long ago. *What a weird start I had*, she mused, thinking of her own two and how neat their lives were.

The 137 bus jerked her back to the present. 'Minnie' hoisted herself up and moved towards the stairs, and Chess put the beach picture back in her satchel, buckling it carefully. Had that strange little orange bag come with her from Hoarewood? Had a house-mother rummaged around in a box of cast-offs and found something pretty to give to her to make her feel loved, before anyone knew she was going to be loved anyway? Or was it the one thing that might have belonged to her real beginning, when she was Frankie? Or had Honor bought it for her? There was no one left to ask any more.

She looked out of the window and saw a well-dressed woman holding the hand of an equally well-dressed child. Would any of the parents at Kezia and Sam's school have riddles inside them too, or did they all come complete with off-pat answers – for that was how they looked. What about this old flip-flopped lady, who was now on the pavement, checking her purse. Did she have any stray grandchildren out there she'd forgotten about who couldn't understand patois or cook sweet potatoes either? Where *was* Minnie now?

She suddenly realised that the long brick building she was staring at through the grimy window was the Chelsea Barracks, so she swayed her way hurriedly down the aisle and waited by the conductor for the next stop.

On the phone last night, Morgan had been vague about who would be at the gallery to greet her. 'It might be me, but it might be Dan – we haven't worked out who's doing what yet. He's had his navel pierced, so that should give you a laugh.'

Good old Dan! He had made his parents pay heavily for their reckless use of contraception one fertile month in 1979. As soon as the late surprise pregnancy had been confirmed, Morgan dropped her long-held claims that she had never wanted children and the baby became her life. When the baby became a boy and the boy became a liability, she sometimes joked she had been right in the first place, but you could see in her eyes she didn't mean it. Honor had wasted a lot of breath in her lifetime reassuring her that Dan's behaviour – at two, and eight, and twelve, and fifteen – was just a 'phase'. But he was twenty-one now and still showed no sign of toeing the line. Chess treasured him for that because it made anything she did

– or had done – pale by comparison. He held the family prize for delinquency, maintaining that *someone* had to test his mother's incessant claims of tolerance.

Chess could tell Dan was there as soon as she approached the gallery's back entrance. Morgan had given her a security card, with lots of advice on what to do should she lose it and which buttons to press if she ever had to leave the building unattended, but this morning the door was propped open with a crackle-glazed ceramic hare which probably had a price tag of five hundred pounds or more round its precious neck. She picked it up and put it carefully on a table, letting the heavy door slam behind her.

Dan's voice was coming from the showroom. It still had the same lazy delivery that it had when he was six. He was very good at coming over both cool and knowledgeable, which was a near-perfect combination when it came to selling art. In reality, most of the stuff his parents chose to sell – in particular the artist Chess could hear him currently extolling – he thought too tedious by half. Even Damien Hirst was too mainstream in his book.

Two drab watercolours of rooftops that were leaning precariously against the beech desk slid to the Venetian marble floor as she walked in. The concrete and steel from the 1980s had been banished in favour of natural stone and smooth wood, but the Hanlons now had the money to change the look at their whim.

'Wasn't me!' she disclaimed, putting her hands up and smiling. She caught Dan's eye and pulled up the hem of her white jersey top with a wink. 'How's your tummy button?' she mouthed.

'Good morning, Ms Jacoby,' he said, tweaking his shirt apart with an imperceptible sleight of his hand and giving her a glimpse of gold among the dark hair. 'Check that the paintings aren't damaged before you pack them, please. Mrs Blair wants them hung today.'

'Yes, Mr Hanlon. Don't forget your meeting with Mr Hockney at ten today, Mr Hanlon.'

It was round two of a silly game invented when she'd popped in last week, and the browser had suspected as much, especially when she'd gone too far and invented a phone call from the Barcelona Guggenheim and a fax from the US billionaire art dealer Gene Liechtenstein within the space of ten minutes.

Morgan had threatened to withdraw the job offer if they couldn't be sensible, but not before correcting Chess on her facts. 'It's Bilbão, not Barcelona, and it's Alex Wildenstein, not Gene Liechtenstein. Do you speedread the papers or what?'

Now, Chess scanned the watercolours for any scratches or dents and began to parcel them up as quietly as she could so she could continue to listen to Dan's selling technique. Every time she pulled a strip of wrapping tape off the roll, she missed a bit.

'Already sold, I'm afraid . . . commissions, but there'll be a wait . . . incredibly nice guy . . . only started painting two years ago . . . already had an exhibition in . . . yes, clever use of colour . . . oils mainly . . . investment really . . .'

She would have stopped wrapping altogether if she hadn't been asked to deliver them to Chiswick before the school pick-up. Dan was on blinding form.

'. . . from about a thousand . . . just a chance there may be one in store. Francesca? Is Robert Crow's *Koi Carp* still with us or has the exhibition already picked it up?'

The painting he meant was propped against a wall in the tiny storage room and every time Morgan saw it she said, 'Ugh! We must get Robert to come and get that thing, I can't bear it looking at me any longer.' There was no exhibition that Chess knew of.

She waited a moment and then, popping her head round the door, she said, 'It's still here, Mr Hanlon.'

'Excuse me one moment,' Dan said, gliding into the stock-room. 'Of course, I would have to telephone for sale approval.'

'Watch this,' he whispered round the corner, dusting the glass and revealing even more vivid orange gill than Chess suspected. 'A fiver he buys it.' Fifteen minutes later, she was being forced to cough up.

'I can't believe you. There must be a professional code of conduct or something.'

'Beauty is in the eye of the beholder,' Dan replied. 'He loved it.'

'Only because you told him he did.'

'Well, some people need to be told,' he said, watching Chess finish her wrapping. 'And anyway, what were we going to do with it? We couldn't hang it alongside all this monochrome crap, could we? I mean, my God, it was orange!'

'I need more tape,' said Chess, rummaging in a drawer.

'What's with all this grey anyhow?' Dan continued, sweeping his hand crossly around the room. 'Is Mum going through her bleak period? Sixteen hundred pounds for something that looks like the chimney-sweep scene in *Mary Poppins*. It breaks my heart.'

'Right,' asserted Chess, finishing with two loud slaps as she stuck *The Wall Space* labels on each one. 'What are you on about, Dan?'

'That if I had sixteen hundred pounds, I'd–'

'Buy more drugs?'

'Maybe.'

'Anyway, I applaud your sales technique in one so young. I was a disaster when I first tried.'

'That's because you were too busy buyin' and sellin' elsewhere,' he said in a passable West Indian accent.

'Sorry, not funny.'

'Not at all?'

'No.'

'Oh well, how should I know? I was only six.'

'Quite,' said Chess. 'So shut it. I'll see you later.'

'Hold it, Mum told me to give you this.' He tossed her a cassette from his shirt pocket.

'What is it?'

'Some discussion programme she heard on Radio Four and taped.'

'About what?'

'Dunno. Sense of humour loss in your thirties?'

'Oh, piss off!' she laughed, lugging the pictures single-handed from the storeroom into the open boot of Morgan's Golf. 'It's OK,' she shouted as he drifted back into the showroom. 'I can manage.'

The terraced house in a leafy avenue off Chiswick Park that she was delivering to was more or less identical to the one she had double-locked in Clapham a while previously. London properties looked nothing from the outside. Actually, they looked nothing much from the inside either. It was all such silly money. A note flapped from the letterbox which said *Back soon*.

She returned to the car and pushed Morgan's tape into the stereo. It was tiring, all this attention to her welfare, but she thought she'd listen anyway, while she was waiting. Radio Four wasn't really her thing. She tried it sometimes, because she thought she should, but she always flipped back to music, usually Radio One.

The recording started with the last item of a news bulletin about a breakthrough in cancer research. For a moment, Chess thought that might be it, but then a male presenter introduced a panel of names in a voice ominously thick with sensitivity.

'My guests on Past Policy *this morning have never met before and yet they already share an understanding. Their lives have all been defined by the same experience . . .'*

Chess winced, and pressed the eject button. She wished someone could say her life had been defined by something. She had never had a sense of clarity about how others saw her, or even how she saw herself, and people who did were usually smug. Ten seconds later, she leant forward to press play instead, annoyed with herself for being interested.

'Trans-racial adoption has never been more controversial. Sarah is a wife, mother and special needs teacher in Birmingham who after much deliberating successfully traced her birth mother last year. To date, she has done nothing about actual contact. Sarah, why not?'

Something in Chess went ping. She pushed the pictures off her lap and turned up the volume.

'Because my adoptive parents have been good to me. It can't have been an easy ride, adopting a black child in the early 1960s, and I don't want them ever to regret that.'

Other guests started to join in.

'My father was an accountant, and yet I was the only one who could never pass a maths exam. Mind you, I'm the only one who can dance.'

'When you start growing breasts, no one knows how big they're going to get.'

'Once someone mistook me for my mother over the telephone. It felt like Christmas and birthday rolled into one.'

Chess picked at a loose stitch on the leather steering wheel. So, her own 'unique' situation was universal.

'How did your adopted parents feel about you tracing your natural parents?'

'Defensive.'

'Threatened.'

'Rejected.'

Just as the presenter introduced an adoption counsellor, she glanced in her rearview mirror to see a young woman in a sleeveless dress letting herself in through the red door. The last thing she felt like hearing after so much gut reaction was a professional opinion, not that she held anything against Jeeva in the same determined way that Judith did, but all the same, she really did press the eject button this time.

Time was tight when she got back to the gallery if she was going to make it to school for half-past three, but she still dashed inside to find Dan. She wanted to apologise to him for being touchy about his little joke. She popped her head round the stockroom door.

'Dan?'

He was busy contemplating his New Look navel. 'Yeh?'

'Let's see it properly then.'

He gave her a flash of flat tummy with a line of dark almost brushable hair rising up from the waistband of his suit and parting round the band of gold.

'Sexy boy. Don't get it caught in anything, will you?'

'Like what?'

'A woman's tongue?'

'Or a man's,' he ventured.

'Oh, you're so *fashionable*.'

'That's me.'

'Really?' Chess was floored. She could never be sure with Dan.

'Yeh, why not?' he grinned.

'OK, so when you've told me, I'll tell you.'

'Tell me what?'

'About why your crack wasn't funny earlier.'

'Sure. It would be good to hear it from the horse's mouth. I've heard everyone else's version so many times, I feel like I've seen the bloody film.'

'Just listen to this,' she said, tossing him the cassette.

He caught it and realised it was the same one he'd been instructed to give her earlier. 'Can you dance to it?' he asked, giving her a smile so hedonistic she forgot how amazingly insensitive he could be.

Chapter 10

Nick Jacoby was the antithesis of Dan Hanlon. He was so good at saying sorry, he even apologised for it. He said it whether it was his fault or not, because the one thing he couldn't live with, and which his parents still couldn't live without, was domestic tension. He'd once tried to cure himself of his tendency by going on an assertiveness course, but he'd sneaked off after lunch on the first day and sent an apology to the tutor by return of post.

At least he laughed at himself, and it was this, coupled with his constant orbit around any sort of conflict, that had earned him such an easygoing reputation. Not so deep down, however, he did a great line in martyrdom, believing that it was his tolerance that made life run smoothly for all sorts of people.

His upbringing had been in the climate of one long repressed argument. Friends' parents all around him divorced and managed to live in estranged harmony as if there were no tomorrow, but his parents just stuck with their hateful marriage through gritted teeth and entirely overlooked their only son. This should have made him determined not to stifle anything himself but it didn't. If anything, it had the opposite effect.

He wanted a life without strain and yet he was and always had been attracted to complex women. When he first met Chess, he had been struck by how refreshingly simple she was – which was true in a way. She had no career agenda, she didn't feel the need to prove herself, she didn't want anything different to him, she was just happy being happy. And yet the more he got to know her and the more complicated he realised she was, the more he fell in love with her. The thing was, she *noticed* him.

'Do you sometimes wish you had someone more exotic?' he'd asked once in an insecure post-coital moment.

'Do you mean exotic, or black?' Chess had replied. Not that she would have been able to tell him the truth, that sometimes she would close her eyes when they touched and she would be massaging ebony flesh, glistening dark smooth skin, and not the light golden limbs that Nick hid under his linen sleeves and cotton drill trousers.

Still, he often thought, at least she wasn't as complicated as Sonya, the mother of his first child, Vienna. Nowadays, Sonya's illness displayed itself in something called 'compulsive nervous correspondence'. In other words, four days out of seven, he would get a letter from her relating some invented convoluted drama that required his immediate attention. She phoned too but always hung up without speaking. It was now just a part of everyday life, like cold sell double-glazing calls at suppertime, although Nick, of course, continued to apologise for it all the same.

He was orbiting now, mitigating his way out of yet another development in the long-running saga of his 'other' life, as he called it. Chess was retrieving bits of onion from the kitchen sink and slowly losing her patience.

'Stop it,' she said, pushing back her corkscrew hair which was now past her shoulder blades and the longest it had ever been in her life. It hadn't been straightened since she had poured Della's potions on it in 1984 but at least now she knew how to stop the frizz. Coconut oil had become her follicles' best friend. She pulled an old cotton scarf from the belt loops of her jeans and executed a quick ponytail to stop it getting caught up with the onions. 'You do this every time you hear from her. Sonya is not going to go away, and you wouldn't want her to anyway because then you'd risk losing Vienna. I've told you hundreds of times it's OK with me, so there is absolutely no need to justify yourself.'

Nick looked grateful but unconvinced. It was fair enough to

expect his wife to put up with his even-tempered nineteen-year-old daughter, but it seemed a tall order to have to contend with the less yielding ex-girlfriend too, especially since she'd been an ex since the night of Vienna's conception. The latest request was for Vienna to come and live with Chess and Nick for the summer, while Sonya went to Greece on a motorbike with her new lover.

He'd realised Sonya was eccentric right from the very first time he met her. The problem was, by the time he'd discovered it was a clinical eccentricity best controlled by drugs, it was too late. He'd been hooked, genetically speaking.

Looking back, their beginning should have told him, when she'd taken off her dress to dance under the stars at the school Whitsun Ball and revealed a torso covered in intricate biro squiggles. She had lured him into the cricket pavilion and spent the rest of the night tracing the marks round her navel and over her breasts with mottled pink fingers and explaining the spiritual significance of every dot and doodle in a voice carefully modelled on Marianne Faithfull's. While the rest of the sixth form were enjoying clumsy gropes in the rhododendrons, he was being given a squiggle-by-squiggle tour of Sonya's scrawny body in a prick-tease to end all prick-teases.

It was a shock for him to be singled out like that by such a powerful presence. He had never thought of himself as interesting enough – an imagined shortcoming that lasted his entire life. His parents had certainly never found anything he had to say worth listening to, and the girlfriends he had pulled until then had all been quieter than church mice.

One thing he could say about Sonya was that she had never been remotely mouse-like. They had made love just the once, in her bedroom, on a white sheet on the floor while her parents played Mah Jong downstairs. She had painted a red line down the middle and insisted they both undress and lie either side of the line without talking.

'So our minds can make love before our bodies,' she'd told him, and Nick had lain there, erect and feverish until eventually she'd climbed on top of him. No more than three minutes later she climbed off, rolled his hot body off the sheet, cut a snick in it, ripped it in half and given him the side that had been his.

Despite his efforts, that was the last he'd seen of her until she'd turned up at his new halls of residence four hundred miles away three months later to tell him she was pregnant. From then on, his University years were swallowed in one gulp by her derangement.

Sonya had taken to the role of motherhood as if an Oscar depended on it. If he didn't marry her, she'd shouted in the echoing corridors, she would kill herself with the pills she had in her pocket. A week later, when he *did* ask her to marry him, she said he must be joking and she was going to have an abortion. When he offered to pay for it, she condemned him to eternal shame for forcing her into it against the will of God.

Once, after hearing nothing from her for two months, she burst into a lecture theatre and threw a sack of jumble sale baby clothes at him, screaming that he would have to bring the child up alone. Later that same day, she vowed she would never even let him see the baby because all men were evil.

By the time the baby was due to be born and he'd been hauled out of a tutorial to take an urgent telephone message, he was almost immune to the tension. 'I'm in labour,' she'd hissed, 'the baby is in distress. Neither of us are going to live. You must come.' She'd given him the name of a hospital which he discovered, after hitching there in the rain, didn't even have a maternity wing. He was directed to another hospital the other side of town, but when he got there, they told him Sonya had gone home two days earlier, having given birth a week ago.

The baby was named Vienna after the hit by Ultravox – which apparently, so Sonya broadcast later, was the song to which she lost her virginity, only not to Nick. One day, she sent him the record wrapped in black paper with a photocopy of a tiny sick baby on a life support machine taped to the front. When Nick phoned her parents to ask what was going on, Sonya's mother had talked obliquely about post-natal depression. The picture had been torn from a parenting magazine and apparently he wasn't the only one who had received it. 'Can I do anything?' he'd asked.

'Not phoning all the time would help,' Mrs Tate had snapped abruptly and hung up.

With Sonya in and out of hospital, never quite managing to control the depression, and her parents never quite managing to accept it wasn't all Nick's fault, his role as a young father had been far from easy. The rift grew larger and larger and by Vienna's sixth birthday, much to his regret, he had more or less lost touch.

Then, thank God, he met Chess, another powerful presence, another girl who couldn't possibly ever be called a church mouse, and his life changed for ever.

'You must contact her,' urged his new wife, who knew only too well how easy it was to lose touch. 'If you don't, she'll grow up thinking you don't care. Press for access, go and stand on their doorstep, anything, but just let her know you want her.'

'I will, I will,' he'd promised.

But in the end, he didn't have to. Two weeks after the birth of Chess and Nick's first baby, Kezia, Sonya arrived on *their* doorstep, fuelled by the thought of Nick enjoying a more serendipitous version of fatherhood than the one she had offered him. In velvet patchwork jeans, a white embroidered bodice and with her blonde curly hair pink at the tips, Nick could see she was haunted by the emaciated look that comes with nervous disorder and excessive smoking. Then, from behind, his daughter appeared.

'This wasn't my idea,' the eleven-year-old Vienna had said in a strong Lancastrian accent. It was the first time her father had ever heard her talk.

Even now, eight years on, he always thought of his eldest girl the way she'd looked that day – her hazel eyes looking through long brown hair parted in the middle, freckles across the bridge of her nose, her big front teeth, flowery Doc Martens, yellow leggings and black denim jacket. Her hair was still long and her nose was still freckled, but she wouldn't have worn leggings now, not even for a bet.

She stuck to baggy checked trousers and big fleeces in the winter and baggy checked shorts and fleecy T-shirts in the summer. If ever she wore a dress, it was a baggy pinafore. She spurned make-up, perfume and most jewellery, but this only served to make her seem even more adult. Her maturity would have been wretched if she hadn't been so full of such positive energy.

Nick had described his daughter to Chess one night as 'transitional' but the word hadn't been in his wife's vocabulary.

'What do you mean?'

'That she's somewhere between a child and a woman but too far removed from either to be predictable.'

'Why would you want anyone to be predictable?'

But anyway, Chess disagreed. She thought Vienna had skipped adolescence altogether in favour of early womanhood. When she thought back to the way *she* was at that age, the contrast made her cringe. Would Vienna ever think she could just nip into Harrods and nick a dress like she had?

'Er, no, but then nor would most sane people,' Nick had said. He'd never learnt that flippant, as far as Chess's background was concerned, was not good.

'So what do you honestly think?' he asked her for the umpteenth time that evening. He'd been for a run and was showered and barefoot, and Chess felt like stamping on his toes to get the message across.

'Ask Vienna.'

'About what?'

'About whether she *wants* to come and live here for the summer.'

'It's not Vienna's concerns I'm worried about. She could have the attic room – it's big enough for a bed and a sofa, and we could get another phone line put in. She would have her privacy, we'd still have ours.'

'Fine. So who *are* you worried about?'

'You. I'd hate to think I might be doing something you secretly would prefer me not to. I mean, some of the stuff you've had to deal with because of Sonya in the past has been completely over the top, and you've never objected.'

'It's called acceptance,' Chess said cautiously, reaching for the wine to top up her glass and pour him his first. He'd finish the bottle now. She liked two glasses before nine, but he would go on until midnight. They sat down and their legs intertwined under the table. Physical intimacy was like the bottom line. Everything bounced off it. How could she even think of stamping on his lovely feet? Her irritation could be so unwarranted.

'No, but really, it's your life Nick, not mine. Who am I to lay down laws about things that don't concern me? If I wasn't here, what would you do?'

Nick shrugged and looked aggrieved. He even shifted his legs so they were no longer touching, although he disguised it as a natural adjustment.

'What?' she asked. When he withdrew his touch, there was always a reason.

'You sound so perfunctory.'

'Hold on, I'll just go and look that up.'

'Detached, indifferent.'

'Well, I don't mean to be.'

'But we're married, Chess – my decisions *should* affect you. I even *want* them to affect you. I don't like it when you claim you don't care – it makes me feel like we're not so close.'

'Your decisions do affect me; I just don't think I have the right to influence them before you've made them, that's all. There are things I want to do that you might not like, and I still think I have the right to do them anyway, so it's not all one-sided.'

'Like what? I don't really mind you working at the gallery.'

'I know, but it's one example.'

'Give me a better one.'

'OK,' she said with a hint of challenge. 'Suppose I wanted to check out my real family again.'

'Why wouldn't I like that?'

'Would you?'

'I don't know,' he said. His mouth twitched a little and he ran his finger around the rim of his glass.

'Because I'm thinking I might just do that,' she said tentatively.

'I know.' He looked at her sideways. 'Judith told me. She read your letter out to me over the phone. She said she thought you would have already discussed it with me.'

'Well, bloody great. That makes me really cross. I told her in *confidence*. Anyway, all I said was that I was thinking about it. And it was only a throwaway line at the bottom of the page, to give her something other than Mum to think about.'

'A throwaway line?'

'Sort of. OK then, I *am* thinking about it.'

'Well, think hard then. You've got a lot more riding on it now than you did when you were eighteen.'

His words were like a slap across the face, and the sting was so sore she got up from the table and returned to the sink. When she'd scrubbed everything she could and still couldn't bring herself to talk to him, she went to the phone. Judith deserved to be confronted, mad with grief or not. She didn't really feel like another clash but at that moment, her sister – depressing, pregnant and all – felt like the lesser of two evils. At least if they had a row, it wouldn't last long. She and Nick could seethe for days.

But Judith wasn't in and her husband Tim, the giant of a boyfriend picked up in Turkey fifteen years previously, answered instead.

'Hi Tim, it's Chess. How are you?'

'Fine. You?'

He was monosyllabic as always – his capacity to chat was nowhere near as lengthy as his inside leg measurement. The ponytail he had sported when Judith first met him had bitten the dust long ago and Chess always thought it had gone a long way to make him seem more interesting than he actually was. Lately, she suspected that what little personality he'd been left with was now disappearing at the same rate as his remaining hair.

She had never quite understood his job with the National Rivers Authority, which was something to do with testing contaminated water, and the only time she'd ever asked him to explain it in layman's terms, he'd lost her after the first sentence. Nevertheless, she was still smarting from Nick's verbal swat, so she tried her best to get a conversation going.

'How's Judith coping then?'

'Oh, good days and bad, you know.'

'And how about the pregnancy?'

'Much the same – bit sick, bit tired.'

'Should she really still be at work at this hour?'

'Probably not, but it takes her mind off Honor.'

'Yes, well, something has to,' Chess said, thinking it almost certainly wouldn't be the scintillating company of her husband. 'Can I phone her at college? Has she got a direct line?'

'No, and the switchboard will be shut by now. I'll tell her you phoned.'

'OK. Give my love to the nippers.'

'Right you are. See you then.'

'See you.'

It didn't dawn on her that Tim was like that with her on purpose. When it came to the relationship between his sister-in-law and his wife, Tim Law had learnt to behave in the same way as the high performance water filters he fitted in the course of his work. The more crap he could trap before it reached Jude, the better – and as far as he could see, Chess at the moment was the main source of pollution. Anyone could see his pregnant wife was in no fit state to take on board any more crises at the moment, so why her bloody sister thought it was a good time to write to her and raise the old chestnut of contacting her real family, he didn't know. The letter had sent Judith into a panic which had wiped out an entire weekend. 'That's it,' she'd cried all over the house. 'Not only have I lost Mum and Dad but I'm about to lose my only sister too.'

'Come on, you know Chess will always come running when she wants something.'

'You don't understand, Tim. We look after each other. It's

always been like that.'

His view of Chess had been prejudiced from the outset. Christmas 1984 in the Lovell household – his first experience of life with his new girlfriend's family – had been about as festive as tinsel in June. The eighteen-year-old Chess had spent most of it in her bedroom pretending not to give a damn about her recent shoplifting conviction, Honor had spent most of it in the kitchen pretending not to cry, and his lovely Jude had spent most of it running between the two pretending they were all still having a good time.

She'd been at great pains to show him that it wasn't always like that, that they were really a close loving family with only the normal tensions, but he'd never really been able to accept that. In his eyes, the family ties were there all right, but they were so tightly bound, he expected them to snap at any minute. And Jude *would* keep tightening them further still, even now, when the one woman she'd done it all for was dead and gone.

Living with his wife lately was like walking across one of those dilapidated jungle bridges – put your foot on a rotten slat and whoosh, you'd be in the swamp before you knew it. He felt more justified in keeping Chess at arm's length just now. Someone had to safeguard Jude from falling into a torrent of such unnecessary concern.

If Chess wanted to trace her family, fine, she should trace her family, but she should leave Judith out of it. If his wife *had* to worry, and he was realistic enough to accept that she probably did, then he would rather she worried about what was going on in her own home – or even her own womb.

Judith's three born children didn't do badly for attention, but as for the nameless little life trying to grow inside her, it hadn't even got a look in so far. But his demanding sister-in-law had got one thing right – Jude shouldn't be at work at this hour. If she wasn't back in half an hour, he'd page her and tell her as much.

Only one strip light in the English department of Norfolk's largest higher education college was still on. As a senior lecturer, Judith Law wasn't single-handedly responsible for keeping the electricity bill down, but she had worked her way systematically through the corridors turning unnecessary lights off nonetheless. It was good to feel she could turn some things off at the flick of a switch.

Her desk was tidier than it had ever been in her life. She'd already marked six twentieth-century American literature essays, planned tomorrow's tutorial on Saul Bellow and put in a bulk order for more copies of *Tender Is The Night* so she could pass the discount on to her students. She'd written a reference for a girl applying for a holiday job with the Tourist Board and deleted the backlog of unwanted files on her computer. There was nothing left to do. She didn't even know why she'd bothered to come back in really, except that it was a relief to be alone. Anyway, maternity leave was looming, which meant this sanctuary wouldn't be available to her for much longer. It was the only space left where she was neither a mother, a sister or a daughter. Here she was just another member of staff.

Judith leant back in her blue woven swivel chair and looked at her pregnant belly. For twenty-nine weeks and a fourth child, it wasn't very large. Perhaps it was feeding on her emptiness. All her other babies had been the subject of so much rejoicing they'd each tipped the birth scales at more than nine pounds, even her daughter Kate.

This one though, caught up in so much sorrow, had been the subject of a great deal of midwifery consultation about fundal height and placenta deprivation. 'Small for dates,' they kept telling her, not that she could do much about it.

Last week, she'd been sent for a scan, except she'd forgotten to go – sort of. The truth was, she didn't really want to see the evidence, not even by ultrasound, because then it would *be* someone, and she'd have to start to try and love it. She didn't have the energy to dig around for anything like that yet. There was always the chance that by the time it was born, she would have grown out of her old vision of what a family should be, and have built up a new one.

A new one without Honor at the head. Seemed unlikely, even pointless, to be honest. 'Sorry,' she said very quietly, running her hand cursorily over her eight-year-old needlecord maternity pinafore, but even that was said with a shrug.

The baby had been unintentionally conceived just as Honor's illness was labelled terminal. Deep down, Judith had suspected she was pregnant from day one, but she chose to pretend that her lack of appetite and tiredness were as a result of shock from her mother's prognosis. When she missed her second period, she lied to Tim that the doctor had diagnosed stress, but her husband had already noticed the telltale dark brown line rising up her distended tummy and he'd told her it was time to change doctors.

'OK, OK, just don't tell Mum,' she'd begged.

'Why not? The idea that you conceive as easily as she miscarried makes her happy.'

'Because there's no way she's going to live long enough to see this one born, is there?'

Tim and Judith kept the news from the family until after the funeral, by which time the baby had already been in the womb for twenty-one weeks. Much to Tim's exasperation, Chess replied flippantly with, 'Do you think we didn't know? Even Mum guessed, and she was the only one who didn't know you were off alcohol.'

So then Judith had just swapped one misery for another, beating herself up with the guilt of sending Honor to her grave being shut out of something she would normally have been central to. Her mother had been present at the birth of all her other children – George first, then Harry, then Kate, supposedly because Tim was squeamish and needed support but really because Judith had thought it would make her happy.

All her life, Judith had acted to please Honor, to the detrimental extent that it had almost become her principal work. What she failed to realise, and what Tim had tried to tell her lately, was that no one, not even a daughter, could be solely responsible for another woman's happiness – or a man's for that matter.

'Just tell me, could Kate ever save you from feeling the way you do at the moment?'

'She's only six,' Judith had answered, pretending not to have recognised the heart of his question.

'And when she's sixteen? Or twenty-six?'

'No.'

'And does that mean perhaps that you don't love her as much as Honor loved you?'

'No.'

'No. So you should try and stop living other people's lives for them, because they're more than capable of living them themselves.'

Judith could see now, in the solitude of her deserted English department, that Tim had been warning her off Chess, not criticising her over Honor. She had always reacted with excessive panic to her sister's predicaments, even before Tim was on the scene. It was just habit.

When Chess grew breasts at eleven but refused to wear a bra until her sister did, Judith had worried. When Chess couldn't pass her exams and *she* couldn't fail, Judith had worried. When Chess came back from London with a criminal record, Judith had worried. She'd even worried when Chess chose to marry the seemingly harmless Nick on the grounds that he had a daughter by another woman and therefore came with emotional baggage.

Maybe Tim was right, maybe it was time to stop worrying. But that was like asking the tide to stop turning.

Tim and Chess didn't really despise each other – at times they even had a good laugh together – but there was a lack of trust or a mutual suspicion, certainly. And she didn't help matters. Tim could now see her losing precious sleep over Chess's latest confidence.

'Your sister is always saying she's going to do something and then doesn't.'

'But what if she does? I'll lose her.'

'You won't.'

'I will. She's got replacements all lined up. I haven't. She's all

I've got.'

'Er . . . hello?'

'Sorry, I don't mean you and the children don't count, of course you do, but I mean, she's all I've got left from the past.'

'Why can't you fret over something that matters?' Tim had barked in exasperation. 'Like our "small-for-dates" baby, for example?'

He was right. Sitting in her still office, she promised herself she would give it a try. From the depths of her bag dumped by the photocopier on the other side of the room came the muffled ring of her mobile phone, and because she was accustomed to life being a cycle of bad news, she immediately decided it was an emergency.

It nearly was. As she heaved herself up from the chair too quickly, the swivel mechanism span round and she stumbled into the open bottom drawer of her desk. She hit her shin badly and the knock toppled her over. Her centre of gravity had changed of late and she ended up on her hands and knees feeling silly. It wasn't a bad fall, but the baby inside her screamed.

'I don't like it in here,' it was saying. 'I want to get out.'

If she'd been more in tune with her pregnant self, she would have heard the cry. Instead, she pressed her hand against the pain until it subsided and puffed her way to the bag. By the time she'd pulled the phone out, it had stopped ringing, but the LCD was flashing a familiar number and she knew it was Tim, calling her home.

Chapter 11

Not being able to contact Judith just made Chess want to speak to her even more. She tried the next day and the day after that, but she was left with the distinct impression that Tim was fielding all calls.

'You ought to re-train as a doctor's receptionist,' she told Tim.

'That's a good idea. Do you want to make an appointment then?'

'God, Tim, I only want to talk to her. I need her thoughts on something.'

'The problem is, Chess, I'm not sure she's got any sane ones left.'

'Is she that bad?'

'She's not good.'

'Then maybe she needs something else to think about.'

'Like a baby maybe?'

Chess stopped for a moment and then said, 'You think I should leave her alone, don't you?'

'No, no, I don't really,' Tim replied, his voice softening. 'She'd hate that. I'm just trying to protect her, that's all. You must know she doesn't find the idea of you tracing your real family again that easy.'

'Then tell her she can't get rid of me that easily, will you?'

'OK.'

'And give her a big hug when she gets in.'

'I will. Cheers, Chess.'

'Cheers.'

He can be quite nice sometimes, she thought as she put the phone down. He's good to Judith anyway, and Mum liked him. I won't mention it again then, I'll sort it on my own. Well, I'll have to, because if I can't talk to my sister about it, and my parents are both dead, then who can I talk to? Nick, a voice screamed in her head. Nick, Nick, Nick.

But deprived of a second opinion, Chess's mind played an increasingly frantic game of mental pinball for nearly a fortnight, batting the idea of a reunion with Minnie backwards and forwards until it nearly drove her mad.

It was Dan who eventually bore the brunt and his twenty-one-year-old patience just wasn't up to the task.

'Just pick it up or let it drop, will you?'

'You're right. I will.'

'Pick it up?'

'No, let it drop.'

Several times she thought she had made that final decision, but then those two little flippers of curiosity would bat the idea right back, and she would be on with the game again. Nick was left to guess what was bothering her, because she certainly had no intention of telling him, not after his last reaction. It was a stubborn stupidity, and even she knew she might be cutting her nose off to spite her face, but his words had hurt and she wanted him to realise that.

One evening, when the children were in bed and it was still only eight o'clock, she could feel herself brewing for a row just for somewhere to dump her frustration. She prowled around the kitchen like a caged tiger.

'Do you realise we've only been out once since we moved here?'

'Why? Is there somewhere you want to go?'

'No, but come on, we're too young for carpet slippers just yet.'

'Give us a chance, Chess. We've only just moved.'

'But I miss going out, don't you?'

'Out where?'

'You know, just out.'

'Geoffrey and his wife invited us round for supper, and you told me to make up an excuse.'

'He's *sixty*, Nick, and she plays golf.'

'It's a start.'

'I'd rather start somewhere else.'

'So would I, but–'

'There's always a bloody but with you.'

'Oh, I see. You want a fight. Well, why didn't you say?'

To prevent anything angrier escalating, Chess grabbed her swimming things from the laundry basket and threw them into a bag.

'Well, I'll go out on my own then.'

'Where?'

'For a swim. I'll go and check out the Leisure Centre.'

'If you want,' he said, pretending to accept her behaviour as quite normal. 'If you meet anyone interesting, why don't you ask them if we can come to dinner next Saturday?'

In the car, she smiled at his comment. He was cool really. And anyway, swimming wasn't what she intended to do for one moment. She did almost three complete circuits of Clapham Common trying to pluck up the nerve to drive on through to Notting Hill and Minnie's old address to see if it was still the same as she remembered it.

If she did make contact, what then? A family Christmas perhaps, with Della rolling her weed at one end of the table and Judith reading out terrible cracker jokes at the other? Building bridges only *she* wanted to cross seemed entirely pointless. Was there anyone else in the entire equation who would benefit, or even welcome, a merger?

Yes, the children, she could claim she was doing it for the children. It was their birthright – but even as the idea came to her, she knew that was a political correctness too far. If she *did* ever do it, she would have to come clean as to the motive – that she was doing it entirely for herself. And just maybe, possibly, hopefully, Minnie – perhaps.

The traffic was heavy for eight o'clock in the evening and it was easier to keep on driving than make a decision. She crawled down Brixton Hill in second gear, slow enough to take in the faces of people milling around, but she could see nothing familiar in any of them.

Her grandmother would be well into her seventies by now. Chess imagined her plodding up this very pavement carrying her shopping and wearing a felt hat and tightly buttoned coat. Then she saw her at her small kitchen table, chopping or sipping, listening to music and wondering. Wouldn't it be good if thoughts bumped into each other, if Minnie was thinking of her too? Or had the old woman consigned Chess to the already full bin of people who had abandoned her in search of an easier life?

Fifteen years was a long time, almost as long as their first separation. The words spoken by her one and only counsellor came floating back to haunt her. *'Minnie might not be alive, she might not want to know, she might be mentally ill, there may be many reasons why she doesn't want to see you.'*

Chess banged the steering wheel in frustration. She detested the way she was so easily withered by rationalisation. 'Better not', 'my life's in place', and so on. It was as if her heart had no direct line to her head any more, and vice versa. On automatic pilot, she followed the battered VW Beetle in front which took a right-hand lane and turned off the main road. She hadn't meant to do that, and for a moment she was lost. 'Bugger, bugger, bugger.'

When a sign to Brixton Leisure Centre pointed to the left, she took it and wondered if she was brave enough at least to strike a reasonable compromise. Why not really go for a swim and actually do something she said she was going to do for a change? OK, so it wasn't the local pool, but at least she could go back with wet hair. She felt suddenly vindicated, cross with Nick for being flippant, half-believing she had meant to do this from the outset.

She pulled her car up alongside a row of shuttered shops built into the arches of a railway bridge and fixed her steering lock. Some of the assorted businesses – a florist, an Italian food store, a second-hand furniture shop – had NO PARKING warnings daubed in big white paint across their boarded fronts, but since no one else was taking the directive seriously, she didn't either.

A group of women and children were walking up a flight of concrete steps to a large redbrick building, so she followed. They were speaking noisily in a language she didn't recognise but she listened to their gist all the same. Whatever they were talking about, it both amused and shocked them.

She followed, pleased to have someone else taking the lead. Soon, she was through the turnstile, up the escalator and into the female changing room.

As she picked her way across the wet tiled floor and to the ranks of metal lockers, she felt an odd kind of weight leave her, one she hadn't realised she was carrying until it was no longer there. Her self-consciousness dropped to the floor with her clothes and a lightness she hadn't felt for months came over her.

She changed in the open benched area, enjoying not bothering to hide behind her towel or struggle discreetly into her costume like she normally did. Other women were drying themselves with one foot on a bench or rubbing a towel across their backs whilst their breasts jiggled for all the world to see. Dark nipples, plaited hair, big swinging bottoms, high-hipped slender legs and tight protruding tummies – everyone the same and everyone different. She was anonymous in a sea of bodies, in the majority at last. Every now and again there was pale skin, but in all directions she saw an echo of her own shape, and varying shades on her own colour.

I'm going to pretend I'm you, she thought, watching a woman her age attempting to fit wet legs into tight leggings. I'm going to pretend I have a black husband and matching children at home, an employer, neighbours and friends who look like me, a whole extended family who all live and shout and fight and love on top of each other in high-rise flats, that I am wholeheartedly and completely black, like it doesn't even occur to me that I am.

Chess stepped through a foot bath and into the water behind a wide-hipped woman in a pink shower cap and frilled costume whose bottom moved in an opposite direction to her top. It was shallow at first but once you ventured around the central isle, the pool was divided into lanes. She swam up and down, alternating between breast- and back-stroke for an hour without being noticed.

On the floor above, separated by glass panels, was a gym. People pounded on running machines and pulled on rowers. Some were fit, others looked fit to drop. No one was taking the blindest bit of notice of her and it was bliss. A lifeguard in very small silver trunks paraded up and down the side of the pool. He looked like he loved himself, but then Chess rather loved him too. His body was good enough to eat. A girl he obviously knew sidled shyly past him and he spun round to block her path in jest.

His movement, the way he turned on his feet and pinned his glossy arms either side of his girl to show off his six pack made Chess think of Poncho, her fifteen-year-old recurring fantasy. She parted her lips at the memory and inadvertently took in a mouthful of chlorinated water which made her cough and splutter, but even that didn't bring her back from her dreams.

It was the way her young body had been camouflaged against his that she liked to remember, the way her eyes in the half-light of the gallery stockroom hadn't been able to work out where *her* curves ended and *his* began. It had been the perfect way to lose her virginity and sometimes, like now, the muscles of her vagina contracted when she thought about it.

She played around with the scene in her head as she continued her lengths. If they met again, would their craving be instant and mutual? What would they be like together now? His body would have filled out, he might wear glasses, have a few grey chest hairs. He'd love the meandering stretchmarks that ran over the humps of her behind – they were just his kind of thing. He would want to run his tongue along them, trace them with his fingers. It was fun to elaborate, to build the vision into something more. He'd been painting abroad somewhere all this time, say South Africa, yes, the townships, and then once he was back in London, he'd not been able to shake the image of her out of his head. Maybe he'd even started painting her, young beautiful nudes running along night-time pavements. Then, desperate for her, he'd finally found the courage to come into the gallery to start his search, and she would be the first person he'd see . . . she would just appear from the stockroom, a mature woman, no longer the inexperienced virgin.

What would they do? They'd kiss, and the kiss would turn quickly into an intense ravaging of each other's bodies. They wouldn't speak, not until afterwards. Where would they do it this time? In the storeroom again – she could lead him in there like a re-enactment of the first time and strip without foreplay while he did the same. Would anyone else be there? Maybe Dan, in the showroom, half aware. How would Poncho feel inside her? Bigger than Nick. Would she put him in her mouth? Yes. How on earth could she begin to find him?

A few more lengths of rhythmic slow swimming helped her back down to earth and by the time she got out of the water, she was in control of her thoughts again, amused and a little surprised by them. Her body, though, took a little while longer to settle.

When she got home, Nick was puzzled by her sexually flirtatious mood. He had no idea what had triggered it – after all, she had left the house in a strop – and he had even less idea where it would lead. But Chess knew exactly.

'You must take more exercise if it makes you like this,' he said, finding her naked at the kitchen sink.

'Like what?' she said, smiling with fake innocence as she swilled her costume in front of him so he could smell the chlorine.

'Well, I can't remember the last time you did the washing with no clothes on.'

'That's only 'cos you're not here to see me,' she whispered like a hussy, turning round and pressing the small of her back against the stainless steel. She spread her arms across the units and put one leg across the other.

'What a terrible waste,' Nick said, approaching her and unbuttoning his shirt. It was on the chair before he reached her, and he was unbuckling his belt.

'But you're here now . . .'

'I am.' He took her hand and put it firmly on the seam of his flies.

'So you are.'

'You'd better get on with the washing-up then,' he murmured, turning her round and kissing her neck while undoing the last button of his jeans. 'I wouldn't want to . . .' She felt the mat of chest hair against the skin of her back and his penis brush her buttocks '. . . disturb you.' He slid his body down hers until he was on his knees and turned her round to kiss her hip bones and run his tongue around her navel in the way she liked.

Poncho, she thought wickedly to herself. Poncho in the storeroom. Nick wouldn't mind. She felt her indulgence in keeping her eyes closed was quite justified. Sex with her husband was always good, and if it was sometimes shored up by fantasy, so what? That was healthy. *Cosmopolitan* said so.

Having the sense of purpose to seduce her husband was nothing to the amount of resolve she needed to take her to Minnie's, and a week later she still hadn't found that extra surge of confidence necessary to get herself there.

At last, Dan made the decision for her. They were indulging themselves with ice creams on the Chelsea pavement outside the gallery, and warming up in the baking sun. Morgan's re-hauled air-conditioning was working so efficiently that the showroom now enjoyed practically sub-zero temperatures.

The mood was very relaxed for London, as if the heatwave made it too damn hot to be aggressive. Passing voices talked convivially about Wimbledon or clearing off to the coast, but Dan, using a voice borrowed from the world of alternative stand-up comedy, was busy recounting the repercussions of the bi-sexual bombshell he had just dropped on his parents. 'So I say, "Mum, what I'm trying to tell you is that I'm bi-sexual," and she says, "Oh, for God's sake Dan, I can't keep up with you. One minute you're all over women, and the next, you're into men. I wish you'd make up your mind," and so I say, "Er, but Mum, that's what bi-sexual people *do*," and then – get this – she says, "I don't care what bi-sexual people do, Dan, I care what *you* do," and so–'

'Dan,' Chess interrupted eventually, crunching the last tiny cone of her coconut and black cherry cornet and feeling dissatisfied with it, 'it's not a joke.'

'Yes, it is. It's laughable.'

'No, no, look, believe me, not everything in life has to have a catchline.'

'Oh, *really*?'

'For a start, you could have waited until your boyfriend had left the house before broaching it with Morgan.'

'But I was only telling her to save her the embarrassment of catching us at it.'

'You have your own separate flat.'

'Yeah, sure, but she has a key.'

'What? So she can let herself in to see who you're sleeping with? I think not. It's much more likely you were just inventing a new way to shock.'

'You think I slept with a man for the sole purpose of some mental sport with my mother, do you?'

'I wouldn't rule it out.'

'Well, she has gone mental about it, that bit is true enough.'

'It's probably the way you did it rather than the issue itself that's making her react the way she is. Morgan's really tolerant, you can't keep blaming her for all the drama. You're going to have to start taking responsibility for your own actions.'

Dan laughed, and threw the rest of his ice cream on to a drain in the road.

'Yes, Mummy. Remind me not to have Tutti-frutti again. I always forget it starts to taste like sick after the first mouthful.'

'Don't even say it,' Chess warned, seeing his mind working towards some vile conversational link. 'Hey, tell me, is it an on-going relationship, this thing with Todd?'

'Let's not rush things, eh?'

'Oh, right, 'cos you never rush things, do you, Dan?'

'You're being very judgmental for someone who doesn't

have all the facts. That's like me saying the only reason you have suddenly decided to do something about re-tracing your grandmother is because Honor has snuffed it and you thought it might be nice to find a replacement.'

'Who says I've decided?'

'Me. Come on, you know you want to.'

'Is that the line Todd used with you?'

'It wasn't that way round actually. Anyway, we're not talking about me any more, we're talking about you. Have you even tried to find out whether or not Mickey is still alive?'

'Minnie,' Chess corrected him.

'Oh, God!' he screamed, performing an excessively camp gesture, hands to side of mouth, lips open in cartoon gasp. That's a new one, thought Chess. He's just like a sponge, soaking it all up until something else comes along and squeezes it out of him to make room for his next fad.

'I really wasn't trying to be funny then. I've always got the two of them confused – big ears and high voices and . . .' he carried on.

'One is a boy and the other's a girl,' she helped.

'Er . . . so?' he asked, with perfect comic timing.

Chess hit him across his flat stomach. 'This is Dan Hanlon saying goodnight – goodnight!'

They both cheered and Dan leant against the gallery wall, tilting his face towards the sun. 'But have you?' he asked, taking his sunglasses out of his shirt pocket and putting them on.

'Have I what?'

'Done anything at all to try and find out if she's still around?'

'No, but partly because I don't know how to.'

'You've got her address, haven't you?'

'Yes.'

'Well, just go and knock on the bloody door then.'

'She won't be still there, she'll have moved.'

'Oh, right, you can see into the future.'

'OK, then I'm just not ready for it. Is that what you want me to say?'

'Say what you like – she's *your* grandmother. Do it now, the next free cab that comes along. You've got enough time before the kids come out of school.'

'Dan, you come out with such bull sometimes. How can I go? I'm supposed to be working.'

'Yeah, and we all know the business would fold immediately if you took the afternoon off, don't we?' He was still holding his face up to the sun. His eyes were shut and his voice trailed into the air.

They stood there, Chess thinking and Dan not, until a cab with a 'for hire' light really did come towards them. Like a flash, her hand went up.

'OK, I will then,' she said, as the black cab drew up.

'Good,' said Dan lazily, as if they had settled an argument.

'No, wake up, look, I'm going.'

Dan pushed himself away from the wall with the flat of his left foot and took off his glasses. 'Fuck, how did you do that? Are you magic?'

'No, but you are,' said Chess. 'Cover for me, won't you?'

'I'll say you got hypothermia from the air conditioning.'

'Ladbroke Grove please,' she said through the open cab window, shaking with her impulsiveness.

'Bottom or top?' grunted the cabbie.

'Oh, I'm not sure. I don't live there, I'm just–'

'I don't want your life story, love,' he said bluntly. 'I just want to know where I'm supposed to be going.'

'The bit beyond the bit where it starts to go downhill,' Dan told him over Chess's shoulder, 'where the real people live.'

'Oh, my bag!' she cried. Dan spun back into the gallery, grabbed her leather backpack and hurled it through the pushed-down window.

'On your head be it,' she said, grabbing it. 'This is your idea.'

'Not at all,' he replied. 'You can't keep blaming me for all the drama – you've got to start taking responsibility for your own actions.'

'Touché,' she mouthed back, flicking two fingers at him as the cab pulled off.

Twenty minutes later, she placed the exact fare in her unpleasant driver's expectant hand and stood moronically on the pavement as people walked around her, feeling like she'd been beamed down from a distant planet. It was a very different pavement to the one she'd just come from. Well, the pavement was more or less the same, save the proliferation of chewing gum and cigarette ends, but the shoes that walked it were certainly different. She didn't know which was more preferable – to be outclassed in Chelsea or an outlander here.

It took her a while to get her bearings, to realise that she was on the opposite side of the road to the one she wanted, and that if she walked up, and not down, she would find the landmark she knew she could work from – the grimy post office Minnie used to collect her Giro from.

As she approached it, everything else slowly came into focus. There was the crossing, the three telephone kiosks, the concrete ramp – and the tower block. The scene looked just a little smaller somehow, and emptier – the entire community must have gone in search of air and shade.

Chess saw herself aged eighteen, running across the four-laned road, dodging the traffic with her Walkman plugged in. The little purple and yellow machine was still at home, in Sam's bedroom, the eject mechanism broken and the headphones bent wildly out of shape.

She walked purposefully up the road, looking into any faces that passed, just in case. As she opened the post office door, she caught a glimpse of herself in the glass. She looked a bit much in her black linen top and trousers, a new image spurred on by Nick. Taking a magazine – any magazine – and standing in the queue, she managed with one hand to whip off her silk scarf and put it in her bag, then she did the same with her earrings. Giant bars of Bourneville were still being displayed. Minnie used to be addicted to the stuff. Maybe they only kept them in stock for her weekly chocolate fix. She picked one up for old times' sake.

Do you know Minnie George? she wanted to ask the woman at the counter. What about Della George? Do they still live up there, in the St Paul's Building, A block, number 238? Only I'm Minnie's granddaughter, adopted, you know? I came back for a bit, before I had to go back where I came from and we've lost touch. Well, I'm married now, and I've got children too. Look, here's a picture, taken last year. Minnie would want to know. Can you help me?

Instead, she paid for her magazine and chocolate without a word and walked back outside, where she undid the buttons on her black mandarin collared sleeveless jacket and let it flap about to reveal an old rust Lycra vest. Then she pulled a silver skewer from her hair, letting the curls spring madly in whichever direction they wanted to, and put the slide in her bag with the scarf and earrings. Not so well-groomed now but a little less out of place maybe.

The redbrick buildings were still screaming for vast injections of council money to be re-roofed, re-glazed or re-pointed. Really, they needed to be pulled down and re-built. She peered in through the grey nets and the limp unlined curtains and felt angry on behalf of the occupants. There were not too many people-carriers parked around here, that was for sure.

The concrete wheelchair ramp leading to Block A, St Paul's Building, was being used by two children as a skateboard track. They couldn't have been much older than Sam, and more than once they overshot the end and had to jump off before their boards skidded off the pavement on to the road. Sam wouldn't even have been able to balance on the things standing still. Four years living here taught you different skills to four years in a Norfolk village.

She opted for the stairs rather than the lift. They still smelt just as bad, although there had been an attempt at brightening them up with murals since she'd last climbed them. Nothing could stave off the lure of graffiti though, and plenty of black pen and green spray paint had superseded the worthy if futile effort. If anything, it made the stairwell look worse.

A teenage mother with a sleeping child in a buggy emerged from the lift – working at last – and Chess tried a smile which, this time, was returned. The child had on a nappy and vest, and the soles of its tiny feet were filthy. A grubby dummy was tied on to the buggy handles by a piece of ribbon and a half-full baby's bottle of orange juice was tucked between the child and the canvas seat. For some reason, the snapshot spoke of care, not neglect.

The tower block felt more familiar than it should have done. It had only been in her life for a pitifully short time, but then she'd left a part of herself there, she could feel that now. That's what comes of unfinished business, she thought.

The heavy swing door leading to Level Three was propped open with a cardboard box full of empty cans. Chess stepped out on to the concrete path which looked shorter than it was in her mind. God, every detail of the last memory was still there. Her heart thumped and her throat dried up as she walked past the first door.

She coughed for no reason. Strong spicy smells seeped out from underneath the neighbouring flat and she could hear a child shouting happily inside. The door had a hole near the bottom as if someone had tried to kick it in and the window was covered in children's stickers. The door at the end was shut firm. Three metal numbers, 238, were now screwed firmly to its centre.

She knocked but she could already hear the stillness. It might have been disappointment or relief that made her sigh, but whatever the reason, she stayed where she was. She was shaking now and felt cold, or at least less hot.

The flat was empty she could tell, although who had just left it or was about to return was still anyone's guess. Peeping through the letterbox, she could just make out four pairs of trainers lined up against the wall and a clutter of roller blades next to them. Della used to be passionate about trainers. No doubt she would have favoured roller blades too, if they'd been the thing. Chess tried to work out their shoe size. They were bigger than Kezia's, but not adult's.

Why didn't she feel as if she was trespassing? She noticed that emerging from the doorway of the kitchen was the wheel of a mountain bike with a fat tyre and a coloured mud guard. Della had always kept her bike in the kitchen, always always always. But this was hardly a clue – keeping bikes in hallways was normal practice in flats all over London, wasn't it? This is not the flat of an old woman, she told herself, but try as she did to accept it, the disappointment wouldn't quite sink in.

The real evidence would be in the kitchen, of course, but the window couldn't be seen from the balcony, not even if she hung over the edge. Would there still be a big bowl on top of the fridge, and if Minnie had been to the market would it be full of yams and plantain and okra and baby chilli peppers? On the stove, would there be a huge Dutch pot of rice 'n' peas and chicken, and if Minnie arrived home now, would she insist on Chess coming inside and having some? She thought about her grandmother ladling it into a chipped china bowl and pushing it in her direction, saying something like, 'Where's all de meat on you gone, Frankie? You need feedin' up, you wastin' away.'

She stood back, leaning against the railings opposite the door and wondering what she should do next. Even when the sun was as hot as it was today, the concrete always got the better of it. She sat down with her knees against her chin in the only triangle of warmth, hoping that if she sat there long enough, someone might return home. She imagined Minnie appearing from the stairwell and dropping her heavy bags when she realised who was waiting for her, and coming to her with that big, big smile and wrapping her up in her arms. There was safety in a fantasy that simply wasn't going to happen.

The patch of sun went in search of another corner and the cold concrete started to nip through the seat of her thin trousers. She got up, pushed the bar of Bourneville through the letterbox, deciding against any note of explanation, and walked away, down the passageway, into the smelly lift and on to the busy street.

The blow was, she felt even more an imposter in these parts than she used to be.

'Clapham, please, Cowper's Prep School on Streatham Road,' she said to a cabbie as she climbed in. He looked at her in surprise.

'Got kids there, 'ave you?'

'Yes, two.'

'I only ask 'cos we don't get many fares to private schools from this estate like.'

'No, I don't suppose you do,' Chess replied, in a way that discouraged further conversation. His unsuspecting comment alienated her even further. What would Kezia and Sam ever know of the kind of lives that were lived around here? She and Nick had discussed at length the effect the move to London might have on their children. They kept careful parental eyes on mood swings, signs of bullying or any small confusions creeping in. But in reality, very little had changed. It was not such a different climate after all.

It was true that Kezia and Sam's mixed-race skin colour – a milky cappuccino – no longer labelled them as 'dark' in the way it used to in Norfolk, but other than that, it was business as usual. Cowper's had a healthy racial mix with children of all nationalities, but the pupils were still all linked by the same thing – privilege. The atmosphere of life at school was protected by money and class. It was light years away from the experience the children living round here would be dished up.

Was that Minnie's flat? she wondered as the cab crawled in the traffic back to Clapham. Was that Della's bike? Was anything she'd seen today anything to do with her at all, or would some complete stranger be left puzzling over a mystery delivery of Bourneville chocolate for ever more?

Sitting on the seat next to her was a discarded flyer on yellow paper with black print which she picked up and started to read. It was advertising the *Pinegrove Community Arts Project* just off Portobello Road, an initiative trying to encourage schoolchildren in the area to learn to play the steel drums or make a costume for the Notting Hill Carnival instead of staying inside and staring at a computer game all summer. A whole programme of workshops was planned, from street theatre to stilt-walking and mask-making. Something in the happy Afro-Caribbean lettering made her put it in her bag.

Kezia and Sam broke up from school soon, which heralded weeks and weeks of trying to find something to do. In Norfolk, the summer holiday meant beach picnics and trips on the broads, but what families did in London, Chess had no idea. The other disadvantage to their impending break, of course, was that she now had no further opportunity to repeat today's experiment.

That evening, as another direct result of her frustration, she and Nick fell out again and, for once, he wouldn't let her win.

'I know, let's go to the Notting Hill Carnival this year,' she said after supper.

'You've got to be joking,' he replied.

'Why? It'll be fun.'

'No, it won't. The children hate crowds.'

'No, they don't.'

'Yes, they do.'

'The costumes and floats are apparently out of this world, and–'

'No.'

'*You* don't have to come.'

'True enough.'

'Sometimes, you know, you can be so *boring*!'

'Look, I don't want an argument,' Nick said, throwing the *Law Gazette* he was pretending to read on the table in resignation. 'I wanted to go to the Science Museum last weekend, and you didn't, so fine, we didn't go. Did I make an issue of it? No, because it was just an option that didn't get taken up, and we did something else instead.'

'But we can go there anytime we choose. The carnival is one weekend a year.'

'You go. I'll stay and look after the children.'

'I might take you up on that. I could ask Dan. He'd come with me.'

'Fine,' he said, and walked out of the house without saying where he was going. When he came back twenty minutes later bearing the red wine she liked best, Chess had already gone to bed. Kezia was in with her, curled happily in her father's space, asleep again now. The child had woken thinking she was in her old bedroom at Norfolk.

'Do you wish you were?' Chess had asked her gently, letting her clamber over her on to Nick's side.

'Do you?' Kezia asked.

'A bit. And then a bit not.'

'Me too.'

Nick peeped in, saw he was surplus to requirements and assumed Chess had engineered it on purpose. In fact, his wife had stopped sulking as soon as the phone had rung. A note left for her husband on the kitchen table said that Vienna would be arriving this weekend. Chess had added a point-scoring P.S.

If it's what you want, then it's what I want too. She hoped the words would stick in his mind until she needed him to say them back to her.

Chapter 12

By the time the end of August arrived in a blaze of sunshine after weeks and weeks of rain, Chess was already deeply in Vienna's debt. Since the arrival of Nick's mellow sweet teenage daughter, the word 'bored' had fallen miraculously from the children's vocabulary and they had all somehow steered the course of the summer holidays without so much as a glance back to the distant shores of Norfolk.

Other than a slight tautness in Nick's face every time Chess spoke about it, her resolution to go to the Notting Hill Carnival – or 'play maas' as Dan said she should say – showed no signs of turning into the defiant monster she'd been afraid of. At first, when she was so sure she really did want her family to come with her, she did everything in her power to persuade Nick to change his mind. She courted and cajoled often in the run-up to the Bank Holiday weekend, the traditional date of the second largest street party in the world, but her perseverance had little effect.

'It says here there'll be hundreds of street stalls selling exotic snacks from all corners of the globe,' she reported from a free sheet.

'And hundreds of cases of salmonella the next day,' he mumbled back.

When she found another flyer about the carnival hosting the biggest steel-band competition ever held outside Trinidad, she tucked it under his wipers with a big biro kiss on the back but he never even mentioned it. As a final ditch attempt, she appealed to his burgeoning city slick vanity.

'It's not an event any self-respecting London dweller can

ignore, not if you're serious about living here. It's not just a load of floats, you know, it's a huge arts and music festival, very right-on stuff. All your colleagues will be going – even the ones who wear double cuff shirts.'

'It's not going to work,' he replied good-naturedly, 'but if you really want to go, then go. I've said I'll look after the children.'

Vienna had finally been the one to justify it. Chess had been apprehensive about going on her own – her efforts to get Dan to take her had fallen on stony ground, although he'd been keen to show off his knowledge with bucketloads of advice – and Nick had been taking advantage of her uncertainty by suggesting alternative days-out.

'We could do a picnic in the park? Go back to Norfolk for the weekend? Take the children to the Natural History Museum?'

He hadn't reckoned on his eldest daughter though.

'It's supposed to be a celebration of tolerance, did you know that?' Vienna said one night.

'How do you mean?' Chess never hid a lack of knowledge. It had been pointless, growing up with Judith.

'You know it started as a response to racial attacks in the mid 1950s? The black immigrants from the Caribbean were all having a really hard time – bad housing, no work, lots of racial tension and everything, so they started organising dances for themselves. I think they had the first one in a hall in North London or somewhere, and then at about the same time, a bunch of people from Trinidad started up a steel band and did a gig at a pub every Sunday, and then – I can't remember how, but I could find out – the two ideas kind of merged. It was like a sort of image-building exercise, you know, to help the white people see who these black people really were, or what their culture was really like anyway.'

'How do you know all this?' Nick asked, prickling with pique and pride.

'I found the website on the Internet. I thought Chess might be interested.'

'Oh, that's really kind,' Chess said, moved. 'I sort of knew, but . . .' She paused, and then added quickly, 'Hey, d'you want to come?'

Vienna looked at her father for approval.

'Come with me, please. Come with me.'

'Well, if that's OK with Dad . . .'

'Sure, sure, why shouldn't it be?' Nick replied quickly, in case any hesitation gave him away. 'You can both look after each other.'

Chess was swamped with relief, not just because she now had a chaperone but also because she had just realised how awful it would have been if Nick had given in to her quiet pressure to come too. She knew from experience the horrors of feeling morally responsible for his enjoyment. Going with the blissfully open-minded Vienna was infinitely preferable.

The nineteen-year-old had arrived to live with them with just one roll bag of clothes, a portable CD player and no idea of how long she was going to stay. But she had also unconsciously brought with her a kind of symmetry, which had helped no end.

To Chess, Vienna represented botched pasts and healed presents – or Nick's botched past and healed present, to be precise. And because Chess's own past was so botched and she was currently fixated with healing her own present, it was a comfort just having the girl there, pottering around the kitchen or dripping over the bathroom, a living example of the turns of fate. Every time Chess thought about Minnie – which was more than ever lately – she quietly thanked the persistently mad Sonya for creating the balance in the first place.

Nick, however, saw the flipside. To him, Vienna represented a monumental cock-up all right, but having her with them was somehow just an extension of the disorder. He cherished his daughter almost more than most fathers do, but he wished, sometimes prayed, that his life was more conventional. Neat and tidy, that's what he secretly longed for. In that way, he and Judith might have been ideally suited.

In his fantasy, Sonya had emigrated to Australia years ago

and he had taken over both parental reins. Then, when colleagues asked embarrassing questions at parties like, 'And how many children do you and your wife have?' he could honestly answer, 'Three,' instead of embarking himself on the convoluted explanations he currently fell into.

Not that Vienna was a child any more. She was a tall and, Nick pretended to think, still-virginal teenager, but there was an undeniable motherliness about her, a by-product of life with Sonya, which Chess almost came to rely on.

On Carnival Day, this was more pronounced than ever. Once they were both ready and sinking a quick can of Diet Coke in the kitchen, Vienna was the one to instigate the familiar 'leaving house for day out' routine. Money? Yes (stuffed down the front of the body belt Dan had advised her to wear as a security measure). Camera? Yes (bottom of back pack). Sunglasses? Yes (on cord round neck).

'Right, now, who wants us to bring them back a whistle?' Vienna asked the loitering children.

'Me!' said Sam. 'What kind of whistle?'

'Like the one your PE teacher wears.'

'Oh, cool!'

'They're everywhere,' she said to Chess. 'You peep them in time to the music. We should be able to buy them easily – it's how people make money. They thread the whistles on to ribbon and hang them round their necks and–'

'Internet?' asked Nick, passing.

'Might be.'

Kezia sidled up to her mother. 'Can I come?' she whispered.

'No, darling. Daddy doesn't think you'll like it. There are loads and loads of people, it's noisy and you have to walk for miles and miles and–'

'But I'll miss you.'

'No, you won't. I'll be back before bedtime.'

'You're not going, Kez,' said Nick, who had spent the morning in concocted activity pumping tyres on bikes ready for his planned day out. 'We're going on a cycle ride. Come on, we're off to the Common.'

'There's a fair there,' Vienna encouraged. 'I saw them setting it up last night.'

'Daddy, can we go to the fair?'

As well as the advice about wearing a body belt to keep her purse safe, Dan had warned Chess that the Tube stations nearest Notting Hill closed at lunchtime to control the crowds.

'Oh, is Dan going?' Vienna tried to say casually.

'Probably – he said he was.'

'We should have arranged to meet up.'

'Oh yeah?' Chess looked at her stepdaughter for a hint of the coy, but there was none.

'Well, at least he knows his way around.'

'But you never know where he's been, that's the problem. Don't tell me you fancy him.'

'OK, I won't,' Vienna laughed in a way nobody could read.

They could have taken up the offer of a lift from a parent from school who lived in the next street and had – surprise, surprise – a people-carrier, but Vienna had acted her age just for a minute and refused to go anywhere in a Renault Espace on the grounds of street credibility. So, much as Chess hated being crammed into small spaces, she agreed to brave the Underground.

She had her face in someone's shoulderblade the whole journey until they all disembarked. People elbowed to get to the doors first, as if a head's advantage over the next man would make any difference at all to the quality of their day.

There was little evidence of the family atmosphere she'd imagined and it was with a sense of anticlimax that she realised most of her fellow passengers didn't see it like she did – as if they were all in this together, on a kind of joint ticket to participate in the same experience.

The local antagonism was coming from a cluster of arrogant twenty-year-olds who were already drunk. They were grabbing at flowers displayed in buckets outside a shop, and throwing them at passing crowds in the road. Two police officers held them at the side of the road and preached insistently at them for five minutes, ignoring the jeering protests. 'C'mon, we're only having a laugh, we're not hurtin' anyone. We want to get a good view, you're 'oldin' us up, we're not out to make trouble, we've got here early specially, to see it properly, let us get on with it.'

'Early? You're a bit bloody late for early, mate.'

Some people had been there since breakfast, and since then, hundreds and hundreds and hundreds more had arrived by the hour, and thousands were on their way, on buses, in cars, on foot and on bikes, and at the end of the day there would be nearly two million party-goers in the vicinity. Posturing for position was futile.

Chess saw two of them with their hands pushed aggressively up behind their backs and steered into a waiting police car and she was grateful again that Nick had stuck to his guns. It wasn't a place for the children, not yet. Maybe when they were older.

It wasn't the best start and she was determined to shake off the disappointment. Vienna was still coming up with snippets of information she'd gleaned from here and there, and gradually, at the same steady speed with which they all shuffled out from the tiled coldness of the hostile underworld, Chess's frustration lifted.

'Carnival is we t'ing!' someone sang from behind.

'Riddim is de beat to make you sweet!'

Chess took a gulp of the late summer sunshine. The aroma of marijuana, tinged with coconut and fried fish and pineapple fizz, began snaking its way through the throng, up people's nostrils and into their lungs. The approaching beat of steel drums began hammering into her heart. Limbs around her loosened, walking turned to dancing – it was just as if a huge imaginary spliff was passing between them. She remembered her brief attachment to the weed. She tried to recall how to roll a joint – tobacco into Rizla, add the weed – or did you add the weed first? – cardboard tube at one end – the 'roach'. God, it was amazing how you could suddenly remember things you were sure you'd forgotten – light it up and there it was.

She wondered if she would smoke again if it was offered, or

if Vienna might be the one to offer it. She would have to discourage it – no, she wouldn't, yes, she would, no, she wouldn't – then she laughed out loud at the absurdity of such a dilemma.

'Do you recognise the smell?' Vienna smiled as they shuffled their way under the bridge.

'Well, you obviously do.'

'Only second-hand. You know, medicinal purposes for Mum's condition and that.'

'Really? She smokes at home?'

'Only joking. We should have a plan if we get separated,' Vienna said, changing the subject. She was, after all, talking to her stepmother.

'Should we?'

'Don't look so worried. We don't have to, but . . .'

'How about back here on the hour then?'

'Oh, I was going to say that if we lose each other, we'll see each other back at home.'

'Your father would kill me if I turned up without you.'

'Would he? I keep forgetting he's not Mum.'

'That must be hard.'

They laughed easily.

'Vienna, are you saying you would quite *like* to lose me?'

'No, course not, but it shouldn't be a major cause for panic if we do.'

Chess loved it that her stepdaughter was bursting with such independence – it made her feel completely unconstrained herself, emancipated, exonerated from her usual obligations of marriage and motherhood, free to dance, or smoke if she felt like it, or pretend to be anyone she wanted to be. Vienna was lost in a world too, moving to the music, singing to herself.

The narrow streets were lined, or jammed, with people waiting for the procession to start. A big-hipped black woman exposing an ample cleavage and wearing a pink sarong was being ordered to move her trestle table on which she had enticingly displayed home-made cakes and biscuits covered in cling film. The TV cameras were out in force and, to detract attention from the policing, a member of the Constabulary started dancing with a nearby dazzling silver moon. The crowd suddenly started to cheer and clap.

'There's a woman losing her weekend's business,' said Vienna, 'and the cameras catch the cliché instead.'

'You'd be a good documentary-maker,' Chess replied, spotting a good vantage point on a step up to one of the terraced white-painted Georgian houses. 'Up there,' she said, taking Vienna's hand.

She nudged her way into the identified space and thanked a woman wearing accessory spectacles and a grey bun for shifting over a bit. The woman, straight from the corridors of sexless academia, was obviously grateful to be spoken to, and she started, unprompted, to try and draw them into a discussion.

'I'm doing a thesis on natural responses to oppression, so this is right up my street, of course.'

'Oh, I see.' Chess made a point of looking elsewhere, but the woman carried on.

'During the days of slavery in Trinidad, the indigenous population were forbidden from playing any kind of music or wearing any kind of costume apart from at a carnival six weeks before Easter, which was a terrible oppression of their own wonderful sense of celebration, don't you think?'

'Terrible,' said Chess, despite an elbow and a shake of the head from Vienna.

'So you see, this carnival became the only way for black people like yourself to express their anger against their slave-masters, but instead of making it an aggressive event, they saw it as an opportunity for satire, and created the most elaborate, colourful, fanciful costumes and played the noisiest happiest sound they could.'

'I thought it started in the 1950s,' Vienna butted in, 'as a result of racial attacks from white people *like yourself*.'

'Well, that's the popular view.'

There was something about the woman's delivery, as if she was looking at something small and diseased through a microscope and found it fascinating only because she'd discovered it first, that Vienna found deeply offensive.

'Uh, we need space to dance, this is no good up here,' she said, climbing down. They made their excuses and crossed the road to stand around the corner. Not such a great spot, but more spontaneous company since everyone around them was laughing and swaying to the cacophony of Soca music – a fusion of Soul and Calypso – that was wending its way through the streets from the parading bands.

Old men, huge women, young boys and sexy girls all with different-sized drums around their necks came first, tapping and beating and trying to balance their warrior head-dresses to the rhythm. Mingling in confusion with the last few warriors were some yellow stars, and more moons, being shouted at by a young girl with a megaphone to get back in line. Her voice came to nothing above the blare of the sound systems, so she encouraged her other dancers to grab the drifters by the arms and yank them back to their own group. Then, slowly and vigilantly, in case any stars or warriors or moons or drifters were caught under the heavy wheels, a giant pair of lips fixed to the grid of a lorry came round the corner.

The driver beamed through a thick layer of bronze and blue face paint as he took his unwieldy lorry through the parted mob, keeping his eyes on the group of revellers who were dancing the vehicle through. They were joined by a piece of thin rope which was somehow woven through their twisting, shaking bodies, fusing them together and making them move as one, keeping the crowd out and the tempo in.

As the lips passed, the crowd were treated to their first stage – from last year's winners, a glittering Egyptian tableau in melting gold and blazing sapphire, the huge familiar mask of Tutankhamen dwarfing even the biggest men on board.

The slinky, sinuous women stepped around them, their right arms out at the front, palm down, their left arms out behind, palm up. 'Walk Like An Egyptian' by The Bangles blared from an open-deck speaker, not that you could hear it. Chess realised the four statues at each corner were not cardboard as she'd first thought but children, and she wondered how they managed to stay so still and keep their balance at the same time. One of them broke a rule and waved to someone in the crowd.

Another lorry, festooned with red and gold drapes, came past. It had a huge bank of speakers tethered to its top, and a fat black DJ on board was shouting 'Jump, an' wave, an' misbehave,' egged on by three young dancers. His baggy T-shirt jumped up and down with his beat, revealing an undulating belly painted with red, yellow and green stripes.

'I've got to see the static sound systems,' Vienna shouted in Chess's ear.

'The what?'

'The static sound systems. They're not allowed on the main carnival route, because they're too loud – they drown out the costume bands. They're on the side streets – about fifty of them, I think.'

'Hell . . .'

'It's where the funksters go.'

'That counts me out then!'

Each float looked as if it had cost a fortune. Chess's favourite, or at least the one she remembered because of the cute factor, was one put up by a local nursery. There were thirty or so children under five on the back of the lorry, all dresses as bumble bees, dancing in and out of sunflowers on a carpet of green. Again, only at the last minute, did Chess realise the sunflowers were people, adults this time, their faces happy through stiff paper petals. One bumble bee, the smallest, was in a sunflower's arms, tired of buzzing and being rocked in time to the music. A shooting pain of envy ripped through her body and she thought of her own two. Sam was five, too big now to be a bumble bee. She suddenly missed them and thought of them on their bikes in the park. Should she be there? Or should they be here?

A Space Age float thundered by – all silver and lasers – and they moved to the back of the crowd where it thinned out enough to be able to put one foot in front of the other, and bought tubs of frozen yoghurt from a single unmarked deep-freeze on the pavement. They caught up with the bumble bee float again, but as it turned the corner to the left, Chess spotted a hat stall.

'Down there?'

'The sound systems are this way. Can't you hear them?'

'Be careful then,' Chess said.

'You too. Back at the Tube at seven?'

'If you're not there, should I worry?'

'I *will* be there.'

As they went their separate ways, Chess realised it had been Vienna's intention all along. No doubt she had planned to come on her own weeks ago, and agreed to join Chess just to smooth things. The hats on the stall were colourful and fun, but nothing you couldn't have bought at Covent Garden, so she ambled on, wondering if Vienna would remember to buy the whistles and deciding that she would anyway – the children could always have two each. There was plenty of time to do that – every other person she saw seemed to have bunches of them around his or her neck, threaded on to Rastafarian ribbon.

She looked up at the street name and saw she was on Portobello Road, not that she would have recognised it even if the market had been up and running. Still, she got a little kick from it all the same, like she was having a little piece of today's action at any rate.

Away from the procession route, there was a little more opportunity for taking in the buildings and the bodies waving through the windows or dancing on the occasional balcony. An old chapel, behind railings, seemed a hip place to be, judging from the mix of people coming in and out. A theatrical dragon's head, not quite Chinese but of that same serpentine frame and trailing coloured cloth, was hanging, fixed somehow from above the arched door, its lolling jaw and flimsy flames swaying in time to a blend of beats going on around it.

People, not all young and black, were sitting on the four or five front steps to the building, smoking, eating and laughing. A barbecue in one half of the forecourt was unmanned and sizzling with something that smelt fantastic. A big grey dustbin was next to it, and a lanky boy in a black string vest dipped into it and pulled out a can dripping with melting ice. On the other side of the yard were five deserted steel drums of different sizes, some of the discarded sticks lying in the drum bowls, others criss-crossed on the ground. Chess could tell from the relaxed but energetic bodies on the steps that it was hunger rather than lethargy that had stopped play.

There was something about the scene, or the structure of the building with its small pitched roof over the entrance, that she recognised – then she realised it was the place on the leaflet she had picked up in the taxi – the Pinegrove Arts Project and Community Centre. She noticed now that it said so in big splashy letters behind the dragon's head, and she was disappointed with herself for not being brave enough in the last few weeks to sign Kezia and Sam up for the puppet-making. Maybe then she would have had that little extra confidence to take her through the opening either side of the railings and towards the delicious-smelling food.

Someone spotted her hesitation and thrust a pamphlet into her hand.

'Come see us soon!' the woman in khaki fatigues and a tiny white bandeau across her flat bosom smiled before going back to her group.

Chess was starving now, but determined not to eat chips. Boards offering curried goat, chicken, rice 'n' peas and fried fish were everywhere. She'd watched people tear hungrily into spicy meat pittas and coconut cakes and the only thing that had stopped her from buying something so far were the queues. A big handwritten notice in front of the chapel said *Come In and See Us* and she wondered if, perhaps on her way back from wherever she was going, she would.

Then, through all those noises, through the steel drums and whistles, the distant tinny irritation of a radio outside broadcast, the pulsating thump of Vienna's sound systems, through the laughing and the chatting and the singing, came a single shout.

'Della lost de dog!'

No one else heard it, not even the person who was supposed to, but to Chess it was so loud, so piercingly loud, that it stopped her immediately in her tracks. She got bumped by a thin old man in a tweedy hat who put up his hand apologetically and walked round her in a kind of step dance. The shout came again, closer.

'Della lost de dog!'

She tried to hang on to the words again – to work out if the caller was shouting for Bella or Donna or Taylor, not Della. It was a young voice but not a child's, and with a lurch Chess thought about all those trainers and roller blades lined along the hall in Minnie's flat which was probably only a stone's throw from where she now found herself.

She had known of course that there was every chance she could end up at the flat again today – that was a big part of her desire to be here in the first place – but she hadn't reckoned on something as fateful as a chance encounter. She swivelled to see if she could see where the shout had come from, and then she heard it again, even nearer this time, almost in her face.

'Della lost de dog!'

No, whoever it was was definitely calling for Della, clearly, unmistakeably Della. A boy of about thirteen ran past her and she looked at his feet. Nike. He was wearing a Fila sweatshirt and a cap to match. Three times she'd heard him say the name Della.

Aware that she was building herself up only to knock herself down again, she dodged a few bodies to keep up with him, just in case. Her Della could not possibly be the only Della in London, but this was *her* neighbourhood. It wasn't entirely mad to assume . . .

The boy stopped a few yards past the Pinegrove, at another little encampment, this time on the corner of a road, and he spoke to a woman.

Chess thought it must be his mother, the way she pulled away the foil from a barbecued parcel she was eating and gave it to him. The boy took it and ate it greedily, scrunching up the empty foil and giving it back before pulling a ring on a can that he had also been handed.

'She never!' said the woman.

'She did! It jus' went off and she t'inks she c'n find it!' the boy laughed. 'I say she won't see it no more! Mercedes gonna kill her dead!'

Peep! Peeeeeeep! A whistle blew in one of Chess's ears and a woman shouted a name Chess didn't catch in the other. Their bare shoulders brushed against each other and the whistles around the woman's neck clanked. Chess stood back and the whistle woman, in a red satin bra top, black Lycra cycle shorts and silver platform trainers bounced past. She was cradling something in the hammock of her top. She looked the right age. Is that my Della, Chess asked herself, or am I telling myself it is because I want it so much?

'Della?' she shouted, not loud or sure enough.

There was no recognition in the woman's eyes – but maybe that was because of the sheen in them, a glossy indulgence that made her look festive and sleepy. It was the way she pulled the puppy out that convinced Chess.

'Told ya!' she said, triumphantly producing the tiny black thing with a flourish and handing it over to the boy. Chess watched and remembered the black cashmere dress, pulled out from under a denim jacket to an imaginary fanfare fifteen years ago. It was her! It had to be! Was it? *Did* it have to be? Did she *want* it to be?

Now what? The opportunity to find a way to Minnie was being presented to her on a plate. She mustn't let it go. She had a choice – she could either go over and say something and risk the misery of rejection or embarrassment, or she could walk away and pass up the chance. If it wasn't Della, and there was less and less of a possibility of that being the case the more she watched her, then all she had to lose was a moment's composure. If it was Della, she could lead her to Minnie.

Her tummy turned over. Still in the process of plucking up the courage, she started to walk in a direction that could look as if she were just passing. Maybe, by the time she got there, she'd have found the nerve to say something. But then suddenly, the choice was no longer hers.

'Hey, is dat you?' Della called towards her, but the words reached Chess in disarray, and she flushed with confusion, not knowing what was being shouted.

'Chess?' Della shouted again, coming over and hitting her with the flat of her hand against one shoulder. 'Are you Chess, is dat you?'

Chess tried to look more surprised than terrified. 'Della?'

'God, where you bin', what you a'doin? Chess de Dress, I call you to Granny, and she get so mad! Granny t'ink she never gonna see you again . . . she gonna go crazy when she see you. It is you, innit?'

'It is!' Chess laughed, and put her hand against her mouth and then ran it through her hair. 'So does that mean it's you too then?'

They stood grinning insanely at each other and then Della pulled her over to the pavement by her arm and made a cursory introduction to the woman on the corner that the boy had spoken to, but everyone was still pestering her for the dog story. Della told it, hanging on to Chess all the while, in case she slipped away.

It was the oddest thing, but now Chess was there, she knew that she'd been expecting this to happen all along. It just didn't feel like her day had taken an extraordinary turn at all, not even when she took a can of lager from someone she didn't know, and clinked it against her sister's, someone she hadn't seen since the worst day of her life, and said, 'Cheers!' She was deliriously thankful for it though.

The woman, called Maz, wore a tight short dress and a flashy gold belt that spelt Moschino. A young girl with pierced ears and lots of free-formed baby dreadlocks took the puppy off the boy and began playing with it. He was on his way somewhere else when Della shouted at him to come back.

'Dis a' me boy, Tyrone,' she said proudly, clipping him. 'He's ain't no good. Dis yuh auntie what lives with dem white people in de country.'

'Not any more,' said Chess.

Tyrone gave a flash of white teeth but obviously had no idea what his mother was talking about, and said he was going to find someone called Shane.

'Yours?' Chess smiled as he bounced off. 'He's huge!'

'Yeh, an' I got Mercedes, but she's littler. Where's Mercedes, Maz?'

'Wid yuh yardie,' Maz replied, making the last word sound like a term of abuse. Della looked at Maz as if she shouldn't have let her go with a 'yardie', whatever a 'yardie' was.

'God, I can't believe this,' Chess said. 'I went to the old flat the other day. Is . . . is Minnie OK?' There was a clawing of anxiety inside her as she braced herself for the answer.

'Still kickin' – I t'ink she's makin' more curry wid Dora. Come on, seckle wid me here and tell me where you been, then we mus' go look for her.'

Della made a little picnic on the floor for them from the foiled parcels on the barbecue, pieces of chicken and another meat, possibly lamb. As they ate, Della told her about the mermaid costume she had made Mercedes by sewing sequins and cardboard shells on to her swimsuit, and Chess told Della about Kezia, Sam and Nick, and living in London, and coming here today with Vienna.

She started telling Della that Honor had died before she realised that Della wouldn't even register who Honor was. It was a world apart, always had been and maybe always would be. But now, it was like there was a world in between too.

'I went to the flat the other day,' Chess repeated as she watched Della roll a joint for pudding.

'It helps digestion,' Della laughed, aware of eyes on her. 'Carnival time is de only time you can do it on the streets and not get arrested, so I like to make de most of it! Wha' flat?'

'Minnie's, the one I lived in for a bit, before, you know. Does she still live there?'

'Yeh, wid Tyrone and Mercedes. My man, my yardie, he likes me on m' own. We got a flat just down de road. Minnie look after de piccanee dem . . .' Della paused, and realised she had lost Chess with her patois '. . . de kids, when I went inside four years ago, and I din't never go back, not properly. She likes it like dat. She loves 'em.'

'Do you? Like it like that, I mean?'

'Ah, y' know how it go.' Della shrugged, as if to say she didn't have much choice.

'What did you go inside for?'

'Sellin'. What else?'

Della laughed a smoker's laugh and showed a gold tooth, but then her laugh faded and she scrambled to her feet. A tall man in three-quarter length khaki shorts and a matching shirt was suddenly towering over her, puckering his lips and looking displeased. Chess got up too, although she didn't know why. His hair was cut to within an inch of his head and she noticed the precision with which a Nike Air tick had been shaved into the back, just above his collar. He had gold rings on each finger – three or four of them were inset coins, and he had more gold hanging around his neck. She had never seen anyone in a safari suit look so sinister.

'Bring de food, come,' he said to Della, taking the spliff out of her hand and drawing on it. 'Make haste, y'hear?'

Della went over to the barbecue and spooned out a bowl of curry from a steel pot. 'Where's Mercedes? Maz said she was wid you,' she asked, not looking at him.

'She went wid Dora. I got business to do.'

'I better go check,' Della said, handing him his food. 'You come round to de flat yeh?' she said to Chess. 'I tell Granny you here again. An', hey, I bin wantin' to say sorry for all dat grief when we was kids, y'know?' She ran down the street without waiting for an answer, off in search of her child, and as Chess stood there hopelessly, next to this mountain of a man, she could feel the threat he represented seeping out of him. So that's what a yardie was. She was suddenly out of her depth. She wondered about following Della, but worried about getting lost too.

'Where's Dora?' she asked casually, not wanting to talk to him but feeling too vulnerable not to, 'I'll go too,' but she could tell by the way he was studying her that it wasn't going to be that easy. She half-expected him to yank her head back and inspect her teeth or check her hair for nits. He was Della's slave-master, that's what he was. He ignored her question. 'So, where you a' go? Wha' you a' do?' he said, opening his palm up and pushing it towards her. He was using a different tone to the one he'd used with Della, less bullying.

'Oh, I've got to go and meet someone. I'll see you,' she mumbled, not quietly enough to disguise her accent.

'You know Carnival finish at seven?' he asked, throwing the remainder of his food under the barbecue. 'We can link up, yes? You smoke a weed?' He dipped into a side pocket on his shorts and pulled out a bag and started to build a smoke, not bothering with any tobacco as far as Chess could see. When he'd finished, he held out what was left in the bag. 'For you, a lickle spice for the carnival spirit.' He smiled, and she saw he had a gold tooth too, like Della.

If she refused, which she wanted to, he might show the side of him that Della was so obviously afraid of. If she accepted, well, what would she do with it? What was it and how much was it worth? What would happen if she was found with it? Could she dump it? She didn't want it, she was afraid of it.

'Thanks, I really appreciate the thought, but I don't smoke.' She smiled apologetically, he laughed, and put it back in his pocket.

'What dey call you?'

'Chess. Short for Francesca.'

'Dey call me Bear, but I'm not so grisly,' he said. They stood on the corner for a minute longer with the cultural barrier well and truly up until another woman came wheedling to his side. Rescue me, Chess pleaded with her silently, rescue me, but the girl obviously needed no encouragement.

'Star,' she drawled, stroking Bear's arm. 'You havin' a happy Carnival?'

'Kim,' he droned back. Her hair was pulled so severely off her face that it changed the shape of her eyes. She reminded Chess of a cat in need of food.

'I'll see you,' Chess said, finding the courage to start walking away.

Bear didn't want Kim pussyfooting around. He preferred his new find. He liked the backs of her calves and the way her hair was tied. She looked a clean woman. He must talk to Della.

At home, Nick had rigged the slide to the climbing frame, put the paddling pool at the bottom and fitted the hose to the outside tap. He had lit the barbecue, opened a bottle of wine for when his wife and daughter came home, and bought some lemonade for the children. Kezia had found an extension lead and carried her waterproof CD player outside. When Chess and Vienna got back, the kitchen surfaces were scattered with hastily opened packets of bread rolls, frozen chicken burgers, and crisps – processed, purchased rubbish, the customary fodder of impromptu family barbecues the country over. No unidentifiable meat on offer here, thought Chess, thinking about Della's foil parcels and Bear's plastic one. She hadn't mentioned a word of it to Vienna, but then there had hardly been an opportunity. Vienna had been so full of it herself.

She took off her back-pack, glanced out of the window and saw Sam hurtle down the length of bright blue plastic, Nick carefully aiming the jet of water away from his son's face, over his legs, where he could cope with it. Kezia was in her outgrown swimming costume, her hair and wet lips chattering. Nick threw her a towel, Kezia caught it clumsily, wrapping it tightly around her. Everything looked so safe, so unreal out there.

She stood and watched them for a while longer. They were just as mesmerising as any float, and passing her by just as quickly. One minute they were babies, now they were schoolchildren – worse than that, Kezia was five years off being a teenager. Pinch yourself, Chess, she thought. This is all yours. Life doesn't get much better than this. Stop looking at it from the outside in. Get up on that lorry with them.

Vienna was in the loo and, thinking it was a dependence too far to wait for her to come back before going out to join them, Chess propelled herself through the French windows, blowing a tune on one of the whistles, not quite knowing how to slot back in.

'Mum!' Kezia shouted, running to her and skidding on the wet grass. Her long light body glided gracefully for a few feet but came to a stop as she hit the edge of a low wall around a flower-bed. A sharp stone stabbed her and she screamed out in pain.

'Oh! Hold on. Count to ten – one, two . . . ouch ouch ouch ouch,' Chess soothed as she ran. She got to her daughter quickly and eased her off the ground. The injury – a puncture wound in her buttock and a gritty graze down the back of her thigh – was a first-aid-box job.

'Ooh, little one, I bet that stings.'

Kezia sobbed and clung, digging her nails into Chess's back. Her bizarre day blew right away and she was back in the front line of parenting again. After a quick kiss in the direction of Sam, who hadn't even noticed her reappearance, and Nick, who obviously had, Chess took her injured baby inside to clean up. It was just what they both needed, some mutual affirmation of what a mother was.

By the time they got back outside again, creamed, plastered and Arnica tableted, the action had calmed down and the burgers were ready. Sam had the chivalrous idea of running in to fetch his sister his bean bag so she didn't have to sit on the scratchy lawn like the rest of them, and when he came back, he knocked over the bottle of wine. The blanket, soaked in Rioja, had to be hastily pulled up and replaced with an old throw from the breakfast room. When at last they were all sitting comfortably, Nick said, 'Now, can we start or is there some other drama on the horizon?'

It was just a throwaway line, but Chess, who anyway hadn't been too sure of the reaction she would get if she gave a full and honest account of her day, decided that, for the moment, she would stick with some simple frothy enthusiasm about the costumes and let Vienna do the rest.

At another barbecue on a street corner, Bear summoned Della away from her children with his index finger.

'We can make a' money wid dat girl,' he said.

'What girl?' Della asked, as if she didn't know.

'Wha? You nah know? Wid her looks and dat chat, nuff t'ings can gw'aan. Me 'ave one bredren me waan see now. So you know what you 'affe do? You mus' bring her come.'

'But I don't know where she is or where she go.'

'You bring her come, y' hear?'

Della looked away and saw that Minnie had arrived, large and limping, with more food. She understood enough about Chess to wish now that she had told her Minnie was dead and gone. Maybe then, she wouldn't come looking. Maybe then, she'd be safe.

Chapter 13

Minnie put obstinate strain on her arthritic knees and heaved herself vertical again. Reuben worried about her knees, or rather he used them as grist to his mill. *Come home,* his letters would say, as if they had once shared one there together. *The warmth of our island sun will make them better.* I'll *make you better. Come home.*

The two shoe-boxes of airmails had grown in the last eight years to four shoe-boxes, and the postman was still delivering. Destiny, or maybe an answered prayer, had offered Minnie George and Reuben Fisher a blessed fleeting reunion and they hadn't gone a day without putting pen to paper since. But for reasons Minnie couldn't explain, she still kept him secret and hidden, under her bed. There was really no need, because Gladstone, her bullying husband and the man who had curtailed her life, was by now long gone, in body if not in spirit.

In 1992, when Della, the first of Christine's illegitimate children and, in liability terms anyway, a chip off the old maternal block, had produced yet another tiny mouth to feed, Gladstone had moved out in fake disgust. He had been looking for a reason for years, and another baby in the house suited him well enough. A man can take only so much female stupidity, he justified to his card-playing friends at the bus depot. He claimed the squalling child Mercedes had squeezed the very last drop of space out of their already claustrophobic council flat and so he went to live half a mile away with what Minnie called his 'fancy woman'. He'd set up home in the same polluted terrace he had first imprisoned his hopeful new wife in, and his long-awaited departure left a browbeaten Minnie free to take the first holiday she'd ever had.

She'd gone to Jamaica of course, and when she'd heard the mixed news that Ivy Fisher had died six months previously and left her husband Reuben to run his successful retail business alone, Minnie had decided it was time to do a little shopping.

He'd been behind the counter, and from the moment his eyes looked up at the clang of the bell that alerted him to custom, they both knew exactly that their time together had come. But now, eight frustrating years, one more visit and nearly two hundred love letters on, she still couldn't give Reuben the answer he wanted to hear. *Come home,* he'd write. *You know I'll look after you.*

Gladstone wasn't the problem any more. It was Della. Minnie tried her best to make Reuben understand that her granddaughter probably needed her here, in London, more than he needed her there, in Jamaica, but it was hard. She had kept him on a string all those years at the beginning, and she was leaving him to dangle even now, when time was no longer on their side.

Della have no one else. Her mother Christine is Gladstone's daughter for sure. How else could you walk out on your baby when she still too young to feed herself? If that girl of mine came home now, I'm telling you Reuben Fisher, I would turn my back on her, blood or no blood. Della says she do have someone in Bear, but I see him the problem, no way the answer. She have her children, Tyrone and Mercedes, but they still young – young enough for me to teach them better ways, like I should have done with my own. And now, in the way the Lord has of making me sit up, there's a chance he might bring me Frankie again, the girl I truly thought I had lost for ever, the baby Christine deserted, and the child I had to give away in our empty years, you remember? she wrote.

Of course I remember, he replied return of post. *I remember everything about you.*

Minnie still couldn't believe what Della had been telling her, that her other granddaughter Frankie was back once again, and had come looking. She wouldn't believe it until she saw her with her own eyes. Her second chance at a happy family was here in London and it was the one incontestable reason why she, Willimina George, felt she had to stay where the *Empire Windrush* had brought her fifty-two years ago – arthritic knees, Reuben Fisher and all.

Minnie was absolutely right to think that Della needed her more than Reuben did. At the very moment that she pushed her updated shoe-box of airmails back under the bed, another much less romantic kind of pushing was going on in a flat just around the corner.

Bear, growling and lumbering around his darkened cave, was busy punishing Della for failing to bring Chess to him as requested. If anything really angered him, it was his woman showing disregard, and she seemed to be showing more and more of that lately.

He'd detected Della's reluctance to obey him over the girl the very first time he'd mentioned it at the carnival. He could have slammed her fragile bones into the wall then, but instead, because the good weed had taken the edge off his temper, he'd put her hesitancy away for future reference. When Bear filed away a grievance, he never forgot it was there. Plenty of people could testify to that.

'You mus' bring her come,' he'd said at the carnival barbecue, gnawing on grilled chicken, pointing the bone at her and letting some of the chewed flesh fly off towards her to emphasise his command. Her devious reply had made him immediately suspicious and he'd made sure he was extra rough with her in bed that night, tying her feet with head scarves to the bedposts.

A whole month later, just as he'd calculated, his bad woman had neglected to come up with the goods. That meant he had no choice. It was time for a spot of discipline, to teach her again that Bear did not suffer defiance.

'Where's dis girl I ask for?'

'Oh, her. I don't know, man.'

'Someone say she is yuh sistah. You should know where yuh sistah is. Bring her come.'

Della had tried to appease him with money – her debt-collecting skills were almost as good as his and she only *threatened* the violence. She'd freely given him all the sex he'd wanted, and she'd complied with every other dirty deed he'd asked her to do. But nothing could sway him from his wish. He wanted the smart girl. Well, for once, he wasn't going to have her – not through Della, anyway.

Initially, Bear had required Chess because she was different. She spoke differently, she wore the clothes of a white woman, and to his calculating eyes she looked about as likely a lawbreaker as the Queen. He knew he could use her well. If he asked her to do a bit of running around for him, fetching and carrying, nothing too heavy, and the police stopped her, all she'd have to do would be to open her mouth and speak and they'd let her go. They certainly wouldn't think she was connected to someone as criminally significant as him. Women like Della, with their gold teeth and showy clothes, were easy to pick up. No, he wanted Chess to work for him real bad. And now, because Della was being tricky, he wanted Chess for another reason too. He needed to teach his bitch of a woman a lesson.

'No one holds out on Bear,' he thundered. 'No one.'

'But I don't have knowledge, man, honest,' she said.

'Den you bettah go get it.'

For once in Della's life, because she felt she owed her half-sister something from all those years ago, she was determined not to yield to his threats. The injuries she wore as a result – one cut lip, a black eye and a dull ache in her head where a table lamp had been cracked over her skull – were not actually the worst she'd ever received from his hand. Instead of going to hospital, where they would probably keep her in for observation because of her obvious agitation, she went round to Minnie's, who was an experienced nurse in such matters.

The fact that Chess chose that same day to re-establish contact with her grandmother was on the one hand extraordinary and, on the other, amazingly ill-fated. Extraordinary because she set foot back into the flat at the very moment her name was leaving Minnie's lips, and ill-fated because her sudden presence only served to jeopardise Della's safety further.

She'd been delivering one of the most boring pictures she'd ever seen to an elegant address in Holland Park – an unframed canvas rectangle with ten squares in graduated shades of beige, like a giant paint chart. When she worked out that the price was enough to keep a family of four fed and watered for six months, she felt like asking the customer to match the sum for charity. It was the imagined response that pushed her the extra half-mile into Minnie's neighbourhood.

It had taken a fortnight to find the nerve to do it, and when the moment of resolution finally came, she acted on it almost without thinking. Dan had been giving her lessons on spontaneity – he claimed that the only way to deal with complex choices was on impulse.

'I can't just *go*,' she'd kept telling him. 'I've got other considerations, like Kezia and Sam for starters. They need me to be me.'

'Isn't that the whole point?'

'But they know nothing about my black family. I can't just suddenly throw it at them.'

'Yes, you can.'

'And how?'

'Chess, they're *kids*. Can't you remember being a kid? Kids will accept anything.'

'Then Nick. What do you suggest I do about him?'

'Well, telling him how you feel would be a start.'

She could weigh up the pros and cons for ever, but Dan was her only confidant, so his wisdom – and she used the term loosely – stuck.

Anyway, eventually, not only did she find the resolve to enter the neighbourhood, but also to mount the stairs to the flat and knock on the door. Her timing was good in that she caught both Della and Minnie there together, but it was bad, very bad, in that Bear was on the prowl. It was lunchtime when she turned up, not that she could have eaten a thing. Her stomach was grumbling, but the thought of putting anything in it made her feel sick. Nothing more than nerves, she knew.

The door was answered quickly by Della's eight-year-old daughter, Mercedes. She had her hair up, formed into a perfect pin cushion on the top of her head and held down by a beaded gold plastic cage, presumably bought, Chess imagined, at a market stall full of hair accessories for young black girls. She had spotted similar things on little heads all over London but she'd never seen them anywhere on sale. Even if she had, she would need lessons to coax Kezia's hair into one.

'Hi. Are you Mercedes?'

'Yeah.'

'Is Minnie in?' she asked, perfectly in control. She'd been through this moment so many times in her head, and so very nearly lived it for real a few weeks ago, that she wasn't as awkward as she'd imagined. In fact, her confidence was soaring. Since her last abortive visit, she'd bumped into Della and heard news of Minnie. All she had now was an urgency to be welcomed in.

'Yeah, she is fixin' up Mummy,' said the girl, giving her the once-over. A bicycle was propped against the hall wall with a leather jacket hung over one handlebar. 'Come with me.' Mercedes turned and clomped back down the hall on roller blades, flipping her hand against the jacket as she passed.

'Dat's my mum's new bit of leather,' she said. 'I'm gettin' one next week.'

She showed Chess into the kitchen, where Della was sitting at the table, having her wounds dabbed with a flannel by her grandmother. Mercedes made no effort to announce Chess's presence, and rolled off once again into the sitting room. Neither Minnie nor Della looked up. Chess found herself staring at a cameo from an afternoon she'd tried her best to forget. This time though, the nurse was administering to the attacker, who was now the attacked. How much blood did this flat have to see, for God's sake? But forget all that. There was Minnie! She looked well – a little stooped, but fatter and more than capable.

'I'm back, Minnie,' she wanted to cry out. 'Just hold me. I'm back. Claim me again, please,' but she remained still, fixated, churned up.

The flat still had the same fridge – the dent from the iron had gone rusty and blistered around the edges, but the damage was discernible, all the same. A bowl was still on top, but it was a yellow mesh one, not wooden any more.

The two women continued to concentrate on the job in hand, aware that someone was in the kitchen with them but assuming it was a child. Frequent unannounced visits were still commonplace anyway.

Chess found her voice eventually and, dispensing with the formalities of preamble, she said, 'What's happened?'

'Choh . . . I tell her time and time he is no good, but . . .' Minnie still didn't look to see who was speaking. She guessed it was a friend of Della's, someone she hadn't met.

'Oh, hey, you, I t'ink you better get out here, y' know? It's not a good place for you to be,' Della said darkly, glancing up only briefly. Her top lip was swollen and she found speaking painful. She was mumbling.

'But–' Chess wasn't sure if she was hearing a threat.

'But de girl only just got here,' Minnie said, and then turned to apologise to this stranger in her kitchen on her granddaughter's behalf. The fifteen years of absence had done nothing to Frankie's face that Minnie didn't recognise immediately, and she threw her arms up into the air and then around Chess's shaking body, patting her and stroking her to reassure herself this was not a figment of an overtired imagination.

'Oh, oh, is it you? Eh? Is it? Is it?'

The noise of Minnie's recognition reached Bear's ears in the concrete corridor, even before he pushed open the front door left unlocked by Mercedes.

Della heard her boyfriend's presence before she saw it. He hardly muttered to his little daughter as she passed him on her way out, but only a few men can growl deeply enough to make the air around them vibrate. Della winced in the anticipation of more pain. He would wrongly assume that her claims of ignorance as to Chess's whereabouts were false, that she had lied in his face. A fellow drug dealer had gone on a life support once for committing a lesser sin.

As soon as the bulk of Bear's body eclipsed the kitchen doorway, she knew she hadn't yet been given the beating of her life. Quickly turning to Chess, she mouthed, 'Say I sent for you.'

Chess, still swamped in Minnie's embrace, caught the words but didn't yet understand them. She nodded reassuringly though, and then, abruptly, her grandmother dropped their hug and started flailing her arms in anger. Her rage was directed at the same man Chess had been left with at the carnival, although today he looked dirtier and even more dangerous. She also knew, once Minnie had started shouting, that he was Della's attacker, the man who had spilt her sister's blood.

'Who is you to be doin' dis to my girl? Who is you? You go hit her one too many times and find yourself on de wrong side of de law. You better mind. I want you OUT! You not welcome in my house, not now or ever.'

Echoes of the past span through the air again. Chess had hoped she would hear Minnie's voice still singing, not still shouting.

'Eh, Moom, no worries, everyt'ing goin be a'right, you know seh de girl love me,' Bear started in a honeyed voice. Della knew exactly his tack. He was an evil charmer, and he wanted Chess under his spell. Her head hurt too much at the moment to think of an antidote to his black magic.

'Granny,' Della whimpered, 'you gonna make it worse for me if you not careful.'

'Choh,' said Minnie, 'I not even know what for me to say.' Inside, she felt scared. Bear was bigger than Gladstone ever was, and she knew how easily brutality came sometimes. She turned her attention to Chess, the girl who'd been blown in on an ill wind if ever there was one. When Della had staggered through the door fifteen minutes previously, she had tried, through the blood spit and tears, to explain why Bear had beaten her up. 'He wants Chess,' she'd kept repeating. 'Why?' Minnie had wanted to know. 'Because she's different,' Della had sobbed. 'Different how?' 'Just different,' Della had moaned. Well, this monster wasn't going to take both her girls. Not if she could help it.

'I only come to say I'm sorry,' Bear droned. 'I should never hurt my queen like dat. I cry tears on de ground if you ever know. Me a go make it up t'you, y'hear?'

Della stayed quiet. She wanted to believe him for real, but that was just plain stupid. If she at least pretended to believe him, then there was a chance he wouldn't thump her again for a while. Maybe Chess, now that she was here, could be a trading point.

'Sorry is not good enough,' Minnie snapped. 'You leave her alone, y'hear me? An' if you lay anudder finger on her, me a go send police for you.'

'Granny,' warned Della as Bear approached her. He took the flannel from the table and started to touch it against his girl's cut eye.

'Eh, sis, you know seh I man is a warrior, an me affi teach de girl a lesson sometimes,' he said, in Della's face. His breath smelt of marijuana. 'But I'm glad I com,' his eyes flashed demonically at her, ''cos look what I find here?' he whispered.

'I sent for her,' Della whispered back. 'Ask her, she'll tell you. I did what you said. I obeyed you.'

Chapter 14

Judith sent for Chess too that week, in a plaintive little e-mail. She no longer trusted the phone to carry her words without putting a pause in the wrong place or an inadvertent sigh, to make her seem more desperate than she was.

Anyway, she was sick of being the one to make the first move, and even if her calls were returned – and that was a big if lately – Tim did his best to block them. There was no secrecy about it – she could be standing within a foot of him and he'd still have the nerve to make up some cock and bull story about her being in the bath, or resting, or still at work. He did notice though, with satisfying reassurance, that his wife only challenged him after he'd put the phone down.

'What did you say that for? I don't want Chess to think I don't want to speak to her.'

'Well, let her think that I don't want you to speak to her then.'

'She's my *sister* Tim, we need each other.'

'You need her like a hole in the head at the moment, Jude, believe me.'

But the hole in Judith's heart was much bigger than any hole she could ever imagine in her head, and so she didn't listen. There wasn't anyone left on earth to fill the yawning chasm left by Honor's death, but she still had Chess, the only person who could at least stand on the crumbling edge and stare into the deep dark hole with her and know what they were both missing.

Judith imagined she and Chess were still tied together at the waist like rock climbers, although the rope wasn't as thick as it could have been and it sometimes felt like they were climbing entirely different mountains. Her faltering footwork wasn't helped by a growing fear that even this tentative safety harness was about to be unhooked.

Over-protected by Tim and under-contacted by Chess, Judith resorted to cyberspace where the confidence of being in control revived her spirits. At least computers didn't yet know how to purposely misinterpret.

Hi Chess. I miss you! I've got time on my hands now I'm on maternity leave – how about meeting me in the Countryman next week?

Chess took two days to reply *Where the hell is the Countryman?* but she knew that wherever it was, it would be somewhere significant, a salute to history, another patch on Judith's security blanket, another straw from her youth to clutch at. Chess's first reaction to such relentless loyalty to the past was to water the sentiment down, usually with mild facetiousness. But later, when she thought about the hows and the whys, she loved her sister for it and realised she valued it. She knew that if Judith ever stopped, their world would be poorer.

She was right about the Countryman though. It turned out to be the Lovell family's traditional journey-break between Norfolk and London whenever they used to go en masse and stay with Morgan and Brian. Honor would always greet the landlord and landlady as if they were old friends, clapping her hands in grateful relief when she discovered their home-made smoked mackerel pâté was still on the menu, as if they did it just for her. When the girls got older, they were allowed lager and lime shandies.

Chess, who was car sick as a child, was always given special attention at the Countryman – a cherry in her lemonade or two sachets of ketchup instead of one. Judith had once pretended to feel ill too, but it didn't have anything like the same effect.

Meet you there on Wednesday at 12 then. First one to the bar gets in the shandies.

Judith arrived at the pub first, of course. She had a

pathological inability to be late for anything anyway, but when it was for pleasure rather than duty, her timetable carried an unnecessarily large contingency. This time, she was forty minutes early.

To Chess, the lunch was a last-minute arrangement. To Judith, it was an engineered opportunity to re-live the memories of what everyone else around her took for granted – a family with all its members present and correct, as represented on televisions at Christmas. The journey hadn't been long, but the way she'd been sitting, or the position the baby had been lying in, had made it a particularly uncomfortable drive. Swigging a personal sized bottle of Evian water was her usual recovery technique, but as she pulled into the pub car park it was still all but untouched on the passenger seat.

At one point, when she'd had at least another hour's driving still ahead of her, she'd pulled into a motorway service station and twisted open the blue plastic cap, thinking she could hardly wait to drain it, but after just one sip there had been no room left in her stomach. She'd felt fit to burst.

Now, as she walked round the Countryman's empty courtyard, scuffing up yellowing leaves into heaps, the nagging pelvic pressure became worse, as if the baby was pushing down more than usual. A wave of tiredness swept over her. The last two months were always the worst and today's discomfort just signalled more of the same between now and her due date, which was still too far away to get serious about. Piles, varicose veins, constipation, oh the joys of pregnancy, wanted or otherwise. She put the low, dull backache down to sitting in a cramped car for too long.

She was so busy lugging around her twin suitcases of emotional and physical baggage that she didn't notice her sister's belated arrival. Chess almost missed the turning and swung her Golf wildly to the right at the last minute, poking her tongue out in response to the long indignant honk of a car's horn coming in the other direction.

She was running over to Judith in less than a minute, looking thinner and a lot more London in a black woollen pull-on ski hat and a sleeveless black fleece over a red skinny rib polo neck – a world apart from the same old needlecord pinafore her sister had put on that morning. There was something rebellious about her mood, but Judith was still filled with relief to see her familiar bouncy shape. It brought back her entire childhood.

'Where is it?' Chess laughed, putting her hand on her sister's tiny bump.

'In there somewhere. It's still got another seven weeks to go.'

'But you were *huge* by this stage with the others. Tank Woman, I seem to remember.'

'Thanks.'

'No, it's good, you should be able to shift the weight a bit easier this time. It took ages after Kate, didn't it?'

'Why not go the whole hog and tell me I was a fat cow?'

Chess just raised her eyebrows. She was going to tell her sister to cheer up because it might never happen, but then she remembered that it probably already had.

'Let's go in. I'm starving.'

'I don't think I could eat a thing.' Judith suddenly felt queasy at the thought of food.

'Are you OK?'

'Not sure. I don't seem to be able to tell the difference between feeling good or bad any more.'

'Oh, this is going to be fun!' Chess said more sarcastically than she intended. A flash of tear crossed the surface of Judith's eyes. 'Sorry. Hey, come on, we haven't both driven all this way just so we can get on each other's nerves, have we?'

'Course not. Anyway, it's lovely to see you, you look great. Your face always makes me feel better.'

'Which is more than I can say for yours,' Chess said, tilting her head and looking into Judith's drained expression. 'Are you sure you're OK? You look knackered.'

'Oh, thanks again.'

'I was only trying to be sympathetic.' She put her arm around her sister's shoulders and walked her towards the pub. Judith was moving awkwardly, but she relaxed in Chess's embrace and felt a little better.

It was easy being together, and Chess thought of her brief moments lately with Della, which were still exercises in careful thinking and plagiarised behaviour, borrowed mannerisms and adopted views. With Judith, she felt free to say anything she wanted. There was no point in pretending to be what she wasn't – diplomatic, responsible, mature – because Judith knew the truth. And anyway, their lines of communication would always be clear, unlike the newly re-opened route that was leading back to Della. Experience there told Chess that one false move could lead to immediate shut-down again.

'I've got loads to tell you,' she said, smiling. She'd come armed with her own agenda. She would do so much of the talking, there would be no time for her sister to sink into an even remotely maudlin decline. It would do Judith good to think that life just has to go on. Chess saw her plan as a kind of therapy, for both of them.

'I haven't. Absolutely nothing nice has happened for ages.'

They walked inside the familiar swing doors and their reminiscences were suddenly snatched from them. The Countryman had been gutted – it wasn't even called the Countryman any more, not that either of them had taken any notice of the Fryer's Tuck Inn board swinging in the car park or the new management's words on an easel just inside the door. *We apologise to customers for any inconvenience caused during our re-fit.*

The three small interconnecting rooms with slate floors and tatty leather armchairs of their adolescence were now one large carpeted space with a raised eating area sectioned off by a varnished wooden railing. The matching oak-effect tables, placed one after another along the front wall which looked out on to the road, had brass numbers screwed into their tops and identical dried flower baskets plonked next to ketchup bottles in the centre.

One long bar, staffed by three young men in red polo-shirts, ended in a cold counter for mass produced gâteaux. Another polo shirt, grey and female, was standing unenthusiastically by a coffee, tea and hot chocolate machine.

'Oh, God! They've ruined it!'

'Understatement of the year . . .'

It was comforting to have something in common to moan at and, to Judith's surprise, she found the complete dearth of nostalgia a peculiar relief. There was nothing left to compare with the past.

They chose a small table next to a fruit machine – or rather, it chose them. All the others were laid up for four or six diners, yet to materialise. Chess scrabbled in her bag and pulled out a packet of Silk Cut. Judith pulled a disapproving face.

'Stop frowning. It's bad enough having Nick on my back the whole time about it, without you.'

'Was I frowning? It's not the smoke, it's just that I keep getting this odd ache – not a pain exactly but a kind of nagging pulling sensation just–'

'Probably the long journey. Hey, you'll never guess what.'

'What?'

Chess exhaled excitedly, not seeming to notice that the smoke went straight for Judith's face. 'It's a secret, OK?'

'You and your secrets,' Judith said, digging her fingers around the skin at the top of her bump to ease what felt like a muscle spasm.

'Well, it's amazing. No, I'm not going to tell you until you're listening.'

'I am listening.'

'Promise you won't tell Nick? Dan knows, but he won't say anything.'

'That all depends on what it is you're going to tell me.'

'You sound like Mum.'

They smiled affectionately at Honor's memory, enjoying the idea that a little of her lived on. Judith would have liked it to be a lot more.

'She made me promise I'd keep an eye on you,' she said.

'And she made *me* promise not to let you boss me around too much.' Chess laughed because Judith was showing signs of her old self, and Judith laughed because Chess laughed. And because they were talking about Honor, of course.

'Mum would be pleased to think we were doing this.'

'Yeah . . . she wouldn't be pleased to see what they've done to this place though, would she? Anyway, let me tell you my news.'

'Well, get on with it then.'

'OK. You know I went to the Notting Hill Carnival with Vienna after Nick made a big fuss about not wanting to take the children?'

'No, but–'

'Didn't I even tell you that?'

'Not about Nick.'

'It's not important. We – as in me and Vienna, er, no, Vienna and I – got separated and I – it's almost too far-fetched even for me but you have to believe me, OK?'

'Mmm.' Judith was chewing her lip, trying to take the edge off the knot in her stomach. She heard every word her sister said but it didn't quite connect with her brain. She took in only a fraction of the tale, the sort of story she had dreaded hearing, a chance reunion with people who could so easily whisk Chess away for good. The gist of the excited blather seemed to be a confused tale of dogs and whistles and barbecues, but it was all a bit too much to think about.

'Did you hear me? I said I bumped into Della again at the Notting Hill Carnival,' Chess repeated.

'Really?' Judith tried her hardest to put some zip into her reaction but the revelation had remarkably little effect. A timid sip of her white wine and soda didn't make her feel any better.

'Yes, and I'm back in touch with Minnie again, and this time Della and I are getting on really well. The first time I plucked up the courage to go and see them – well, the second really, because the first time they weren't there, but it was so . . . well, actually, it was terrible because Della had been beaten up by her boyfriend and there was blood all over her T-shirt, although Minnie was just so pleased to see me she–'

But Judith wasn't listening. She was too busy glancing around her to look for the loos in case she had to make a hasty exit. She didn't exactly feel like she was going to throw up but her tummy was definitely griping now.

'Hello?' Chess asked, waving her hand a little aggressively in her sister's face. 'Some sort of reaction wouldn't go amiss.'

'Sorry, I'm lost.'

'What?'

'Just remind me a minute – is Della the one who attacked you?' Judith clutched quickly at any question she could come up with. 'It's been so long, I've forgotten who's who.'

'Della's my sister, Minnie's my grandmother,' Chess snapped. 'And anyway, that's in the past now, OK?'

'Half-sister,' Judith corrected.

'What?' Chess said again.

'Della is your half-sister.'

'OK, half-sister, just like you are my *step*sister,' Chess emphasised unpleasantly. 'Do you want to hear this or not?'

'Yes, I do. Go on.'

'Well, that's it. I bumped into Della and she recognised me. I couldn't believe it, there were so many people around, and I caught a glimpse, and thought it could be, but just as I was going to go over and ask her, she called out my name – and do you know what? There was absolutely no awkwardness – not a bit. You promise you won't tell Nick? I haven't said anything yet because he'll go into overdrive about it, I know he will. He'll try and stop me seeing her, or start quizzing me about where I've been, or . . . well, anyway, I just don't want him to know yet, OK? He'll complicate things. It's got to be easy this time. It just has to be . . .'

Judith was nodding as Chess continued at full pelt, but her mind was elsewhere. There had been fairly strong Braxton Hicks, or 'practice', contractions with all her other children, but none as unpleasant as these. Her doctor had warned her that everything happened faster with a fourth child. Perhaps the head was engaging or something, which would suggest the birth could be next month, not the one after. A film of perspiration shimmered above her top lip.

'And she told me Minnie was still alive and living at the same flat and everything, so I went to see her. It was amazing – God, it felt like we'd never been apart . . . she'd been waiting for me all that time. It made me feel so awful, though, you know? I'd just delivered this ridiculously expensive picture for Morgan to some fuck-off flat in Holland Park and then just down the road, I find my sister bleeding all over a Formica table in a grotty little flat no one should ever be expected to live in and–'

'That's nice,' Judith managed to say.

'That's nice?' Chess repeated. 'That's nice? Is that all? Are you in the slightest bit interested in this? It may not be much to you, but these people are my family, Judith.'

'No, look, I'm sorry, I am interested, and I don't mean nice, I mean amazing, really.'

'Oh, forget it. This was your idea.'

'I do want to hear more, it's just . . . will you come with me to the loo? I don't feel very well.'

The argument was stopped in its tracks. Chess looked at her sister's drained face and forgot everything. She leapt from her seat, put a mothering hand to Judith's head, felt the clamminess and led her to the loo. There, she damped a few paper tissues and wiped them around her pale features, soothing and apologising. It was the way their relationship worked. Judith was Chess's spiritual welfare, and Chess was Judith's nurse. When Judith was sick as a child, Chess thought nothing of holding the bucket for her, and she would always wipe her face for her afterwards, whether Honor was there or not.

For a little while, in the Countryman loos, Judith felt the balance of her old life return again. She thought for a moment she was going to vomit, but then the sensation subsided into something like wind or a griping bowel. Accepting a mint from the gritty depths of Chess's handbag, she splashed her face with water and they decided to leave.

'Better now?' Chess asked in the fresh air, still guiding Judith with a protective arm.

'I think so. Sorry, I don't know what . . .'

'It's probably stress. You've taken too much on board.'

'Like I've got a choice? Death isn't an option.'

'Pregnancy is.'

'Not this one.'

'You did choose to keep it though. You didn't have to.'

'I didn't want to.'

'No?' Chess was amazed. Her sister had always been rampantly anti-abortion. Rampantly anti-anything upsetting really.

Judith sighed. 'Only for a while, you know. Anyway, let's change the subject. This isn't making me feel any better.'

Chess opened the boot of her car and handed her a huge bunch of autumn berries. 'I thought you could put these on Mum's grave if you're passing back that way.'

Judith took a deep breath, felt the minty taste of her sweet fill her lungs and became so ridiculously grateful she couldn't speak.

'Don't make a special trip,' Chess said, recognising the swell of danger.

'Oh, I want to, I'd love to.'

'Well, send a little prayer up from me then.'

Judith made a superhuman effort to smile, but Chess could detect the struggle and she suddenly couldn't wait to be back on the road, driving away from the gloom. She kissed her hurriedly and said goodbye.

'And promise not to tell Nick what I told you, will you?'

'I promise,' Judith answered quietly, but under the surface her body was too busy gearing up for a superhuman effort of another kind to really care.

As Chess put the car into cruise control on the motorway back to Clapham, she went over it all again. Her fleeting concern over Judith's funny turn was starting to curdle into anger. Judith had shown absolutely no interest in her news about Della and the carnival at all – not even a glimmer of panic. In fact, she had been completely bloody anaesthetised, which was a bit rich when she was always going on about supporting each other in the way Honor would have done if she were still alive, how they should each try and fill that role for the other, how their mother's death could bring them closer. But the first big challenge that comes along and all she can do is shut down.

'She should practise what she bloody well preaches,' Chess said out loud, taking her Golf way over eighty-five and being flashed at by a speed camera. 'Bugger!' A wave of self-righteous self-pity came over her. Everyone was against her. Nick didn't understand, Judith refused to listen, Dan took the piss. No one knew what it was like to want to belong.

She imagined Judith at Honor's graveside now, having a nice cosy chat. At home, Nick had Vienna. Well, who did *she* have as an adult confidant? As she put her foot on the accelerator again, assuming that there would be no more speed traps for a while, she decided she would make Della and Minnie a priority, disapproval and difficulty from certain quarters or not. And I'll start as I mean to go on, she promised herself, fumbling with her left hand inside her open bag on the passenger seat. Glancing down to switch on her mobile phone, she dialled home. Vienna had promised to pick up the children if she ran late so there was one immediate opportunity to fulfil the commitment already.

'Vienna, it's me. I'm still on the motorway and the traffic is quite heavy so I might not–'

'You want me to do the children?'

'Could you? If it's raining, get a cab. Put it on our account.'

'Sure. How did it go with Judith?'

'Not exactly a riot. Are you OK until early evening? I've got a few things to do in town.'

'Yup. Don't hurry.'

'I'll be back before bathtime. Are you in tonight?'

'Not sure, why?'

'Just that I could do with a chat. I'd like your opinion on something, if that's OK.'

'Of course it's OK. Anytime, you know that.'

The boy lying fully clothed on Vienna's bed shrugged. He had only known her for a few days, since they started their textile course together at the art college, but he already knew he was too ordinary for her. She smiled at him and shrugged back.

'Family commitments,' she explained, relieved to have an excuse. She felt too old for him anyway, or too knowing, or too something.

Seventy miles away, as Chess switched the power off with her thumb, she spoke out loud, 'You see? That's what being supportive is, *Judith*.'

Judith was touched to see that someone from the village had put fresh water and some evergreen foliage on her parents' grave. On John's death, Honor had secured a double plot in the churchyard so she could be buried next to him, although at the time, the prospect of her demise was hovering way the other side of the millennium, not before it had even happened, as it turned out. At the time it felt as premature a plan as putting the three-week-old Kate's name down for St Hilda's, and Judith had teased Honor gently about it. It was easier to make a joke than contemplate the spectre of *her* death too.

She felt disappointed that a stranger would never be able to tell it was the final resting-place of two such special people. The earth had only just bedded down enough to banish the memory of the chilling mound of soil that had been so hideously corpse-like in the first few weeks. Then, it was as if her mother's scrawny body was only just under the surface, so that when Kate ran across it, she was bringing her foot down on Honor's stomach or chest.

The headstone was still at the mason's having the extra wording engraved on – not that it mattered. Judith didn't need to be told where her mother lay. She had stopped equating the grave with Honor's physical remains now.

Most of the time, she imagined her mother quite close, existing in a different spiritual plain, a cancer-free, regret-free, pain-free zone, but one that, despite those vast discrepancies, still bore a passing resemblance to life on earth. In Judith's mind, Honor was in a beautiful floating bubble, looking down with a love without longing. It sounded so good, she sometimes wanted to be there herself.

She crouched down next to the sunken steel flower arranger

to inspect the leaves to see if they would last until her next visit at the weekend, and that was when it happened. As her compact bump came into contact with her cold thighs, she first felt an almost pleasant sweeping compression of her uterine muscles, then, a split second afterwards, she was shot through with a sudden sharp crescendo of pain.

'*No!*'

Judith clutched at her tummy, bunching the needlecord, and fell to her knees in a scream of agony. Her waters broke in an unmistakeable gush and the cloudy amniotic fluid ran down her legs, soaking her maternity tights and seeping into the heels of her shoes. On all fours now, she lifted her palm to her mouth and licked it in the bleak hope of tasting urine. Her noise – an excruciating involuntary wail – travelled across the graveyard and reached the ears of the woman responsible for Honor's fresh foliage. Mrs Kingsley had known Judith since she was eight, when the Lovell family first moved into a cottage by the school before buying the farmhouse on the outskirts, but she mistook the hunched figure for a stranger all the same.

What she thought she saw was an older woman on the brink of some personal tragedy, perhaps asking her dead friend for guidance. Mrs Kingsley knew the feeling well, because she'd behaved in the same way over her own sister's grave once or twice, when she'd been too frightened to leave her foul-tempered domineering husband for the chance of a peaceful life alone. He'd gone now too, thank the Lord. She thought it would be tactful to leave the woman to her own private desolation – it didn't look the sort of pain she could help with. 'Time will heal,' she could have said.

Minnie's was hardly on the way home, but it didn't matter. Chess's mind was made up. Her other life was going to have to start taking precedence for a while. It was easy to justify. The children seemed settled at school, Nick worked long hours, Vienna was brilliant at filling the gaps – what difference would it make if she prioritised a little? No one would probably even notice. Slowly but surely, her father used to say to her, and she thought for once she ought to heed such advice.

It was a lonely journey back to London for the best part, spent feeling misunderstood, in need and without support. The more disconnected from Judith and Nick she felt, the more she felt the need for her grandmother. To be given unconditional approval from *someone* would be so good, and there *had* been something unconditional in the way Minnie had embraced her again, like a coming home. The cramped flat was at present the only place she felt entirely relaxed in, and she had imagined herself there more often than not lately. Everywhere else turned out to be between a rock and a hard place, made all the more hostile by the kind of thorny reaction she got from her sister and husband whenever she made even the flimsiest of overtures about awakening that dormant part of her life.

The hit of comfort from being able to shout 'It's only me!' through the letterbox made up for it though. Finding Minnie exactly where she had assumed she'd be – in front of the television, watching a tea-time soap and not leaping to stand on any kind of ceremony – made up for it even more. Della's daughter Mercedes, who had answered the door, was back at her great-grandmother's slippered feet, cutting figures out of magazines.

The room was dominated by Minnie's pride and joy, a brown and orange velour three-piece suite with wooden trims. She had bought it brand new two years previously and she still hadn't removed its plastic covers because she knew the moment she did, someone would spoil it with a cigarette or a spilt drink. She was still cross about the spring that had torn through the fabric at the back of the chair and was quietly saving her money for an automatic recliner to help her knees, but that little dream was still on the far distant horizon.

'I brought you these,' Chess said, holding out a small bunch of orange gardenias and contorted hazel twigs she had bought from a ridiculously expensive florist on the way.

'Hey, curly twigs! Cool!' Mercedes laughed, taking them from her.

'You don't need to bring me t'ings to come here, my darlin','

Minnie told her, shuffling Mercedes out of the way with her feet. 'You be careful wi' dat glue on my carpet, chile!'

Chess wished she had turned up empty-handed. Bringing flowers was the gesture of an occasional visitor, not a member of the family.

'No, I know I don't, but I wanted to.'

'Well, t'ank you, eh? I t'ink dere *lovely*. Now what you doin' here at dis time of day?'

'I just wanted to see you.'

'I stay here all day every day, darlin'. You come when you can, but don't you go disregardin' your own now.'

'You are my own.'

'And so am dey, so am dey.'

Chess waited for the credits of the soap to scroll up the screen and for Minnie to press the little green button on the remote control to cut the sound. She never actually turned it off, but let it flicker in the corner like a permanent window to another world.

'Tell me something about Jamaica,' Chess said impetuously, sounding like a child. Minnie had that effect on her. She only half-wanted to know, but every single tiny little bit of her wanted to find a reason to stay.

Her grandmother chuckled. 'How say I tell yuh anudder time? I'm lookin' at de clock and yuh girl and boy will be out of school now.'

'They're fine, someone else is sorting them out. Don't worry.'

'Well, I jus' do, I jus' do.'

'Why not tell me about Jamaica instead?'

'Choh! It make an old woman cry, darlin'!'

'You're not old.'

Minnie pulled herself and her cardigan together. She disapproved of her granddaughter being here when she should be with her children. It didn't seem responsible. She understood that Chess needed these building bricks, just as she hankered for the concrete details of the years she had missed in Reuben's life, but it wasn't wise to accrue them at the expense of her other foundations.

'I headin' fast for seventy-t'ree. I t'ink dat's old enough!'

'When's your birthday?'

Minnie smiled indulgently. Birthdays for her had no significance, other than the precious knowledge that they brought a single card from Jamaica. Della sometimes remembered and gave her clothes, but they weren't the kind she could take back.

'Sagittarius,' she said mischievously.

'November or December?'

'Dat's my secret.'

'I'll find out.'

'Don't yuh go makin' a fuss now. Yuh grandmudder is too old for fuss.'

Mercedes liked talk about birthdays. She chipped in. 'What'd you choose if you c'd have anyt'ing you wanted in de whole wide world?'

'A new chair dat takes me up and down at de touch of a button,' she said.

'Out of anyt'ing, you'd have dat?'

'Not really.'

'What else den?'

'Dat's my secret too,' Minnie said, because what she really wanted, had always wanted, couldn't be gift-wrapped.

Chess looked at her with a question mark and Minnie nodded as if to say, yes, really, it is my secret, and that's how it is going to stay. Then she patted her broad thighs with the palms of her hand and bent forward in her chair to see what the child at her feet was up to.

'What yuh doin' dere?'

'A projec' on families. I cuttin' out a Mum, a Dad, a brudder, a Granny an' a Grandad. But this lot all live in de same house, wid a garden,' Mercedes informed her categorically. 'Like you do,' she added, looking in admiration up at Chess.

'You still haven't told me about Jamaica,' Chess said, getting off the arm of Minnie's chair and sitting on the shrink-wrapped sofa.

'Tell me some news about yuh piccanees first . . . when you goin' to bring dem to see us, eh?'

'Soon, soon. It's school and stuff. Life is always so busy.'

Minnie smiled. She knew the real problem. They would come when Frankie was ready to bring them, and she shouldn't force it.

'You know what I t'ink?'

'No.'

'I t'ink you should go home an' feed yuh family, kiss yuh husband and save me for anudder day.'

Chess could see the concern etched in Minnie's face so she got up and rattled her car keys. 'If it makes you happy, I will.'

But outside on the concrete pavement, Chess wasn't ready to go home and feed her family or kiss her husband, and the very idea made her feel like screaming with the frustration of it all. Dan, she thought. I'll go and see Dan. He won't tell me to go home.

It wasn't until Judith hauled herself up and began to stagger back towards the church gates that Mrs Kingsley realised her mistake. The face was the same as it always had been, if a little slimmer and sadder than it had been as a child. Her doddery seventy-five-year-old legs took her across the slippery paving stones to the corner plot at a speed that surprised her and, before she even got there, she could see Judith was in labour.

'This shouldn't be happening yet,' Judith cried. 'I've got another two – *uugh* – months.'

'It doesn't look that way to me, dear. Now, just you hang on to me and concentrate on your breathing. Do they teach you breathing nowadays?'

Together, they made it across the wet grass to the churchyard's side entrance, and then somehow Judith managed to propel her increasingly uncontrollable body around two sides of the village square to Mrs Kingsley's terraced redbrick cottage.

Inside, instinct took over and she knelt backwards on the tidy two-seater tapestry sofa, filling the space entirely as she draped her arms and head over the back and pressed her contracting womb into the cushions.

'I can't stop it,' she cried, as the plates on the dresser rattled and the cat ran out of the room. 'I need to hold it in.'

'I don't think you've got the choice, dear,' Mrs Kingsley said. 'Now, we'll just keep calm until the ambulance gets here, won't we? How about I tell you what I remember of you as a little girl? There was one Harvest Festival when you and your sister decided to decorate the entire village with cooking apples . . .'

'Shop!' Chess called as she stood in the vacant showroom thinking it was just as well all the paintings were alarmed. 'Morgan? Dan? Is anyone here?'

A vague pop of a wine cork came from the stockroom and Dan appeared in the doorway, somehow managing to smile and swig at the same time.

'Thirsty, are you?' she asked. 'You piss artist.'

'God, that's better,' he said, wiping a drop from his mouth on his suit sleeve. 'You know what it's like when you start drinking at lunchtime. It's really hard to stop.'

'Now *that's* worrying,' she told him. 'Put the bottle down and get back to work.'

'But Doctor, I can't function if I'm sober,' he said, choosing a Scottish accent.

Chess was ninety per cent sure he was joking, but because it was Dan, the ten per cent scope for doubt was Tardis-like in its proportions. Nothing with him was beyond the realm of possibilities. She took the bottle off him, pushed him affably out of the way and put it on the storeroom desk. There were two others there already, both empty. 'Don't tell me this is your third.'

'Get real,' Dan smiled. 'I've had the best part of a glass and a half, I should think. Mind you, Mum and Dad had some fuck-off buyer here earlier and they were chucking it back. I was just a bit bored, that's all.'

'Let's smell your breath then,' Chess teased. He blew in her face. 'Phew! It stinks!' It didn't actually, but the storeroom did. The waft of old cigarette smoke and wine dregs hung in the air and, for a moment, the present airbrushed itself out and she was eighteen again, on the brink of her most prized sexual adventure.

'Bloody hell,' she said. She always swore more when she was in Dan's company. 'I've just had a déjà-vu.'

'What about?' Something in her laugh gave the game away and Dan's interest was aroused. 'Go on, what about?'

Chess took the bottle and had a swig herself. 'I lost my virginity in here,' she smiled. 'It smelt of booze and fags then too.' Her mind had scrambled the run of events and it had long told her she'd made love with Poncho among the debris of the first party. 'And dope.'

'Yeah?' Dan asked, his eyes narrowing. 'How?' He took the wine off her and drank some more. His Adam's apple moved up and down twice, and Chess was mildly shocked to find herself enjoying watching it. There was something libidinous about him. The thought of fancying him had occurred to her once or twice before, but only out of curiosity. This was something just one notch further up.

'You're not the only one who takes risks, you know.'

'I love risks.'

'Really? And I had you down as Mr Missionary Position.'

'Only when I'm fucking tribesmen.'

'It was with the most beautiful black man I'd ever seen,' she said, not wanting to spoil the accolade with the codicil that Poncho was the *only* black man she'd ever seen, still.

Dan let out a carnal little groan of imagined pleasure, and she realised she was playing with fire. On one level he was her kid brother and her employer's son, and on another, he was a bi-sexual gypsy, ecstasy on legs. She should turn this new undercurrent between them around right now and go home like Minnie had said. She was in a funny mood, it wouldn't be wise to test herself, she might just go all the way.

'How great?' he asked.

'Fantastic great.' She heard the dreaminess in her own voice and it turned her on a little more, reminding her of the kind of mindless murmurs she uttered during lovemaking. How far should she go with this flirting? She could feel his recklessness.

'What did he do?' His snaky hips brought him a pace nearer. He loosened his tie and, before she could reply, he had his hand on the side of her neck.

'Did he do this?' he asked, and kissed her skin. His lips delivered a mild electric shock.

'I think so.'

'And this?' He took the ridge of her ear in his teeth and ran his tongue around it.

'Yes, he did that.'

'What about this? I bet he did this.' He manoeuvred her skilfully against the only piece of bare wall and lifted her top. With the wine bottle in his hand, he rolled it against her nipples. The cold glass hardened them even more and Chess was mesmerised. They looked delicious, he looked delicious. How crazy must she be?

The door to the gallery was still open and they both heard someone, probably a customer, walk into the showroom. The polished wooden floor creaked under the slow squeaking of expensive leather. With his free hand, Dan gave the door a gentle push shut and lowered his voice.

'And this?' He rolled the empty bottle down her stomach and traced the line of her pubic hair with its rim. She pushed her pelvis forward so her hip bones protruded and her stomach flattened. She saw the cameo from above, like a scene from some film that she had only just started watching.

'Yeah.'

'And was he hard, like this?' He picked her hand off the table and took it towards his groin, but it was a move too much for Chess and she sprung suddenly out of his hold.

'Probably harder,' she breathed in a more familiar tone, knowing she suddenly wanted to diffuse things. 'He was *black*, Dan, you know.'

'Oh fuck, that's so unfair!' he said, dropping the bottle on its side on the table and allowing it to roll into a pile of papers. 'That would have been so good.' He made no attempt to retrieve the moment.

'Sorry.'

'Never apologise,' he told her, stuffing his own hand down the front of his trousers and giving a slinky wiggle to rearrange himself. 'These things either come off or they don't.'

'It hasn't come off, has it?'

'Well, that's what I'm checking.' And so they switched almost immediately back to the roles they were more used to playing. His body movements reverted to the languid again as he lit a cigarette. Hers became more functional, less giveaway.

'It would have been a disastrous mistake,' Chess told him, rearranging her top. She didn't feel in the slightest embarrassed, although she *did* feel wet and a little unsteady. If Poncho had walked in just then . . .

'Well, worth a try anyway,' Dan shrugged, taking in another mouthful of wine.

'You'd try anything though, wouldn't you?'

'Yep!'

They looked at each other and shared a smile at their momentarily aberrant behaviour.

'Go and see what that customer wants,' Chess said affectionately, patting him on the bottom. 'You could be losing precious commission.'

'I will in a minute.' He leant against the desk and offered the bottle. 'Want some more?'

'No, thanks. God, I really don't know why I did that. I must be going out of my mind.'

'Just pushing the boundaries, weren't we? Just pushing the boundaries.'

'More like losing the plot,' she replied, grabbing her keys.

Judith's ambulance screeched to a halt in front of the same hospital that had tried in vain to zap Honor's cancer only months earlier. She tried not to look up at the window of the same ward she had looked out of in such despair so many times, but her eyes were drawn there all the same.

Over the paramedic's shoulder, she could see the car park where she and Honor had sat dumbstruck after the first terrible

X-ray results, unable to find enough composure to start the engine and drive home. How many times since had she parked there, scrabbling for a pound coin, to bring fresh pyjamas or a tempting Marks and Spencer's salad for Honor to force down? And then her mother had eventually found the courage to speak of death openly, begging her family to take her home, to scrap the treatment, to let her die in her own bed. That had been the last visit. It was strange to think that this place could exist without all that.

Cramped with contractions that came every minute, she was hurtled in a wheelchair through the carpeted reception and the tiled beyond. As she looked at the signs – Oncology, Cardiology, Haematology – she tried not to breathe in what smelt like the fumes of death. Flashbacks of subdued consultations, no-hope diagnoses and worst-case scenarios flickered through her mind. It was all there, in horrible living memory.

Thank God for the gas and air which started to take the edge off her clarity of thought, and even more so the pethidine, which was making up a rationality of its own. What was she here for? Should she phone anyone? What was it that Chess didn't want her to tell Nick? Maybe she had dreamt Honor's death. Was she herself still living or had she too died somewhere back in that churchyard or in the ambulance?

Then, with one terrible spasm that sent her back into an arch and her distended stomach pushing into the air, she remembered. Mum was dead, she was alive, and hopefully, the baby was still somewhere in between.

You've got to get on with it, she heard a voice say in her head. *You've got to, because no one else can do it for you now.*

Chapter 15

Getting on with it was exactly what Chess decided she had to put her mind to as well. Her wayward behaviour with Dan had shocked her into realising that she was all but off the rails and no longer knew who she was and what she wanted. For a moment in the storeroom, she had been prepared to go the whole way, and that crazy deviation jolted her into action. She had tried really hard to pin down exactly what it was she was after. Did she still want her life, as she knew it? Yes and no. Did she want Nick to help her sort things out? Yes and no. Was she happy? Yes and no. The only thing she knew for sure was that she had to return to the project she'd left unfinished fifteen years ago.

She had begun to think of herself as two separate people – Chess the wife and mum, and Chess the granddaughter and sister. And once she had decided that Chess the wife and mum was more or less fully (and almost perfectly) formed, she was able to focus her energies on building bridges with Minnie and Della.

Almost right away, her life became easier, or at least her head was clearer. And at first, the risks she was prepared to take along the way seemed worth it.

Bending the laws came easier to Chess than it had ever done to Judith. In the same reckless fashion that had led her to nearly have sex with Dan, she parked illegally in one of three disabled parking slots alongside Barker's department store in Kensington High Street right under the nose of a security guard who had started walking in her direction. She wasn't shopping for herself or the children – she was delivering for Bear, the last man in the world she wanted to get to know better. It was hard to believe things had moved on at such a pace, but she refused to question it. Things *were* moving, and that was the main thing.

'Two minutes?' she asked the guard, flashing a smile that usually got her places.

'Yeah, then you get a ticket.'

It was just before ten o'clock, and the shabby glass doors to the market entrance were still firmly shut. A man leaning against the graffiti and grey paint-effect bricks spent the waiting time eyeing her up hatefully, no doubt stirred by a grimy glass panel in the wall displaying the headless torso of a woman dressed in red leather. Buckled leather wristbands and dog collars were pegged like tasteless Christmas Cards down each side, and stilettos lined the sill.

'C'mon, c'mon, c'mon,' she muttered, more worried about the parking ticket and the creepy man than the tin, which she held tightly in her hand as she peered into the gloom.

The neon striplights were on and she could see someone pulling up the steel shutters of a stall. Suddenly the doors opened and she almost knocked over the woman with the bunch of keys as she ran towards the far end of the covered market, her flat suede boots bouncing off the freshly swept black rubber floor.

She had expected to find Dora Martin unpacking clothes or hugging a polystyrene cup of tea as she had been on the last two occasions, but when she reached lock-up G25, the queen of Kensington Market was nowhere to be seen. Worse still, no one seemed to know when she would be, either, and everyone had remained worryingly tight-lipped. There was nowhere to post the tin, or offload it, and no one to help her decide what to do next.

'Dora's a law unto herself,' the woman on the coffee bar with the milk churns for stools had told her. 'But don't go saying I said that.'

Chess toyed with asking if she could leave the tin with her, but a strong gut feeling forced her – very reluctantly – to take it home. She could leave it in the glove compartment of her car overnight instead and deliver it tomorrow, although that would mean it had been in her possession for two nights, not one. That might be extending the rules a little too far. The locked tin was normally only her responsibility for less than a day at a time, and she'd been able to handle that by weaving it almost invisibly into her routine. She would pick it up from Bear and Della's on her way to or from the gallery and make sure she delivered it to Dora Martin's market stall before her first picture drop the same or next day. That really hadn't been a problem until now, when the intricate weaving started to unravel at speed.

'Damn, damn, damn,' she repeated, thinking on her feet.

Dora's absence was just the icing on the cake of her agitation. There had been a close shave at breakfast when Nick had been rummaging in the Golf's glove box for the windscreen defroster and come back in with the tin. His tone hadn't been exactly accusatory, but Chess had decided he could sense something, so she'd gone into lie overdrive. It should have been the perfect time to reveal all, but her bare-faced deception was out before she could stop it.

'Oh, one of Sam's little friends left it in the car the other day and I keep forgetting to give it back,' she'd said, knowing it looked less like a child's toy than anything she'd ever seen. 'Don't bring it in here, Nick – it'll be lost for ever if you do.'

That little lie had told her exactly what she suspected – that she knew damn well the errands she was running for Bear were far from innocent little jobs. With a wad of cash in her bag and the tin tossed nonchalantly on the front seat as if to prove her lie, Chess had strapped the children in and set off for school.

'Can we have a tape on, Mummy?'

'Silly Songs! Silly Songs!'

'No, Professor Playtime! Professor Playtime!'

'My vote,' Chess had ruled. 'And I vote for . . . let's see – both!'

She'd made a monster effort to make the journey fun, all because of that bloody tin. She hated herself for that. It wasn't right to be nice to the children out of guilt. Next on her list after getting rid of it was to tell Bear she was too busy with gallery work to be able to help out any further.

As she inched her white Golf forward in the heavy traffic, both the money and the tin sat on the passenger seat, emanating a silent but malevolent presence. It had to go. Her days had become a series of deadlines. Children to school. Tin to pick up. Paintings to deliver or gallery to watch. Della and Minnie to see. Tin to drop off. Children to pick up. She was hardly ever at home during the day and Nick had started to ask why.

She lied to him because she felt she had to. He didn't fit into the equation yet. If she had felt more secure, more – it confounded her even to think this, but more *sure* she was doing the right thing – she would have told him. At the moment though, her burgeoning identity was too tenuous. And then there was the tin.

But was there another reason why she wanted to keep Nick and the children out of it? She raked over her thoughts time and time again for the answer, but it wasn't there. The only one that vaguely satisfied her in the end was that it was unfair to confuse Kezia and Sam with vast changes in the terrain of their lives until she herself knew how the land lay. And if she told Nick without telling the children, he would assume she wasn't as serious as she was.

Anyway, the secrecy was rather nice. It was a little like having an illicit affair. She hadn't reckoned on Della's 'yardie' to spoil the fun though.

Bear had had plans for her from their first meeting, and the way he eventually managed to drag her into his stinking lair was really quite beastly. She hadn't been quick enough to realise that exploitation of personal weakness was his speciality, and she had made the silly mistake of showing her vice – namely her need for Della and Minnie – from the start. Because it was so crystal clear to him that she would do anything to buy her way back into Della's life, he basically had no problem naming his price.

'You can do somet'ing for me, eh?' he'd smiled at first. 'Make me happy, an' you make Della happy too, y'nah?'

Her visits to both Minnie and Della's flats were frequent but spontaneous, and if she didn't know exactly when she'd be there, then she couldn't for the life of her work out how Bear seemed to, unless he *always* came back to check up on Della with such regularity.

She started to wonder if he had some sort of invisible homing device fitted to one of the many heavy gold chains around his neck, because he always seemed to manage to turn up within ten minutes of her arriving, even when there'd been no previous sign of him.

Actually, it was nothing so mysterious. All the big bully had to do was to murmur a few threats to Minnie's elderly and easily scared neighbour and he had an ever-present spy. One call on his permanently switched-on mobile and he struck whatever deal he was doing quickly enough to come running from his street corner or park bench or pub bar to break up the happy family party.

He played one sister off against the other by growling threateningly to the first and practically lying on his back hoping to have his tummy tickled by the second. Della – who was used to seeing his teeth – was clearly terrified of any swipe of his paw and Bear was amused that it didn't go unnoticed how she visibly cowered when he came near. It was all part of his master plan. Chess had to be so desperate to help her sister that she would do anything. *Anything*. It wasn't long before he could taste victory.

One night, he decided he had done enough groundwork to lay the first foundation stone, so he took his fists to Della's face and temporarily changed its shape.

'Help me, man,' she begged Chess the next swollen-jawed morning, as if she was reading lines straight from Bear's script.

Chess, who had never seen domestic violence in close-up, was nearly sick on the spot with the anger. When she had calmed down, she dug in her bag and found some Arnica pills which she dished out to Kezia and Sam whenever they fell and bruised themselves.

'Take some of these. They can't hurt you, they're homoeopathic.'

'You don't t'ink it's white tablets I'm scared of, do you?'

'Have you told the police?'

If it hadn't been so painful, Della would have laughed, but it hurt less to cry. 'I want him off my case, y'nah? He's getting to you tru' me, Chess and he ain't goin' to stop, I tell you now.'

'What does he want?'

'You, dat's what he wants, he wants you.' Della had pushed her sister gently on the front of her shoulder.

'I don't understand.'

'He t'inks you can do good t'ings for him.'

'Good things like what?'

'Only he knows dat.'

'Well, I can't. He can't have me.'

'Look at dis face, Chess! I need stitches on my stitches.'

'Would it make it easier for you if I played nice with him?'

'It ain't gonna make it any more difficult, dat's f'sure.'

With scenes like that sitting in the front of her mind, Chess felt she had little choice but to go along with it, so she avoided asking herself too many difficult questions when Bear approached her with the first favour. He told her the locked tin she had to deliver to a market stall in Kensington was a cash float, but when she gave it a rattle, all she heard was the dull thud of something solid and soft. So? she tried to tell herself. Cash floats can just as easily be notes as small change, can't they?

'Jus' drop it off for me, save me some time in my hectic schedule, eh?' he'd whispered diabolically in her ear. Even his body odour had smelt dangerous.

I shouldn't be doing this, I know I shouldn't be doing this, she said to herself every time she allowed herself to think about it, so she stopped thinking about it.

The errand barely made a dent in her day. It fitted in easily around the school run, the gallery deliveries and her new-found priority to spend time with Della and Minnie. All she really cared about was rebuilding a relationship with her natural family. If this small favour meant she had the perfect excuse to see them regularly and it wasn't hurting anyone, then where was the harm? In fact, it wasn't just not hurting anyone, it was preventing anyone from being hurt, if Della's entreaties were anything to go by. Saving her half-sister from a death beating seemed like a reasonable way of buying her way back in.

But, of course, it hadn't been a one-off favour, and now it had turned into something of a routine. The good thing was that Bear really had stopped hitting Della, although the truly bad thing was that Chess still hadn't said a thing to Nick. He continued to have absolutely no idea that since the Notting Hill Carnival, half his wife's life had changed beyond recognition, or that she was fighting to keep the other half intact.

It was one of those conversations she kept meaning to have with him tomorrow. At least Judith was in no position to let the cat out of the bag, though God knows, Chess wouldn't have wished that method of gagging on anyone.

'God!' she suddenly shouted, hitting the steering wheel with both her hands. 'How *could* I have let her drive home that day? What the fuck was I thinking of? Myself, as always, my selfish little fucked-up self. Judith wasn't feigning disinterest in the pub, she was in *labour*. I was angry, yes, I was preoccupied, yes, but for God's sake, Judith was in *labour*. And what did I do about it? Go and nearly have sex with Dan! What the hell is going on with me?'

She forced herself to think the most desolate thoughts. What was her sister going through just now? Was the baby still alive? How were Harry and George and Kate coping? Would Tim let her know if there was any change? The gravity of it hit her full on. She reached for her mobile phone and called Judith's home number. Two cards and a feeble phone message was a woeful response and she must put it right immediately. But what was there to say? Sorry? It was a start. But there was no reply, and no answer machine.

This is ridiculous, she thought. My life is spiralling out of control. My sister's baby is fighting for its life and I haven't even spoken to her about it; my husband thinks I am choosing curtain material at John Lewis when I'm really delivering God knows what to God knows who as a favour for a criminal, and I can't even take my children to meet their great-grandmother. I've got to do something. *Today*. She decided there and then that she would drive to Norfolk that evening, whatever happened.

She had decided in the last twenty-four hours that her short career as Bear's courier had to come to a stop anyway. The nagging doubts had started to throb. In fact, if the problem had been toothache, she would be on the dentist's emergency cancellation list by now.

The pain had really kicked in when Bear had given her an envelop containing 'petrol money' as a 'lickle t'ank you'. Twenty pounds would have seemed generous enough, so counting out twenty tens yesterday, once she was out of the dim council flat he and Della shared and back in the safety of her own car, had really unnerved her.

With the money burning a hole in her jacket pocket, she'd gone straight round to Minnie's where she'd tried her best to offload it, but her grandmother had been an unwilling charity case, and the two hundred pounds remained untouched in the zipped section of Chess's handbag. She couldn't actually *see* the notes but she was reminded every second of the day that they were there just by the burning of bile in her throat.

Somehow, when the flashing police car that she'd seen in her rearview mirror edged between her and the car in front and forced her to pull over, she wasn't at all surprised. The same primitive mechanism of the brain which helps people cope when aeroplanes prepare to crash, or muggers pull knives, kicked in, and Chess was suddenly a third person, watching herself through the television screen from the comfort of her own sofa, having put the children to bed.

The world went fuzzy. The noise of the car engine continuing to run reverberated in her head as the inevitability unfolded. There wasn't enough time to pick up the tin and toss it into her open bag before an officer tapped on her window, even though she could hear herself shouting, '*Do it, do it!*'

'Are you aware it is an offence not to wear your seat belt?' he recited loudly. The window pane was still gliding into the door panel.

'I'm sorry,' she said in a strangled voice, yanking the belt down and pretending to think that was all. She even flicked her indicator as if to pull out. 'I usually do.'

'Turn off your engine, please. I'd like to have a look at your documents.'

'What documents?' she asked, chanting silently to herself, '*Keep calm, keep calm, keep calm. Treat it like an episode of* The Bill. *It will soon be over.*'

'Driving licence, MOT certificate, insurance,' the policeman said, but he was talking on automatic pilot. His eyes flicked to his larger, older colleague, who had opened the passenger door and picked up the tin. Her brain refused to register his question.

'Would you mind telling me what you've got in here?' he asked for the second time.

Chess felt a chill in the pit of her stomach. She was the female lead. 'Um, er . . . cash float for a market stall.' She sounded rehearsed, and she caught sight of her own terrified eyes in the mirror.

'Yours, is it?'

'No, I'm just delivering it.'

'Who to?'

'Um, someone called Dora. She sells jeans and things in Kensington Market, the one at the end on the ground floor . . . and jewellery, and . . . er, sunglasses.' Her voice trailed off.

'That would be Dora Martin, would it?'

'Well, er, I don't know her other name. I'm always in a hurry so I just drop it off and go. I just do it as a favour for friends.' The deficiency of her answers was appalling. She tried her hardest to sound polite and educated.

'And can you give us the names of these – er – *friends*?'

Chess left Della out of it. 'Well, he's a friend of a friend really. I only know him as Bear.'

'So you're dropping off a cash float to someone you don't really know as a favour for someone else you don't really know – have I got that right?'

Remembering the two hundred pounds in the envelope in her handbag, Chess's panic began to break out. This was no TV show. This was really happening and she should start to think.

'It's more complicated than that. That is, it's not, but my reasons for doing it are. He threatens her, and she's terrified. I thought if I did it . . .'

'Perhaps you'd like to tell us all this in the comfort of the police station,' the younger one suggested.

'I can't. I'm supposed to be . . . well, I'm on my way to work and . . .' but she stopped mid-sentence, fading into nothing more than a bitten-lipped frown. When she'd had her first brush with the police at eighteen, her father John had written her a long letter about 'the consequences of stupidity'. She should have read it more carefully. He'd be turning in his grave at the moment.

'You see, I've got children,' she said helplessly, as if this placed her above suspicion. 'I was going to take Sam to the doctor's later. He–'

'I'll drive the car,' the older one said through the passenger door as if she were no longer present. 'You call for a van.

'*What?*' Chess screamed. 'What van?'

But the only response she got was a sharp request to get out of her car and stand on the pavement. No more than ten minutes later, before she even had time to collect her horrified thoughts, a plain white Transit pulled up, and she was bundled in through a sliding side door and told to sit on a bench inside.

She was in a metal cage covered by Perspex, and the smell of disinfectant, as if something grim had just been cleaned up, went straight to the pit of her stomach, making her feel very sick. No, this is not really happening, she told herself again. I'll wake up in a minute. She was looking down on herself again, out of body and mind, watching it happen to someone else.

The real Chess was in a department store, choosing curtain material. She should hurry, Sam had to be at the doctor's . . .

The van accelerated and braked its way through the traffic, sending her swaying about in her pound like a stray dog on the way to Battersea. At least if she really were a dog, she'd get a welcome at the other end. Dear God, please let this be a dream. I'll even accept that I have gone mad if You'll say this isn't true, she prayed as her left shoulder bounced rhythmically off a sharp rivet. She didn't have the presence of mind to move half an inch to the right, and she let the pain continue, as if she had no choice.

She tried to concentrate on practicalities. Who would pick up the children? What was really in the tin? How long would it be before she was allowed her car back? But nothing helpful shaped in her mind at all. She was suspending belief. Thank God Nick was away in Bristol until tomorrow. It was tomorrow, wasn't it?

Surges of hysteria kept swelling inside her, but her body kept them down. As she stared into space, her eyes dulled and her face rigid with control, she adopted the unfortunate air of a woman well-acquainted with being handcuffed inside a police van. It did nothing to dispel the prejudice of her driver as he glanced in his mirror from time to time.

'Is this because I'm black?' she asked one of the policemen as she was ordered back out in an enclosed courtyard at the station. It was not exactly a helpful question, and she didn't really know why she had asked it, except that she had some sort of death wish.

'No, it's because we think you're concerned in the supply of controlled drugs,' he replied curtly. 'Through that door, please.'

'But I'm not! I wouldn't do that! I've got two small children, my husband's a solicitor. What does controlled drugs mean?' she asked as she stumbled across the yard in a dream.

The officer was thrown by her believable naivety. Her words kicked him in the backside, and they caused him to look more carefully at exactly what he had here. She was wearing the same Marks and Spencer brown moleskin trousers that his wife had. She didn't have either a black or a London accent, her nails were clean and her teeth didn't have those telltale shadowy lines on the otherwise white enamel that suggested drug use. He was anxious to open the tin to confirm that her arrest was defensible.

'I'll hand you over to the Custody Sergeant, who'll book you in,' he said once they were inside the building. She noticed the softening of his approach. 'Now, if you give me the key, I can look inside the tin and then we'll know what we're dealing with.'

'But I don't *have* the key. I really am telling you the truth – I just deliver this as a favour.'

'We'll be able to find out if you're lying,' he warned.

'I'm not lying. Honestly, I don't have the key. I just deliver it locked. It's a cash float for a market stall.'

'So you said, but you can save all this for the interview. Now, if you could empty your pockets and remove your jewellery.'

The Custody Sergeant took her handbag from the officer and tipped it out on the desk. The envelope with the money stared up at them both.

'How much is in here?' he asked, flicking through the notes.

'Two hundred pounds.'

'Been to the cash point, have you?'

'No, I've just been paid at work. I deliver paintings for a friend's gallery.' It was her first lie.

The Sergeant shook the handbag again. Tampons and loose change rolled on to the floor, and an empty packet of popped pain relievers landed face up by the telephone.

'Nurofen,' she said quickly. A monumental headache was just beginning to develop.

In a Bristol hotel, Nick had only a vague muzziness behind his eyes. He pulled out a padded dining chair and sat down to a lunch he didn't really want. Either side of him, solicitors talked to more solicitors about the morning's lecture, and he wondered if he was the only one to have found it force-fed tedium. He had yet to discover why his firm had considered 'Enduring Powers of Attorney and the Elderly Client' an important enough area of law to put up £800 for him to attend this two-day course in a four-star hotel. The afternoon's timetable, 'Local Authority Provision for Pensioners, and Its Legal Consequences', looked unlikely to provide an answer, and as for the thought of tonight's 'social evening', it actually made him shudder.

He might be required to attend the discussion, but socialising with people he would never meet again was definitely not in his remit. Home was under two hours away – if he disappeared at five, he could return first thing tomorrow, and no one would be any the wiser. He could surprise Chess and Vienna with a takeaway, play a game of Scrabble, see the children, even if they were sleeping. Scrabble? Scrabble? Wake up, Nick, your wife can't spell and your daughter prefers clubbing, he laughed at himself. Being away always made him play safe with memory. There were more dangerous thoughts he could have entertained himself with, like: Did Chess feel the new gap between them too? How secure was their marriage really? What exactly was she hiding from him? But he wasn't in the mood.

Nick stared at the white tablecloth and toyed with his cutlery, trying to summon the effort to talk to his fellow students, although there really wasn't anyone he liked the look of. Just for something to do, he took his mobile phone out of his briefcase and pressed number one on the speed dial, his own home number.

The answer machine cut in – his voice at the moment – but he had nothing to say to himself so he hung up without leaving a message. Then, still bored, he tried Chess's mobile. It rang for ages. He would have expected either a voice saying, 'The Vodaphone you have called is switched off, please try later,' or his wife to answer. She must have left it switched on in her handbag.

He was almost right. Chess *had* left it switched on, and it was in a bag – a sealed contents bag along with the envelope of cash, assorted make-up, the retrieved tampons and her purse, all safely locked up in a Metropolitan police station cupboard in Central London. No one heard it ring. Its owner was currently incarcerated in a cell with a wooden bench and a stainless steel lavatory, and the custody staff were busy dealing with a violent and very noisy drunk who had just vomited all over the desk.

Nick gave up, switched his own phone off, and turned his attention to the menu. Pumpkin soup, followed by roast vegetables, couscous and lamb. A well-endowed woman solicitor in a timeless herringbone suit sat down next to him. Being chatted up was a regular feature of his life – something to do with his friendly face, easy manner and the very obvious fact that he had no idea how attractive he was.

'I do hope they'll deal with foreign residents who are still domiciled in the UK after lunch,' she said, moving closer.

'Quite,' he replied, thinking he might just leave at four, not five.

'Could I at least make a phone call to arrange for my children to be collected from school?' Chess asked the officer who'd just unlocked the cell door. Her eyes were swollen and she had been left in there without a tissue, so the sleeve on her mock suede shirt was marked with mucus and mascara.

'What time are they out?'

'Three-thirty,' she sniffed.

He led her to the custody desk and dialled for an outside line. 'Just the one call then.'

Be there, Dan, be there, be there. In a way that she would never fully understand, their moment of sex had turned their friendship into something more platonic but more solid than ever. Before he had rolled a wine bottle against her bare breasts and tipped its neck into her pants, she might not have been able to ask him this.

The familiar sound of the gallery's answer machine cut in.

'Oh no, please, please . . . Dan? Hi? Dan?'

'How d'you turn this thing off?' Dan laughed down the phone. 'Oh, let's just ignore it.'

'No! Don't let it tape me. Turn it off – have you turned it off? I can't talk properly or explain or anything, but could you pick the children up for me? Something terrible has happened.'

'What?' For once, he sounded ruffled.

'I can't tell you now. Later, later. But please, can you sort the children? Take them back home to Morgan's and I'll call you later, if I can.'

'Are you in trouble?'

'I've been in a police station cell for the last hour. Make sure you wipe this, will you? I'm in a police station, and I–'

'Fuck, Chess . . . are you OK?'

'No, but yes. No panic, got to go. Don't say a word. I'll speak to you later, if I can.' The policeman tapped at his watch. 'I've got to go. Thanks Dan. Don't worry.'

She was shaking when she put the phone back down. 'He'll have to give them their tea,' she said out loud. The officer recognised shock when he saw it.

'You'll probably be able to give them it yourself.'

'Will I? How?'

He looked straight at Chess and said, 'We've opened the tin.'

'Have you?' Her guess as to the contents was very obviously as good as theirs. 'What did you find?' she asked, as if there was any stupid hope left it would be money and not drugs.

'Like you said – cash.'

Something between a giggle and a sob escaped from her mouth. 'Oh, thank God for that, thank God for that.' She steadied herself with one palm against the wall. 'I thought I'd been really stupid for a moment.'

'I think you have, love, but this time, you've also been bloody lucky.'

'Does that mean I can go?'

'If the search goes your way.'

'Search? What are you going to search?' From some dark recess of her mind, she remembered the practice of smugglers secreting drugs inside them. 'Me? Please don't.'

'Not you, love – your house.'

At which point she clung to her hair and pulled it from the roots just to keep herself from screaming.

Nick's forecast for the rest of his afternoon had been horribly exact. He had almost fallen asleep during the discourse on Local Authority provision for pensioners, and as for 'its legal consequences' – as far as he could gather, you could find these out any time you liked by looking them up in a small white Government handbook, which was what the lecturer appeared to be reading from.

The hands on the wall clock reached two-thirty. Coffee with individually wrapped pieces of cardboard was served. Just as he was plotting his escape, the speaker moved in on him and started trying to sell him a ridiculously expensive set of books on the subject, and before he knew where he was, he'd put in an order for his firm. It was a stupid move on two counts. One – he was now destined to become office expert on anything to do with old people, and two – he'd drawn attention to himself, which meant that his breakout would have to wait. He made another quick call home, but got the answer machine again. Chess must have left early to pick up the children.

In Clapham, a small convoy of unmarked police cars made its way around the Common and through the identical streets at the direction of its nauseous prisoner, who was handcuffed to a WPC in the front vehicle. People looked, but only because it was unusual to see three identical Sierras in a row. None of them could possibly have known its mission.

'It's here, the green door,' Chess said, straining to see any activity through the windows of her home. She had tried to persuade the police to let her call home, to make sure it was empty as she thought, but they had laughed at the idea. Thank God Nick was away. She'd been spending a lot of time bargaining or thanking God in the last few hours.

Vienna might just be in, although she was usually good at getting herself to college when she should. Not for the first time, Chess saluted Sonya for giving the child – no, she wasn't a child any more – such a reasonable grounding in bolts out of the blue.

'Is it possible to undo these handcuffs?' she asked the WPC. 'We've not been living here long.'

'I'm sorry, but it's procedure. Stick your hand in your jacket pocket and I'll walk close if you like.'

'Thanks,' Chess said, grateful for small mercies. The attitude of the police had changed significantly since the tin had been opened.

It was still just like a slow nightmare though. Being locked in a cell was bad enough, but it was at least an ordeal she had had some previous knowledge of. Being let into your own home by hostile strangers wearing the badge of authority was ten times worse. Like they had a bigger right to be there than her. Maybe they did. What right did she have to anything any more?

Everything was just as she had left it that morning, although to think it was only a few hours ago was almost inconceivable. It was like one of those experiences she'd read about, just before death, floating up near the ceiling, unable to get back into your own body. It was how she felt almost all the time lately.

The morning's post was on the floor where the doormat would go if she ever got round to buying one, the milk was still on the table quietly going off, and Kezia had forgotten her school coat – it was on top of a heap of tumble-dried clothes on a kitchen chair.

Chess could hardly stand for the weight of love she carried for her daughter just then. Little Kez, her big eyes, her second teeth that her mouth had yet to grow into, her passion for handstands and shells and singing. It was too much to bear to think of her at her new school, trying her best to fit in, to find friends, to belong, and Chess nearly gave in to the senseless urge to run to her, tell her exactly how much she loved her, what she meant to her. She would find Sam too, and let him climb on to her and ask her for chocolate and she would promise him all the chocolate in the world, for ever.

Forgetting herself for a moment, she went instinctively to pick up Kezia's coat but the handcuffs cut roughly into her wrists as her whole arm was yanked back down by her jailer, more by involuntary action than force.

'Ow. I was just–'

'Well, I shouldn't if I were you.'

The vignette had been clocked. Within seconds, another officer was at the chair, rummaging through Kezia's innocent little pockets. A conker, skewered and tied to a dirty piece of string, fell to the floor and bounced.

It was the moment Chess knew should have come a long time ago, the moment the whole ghastly drama became real, the moment the gravity of it all hit home with one fist-clenched iron punch right in her gut. A soft but terrible noise tried to find its way out of her body but she held it in her mouth, along with her breath. Her lips trembled and her tears came rolling down her face one after the other. Eventually, when she finally just had to breathe, the moan came out merely as a long controlled sigh, which the WPC mistook as a kind of submission and ignored.

Chess felt then, possibly for the first time since the chaos had begun, that her life was stretched to breaking point. Any minute now, it would snap and it was too late to do anything to stop it. Well, she would let it snap and then when it was all over, she would sort out the mess. She would tell Nick, tell Bear, take the children to meet Minnie, and get Della in to a safe house. She would go and see Judith, mourn for Honor and John and get to know the new baby. She had to do all this or she would die.

Four other male officers who had disappeared in a starburst effect into the bowels of the house on arrival were now back in the kitchen. They had opened drawers, shaken bedclothes, and undone suitcases. The cistern lid of the upstairs lavatory was still lying on the tiled floor.

The boss, whose wife had the same moleskin trousers at home as Chess and whose children used the same Body Shop play soap he'd noticed in the bathroom, spoke matter-of-factly to her. 'We're not going to find anything, are we?'

Chess shook her head.

'Then we'll get you back to the station, wrap up the paperwork and let you go. Don't worry, we haven't made too much of a mess.'

'Can I leave a note for my family?'

'If you like, but you should be back here in an hour yourself, so you can talk then, can't you?' He bent down and picked up something from the floor. As he uncurled his hand and put it on the table, Chess saw it was Kezia's lucky conker. His radio crackled and he started to speak into it.

'Yes . . . no, nothing here, wild-goose chase . . . Yes, right, we'll come back – over.'

Over. If only it was.

Nick didn't even make it to five o'clock before he took flight, which meant he was home by seven. The lights were out and house was empty and for one unpleasant moment, a sensation prickled through him that they might have had burglars. The videos were stacked in uneven piles on the sitting-room floor and in the upstairs loo the cistern lid was off. But nothing was missing, apart from his wife and children.

Then suddenly, in a flurry of noise and disorder, they were all back. The children were hyper and, for once, Chess made no effort to calm them down.

'Where have you been?' Nick asked, appearing from the darkness of the kitchen and making his wife leap out of her skin. For a moment, she'd thought he was Bear or the detective, back for more ransacking. 'I've been trying to call all afternoon.'

'Don't ask,' Chess replied, praying he'd take her at her word. 'It's been such a bad day we've been to McDonald's for supper. I couldn't face the thought of cooking.' She missed out the fact that it had been a takeaway and that the children had eaten their Happy Meals in the car whilst she collapsed into demented hysteria outside the gallery, trying to relate it all to

Dan. His only reaction was to appear mildly impressed and then to offer her a smoke to calm her down.

'Why? What's happened?' Nick asked. 'I thought we might have had visitors.'

'In what way?' she asked, her throat dry.

'The videos and the airing cupboard – there are towels all over the landing.'

'Oh, that's me. I started spring-cleaning and then it all went pear-shaped. Morgan sent me off to a last-minute frame sale in Brighton. I didn't think you were coming home tonight.' She listened to herself incredulously. What am I saying? Why can I not tell him? I *must* let him in.

Nick listened to her high-speed gibberish and thought about the gap. 'No, nor did I. I just felt this terrible urge . . .' He came over to her and put his arms up her sweater. He needed to pretend everything was as it always had been, even if it wasn't. 'That's better.'

'Daddy!' Kezia shouted. 'I can see what you're doing and that's rude!'

'No, it isn't,' Chess corrected. 'It's lovely.' God, it really was. Too lovely to spoil with the truth.

Nick was amazed – for once, she hadn't wriggled away from a public display of affection. He couldn't help himself collapse inwardly with love for her. It didn't matter what was going on, he would want her for ever, whatever. Devotion beamed out of his puzzled face. She caught the rays and could hardly bear it. Maybe she should tell Nick last. Tell Bear first. Clear the way.

'So what was this frame sale like then?'

'Oh, pretty much as you'd imagine one to be.'

'Lots of frames, and a big board saying SALE, that sort of thing?' Nick teased.

'You weren't there too, were you?'

Confrontation wasn't his style so he pretended to buy Chess's story for the moment. Spring-cleaning in the autumn wasn't so peculiar, but the sale in Brighton Nick knew was a downright lie. Morgan had only just been on the phone saying she had been to it herself and Chess would have to deal with the delivery tomorrow. She would have to cover her tracks better than that if she was going to continue in whatever lie this was.

At three in the morning, Nick crept from the marital bed and went downstairs. He couldn't sleep with his wife tossing and turning as much as she was. It wasn't her movements that kept him awake, it was just that he was too afraid to imagine her dream.

He was starring in it actually, staring blankly at her through the bars of her locked metal cage, shaking his head intermittently as a jailer with a huge bunch of keys read her the charge.

'Francesca Jacoby, on the 23rd of October at Kensington, you had in your possession a quantity of cocaine, a controlled drug of class A with intent to supply it to another, contrary to section 4(1) of the Misuse of Drugs Act 1971. You do not have to say anything but it may harm your defence if you fail to mention something now that you later rely on in court. Do you understand?'

Chess understood only too well. It meant her life had been on the line, dream or no dream.

Chapter 16

Little Will Law's life really had been on the line. He should still have been nestling in his mother's womb, putting on those last few pounds, developing surfactant for his tiny lungs, shedding the furry hair on the surface of his skin, growing nails and eyelashes and taking his nourishment from nature. His ante-natal world should have been full of the sounds of heartbeats and the occasional babble of family life or the gentle singing of his mother as she put his siblings to bed.

Instead, he found himself cruelly ejected from his restful watery pink bed and thrust into a hard white light where everything hurt. His perspex incubator was no substitute for his mother's womb, and his food now came through a naso-gastric tube which had been pushed up his amazingly small nose to connect to his baby stomach. His only lullabies were the bleeps from his monitor. Sometimes, he could feel himself escaping to somewhere more peaceful, but big hands or cold tubes always pulled him back.

Because the first tentative hours of his life had come with no guarantee, his traumatised mother had bonded more with the machine than the baby inside. She would sit at her son's grey plastic cot, staring at the undulating neon waves, the peaks and troughs and the flashing numbers as they flicked up and down at whim, as if she could control them by surveillance alone.

She knew that the triangle of discs on his scrap of a chest were electro-cardiograph leads to check his heart-rate, that the sandwich probe around his foot that made his toes shine with a red light measured the amount of oxygen going around his bloodstream, and that the drip in the top side of his doll-sized hand was called an intra-venous infusion. What she still didn't know was if he was going to live or die.

The doctors and nurses were careful to speak in terms of hope rather than certainty.

'A baby at thirty-three weeks' gestation has a very good chance.'

'But is he going to be all right?'

'He's doing his best.'

'But will he make it?'

'You would be surprised how many do.'

Judith needed Will to live really badly, not least because she considered his plight to be all her fault. The staff on the unit were referring to him as an IUGR baby – inter-uterine growth retarded – which had been loosely explained without apportioning blame. But Judith knew exactly what had stunted her son's development. It was her total lack of ante-natal love. She hadn't paid him any proper attention at all. She had been too busy being a child herself to realise it was someone else's turn, too busy poring over a life that had already ended to divert her energy into one that was just beginning.

The only time she had been allowed to cuddle him – if cuddle is the right word for the way she cased his infinitesimal frame with her hesitant palms – was directly after the birth. It had been a touch and go delivery, but the baby was alive and breathing on his own, so as she held him and tried not to scare herself half to death by his size and his transparent pale skin, the heavy droplets of anxiety and effort hanging in the wet air of the emergency delivery suite had temporarily evaporated. For a while, it had almost been a case of business as usual, but really it was just the lull before the storm, a blessed interlude to hang on to in the frantic times ahead.

It had all been going on at such a medically efficient rate that by the time Tim arrived, his only role as a father was to listen, watch and hope. This last undertaking was the most difficult, made almost impossible when the midwife had produced a Polaroid camera and inadvertently let everyone know just how tenuous their son's life expectancy was. Things were looking pretty bad when even the photographs had to be instant. Then the grunting had started.

'Facial oxygen, please,' the midwife had called urgently to someone in the corridor, 'and let's get this one up to the neonatal unit straight away.'

So the baby had gone one way and his parents had gone the other. Judith was wheeled to a room a discreet distance from all the other mothers to save her from the pain of any referred post-natal elation, and there she and Tim stayed, alone, for a whole hour, waiting. One strange and fleeting comfort occurred to her while they sat thinking.

'There's no one we should phone, is there?'

'Like who?' Tim had asked.

'No, I mean, it's not exactly a question – there really is no one else who needs to be told, is there? It's just you, me and the children in this, that's all.'

'Yeah, that's all,' Tim reassured. 'Just us lot, just the six of us.'

What Judith meant, and what Tim understood, was: 'Is it OK if I leave Chess out of this for the moment?' The fact that she needed permission to accept such a radical thought just underlined it for her. Things had changed. If this same crisis had happened when she'd had Kate, or George, or Harry, the Lovell family emergency hotline would have been in constant use. Not now. There didn't seem to be the same need. For a moment, life had almost seemed simple.

An auxiliary nurse brought them a cup of tea and a midwife popped her head round the door to smile hopefully at them and offer Judith some more Paracetamol, but no one brought them any proper news at all. In that dire dumbstruck time, they'd thought of his name – Will – in the hope that he might just manage to live up to it.

Judith was now something of an instant expert on her son's condition. It had been agony in the first few hours to watch his body struggling to take every breath and she could see the outline of all eight miniature ribs each time he did, but she knew she couldn't breathe for him, so she quickly latched on to the textbook language being bandied about the place and gained strength from that instead.

Her son wasn't breathing too fast, he was 'tachnypnoeic', he wasn't using his tummy muscles to breathe, he was 'employing his sub-costal and inter-costal muscles', he wasn't grunting, he was 'in recession', and he wasn't being fed on mere sugar and water but 'dextrose'. She clung to the medical terminology as if, somehow, her literacy increased Will's chance of survival.

She tried not to look to see which couple the priest headed for when he made his frequent visits to the ward – she was only thankful it wasn't her turn yet. He tried to offer her a reassuring smile on more than one occasion, but so far she couldn't even meet his eye. He was like the Grim Reaper in a crew neck.

Post-natal euphoria had been thin on the ground this time, but when the consultant did his rounds on day two and told Judith she could start feeding him, she could have fallen to her knees and worshipped the God she had lately forsaken. Her faith, however, was short-lived, overtaken almost immediately by sheer panic.

'How?' she'd asked. 'How do I feed him?' The baby was so tiny and her breasts were getting bigger and bigger by the minute. Her nipples were totally out of proportion to Will's minuscule mouth – and anyway, he was all wired up. She could no more hold him to her than climb in there with him.

'You express your own breast milk and we feed it to him by tube,' the doctor said. 'His suck and swallow mechanism has only just developed so he won't be able to take more than 1ml of milk every four hours. You will still be producing colostrum, so he'll get the benefit of all those wonderful antibodies, and then when your real milk comes in, it will be so much more readily absorbed by his gut.'

'Isn't there something safer than ordinary breast milk?'

'There's nothing ordinary about breast milk,' he smiled. He was used to this reaction from even the most pro-breastfeeding mother. It was common for parents to rely so heavily on the medical process that when it came to taking responsibility for themselves, they very often couldn't.

'It's much better for him,' he emphasised, telling her what he felt sure she knew already.

'Than what?'

'Than formula milk.'

'But that is an option?' Judith asked. She could hardly believe what she was saying. She was the archetypal middle-class mother who spurned everything from bottles to dummies to tinned baby food and disposable nappies. At one time she had been the National Childbirth Trust's spokesperson in a media 'Breast is Best' campaign. This was ridiculous.

'Well, it's always an option, but . . .'

The crux was, she just didn't trust herself to do Will any favours. If she had heaped this much grief on him so far, how could she expect him to react favourably to anything else she offered him? Her body had let him down, and it might do so again. What if her milk dried up? What if it was deficient because of all her sadness? What if it just didn't suit him in the same way that her womb obviously hadn't?

Her adamant decision not to breastfeed was completely out of character, but she really did believe that anything she produced would be rancid. As far as she was concerned, this baby had got where he was entirely under his own steam, and much as she wanted to help him, she felt she had nothing to give of any substance. If Will could be sustained in a sterile, antiseptic, decontaminated condition, then he might just have a chance. She certainly didn't want to make matters worse by offering him her own lamentable efforts. Feeding him something from a body that had already failed him would just add to his vulnerability.

Tim had tried to make her see sense. He'd even called her decision irrational, but he'd let her make it all the same. 'Look Tim; formula milk is designed to gives babies life, not to kill them off,' she'd said.

Nevertheless, a breast pump sat next to her hospital bed and she used it three times a day, mechanically and clinically, taking her five or six fluid ounces obediently along to the 'milk room', where she would stick it in a freezer for it to be ultimately thrown away. She sometimes compared it with the other bottles sitting there and decided that hers looked almost green in comparison. Keeping up her milk production was important, everyone said, so that if and when Will was strong enough to feed directly from the breast, she could think again. But try as the nurses and her husband did to persuade her that, ultimately, breast really was best, she remained utterly deaf to their gusts of advice.

Chess on the other hand was more than open to advice, although it just so happened that with Honor dead, Judith ensconced, and Nick too much a part of the problem to be approached, shoulders to cry on were in short supply. The only ones available were Dan's, and she preferred not to get his wet. Although their ten-minute flash of sexual desire had been and very definitely gone, she wasn't entirely unaware it had happened and couldn't be running to him on a daily basis. Anyway, she might need him for the next big crisis.

The day after her brush with the police, she was physically sick with fear. Being in bed had merely made her feel worse and she'd hardly noticed Nick wasn't next to her when she crawled out from under the covers and drifted downstairs.

'You OK?' he'd asked from the sofa when he saw her dishevelled naked body wandering aimlessly through the sitting room at dawn.

'Oh God!' Chess clutched her breasts.

'Sorry, I thought you knew I was here.'

'I came to find you,' she lied, her voice rough with sleep. 'Have you been down here all night?'

'Yep.'

'Why?'

'You were talking too much.'

'Talking?'

'In your sleep.' It was a trap, and he didn't like himself much for laying it.

'Was I? What did I say?'

'You tell me,' he said mysteriously.

She padded over to him and sat on the edge of the cushions until he budged over. Then she lifted her legs and lay next to him and pulled the throw over them both. She lay there stiffly, uncomfortable and cold, wishing she felt like making love. Nick was fully clothed and difficult to touch. She wanted to tell him everything, but he was too remote, unreachable somehow, and the words just stayed inside. If she looked his disappointment in the eye, she would hate herself even more. But how *could* she have risked so much?

'Cuddle me,' she asked pathetically, so he did, as best he could, considering. When she eventually got up, she took the throw with her and draped it round her shoulders like a cloak.

'It suits you,' Nick said. 'You should wear it like that more often.' But even he wasn't in the mood for flippancy and it was no surprise when she didn't reply.

Chess only just managed to feed the children their breakfast and get them out of the house with their father before having to rush for the lavatory. Afterwards, with her forearms resting on the loo seat and her head still staring into the ceramic bowl, she tried to muster enough courage to get through the rest of the day.

'Oh God,' she groaned. Was it too late for prayers? She splashed her face with cold water, and rinsed her mouth. Then she re-tied the scarf around her hair and stared long and hard at her reflection in the bathroom mirror. She hardly recognised herself. She looked ill. Sick in the mind maybe.

'Well, it's your own stupid fault,' she told the stranger. 'You've brought this all on yourself.'

She had forfeited the precious right to look after her children and the privilege of being loved by a man who trusted her. These things were no longer her prerogative. If she lost them, it would serve her right. In some ways, she even thought she should give them up of her own free will.

But the idea of life without them was too much to bear, and it pulled her up, away from the sick bowl and into Sam's bedroom, where she pulled back his curtains and looked out over the family garden. The slide was still out, although the late October days had rendered it almost useless. Her mind flipped back to the barbecue evening after the carnival, when Kezia had scraped her bottom and Sam had fetched her the bean bag. It seemed so long ago. How differently she would do things now.

There *must* be a way to negate my crime, she thought, but if only she knew what her crime actually was. In her version, she was the victim, not the perpetrator – but the fact remained, her stupidity had nearly screwed it for the people she loved best. She still hadn't been to see Judith and the baby – her arrest had seen to that.

'I have to make up for it,' she commanded herself as her tongue caught the taste of sick on her gums. 'I have to.' Maybe when she'd achieved the good deeds she now owed almost everyone she cared about, she could begin to find out who she really was too. Until then, she had no right to even try.

Facing the world was the last thing she felt like doing, but she dressed gingerly, cleaned her teeth and went downstairs. The tin containing Bear's 'cash float' was still burning a hole in her handbag, and as long as it remained in her possession her stomach would refuse to hold down any food. She never wanted to be anywhere near him ever again, but she knew she had to return his money – including the two hundred pounds gift – before she could even begin to claim her life back.

The tin radiated with an evil spell which had so nearly worked on her she didn't have the nerve to even look at it again. Getting shot of it was the number one priority.

Her car lurched through the traffic for nearly an hour. The route to Bear country was no longer a problem – she could almost do it with her eyes shut – but today it felt different. She was acutely aware of her driving. Every time she passed a police car, a belch of yesterday's fear and today's nausea rose in her throat. She scraped her gears, hesitated for too long at junctions and turned on wipers instead of indicators.

As she approached the moneyed enclave of Holland Park, only a gentle stroll from the collective poverty of Della's ghetto, she became irrationally frightened that she was going to collide with one of the chauffeur-driven Jaguars or Bentleys. If the rusty bumper of her little Golf found itself in contact with anything that assertive, she could be back staring at that stainless steel lavatory again.

She passed Ladbroke Grove Tube station where the flower stall was just opening up and she thought briefly of the carnival again. A tear escaped. This was not the way things were meant to have turned out, not at all. Then she swung at the last minute into a left side street, and left again towards the grim tower block that held so many prisoners.

A big white car – a reject from the 1980s – was practically on her back wheels and she glanced into her rearview mirror to see the dual bulks of two men filling the front seats. With her hands shaking and gripping the wheel, she started a tearless whimper. One of them was Bear, it must be. What did he want from her? If the police saw her with him, they could arrest her again, and she'd be back in that . . . her heart was pumping out such an intense adrenaline she no longer felt safe to drive. The road came to an end, so she pulled into a turning space and parked, wondering if she had the guts to confront him.

The white car manoeuvred aggressively and one of the men gesticulated angrily at her, but it didn't matter, neither of them was Bear. Her lips trembled with relief and she sniffed into her shirt sleeve. It was still marked with the mascara and mucus from yesterday and she caught the smell of police cell disinfectant on it too. She'd put it on for penance, to remind her the job was not yet done.

Della's bike was chained to the railings outside her door on the sixth floor and a duvet cover hung over a clothes dryer on the balcony they shared with next door, but that was no evidence that anyone was in or out. Chess sat in the car for a while longer, still not sure that she could face him if he was there. Then she pictured her children at school – Sam in a paint overall, Kezia yo-yoing in the playground – and she braced herself to get out.

One little plan was germinating in her head. Instead of them all being dragged screaming into Bear's dark, unpleasant world, why couldn't she drag Della into Minnie's, or both of them into hers, or at least into a better world than the one Della currently inhabited? Punching a way out of terminal abuse for her sister would make her feel she was worthy again, eligible to take her place in the innocent bubble in which her husband and children still lived. Bear was not the way back to Della, scary as hell or not. Even as the plan pushed its first leaves above the soil, she could see it wouldn't survive. Cross-pollination was not the way.

Up on the concrete corridor, she noticed that someone had kicked in the toughened glass panels between the black railings since the last time she'd been there; one of them lay whole on the patch of grass below. Was it temper? *His* temper?

The flat was in darkness, but a mellow pulsing of music was coming from within. She knocked, then she shouted, then she knocked again. The tin just had to be handed back before she went home, otherwise she had no right to any happiness ever again. If the worst came to the worst, she could just post it through the letterbox with a note explaining.

Eventually, someone came to the door, but whoever it was only opened it as far as the chain would allow. Chess thought she recognised the glimpse of fingers.

'Della?'

'He's lookin' for you,' her sister spluttered with a split lip. 'He t'inks you got his money 'cos Dora never got it yesterday.'

The horror just had no end. Acid fear rose in Chess's throat. 'Has he hit you again?'

'Yeh, and he's gonna hit you if you don' watch it. Wha' you doin' here? You mus' be mad.'

'I've come to return the tin. Look, it's here, and so is the two hundred he gave me for petrol . . . I can't do it for him any more Della, I'm sorry.'

'Wha' happened? He t'inks you might a' give his name to de police 'cos dey come askin' for him yesterday in de road.'

Chess pushed away the thought that she was even deeper in this than ever. 'No, I didn't. I spent the day in the cells yesterday because of him. They searched my house because of him. I can't . . . I just can't . . .' She began crying again, and the chain came off. The door opened enough for Chess to see Della's fresh bloody cut and yellow swollen eyes. 'Can I come in?'

'Now I know you mad. You gonna see a diff'rent side to him now, Chess. You better t'ink of somet'ing to say, quick, or he might beat you like he beat me.'

'OK, look, take the tin – the police forced it open, not me. And give him the two hundred back as well, then I don't owe him anything.'

Della took both without hesitation. 'You and me see each other soon, yeh? When he's got his pennies and he's calmed down a bit.'

'Yes,' Chess wept. 'I think I'm losing my head, Della. I love you, I do, I don't want it all to go wrong, I'm going to help you, I promise I am.'

Her sister was touched but embarrassed. 'You jus' look after yourself, eh? Don't worry 'bout me.'

'Please, let me in. We can sort something out together. I'm desperate, Della. I'm busy screwing up my life here.'

'I'll see you at Minnie's tomorrow den. I'm not in de mood for another beatin' today, know what I mean? It's for yuh own good.'

And with that, the door was shut and chained once more.

Judith Law was beginning to feel almost like part of the furniture in the neo-natal unit. In the same way a nervous flyer latches on to the body language of the aircraft cabin crew, so she had learnt to read the different facial expressions employed by the consultants and junior doctors. Unlike the nervous flyer though, her heart had stopped lurching every time she heard a wing flap – or monitor – make a funny noise, but then, this turbulent flight had already lasted four days.

The sweetest thing was, Will was now allowed to wear his own clothes, and instead of lying there naked, he sported a tiny blue and white striped T-shirt given to him by the children. Tim had brought them in for a few minutes after school to meet their new brother and, in turn, they had each put their hands into Will's incubator and placed them, as instructed by the nurse, on his head. They were told all about minimal handling and how premature babies prefer light pressure to rhythmical patting, and they took every word to heart, terrified of doing anything to make him squeak or squirm.

Kate was sure she saw Will smile when she was allowed to put the velour penguin in with him. Even that had been sterilised by a machine.

The six of them, the new improved version of the Law family, practically filled the place up. Well, the sixth only weighed three pounds and he was the reason they were all there anyway, but Judith did like to think of them like that once they had all left for homework and chips. Four children, two adults. Big enough to fill the table at Christmas, small enough to keep it simple. Oh, it was becoming such a blessed relief, to finally let go. She was even pleased that Chess had kept away. What her reasons were she couldn't guess, but she didn't want to. That kind of stuff was too much like hard work.

A full and healthy life for Will began to look more and more hopeful, which was why Judith agreed to try and catch up on some much-needed sleep by spending a night on the ward one floor below. She had been in one of the bedrooms on the unit until now, but another mother was in more need, and she could see everything was under control.

Her eyes were closed almost before her head hit the pillow and it seemed as if she'd been gone for ever when she caught the lift back up to the unit the next morning, after breakfast.

It was just as well she hadn't witnessed for herself the speedy activity around her son's incubator at 3 a.m. Whilst she'd been flat out with exhaustion downstairs, a vigilant freshly-rested night nurse had looked into Will's cot and noticed the familiar but sinister signs of a distended abdomen. Within the hour, it had blown up like a balloon and given him the scaled-down look of a famine victim. Tell-tale bloodstained bile was detected in his naso-gastric tube and a check of his nappy showed no reassuring black meconium like the nurse had hoped.

As Judith walked over to greet her son, the first thing she noticed was that he had been stripped naked. More alarmingly, his feeding tube had been taken out, and she could see even from a distance that he looked all wrong. Two steps closer, and she discovered that, overnight, he had been transformed from a little mannequin into a bloated sparrow.

A consultant was talking to a junior doctor and waving an X-ray. 'Here, you see? The classic signs of necrotising enterocolitis. At thirty-three weeks, the gut is immature, and its motility is slow, so if you force milk on the baby too quickly, you run the risk of NEC. This mother has chosen not to breastfeed so she increased the risks herself, although it can happen across the board. There are many stages of severity and it is too early to predict the outcome here. All we can do is stop feeding and treat with triple antibiotic therapy.'

Judith remained utterly still. The world had stopped turning yet again. For 'too early to predict the outcome' she heard 'this baby could die'. She had left Will for just a few hours and in her absence something terrible had happened. But then she was wearing a big label pinned to her clothes, wasn't she? *This mother has chosen not to breastfeed.* It was as if every decision she made concerning her son's comfort and survival led to pain.

The noise that came from her belly was not unlike the one she had made in the churchyard when her waters had broken. The consultant looked embarrassed and the student sloped off, leaving the same observant nurse who had picked Will's condition up in the first place to deal with the fallout. She was less well-rested now, but still faultless at her job, and she explained in the mix of layman's terms and medical terminology that Will had developed a gut infection, that he would be nil by mouth for ten days to give his digestion a rest, and that they were all hoping for the best.

'Please may I see the priest?' Judith sobbed. 'Please may I see the priest?'

Chapter 17

The very next post after Minnie and Chess's exchange about birthdays brought a letter for Minnie from Reuben with more than cause for celebration. He was coming to Britain! Not for ever, and not for any special occasion, but just for her! She couldn't remember the last time anyone did anything for that reason alone, but Reuben had finally saved enough both for the flight and to pay someone to run his shop for the sole purpose of being with her.

Minnie forsook the covered food market that week in favour of the West End and the biggest Marks and Spencer she knew. She had in her mind a smart red woollen coat and a black hat. Reuben liked hats, he always had, ever since he'd first seen her in her yellow ribboned straw boater climbing up the gangplank to the troopship in the spring of 1948. There were small mercies in living apart, like the comforting knowledge that he would never see the brown tea cosy she'd been pulling over her wiry hair for the last few winters.

His latest missive had travelled everywhere with her since it had arrived, its promise of reunion changing the colour of her otherwise typically grey days. *I am coming to take you away,* he wrote, bold with fantasy. *We are going to the country to sit in front of real fires and sleep in warm beds and pretend we have been together for ever.*

That particular crazy daydream was now tucked back in its envelope and sat on the kitchen table in Minnie's flat. Also on the table was the shoe-box containing all his other precious flights of fancy. It had made a rare trip out of her bedroom so she could indulge in its years of pillow-talk between the chopping of the lamb and the baking of the coconut cakes. She had needed to find room in her imitation leather handbag for a fat envelope full of money that Della had given her that morning so she had been forced to give up her latest treasure and leave it with its predecessors. Anyway, anything with Reuben's writing on it was too dear to run the risk of losing, especially when she could carry it with her, word for word, in her head.

The notion that they could escape anywhere together was too far-fetched to expect it ever to actually happen, let alone the fact that she had never even stayed in a hotel or spent any time in the countryside. *Her* England was made of concrete. She realised the rolling green fields and the rugged coastlines were out there somewhere because she had seen them on her television, but they belonged to other people, in the same way that the lush hills of Jamaica had once belonged to her. The only open places she ever visited were either in her memory or her imagination.

She had been battered enough by disappointment over the years to know realistically that the dreams Reuben nurtured were mostly just dreams, but even so, the dates of his next visit were now circled in the calendar of her mind, making her feel like a teenager dancing towards her first date. The prospect of them simply being in the same country put a samba in her step at any rate, and like an adolescent in love, she chose to spend the waiting time picking through the minutiae of their every exchange.

The wait seemed eternal but it was made light by the letters, some of which transported her right back to the slatted sea-splashed deck of the *Windrush*.

Reuben's flight came in next Friday. His nephew who ran a taxi firm was picking him up from the airport and taking him back to Portsmouth for the weekend. According to Reuben, he was then borrowing a little runabout from the taxi fleet, driving to collect Minnie and, thereafter, the world was their oyster.

You pack your bag and you wait for me on Monday. You

don't go worrying over your family, you don't go worrying over your pennies, you just put on your smile and bring your heart. We will have this time before we die, Minnie George.

She didn't like that last sentence at all, but he was right. Their love might still feel as new as the day they first brushed hands a week out of Kingston dock, but their bones didn't. One day, time would run out for one or other of them, and they would have to resume things in heaven. At least they could be sure Gladstone would never be able to spoil things for them there.

But for the while, she still trod this earthly soil and at this particular moment, the crowded pavement of Oxford Street. This Marks and Spencer was much larger than she'd imagined and everything she fingered was either much softer or much thicker than anything she had ever worn. If it hadn't been for the money Della had given her this morning, she wouldn't even have been able to afford to look. Most of her clothes came from the market. If they didn't come from there, they came from Della, and when they came from Della, she asked no further questions.

Accepting suspicious gifts was something she had learned to live with, but accepting money when she didn't know where it had come from was something she had never done before. Reuben's words had hit home though. If they *were* going to have this time together before they died, then at the very least, she wanted to look nice for it. In that way, the two hundred pounds in the brown envelope that her granddaughter had thrust into her hand this morning had come along at just the right time. It was odd that she'd been able to take it from Della and not from Chess just a few days earlier, especially since it was the very same package. Della knew she didn't need to buy Minnie's love, and it was important that Chess didn't think she needed to either.

The rows of red coats thrilled her. There were buckles, hoods, fur collars and belts, there were waterproof, shower-proof, wool and nylon, there were padded ones, flimsy ones, long ones and short. What there weren't, not by Minnie's standards anyway, were cheap ones, but for once, she wasn't using that as her guide. She heaped as many of the pretty things as she could carry over her broad strong arm and wandered off in the direction of the changing room, already wearing one of them in her imagination.

Her head was so full of Reuben that she had completely forgotten about leaving the shoe-box full of airmail letters on the kitchen table, but then she never really considered them of any consequence to anyone other than Gladstone anyway, no more than reading a magazine love story would be. It was all pie-in-the-sky, a little bit of harmless delusion to soften the regrets. She and Reuben belonged together only in their joint imagination somewhere over the island sky. She thought she might just buy him a tie though, just in case this hotel had a dress code.

Reuben Fisher's plans didn't seem at all harmless to Della George though, not when most of them seemed to revolve around the planned theft of something that wasn't his.

She'd reached her grandmother's flat early with the intention of raiding the fridge for food if only her cut lip would stand up to the chewing. She was starving, because she hadn't been able to move her jaw enough in the last twelve hours to do anything other than sip, but there was never anything worth eating at the home she shared with Bear anyway. Plenty to smoke, and usually something to drink, but rarely anything as life-sustaining as food.

Minnie was the only source of comfort she had and so Della had beaten the wellworn path to her door, but today the old lady had been in one of her bustles to get somewhere and any sympathetic noises had disappeared into thin air.

'What you doin' here so soon?' her grandmother had asked.

'Meetin' Chess. She wan' to speak wid me on somet'ing.'

'For why?'

'She don't say. Where you goin'?'

'Well, I t'ink it's time I bought a hat.'

'Wha' for? Someone gettin' married?'

Minnie had laughed and laughed about this for the rest of

the time it took her to get ready and go. Della couldn't see the joke and grew irritated by the chuckling, but she missed it once it had gone. The flat had seemed very lonely then.

Mercedes and Tyrone were both at school, no doubt in clean white ironed shirts, polished shoes and well-packed lunch-boxes. Their great-grandmother turned them out well, there was no doubt. Far better than Della thought she ever could. Their school photos displayed proudly on the narrow mantel-piece above the coal-effect electric fire were a credit to Minnie's nurturing skills.

She shuffled through the papers on the kitchen table to see if there was anything – a school newsletter or a hair nit warning – that she should take a look at or sign. She did try to be a mother in her own hopeless way, but their father demanded too much. Thank God Minnie had the womanly knack of dividing herself into enough pieces for everyone.

It was the Jamaican stamp that first caught Della's eye. She knew her grandmother was always sending stuff over there, but it was rare for her to get anything in return. Like other members of her family, Della mostly assumed that because Minnie gained such apparent pleasure from her continual nourishing, she didn't need thanks.

The name on the back of the envelope rang a vague bell, but if ever Reuben Fisher had been mentioned in the past, she was sure it had been as a friend of Gladstone's. Della didn't often read for fun, but her curiosity made her pick the envelope up and open it.

The further she got with the declarations of love, the more she felt as if she had been punched in the stomach with an iron fist. A new voice started to fill her head with a threat she had never even considered before. *I am coming to take you away,* it said. *Don't you go worrying about your family, we will have this time before we die.*

Della read Reuben's letter through quickly, almost without stopping for breath. Then, when she had read it again more slowly, she sat back in the vinyl padded chair in a confounded slump, trying to control the resentment that now boiled within her. She hated him already, this Reuben Fisher of Jamaica.

She was winded with the thought that Minnie had someone else to love. All her life, she had thought *she* was the main love in Minnie's world, her grandmother's sole reason for living – but all this time in the shadows there had been him. This someone, this *Reuben*, was so gentle and he wrote such beautiful things, it hurt. It was painful to learn there really were men like that out there after all. And it was frightening too – he lived in the one place Minnie missed with all her heart. Who *was* he? How *dare* he? Why had Minnie kept him such a secret? What terrible plan was it that she played no part in?

Her first thought was to ring him up and berate him for trying to buy something that wasn't for sale. 'Find yuh own Minnie. Dis one's taken! She's mine!' Then she thought she would wait until he came over to England, do it in more style, with props. It wasn't a comforting thought, that one, because in Della's fearful vision, Minnie wept and clung to *his* arm. In the end, she chose *him*.

Della dragged herself off the chair and marauded through the other congested rooms in the flat just for something to do or somewhere to take herself. It was only a letter, and one she had no business to read anyway. She should return it to its envelope and leave it. If she ignored him, he might go away.

There were no other messages, no cards, no photographs anywhere else, and it calmed her. She was projecting her own insecurities on to something basically harmless. She would show Chess and they could enjoy the secret, tease Minnie about it maybe, get her to confess.

Then she saw the shoe-box stuffed full of identical airmails and an icy loneliness cut into her bones that immediately cancelled all hope of recovery. As she picked out one, then two, three, four, dating back last year, the year before, and before and before, her head went into a silent spin. The correspondence she had uncovered so far was obviously not even the half of it. Pulling a can of warm beer from her bag, she braced herself to digest the full story.

Come home, she read. *Come home to the warmth of my arms and our island sun. Come home.*

So Jamaica really *was* Minnie's home, a foreign country with its own language and people and way of life. And London was hers, the cement city of launderamas and dole queues where there were no warm arms to hold her and no island sun. Her eyes pricked with water.

You say Della have no one else, Reuben had written. *But she do have someone, a boyfriend and her piccanees. These are her family, Minnie, and they need her just like I need you.*

'NO!' she shouted back at the words. 'NO!' Bear wasn't someone to love, he was someone either to fear or to hide behind. OK, so he had thrown a few glittery prizes her way – a hot stereo, a leather jacket, a little weed – and Della had once told her posse of admiring friends she was in love with him, but all that had died with the first slap. He was no father to their children, and he was no husband to her. The word 'family' never entered his speech.

No man had ever whisked her away for a night of romantic love like the one Reuben Fisher was offering. No man had ever even whisked her away for a night of *lust*. Why did the good things always happen to other people? Even to *Minnie*. It wasn't fair. Is that why Minnie was buying a hat? For her own wedding? Was she going to elope? What was the real story behind this holiday in the country he talked about?

The one thing that had just about made Della's detestable journey through life bearable so far was that she and Minnie were on it together, motoring along fuelled by different gas but driving the same road nonetheless. Minnie had the Lord on her side, Della had youth, and then, when those things failed, they had each other. But it wasn't the Lord that Minnie had been trusting in all these years, it was Reuben bloody Fisher. *He* shared her grandmother's map, not her.

Suddenly, a light went on in her mind, illuminating all the dark corners she'd not been able to see into for so long. They were full of broken glass, blood, empty syringes and crushed lager cans, the damage and debris of an abusive existence. Were the corners of Minnie's mind shaped like a distant shore, coloured with the blue of the ocean and the yellow of the sun? An anger that should have been directed at Bear found its target in Minnie instead.

'You a liar!' she screamed into the empty kitchen, swiping a mug of cold tea across the floor. 'A liar!'

Tears fell from her eyes on to the worn lino, a dumper-truck of despair tipping its entire load all at once. The top half of her body sagged forward to hit the kitchen table, her dead weight crushed one side of the shoe-box, sending the airmails flipping all over the already cluttered, tea-splashed table. Her cheek flattened against the pile of Reuben's outpourings and her tears trickled down her skin to smudge the ink. She wished they would wash away his words entirely.

The scar where Bear had brought the lamp over her head began to throb enough to fear it could re-open, not that she cared, and she let her sobbing grow into deep throaty moans. 'How me a goin' deal wid dis? Me 'fraid, me 'fraid . . . when Minnie go, dere's gonna be 'nuff blood shed, y'know. Minnie keep me safe – when she here, Bear caan't touch me. All dese years, I t'ink Minnie love me jus' cos she love me, but now I see she love me 'cos she 'affi. It caan't go so. I need her. She's got her work to do wid me, here, she caan't jus . . .'

The small space resonated with her moaning, which crescendoed into a single piercing wail. She kept her right cheek on the table surface and continued to moan incomprehensibly to herself until the storm passed.

Chess caught only the tail end as she let herself in half an hour later, but even that was enough. The sight of her sister's shattered life was as clear as writing on a page. As she stood in the doorframe surveying Della's broken and unhappy form and heard the unnerving echoes of what could so easily have been her own cries, she knew at once how to negate the crime of two days ago, how to nullify her stupidity, how to start to put things right.

'It's OK, I'm here,' she said, putting her arms around the hunched figure.

'Me 'fraid, me 'fraid. Stay wid me, Chess, stay wid me.'

'I will, I will. Whatever it is, we'll sort it out together.'

'I caan't do it on my own.'

'You don't have to. We can sort it.'

And there they stayed, holding on to each other for dear life, for as long as it took them to build up the courage to start. It took a few attempts at speech before Della could get it across to her sister that it wasn't Bear she was afraid of (although there was that as well) but another man, one she had never met, who lived on the other side of the world.

The story of Reuben came out in fits and starts, in spits of recrimination and the occasional flash of total disbelief. Della showed Chess the letters, but this time they started with the earliest, 1948, more than fifty years ago. It took them a long time to read them all, by which time Della had drunk all four cans of beer and Chess was shaking with caffeine.

'That is a long time to be in love with someone,' Chess said, putting the last one back in the box. She loved the idea that Minnie had been cherished all those years and she'd nearly screamed for joy when she came across her own name. But she had to be careful. It was different for Della. She had more to lose, just like Judith and Honor. It was another gap between them, another unshared experience, another underscoring of their difference, so finally, they dropped the subject.

'Let's talk about you,' Chess said. 'We need to sort you out.'

They both knew their first port of call would have to be Bear. He had to be crossed off the list.

'I caan't leave him, man – he'll kill me.'

'He's killing you anyway.'

'He won' never let me go.'

'Then don't ask his permission.

Chess was suddenly in compelling form. It seemed a lifetime ago that she was being sick in her own lavatory, too weak to get up and grab her own life back. Her good deeds were suddenly shining like a prize in front of her, and this time she wasn't going to let them go.

Minnie had her own prize, sitting in a large green bag by her side as the bus rocked its way through the London traffic to take her home. The pillarbox-red wool peeped out through the rigid plastic handles and she touched it from time to time, holding it between her thumb and her forefinger and massaging its indulgence. It was hard to believe it really was hers.

As she opened the seal on the triangle of Chinese chicken sandwiches she'd bought, she said a little prayer of thanks to God for Reuben. Pampered was not a word in her vocabulary but that was how she felt, not least because she was eating something that someone else had prepared for a change.

The young shop assistant had been so helpful, buttoning and unbuttoning all those coats and fetching and carrying all those cardigans. When Minnie had come over all hot and itchy, the girl had given her one of those face wipes from her own handbag, and when it got to time for her lunchbreak, she even introduced Minnie to the other girl by name.

Then there had been the hats, hundreds and hundreds of them, all perching on mushrooms in such a hypnotising display that Minnie had to work out where on earth to start. She'd even tried on the ones she felt sure she would never buy, no matter how rich she was. There were ones for weddings, ones for church, ones for the sun and a few not unlike her own brown tea cosy. Then, on a high pole topping all the others, there was a velvety black dome with a pleasingly neat brim. It framed her face nicely, according to the security guard who got it down for her.

The bus lurched and swayed and she sat there smiling at people as they got on and off. What a lovely day. She put her dry brown hand into the flimsy plastic pack and tried to pull out her lunch – or was it tea? The bread was floppy and the meat fell back into the triangle but Minnie didn't mind. She could easily pick the bits out with her fingers as long as she remembered to wash them before trying on her coat again.

Bear picked a week's worth of dirt from under his fingernails as he lay in the bath. Early afternoon was normally his busy time but his head was hurting today from either too many transactions or too much weed. He sank his Leviathan body under the murky flat water and held his breath. When he emerged slowly like a dangerous hippo and let the flood from his freshly cropped hair drip down his hard dark face, he became aware of voices coming through the flimsy wall of the sitting room.

'We're safe. He's not here. You can come.'

'I'd come even if he was.'

'Don't you get too brave. You not too big for him to give you a slap.'

'I wish someone would give *him* a slap for a change.'

'No one is dat stupid.'

'Well, I'm not going to give him the pleasure of scaring me.'

'Den you a liar.'

'No, I'm not. He can't touch me, and he doesn't have the right to touch you. Look at your chin. Hold on.'

Chess tipped the contents of her handbag out on the smoked glass table top and found a foil tube of Arnica cream.

'Not more medication,' Della managed to smile. 'You a walkin' bloody chemist shop.'

Bear pulled his bestial arms quietly out of the water and put them behind his head. He snarled his lip in disapproval of the words he could hear and showed his gums to the bathroom tiles. She's not scared of me because I haven't growled at her loud enough yet, he thought. All that purity she'd laid on him at the carnival – he didn't buy that any more. He'd trusted her with money to see if she could be trusted with anything else, but the way it turned out, she couldn't even be trusted with that. Della had tried to sell him the line that it was just fear and inexperience speaking when the girl had let his name slip to the police, but he didn't buy that either. She was trouble disguised as help. Her voice was so clear, she must be just the other side of the bathroom door.

'He's not your keeper, and you don't owe him anything.'

No, but the bitch owes me, Bear snarled only four feet away. If she t'ink she is gettin' two hundred pounds jus' for the privilege of puttin' de law on to me, den she's more stupid than I t'ink. He wanted his gift returned. Even if Della *had* told him she'd given it to Minnie, which had gone completely out of her mind, he would consider it his stolen property.

What was this he was hearing now? What line now was she selling his woman? To move out? To get a job? Della was his. He was the one to make changes in her life, not this white trash in black skin.

He sat upright and a wave of water slopped on to the floor. 'COME!' he boomed, his bass voice rumbling through the small space like an avalanche. 'DELLA, YOU COME NOW!'

The two women jumped, but one stood rooted to the spot. The walls were as thin as set divides and they reverberated with his anger, but the drama was well-rehearsed. The script only varied as to which bone he would try and break this time. Chess watched it unfold as quickly as if the clipboard had come down and someone had shouted, 'Action.'

Della's eyes flashed madly to the bathroom door.

'COME!'

'Don't,' Chess said suddenly. 'We're leaving.'

'I caan't, man,' Della whimpered.

'What are you, chained to the wall?'

'COM! YOU COM CLEAN ME NOW!'

Della knew the cleaning routine. It was part of Bear's slave-master bit. She rubbed the hard skin off his feet, loofahed his back, rubbed oils into his hair and then she undressed too, because when Bear got out of the bath, he had sex.

'Tell him to clean himself,' Chess said, but her sister stood between the devil and the deep blue sea. She neither entered the bathroom nor moved to the front door.

Della was thinking. Chess had told her that afternoon that she was too good to waste on a bully. The revelation that she might be too good for anyone was a new one on her, but somewhere right down deep in her soul, she could see the truth in it. Once upon a time, at school, she had won prizes for her art. Once upon a time, she had sung in the church choir. Once upon a time, she had laughed more than she cried. The words left her mouth of their own accord.

'You can clean yuhself.'

That was enough disobedience for one day. Bear heaved his bulk out of the tub and without bothering to cover himself he flung open the door and stood there in his towering naked awfulness. The rivulets of bathwater trickled like tiny shards of shattered glass through the tight curls on his bullworked chest. He stood with his giant legs astride, his penis hanging heavily between them, and he stared dangerously at the two girls.

'What you say?'

Chess's life was flashing before her eyes again. 'She said you can clean yourself.'

'I don't ask you, I ask her. Now you tell me what you say, Della. NOW!'

But Della's tongue had frozen in her mouth. She shook her head and looked at the ground, clenching every muscle with dread as he took two steps towards her.

Chess's head flung back with referred shock as Bear did what she could hardly believe he was going to do. In a split second, but also somehow in slow motion, he raised his hairy arm with his fist wrapped around a long backscratcher like a giant wooden hairbrush and brought it down with a resounding crack across Della's skull.

'NO!' Chess screamed, but time had stalled and her mind set free an ancient recurring childhood nightmare. At six, she was stalked in her sleep by a house-sized gorilla who was tall enough to push his face against her bedroom window, where he would beg her to let him in. When she wouldn't, he would smash the window with a big stick and she would try to shout for her parents to come and rescue her but she would have no voice. This time though, she found it.

'Della, we're going,' she said calmly.

'You not goin' ANYWHERE,' Bear roared. 'She come here and clean my back, and you, YOU, you leave my house.'

'Della, come on.' Chess picked up her bag, stuffing the items back in as fast as she could, and grabbed her sister by the arm. Della was like a lead weight. Her limbs had forgotten how to move of their own accord.

'She's leaving you. Take one last look at her, because from now on you'll have to find someone else to bully,' Chess spat, trying to sound brave. 'And if you lay one more finger on her, I'll make sure the police know exactly who you are and what you do this time.' Her utterances were not her own. They came from a nauseous pit of loathing in her churning belly and they were spewing out, spiked with the injustice this man had forced upon her sister.

'I warn you, you make grief for yuhself,' Bear shouted, grabbing his towel. 'I know where you live.'

'Then don't you bloody come within a mile of it,' Chess hissed. Her eyes could flash with just as much anger as his.

'You know dis man is a warrior!' When Bear used the term warrior, Della knew he meant there to be bloodshed. 'Dell-ah! You tell dis sistah I will teach her a lesson.'

'Chess, listen . . .'

'No. Della, come on.'

The two of them moved cautiously towards the door, a little quicker into the hall and then hurtled into the fresh air. Hand in hand, they ran down the concrete stairs two at a time, through the dim passages and swing doors and back to Chess's car, parked in full view of Bear, who was eclipsing his own doorway with his enraged but silent form.

The doors opened with a flash at the press of her keyfob. Chess's trembling hands couldn't undo the crooklock first time, but then she flung it in the back seat and she accelerated like she had never accelerated before. The engine screamed and the gears jerked to keep up, but as they kangarooed down an empty side street with the distance between them and the monster growing ever further, their petrified bravery turned to a wild hysteria.

'*Aaaaagggggghhhhhhhhh!*' Chess let the pent-up terror out in one long loud screech, her arms off the wheel, waving frantically as she shook with something that seemed to be laughter but couldn't have been. Della started to scream too, grabbing Chess's left hand with hers and raising it to the car roof in a pyramid of female triumph.

'What me done? What me done?'

'You've left him, that's what you've done.'

'I have? I have? I have! I have!'

The two sisters travelled joined at the fist, Chess steering haphazardly with one hand, her body still convulsing with panic, all the way to the enduring haven of their grandmother.

'Will you be safe at Minnie's? What if he comes round?'

'We can jus' keep de door locked an' he can shout his mouth tru de letterbox if he want.'

'Shouldn't I take you to a refuge or something? A safe house?' Chess knew exactly where there *was* a safe house – in a leafy road just off Clapham Common – but it might as well have been in Timbuctoo for all the help it was.

'Granny's *is* safe. Bear don' hardly come dere when he t'ink Minnie won't let him in. An' Tyrone will see him off.'

It was bravado, and both of them knew it, but what else could they do? And anyway, Della loved Minnie unconditionally again now. Maybe Reuben wasn't quite so terrible a threat as he had seemed that morning. She could afford to be generous now that she had someone as strong as Chess to hold her hand too.

Chapter 18

The hospital priest turned out not to be the Grim Reaper in a crew neck after all. He was called Graham, and when Judith talked to him she felt he really did understand what on earth it was she was trying to say. The more she talked to him, the more *she* began to understand too.

The first twenty-four hours after Will contracted his gut infection looked very much as if they were going to be his last, even to the experts. His soul seemed to shut down, and every time Judith looked into his intensive care incubator, she no longer saw a baby lying there but a tangle of wires attached to the carcass of some sort of bloated featherless bird. She would wander around the unit in her dressing gown for hours, wondering if anyone anywhere in the entire medical profession thought there was any point to all this.

'Of course there is,' Graham said. 'These hospital trusts are tight-fisted buggers, you know. They're not going to throw their budget away on hope.'

'Do all priests know rude words like that?'

'Is the Pope a Catholic?'

How he managed to keep his sense of humour with all the bleeps and buzzers going off around him she didn't know, but his irreverence helped. She was learning to junk preconceptions left right and centre, not least what happy families were all about.

It was easier in this insulated environment not to think of Honor's death at all. It had absolutely no place here, and whilst it still was and always would be a tragedy, it was beginning to bear the hallmarks of a turning point, a watershed. It was just the seed of a new approach, something she had no free headspace to nurture, so she tossed it to the back of her mind to feed off the chance that when she retrieved it, it might have put down some healthy roots.

The decontaminated bubble she was currently living in would one day have to pop and expose her to the real world once more, but for the moment, it was a relief to breathe the only available oxygen of hope.

Her baby Will roamed the entire landscape of her mind at present. Her whole life was with him, here, inside the unit. It was as much as she could do to remember her other three children and her husband from time to time, let alone Chess. Her sister's letter yesterday, full of encouragement and optimism, remained only half-read by her bed. Chess would have to wait for *her* for a change. It wouldn't do her any harm.

Judith knew exactly what she was doing by paring her world right down to the bare minimum. When she'd learnt to cope with that, then she could start building it back up again. The acid test would be to see if Chess still wanted to be part of the foundation.

Sometimes, Judith would concentrate on the stretched skin of Will's miniature face and try to add the layers of childhood on to his neo-natal features. Maybe he would look a little like Harry, but thinner. She saw him in a Cub's uniform aged nine, or as a filthy-faced toddler in Wellington boots by the gate in their garden, waving a stick and shouting at his siblings. Then she would re-focus, fix her eyes on the wired bird, and she would see nothing.

Her third son and fourth born was being reared on a cocktail of fluids low in sodium and potassium that had been made to his own precise prescription, pumped in by long line infusion which entered his body through a vein near his heart. His diet was called total parental nutrition, which seemed to his mother to be the ultimate irony.

She insisted on being there every morning when a nurse took the daily sample of blood for analysis just in case he squeaked and needed her, but he never did. He just lay there quite lifeless, not crying and not looking for food. The unit was full of babies who never cried. They couldn't afford to waste their energy on such frivolous protest.

'Why do you keep saying this is your own fault?' Father Graham asked her when they were by the window that looked out on to the rather uncomfortably placed Garden of Peace one morning.

'Because it is. I ignored him,' Judith confessed quietly.

'Not a medically recognised cause, I'm afraid. Neglect, maybe. Ignoring, no. You don't have to answer, but can I ask *why* you ignored him?'

'The answer isn't very nice.'

'Trust me, I'm a priest,' he smiled, taking the rise out of himself.

Her admission was barely audible. 'I think I was hoping he'd go away. I couldn't see the point in having a baby if my mother wasn't going to live long enough to see it. She died about two months ago. Don't tell anyone, will you? I'm so ashamed.'

Graham paused and, without looking at her but continuing to stare up into the sky, he said, 'And what makes you think she can't see him?'

At that same moment, Judith noticed that the sun came out.

It wouldn't have mattered to Minnie George and Reuben Fisher if the sun had put in an appearance or not during their precious days together, but as luck would have it, the weather was about as near to an Indian summer as you can get in late October. West Indian, that is.

He chauffeured her at no more than fifty miles an hour along the B roads of the south coast, bursting with pride at his organisation in getting thus far, until they reached the seaside town of Weymouth in Dorset. It felt to Minnie like the ends of the earth, but was in fact only a morning's journey from the dock where they had both first set foot on English soil in 1948.

She had forgotten in more than fifty years what the sea looked like, and as Reuben steered his borrowed taxi carefully round the corner on to the seafront, Minnie clasped his hand on the gear stick so tightly he couldn't change into third.

'Oh, Reuben! Open de window.'

'Press your button and it will do it for you.'

'Ooh! Heh heh!' she chuckled with total delight as the glass slid down gracefully and let in the smell of salt and the sound of seagulls. 'Dis am de way to live, eh?'

They crawled along oblivious to the mounting traffic behind them. Their selective vision missed the tacky shopfronts and amusement arcades, the plethora of metal signs to tourist attractions and the architectural lapses that the planners had sneaked through over the years. They saw only the folding waves on empty sands, elegant railings along a Victorian promenade, freshly painted bus shelters and a noble clock tower standing proudly in the middle of the road.

'De King always came here for his holiday,' Reuben told her proudly.

'De King *is* here,' Minnie beamed and squeezed his hand even tighter.

He parked attentively in a side street and they took a stroll. The hotel he had booked looked so grand from the brochure, he wanted her to see it from the seafront, not the car window. As they walked, the bite of winter that had started to set into her arthritic knees in London was taken away on a mild breeze and she walked without pain, or maybe that was just because of who she was walking out with. Their arms linked perfectly together.

She wouldn't believe him when he told her she was looking at the place they were to stay. She pulled on his arm and tried to make him walk on, she pretended to get cross with his nonsense, she even refused to cross the road when he told her they should check in.

The sun was hot and she had taken off her red coat, but once she realised Reuben was serious, she felt compelled to put it back on, just to walk in anyway. Reuben told her she looked beautiful regardless.

'What you say if I wear a sack one day, eh?'

'I would say Minnie George can even wear a sack and look like a queen.'

'And dis a' me kingdom,' she said.

She certainly felt like a queen. The Royal Hotel was just as she imagined a palace must be. It had red carpets even softer than her coat, wide stairs that men in top hats could dance down, wooden lifts that didn't smell, and the biggest cut-glass chandelier in the ballroom she had ever seen – although the comparison didn't stand up to much.

They ate their meals by a huge picture window with views of the American war memorial on the seafront, and if she leant forward, she could see the time on the Jubilee Clock Tower. She knew the names of these landmarks because she had read about them in a book in her room – *their* room. Several times she had to pinch herself to believe that for once in her life, she was looking out, not peering in.

'You t'ink dey t'ink we married?' she chuckled over her kippers on the first morning.

'Newly-weds,' Reuben told her. 'Dey t'ink we mus' be newly-weds.'

Actually, the staff at the Royal couldn't work them out at all. It was like watching the unfolding of a love story, even if the opening credits did belong to the world of comedy.

After hours of deliberation in Portsmouth, Reuben had booked separate single bedrooms. He wanted Minnie to relax on this holiday, he wanted to cosset her, to treat her to every pleasure life had always denied her, and he thought this would probably, on balance, include privacy. But he'd got it wrong – a fact which became clear as soon as the receptionist handed them separate keys on metal balls.

'What you t'ink you doin'?' Minnie had whispered loudly to him by the lift. 'How many nights have you wished we were together when we were apart, eh? We don't want to waste all dis time now, do we?'

So Reuben had returned to the desk. 'I'm sorry, miss, we don't want separate bedrooms any more. We want to be in de same chamber, please.'

'Certainly, sir. We have a twin room on the second floor with a balcony?'

'Not a twin,' Minnie announced proudly from where she was standing ten feet away. Her red coat had given her a confidence she didn't know she had. 'A big bed please, for de both of us.'

Sleeping arrangements were on Nick Jacoby's mind too, but unfortunately, he couldn't just click his fingers to change them. He had always seen it as a barometer of the health of his marriage that he and Chess so rarely slept apart, even when the children had been babies. They always used to feel happily smug and superior when other couples they knew were so depressingly open about the amount of traffic their spare bed saw between them. Used to.

He wondered if Chess guessed he was awake when she crept off in the middle of the night nowadays. He had done it first of course, by sleeping on the sofa that night he first started suspecting the worst, but one night should hardly have set a precedent. She might be next to him now, but for how long?

How could he possibly have known that at that moment, his restless wife was thinking not of some secret lover but the detail of her half-sister's long-fingered hands and the characteristic way she so adeptly fiddled with things like tobacco and Rizla papers? Chess, thinking that Nick had been asleep for at least half an hour, had been idly trying to work out the stages of rolling a joint again. Not that she had any intention of taking it up, but it was more interesting than counting sheep. Then she'd realised that building spliffs wasn't the only thing Della had a talent for. Even in a world where any creative juices should have been immediately sucked dry, Della had always made things – hats and belts from cut-off T-shirts, Mercedes' mermaid costume for the carnival, a muslin roof above the otherwise unromantic bed she shared with Bear. Her efforts always turned out better than they should, given the base material.

Chess was encouraged by her speculation, a cheerful

offshoot from the rather darker mainstream of her Della-focused thoughts, and she tried to stick with it until she fell asleep. As soon as she had consciously acknowledged what she was doing though, the image fell away, immediately replaced by something less restful. Bear actually, and whether or not he had been removed from the equation for good.

Nick suddenly fidgeted and it crossed her mind that he might not be asleep after all, so she stayed as still as she could to avoid any empathetic exchanges of their respective insomnias. She had promised herself to manage at least one whole night in the marital bed, sleep or no sleep. They both needed reassurance that they could still manage it. No doubt Nick had work on his mind – a difficult case that hung in the balance or hinged on some obscure precedent he had just come across in one of his doorstop-sized law books. But what could she tell him of her wakefulness? To him, her distractions must seem simple. A house to decorate, children to organise, a part-time job to keep her ticking over.

How could he know there was so much else going on? An arrest to rationalise, a personal threat to disregard, a whole new world out there waggling its come-hither finger in her direction? Her refusal to tell him the truth had twisted things into an unnecessarily messy tangle, and the longer she left the knots, the tighter they seemed to get. She would need something very sharp or pointed to sort it all out now.

During school exams, her father used to try and coach her by teaching her to use a little mental trick. Don't look at the whole paper at once, he'd always said. Just take it question by question. Resist the temptation to scan it and panic. Nothing ever looks easy from the outset. If you can't solve the first problem, go on to the next. Well, in this test, question number one was Della, because it was one she felt she had the power to answer.

She began wracking her brain, trying to find an avenue that would take Della away from Bear for ever, but any tour of her mind led back to the same dingy dead-end alley. She knew that as long as Della's life remained empty, and Bear prowled around on the hunt for prey, her sister would be susceptible. It was like misfortune had her trapped in the cul-de-sac of life for ever, and would beat her into submissive retreat with a branding iron every time she tried to escape.

Chess's tired mind had leapt from image to image. The walls of the dirty alley became the walls of a prison, and she'd started thinking about people being prisoners, their life choices stamped on their foreheads at birth. She marched mugshots of her family through her ticking brain. Minnie, Judith, Nick, herself. Della had no choices stamped on hers, not even the one between Jamaica and London like Minnie did.

Honor and John must have had truckloads, it occurred to her. Maybe she had only been able to choose her house, her job, the life for her children, all that, because of them. We inherit options, she thought. If your legacy is choice, you get choice; if it's poverty, you get poverty. She had never really thanked them for that.

The living nightmare of her arrest, and how close it had pushed her towards no choice at all, cut a gash through her thoughts again, and she quickly blocked it off, returning to the things about her life she *could* change. Della – she could change Della – but in the same way that the music curdles when a feel-good film starts to turn into a thriller, she realised that those thoughts wouldn't get her anywhere either.

Maybe her sister's fate was already sealed, maybe hope for a happy ending was in vain because the script had already been written. She held a vision of fingers pressed around a pen, dashing words off on a page, and then suddenly she was back with the comforting image of Della's deft hands again, the way she twisted foil into spirals, moulded soft candle wax into shallow shells, wove Mercedes' hair into the maze of pigtails.

That was it! *Della had a skill!* And with a jolt that made her sit up and force the inspiration to stay in the forefront of her brain, the possibilities offered by the Pinegrove Arts Project just off Portobello Road came to her in a flash.

'Come and see us soon,' a woman with blonde dreadlocks

outside the chapel had sung to her on Carnival Day as she handed out leaflets. Della had a skill and she had an invitation. Surely the two advantages were linked.

It was enough to allow Chess to fall back into the duvet and find the curve of Nick's chest and thighs to curl into. The surprise and warmth that flooded through her husband's body as he felt her touch was gratefully received by both of them. They sighed without speaking and then both fell into a sleep sound enough not to hear the children, delighted to find them together, come in and whisper that they were off downstairs to eat biscuits and watch television.

When they *had* woken, Nick was surprised to see her still there too, but not altogether reassured. Maybe they had both been just too damn exhausted to make the effort to move. All these thoughts were still sloshing round his head as messily as the water in the bath he shared with Sam that evening. It was an occasional ritual which was never entirely satisfying. The temperature had to be colder than he would have liked, and Sam had a habit of kicking him just where it hurt, but there was a sense of bonding there nonetheless. Chess still bathed with both children from time to time, but Nick had stopped with Kezia at his own unspoken discretion, and as a couple they mostly showered separately.

Through the open bathroom door he could see his wife busy with handfuls of bed linen, including the big blue checked duvet cover off the spare bed. It always used to stay stripped until it was needed, but now she treated it as part of the general household wash.

'You're not sleeping brilliantly at the moment, are you?' he said when she came to stand in the door and chivvy Kezia into undressing.

'Not exactly.'

'Do you think we should talk about why not?'

'Not at this precise moment, no.' She shook a quilt down into its freshly laundered sleeve.

Kezia was sitting on the loo, picking a transfer off the back of her hand and pretending not to listen. Chess punched the pillows and made a face to warn him off, but he felt safer with the children around, so he went further.

'I used to be able to see right into you. I used to know exactly what you were thinking.'

'Did you have X-ray eyes, Daddy?' Sam asked.

'Yeah, I could see all her guts.'

'Oh, cool!'

Chess smiled awkwardly.

'But I can't any more.'

'Aww.'

Nick flicked a small splash of water in Sam's face and turned back to Chess. 'You're different lately.'

She could never say he didn't feed her the right lines, that was for sure – but now was not the time to blurt out that she had always been different and was ill from the effort involved in forever trying to appear the same. Instead she said, 'Can we have this conversation later?' knowing that if ever there was a good time, it had passed long ago – somewhere around the evening after the Notting Hill Carnival, to be precise.

'So there *is* a conversation to be had then?' he asked, a reddish tinge moving across his worried wet face.

Not just one, she thought, but Nick, oh Nick. She could think of nothing better than offloading, and he wouldn't mind being the dumping ground, she knew that. But to make it all OK, to give it the best chance she could, anything she told him now had to be positive stuff. And there was nothing very positive to report from the Ladbroke Grove camp at present, except, of course, Della's flight from Bear.

Anyway, Chess was still capsized with contrition over her arrest, which turned her upside down every time she thought about it, and it was better she kept that to herself. She didn't know it, but whenever the whole scary mess forged through her thoughts, she winced conspicuously. Nick was getting used to the expression in her repertoire.

'Scrub my back, will you?' he asked, clutching at the straws of tradition. His simple customary request made the muscles in her neck flinch, and all the tiny hairs on her body stand on end.

She heard the crack of Bear's wooden backscratcher come down across Della's head once again and she quailed at the recall. The bastard had turned an act of love into an act of slavery, which meant she couldn't possibly respond to her husband's request, not even for old time's sake.

'Come on, Sam, hop out,' she said, grabbing the nearest towel.

'I get the message,' Nick grunted, but he didn't really, not at all.

Neither of them put their heart into the stories they read the children that night. The universal parental gift of being able to move one's mouth in rhythm with the words on the page whilst the brain undergoes another process altogether came into its own. The longer they each stayed in the separate bedrooms of their daughter and son with their lips on automatic pilot, the longer they stayed safe from confrontation.

Downstairs, Nick gave it another try and this time he actually got somewhere. Not exactly truth junction, but on the map at any rate. One way in was to engineer a conversation about the children.

'I'm a bit worried about Kez,' he said as nonchalantly as possible.

'Are you? Why?' Pounce, she was there like a mother cat.

'Just that she doesn't seem particularly happy at the moment. Has she said anything to you?'

'No.' Chess panicked. She couldn't think of *anything* Kezia had said to her at all lately, or anything she had actually listened to anyway. Her priorities were like frogs in a sack. 'What makes you think there's a problem?'

'A few things. You haven't picked up on it?'

Chess shook her head and looked at him so he could see her shame.

'Has she said anything to you about not knowing how to find a special friend?' he asked.

'No.' Had she? Had she? She might have.

'She says everyone else at school has already got someone, that the girls are all in pairs and the boys don't join in like they did in Norfolk. I said all the stuff about it just being a matter of time and that next term she would probably have so many friends she wouldn't be able to choose who to invite to her party and all that, but it didn't make any difference – she still looked sad.'

'You don't think she's being bullied, do you?'

'I asked her that and she said no. No, I just don't think she feels a part of it yet.'

'Well, join the club,' Chess couldn't help herself saying.

It was the kickstart they needed for the conversation to go anywhere at all, and that was it; Nick pressed his foot gently on the accelerator for the next hour or so.

'How do you mean?'

Slowly, his wife started to emerge from her own shadows. They began to talk more easily, like they used to, and the subject turned, because Nick steered it that way, to getting what you want out of life, that what you reap is what you sow.

'No one does more sowing than Judith, and look what she's got to show for it at the moment,' Chess argued.

'I know. Tim said on the phone today that she really does believe that if she loses the baby it will be all her own fault.'

'Did he? Do you think that's right? I mean, is that just Judith wallowing? Coming out with stuff she doesn't mean?'

'It's hard to tell.'

'You didn't tell me Tim had phoned.'

'He didn't. *I* phoned him, from the office.'

'Did you? Why?'

'Because I had a spare minute and I was worried about Judith and the baby, why do you think?'

'But that's my job – I was going to phone tonight. Do you think it's too soon to go up there?'

Nick shrugged.

'I just want to see Judith, give her a kiss, see the baby. Do you think I should call now?' Chess asked. 'Although I feel a bit pissed, do you?'

'We've only had a glass,' he said, tilting the bottle to see where the level lay. 'But I wouldn't phone if you do. You're not Tim's favourite person at the moment.'

'So what's new?' She pretended the news didn't bother her.

Nick teetered for a moment on the brink of something he hardly dared dip his toe into. 'He said he thought that the lunch you had with Judith on the same day she went into labour upset her.'

'Bollocks. She was feeling weird before I even got there.'

'God, your language, Chess. Anyway, I'm only telling you so you're forewarned.'

'Sorry.' She realised she was sounding guilty.

'And he said you'd confided in her, told her to keep something a secret?' Nick was prodding gently. He wasn't sure he wanted to find what it was he was looking for.

'Really?' She was blushing under her skin.

'Yes,' he said, making an effort to keep his face relaxed and open as he looked at her. 'What was that all about, then? Anything I should know?'

'I can't even think what it was we talked about,' Chess lied. *Tell him, you stupid cow*, the voice in her head shouted, but she continued to ignore it.

Nick shook his head. 'Well, I don't understand that then.'

'Nor do I.'

There was a brief silence while Nick tried to decide how far he should press her, but something urgent and desperate beat him to it. 'Are you sure?'

Chess wrinkled her brow and pretended to rack her brains. 'I don't mind them blaming me if it makes things easier for them at the moment.'

'Well, I do. I'm not having them hold you responsible for something that is entirely in Judith's imagination. Not if you haven't done anything wrong.' It was more of a question than an answer. 'It's just that it's odd you haven't raced up there like you normally would.'

Chess felt like she used to when she and Judith were little. Honor would discover some childish misconduct and holding the broken, squeezed or eaten example in her hand she would ask them equally, 'Who did this?' There was never any doubt it was her, of course, but she would try and deny it all the same.

'Well, for a start, I haven't been asked to, and anyway, when have I had the time?'

'You would normally make time.'

'I know,' she accepted guiltily. 'But . . .'

Forget them, Nick wanted to say. What about this secret, Chess, what about this secret? The core of him told him that whatever it was, it wasn't really another man. She smelt the same as she always had done, wore the same bare look in her eyes, allowed herself to be touched by him in the old familiar style. The fact that the touching more often than not stopped short of sex lately was down to something else, something to do with a preoccupation he couldn't fathom.

They stopped speaking and he tried to hold her gaze. 'Let me in, Chess.'

'In on what?'

'The secret.' An image of their crumpled bed came to him. When he'd gone upstairs to change from his work suit this evening, the phone from the bedside table had been on the duvet impressed with the shape of his wife's lying body. She had been talking to someone privately.

'Are you having an affair?' he asked lightly. She could take it as a joke if she wanted to.

'It is not an affair,' she reassured slowly and definitely. 'It's not that.'

'I know that really. But it feels like one.'

'I'm sorry.' God, she was that close to *telling* him. If it hadn't been for the arrest, she would have done, but the horror squatted like an ugly toad in the front of the picture.

'It is *something*, though, isn't it?'

She left his question hanging there. He was right about his implications up to a point. She might not have been having an actual love affair, but her behaviour had all the hallmarks of infidelity nonetheless – the lies, the covering of tracks, the silent obsessive thoughts, the flickers of impulse followed by the hours of guilt. No affair, but very definitely a secret, and now a plot. Only the very small beginnings of one, but carried out carefully, it could make the jigsaw pieces finally fit.

'Yes, it is *something*. But bear with me just for a little while longer, yeah? There's been a lot to deal with lately and I just need to order my thoughts.'

'Sure,' he said, rocking the base of his empty wine glass on the arm of his chair. 'Sure.'

'All good t'ings come to end,' Minnie sighed as they waited for the restored antique lift to carry them down to reception for the last time. Reuben's flight back to Jamaica was just a day away and their coach was in danger of turning back into a pumpkin.

The way the lift swayed and rattled in its shaft made them both wonder if it would ever deliver them, but then spending the rest of their days in such a confined space with just each other for company wouldn't be such a bad way to go.

'Not dis good t'ing don't come to an end. We are for ever,' Reuben said. 'Besides, we have one more place to go.'

It took him a suspiciously-long twenty minutes just to drive the car from the back car park to the front, not that Minnie was in any hurry to leave her velour armchair placed perfectly by a window to catch the morning sun. The receptionist brought her tea without being asked, served in a dainty floral bone-china cup with a saucer, and as she sipped she decided that even if she died now she would not feel there was any better living to be done.

Reuben was breathless as he lifted their tatty suitcases into the Hoovered boot of the taxi.

'Are you stealin' me?' Minnie asked him. 'Where you takin' me? Where yuh tears, eh? You not lookin' much like you about to say goodbye to me, Reuben Fisher.'

'Don't say dat word,' he said. 'Get in. We goin' to church.'

The Victorian façades of the seafront hotels downgraded to bungalows lining a busy road, the bungalows turned to terraced cottages, and then the terraced cottages became fields. Away from town, then village, then hamlet, the roar of the tarmac stopped and the wheels started to rumble over potholes and stone instead.

They were on a privately owned No Through Road cutting across the open grassy borders of the Dorset cliffs. If the brakes and steering had failed, they could have plunged right over the edge, but Reuben guided his queen's royal carriage and its precious cargo at snail's pace over the foreign terrain. Every time he took her over a cattle grid, Minnie's large bosom and hefty bottom shuddered along with the whole body of the car.

'Where you takin' me, Reuben?'

'I told you. To church.'

The heavens were blue, the carpet beneath their feet was a mossy green and Minnie left her red coat on the back seat when she got out, but because she was going to church, her black hat remained firmly on her head. There was no wind to whip it off, but from behind, Reuben's hands held it down.

'What you a doin now, Mr Fisher?'

'I'm makin' you look like my bride,' he smiled, tucking two yellow gerberas like mini-sunflowers into the narrow band around the brim. At his feet was a huge ribboned bouquet. As he placed it proudly in her arms and she saw it for the first time, she started her familiar laugh-cry.

'No, no, Minnie George, you caan't have wet eyes for dis. You won't see where you goin'.'

'What you a doin? What madness is dis?'

He took her trembling arm and led her along the stony track. There was no spire on the horizon, just gorse and windswept trees and then the sea, stretching on and on towards Jamaica.

A gap in the foliage took them on to a narrow path where they had to duck under branches and pick their feet cautiously over mushrooming roots. The sun might not have been as hot and the plants as tropical, but the echo of their communal childhood adventures rustled through the yellowing leaves all the same.

God's houses come in all shapes and sizes and this one was nothing more than a wooden shack hiding in a thicket clearing. Someone somewhere tended its pocket garden lovingly though, for the borders were clipped and weeded and the plant troughs properly prepared for winter. The tiny double doors were unlocked, and Reuben pushed them open.

They stood no more than twelve feet away from the altar, a modest table covered in a white cloth with two ceramic candlesticks and a large brass cross. A simple arrangement of greenery sat on a white wooden pedestal to the left and the piano lid was up, with sheet music already out. Four shortened pews down either side were furnished with Bibles, hymn books and cushions. Minnie immediately sank to her knees to pray. Reuben stood with one palm over the other and his chin high. When her brown eyes flashed back up a minute later and locked with his, he could see deep into her lovely soul.

'Shall we?' he asked, crooking his left arm and offering it to her.

Their doddery legs walked in time to imaginary music down the aisle, she taking care not to trip over her slim virginal robes and he bursting with young man pride at catching so bonny a wife. Their parents were there, and their brothers and sisters, their friends and their neighbours. They were on the cusp of twenty and knew nothing of what life had in store, only that they would live it together.

When their slow proud procession reached its end, they stood before the minister of their minds and made their vows before God.

'I do,' said Reuben solemnly.

'I do,' said Minnie fervently.

'Now I may kiss the bride,' said Reuben, and their lips met for a moment before they hung on to each other, supporting their old bones and drinking in the fantasy of a marriage that never was, until it got cold enough for the new Mrs Fisher to think of her warm red coat in the back of their car.

Sometimes, bad things come to an end as well as good, because on the seventh day after Will Law's necrotising entero-colitis was first diagnosed, he started to make sucking noises.

'He's hungry! He's hungry!' his amazed mother shouted to anyone who could hear.

'Then he'll just have to wait,' grinned a passing nurse, picking up his clipboard of notes. 'He's nil by mouth for ten days.'

'How about giving him a dummy?'

Was there no end to the number of times Judith Law could surprise herself lately?

Chapter 19

Reports of childish laughter fired out of the Pinegrove Chapel double doors to greet Chess and Kezia before they were even inside the gates. Kezia was pulling down on her mother's hand, skipping and showing no signs of the sore throat she had complained of that morning, which had coincidentally manifested itself on the same day as her spelling test. She had literally refused to get out of the car at the school gates and Chess had, for once, let her get away with it. Normally, such outrageous fabrication would have been entirely ignored, but Kez had been so brave at settling in, Chess didn't have the heart to insist. And anyway, she felt partly responsible for her daughter's qualms over the test, since she was the one who had lost the spelling book in the first place.

She had a horrible feeling she might have left the book in Bear's flat when she'd emptied her handbag to look for the Arnica tablets, but she certainly wasn't going to go back there to take a look. It was no go territory, a hostile environment, not the sort of place you'd ever expect to see a child's spelling book, that's for sure.

She wouldn't have found it anyway. Bear had swiped it the moment the girls had fled, as reparation for the disrespect he had just been shown. The slim red book had the school's name and address emblazoned across the front, surrounded by a collection of stickers including one for an art gallery in Chelsea – two little details he felt sure would come in handy soon.

And it was reassuring to have Kez with her today anyway. It made her forget the darker side of her visit. The Pinegrove doors were ajar, so Chess pushed them open and shouted a polite hello into a deafening gunfire of excitement. The action was very obviously concentrated entirely in one room, but she pulled Kezia into the other, a wide empty space with a wooden floor and cathedral beams. At least there she could gather her thoughts, because she still wasn't exactly sure what she wanted to ask.

Rolls of fabric were stacked along the heavy-duty shelving, and huge drawstring bags hung from the ends, elongated and stuffed with smaller scraps of material. Tall sheaths of pale bamboo and auburn willow were standing by the floor-to-ceiling windows and rolls of wide black gaffer tape sat in a pile in one corner.

Kezia was just saying it looked like the recycling bank they used to go to in Norfolk to get free craft materials for the primary school when something fell off a shelf behind them with a bang. She jumped round to see three latex masks sitting on poles, looking at her with an expression and pallor somewhere between dead and alive. They had no hair, and just holes for the eyes, but their faces had the unmistakeable structure of real humans.

'Oh! Mummy! That frightened me,' she giggled unsurely, taking her mother's hand.

'Aaah! And there was I just thinking how safe it all felt.' Chess was starting to feel excited, as if there was something promising at last on the horizon. 'Come on, let's go and see what all that noise is about.'

They went back into the small panelled lobby full of stilts and paint pots and through another door into an identical space filled to the gunnels with commotion. Little children like ants, with a ratio of maybe one white to fifteen black, were running haphazardly around underneath two huge billowing green parachute silks. Eight adults held the four corners and were flapping the sheets up and down like bellows as the little shapes howled, screamed and wriggled underneath. The volume of noise was incredible.

A woman on the corner closest to them beckoned at Kezia to come and take over. The little girl shook her head and thrust her face shyly into her mother's (or rather Vienna's, since Chess had borrowed a little street cred from her daughter-in-law's wardrobe) purple fleeced tummy. After a few seconds, she resurfaced.

'Shall I, Mummy?'

'Do you want to?'

'Do you want me to?'

'Go on.'

Kezia crept to her position and took over her fistful of cloth with a grave sense of responsibility. As she glanced back proudly at her mother, Chess let out a long puff of air. Even dressed in her private school uniform, Kez blended in without distinction. She could have been coming to the Pinegrove since birth for how real she looked. The little scene had the big impact of a breakthrough, although into what, Chess still wasn't sure.

Drinking tea from a chipped blue mug in the comparative quiet of a small part-wooden, part-glass-panelled room between the two larger spaces, she tried to work it out. The words that were coming out of her mouth were strictly to do with Della and the opportunities for voluntary work, but there was something less easy to verbalise going on inside her head. It felt right, being here.

Jo Storey, the Pinegrove's co-ordinator, sat and listened. She was hard to age. Her face was lined, but she was wearing a tight khaki T-shirt that showed a flat bronzed stomach and a pierced navel, an oversized hooded jacket that flapped around her bony hips, a pair of voluminous sweat pants in washed-out orange and baseball boots. Her blonde dreadlocks looked like they'd been in for some time.

A hand-painted poster above the cluttered desk showed her in crayoned caricature wearing a badge saying *The Queen of Retro Grunge* – whatever that meant. It made Chess feel even safer, as did the little note above the wall-mounted hot water tank reminding people to wash their mugs up after use.

'And there are no opportunities for paid work? I think if Della started bringing home a proper wage packet . . .'

Jo Storey shook her head. 'We do employ people with childcare qualifications, but we're up and running on that at the moment.'

'She doesn't have any qualifications, full stop, but she's incredibly good at making something from nothing. Anyway, voluntary work would at least be something. Does it matter that she doesn't have any experience?'

'No. I was living in an old ambulance on common land in Oxford until two years ago and before that I was a battered wife. That's not much of a CV, is it?'

'Della knows all about being battered, which is part of the reason I want to help.'

Jo's face changed immediately. 'She does?'

The shared ground allowed them to fall into a more relaxed pattern of conversation. Chess got so involved in hearing Jo's story and telling Della's that she forgot Kezia was still in the other room, playing with strangers. As soon as she remembered, she put her head around the glass-panelled screen to retrieve her, but her daughter was no longer at her corner outpost with the adults. She was now one of the children under the parachute. Chess was smiling brightly when she sat back down, but Jo was more serious.

'Bloody men. Look, I think I'd like to pull a few strings and help, if that's OK. Tell Della to come and see me. All she needs to do is turn up and ask for me.'

When mother and daughter walked back down the steps across the tiny courtyard fluttering with items of rubbish blown off from the road, the sun was shining. Chess was suddenly so happy she launched herself off the bottom step and landed in a star shape.

'Mumm*eee*! Why did you do that?'

'I just felt like it.' She very nearly did something even more impulsive. Minnie lived just around the corner. She should be back from her holiday by now and Chess knew how much she would love to meet her great-granddaughter. If they went there now, Chess could talk to Della about the meeting she'd just had, and Kezia could play with Mercedes' roller blades. She hadn't seen her sister since their mad escape from Bear, and neither had she had a chance to talk to Minnie about Reuben. The only thing stopping her was herself, but it was a stumbling block she just didn't know how to budge, so instead they got back in the car and detoured past the tower block.

'I've been up there,' she said, pointing to Minnie's windows.

'Have you?' Kezia asked, only half-interested. 'Why?'

'You'll find out one day.' One day soon, she dared hope.

There she ran out of steam, but the temptation to talk to someone was so great she drove straight to the gallery.

Dan and Vienna stood in The Wall Space showroom in front of a large unframed canvas daubed with trowel-loads of acrylic paint. Somehow, the artist had managed to convey through the sweeping mess an impression of a woman's bare back with her face in an oval mirror beyond, but the more they looked at the seemingly random strokes, the less they could see the trick.

Dan wasn't really that interested, because he knew all about artistic device, but he remained standing there all the same, just so he had an excuse to be that close to Vienna's face. She wore no make-up and smelt very lightly of what he first mistook for cannabis and then realised was patchouli, and there was a gap in her creased linen pinafore which showed where her tight top ended and her pants began. He wanted to slide his hand in and touch it.

'Not your type?' Vienna asked. She meant the woman, not the painting, because Chess had told her about his latest preference and yet that wasn't what she had been picking up.

'I wouldn't rule her out,' Dan said. 'Would you?'

'Er . . . strangely, Dan, I would. She's a woman, and I don't fancy women.'

'Whyever not? I do.'

The flirting was a recent thing. Previously, they'd enjoyed only a cursory knowledge of each other based on the sporadic judgements of their extended family over a number of years. Dan had pigeonholed Vienna as the straight kid of a screwy mother and Vienna had put him down as the exact opposite.

Neither had been particularly intrigued. Then Vienna came to live with Nick and Chess and, as a result of one curious phone call, a fresh approach had come between them and the shock of re-evaluation had sparked both their interests.

She had called the gallery one day to speak to Chess, and Dan, who was there on his own, had been quite wonderfully evasive.

'Er . . . I'm not sure of her hours today,' he'd equivocated.

'But she said she was coming to you straight from school.'

'We don't take kids straight from school. We like our staff to have a few years of retail experience elsewhere.'

'Very good.'

'Thank you. No, I think she must be delivering something en route. I could check the rota.'

'A rota? For three of you? Is life in a gallery that complicated?'

'We lead busy lives. We all have other commitments, you know.'

'Yes, but yours are mostly nocturnal.'

'Ah, we've changed our opening hours.'

First point to him.

'Oh, don't worry,' Vienna had said casually. 'I expect she's with Della or Minnie.'

Second point to her.

'I thought that was supposed to be a secret.'

'So did I.'

'So why did you tell me?'

'Because Chess also told me she'd told you.'

'Ah-ha! She didn't tell *me* she'd told you, though. What are we to draw from that?'

'That she spoke to me after she spoke to you?'

'Excellent, Moneypenny, excellent. So how much do you know?'

'How much do *you* know?'

'I'm not prepared to say over the phone. Maybe we should meet up and compare notes.'

So far, they had managed to keep whatever relationship was

growing to themselves. That wasn't such a feat for Vienna, who was often a closed book, but for Dan not to blab was something else. But then this *did* feel like something else to him – so much so that he had resisted the temptation to offer himself in the way he usually did. His customary habit was sex first, relationship afterwards, maybe. This time, he wanted to play it differently.

Anyway, if any of the interested parties around them had picked up the trace of courtship, they would have soon come up against a dead end.

When Dan called Vienna, it was on the extra line Nick had considerately installed for her in her attic room. If they saw each other, it was on neutral ground away from either of their homes. Neither of them fuelled it more than the other.

Having lived for so many years with Sonya, a woman driven by a destructive need to bombard her men daily regardless of reason or response, Vienna had learned to wait. She very rarely made the first move, and never chewed her nails or had to sit on her hands to maintain that distinction. If someone wanted her, and assuming of course that she wanted them, they had to make it clear. She wasn't going to waste her energy on half-heartedness. Dan, who was used to being the pursued rather than the pursuer, was impressed. He could see as clear as day that she was just doing what came naturally. It was just a pity his own instincts were now so unreliable, as he had no idea *what* came naturally to him any more.

What drew *her* to him was his apparent lack of need, his ability to make choices without reference to anyone else, his confidence in a personality shaped by his own hands. Other people might have worn such accolades with arrogance, but with him, well, it just made him easy to be with.

That the gallery was just around the corner from Vienna's college was a happy convenience. She was there for the third time in a week, supposedly swapping more notes, and Dan had just got round to embellishing Chess's arrest story with a few extras when the talk of the devil walked in with Kezia.

'Oh, Vienna! Aaagh! I'm wearing your top! Sorry, d'you

mind?' Chess laughed happily. It had been a good morning, and she was pleased to see a third party.

'Course not, it suits you.'

'So, what are you doing here?' *Ask me where I've been,* Chess urged silently. *Ask me where I've been.*

'Oh, just chatting up Dan.'

Kezia made one of her yuck faces.

'You and I should have a little talk,' Chess teased, shaking her head at Dan. 'So, what do you want me for?'

'I don't want you. I want Dan.' Vienna did actually, more and more. So far, he hadn't asked her for any advice, he hadn't tried too hard, he hadn't made her feel too wise for her age. He was also hard to pin down, and most boys at college made themselves irritatingly available for her.

'Long shot, Vienna, long shot.' Chess was too excited to pick up any grains of truth in the repartee.

'You just don't listen, do you?' Dan said to Chess, and then to Vienna, 'She's missed the point entirely.'

'Have nothing to do with the boy, he's out of control.'

'Er . . . *man*, please.'

Kezia was hanging on adoringly to her older sister, arms round her waist, face simpering upwards for attention.

'Why aren't you at school?'

'Got a bad throat,' Kezia said through a guilty smile.

'And a bad spelling test,' Chess added. 'I should really take her back this afternoon.'

'Oh, Mum.'

'Is it hurting again, Kez?' Dan asked, egging her on.

'Yes.'

'I'm not surprised, with all that shouting you've just been doing,' Chess told her.

'What shouting?'

Kezia took the cue perfectly, just as her mother hoped she would. She forgot the Pinegrove's name and described it as a nursery school, but spoke poetically about the parachute silks and the way they billowed out and you just knew you had to run under it because it looked such fun but you were a bit scared too because it came down on top of you and it took a while to find your way out.

'Can we go back there soon, Mummy, please, please?'

'Hope so.' Chess turned to Dan. 'I'm getting there, slowly. I've persuaded Della to leave her bastard of a boyfriend, and I think I might have found her a job. Can I give her a quick ring while Vienna looks after Kez?'

He waved her into the storeroom. 'Do it in there,' he winked. 'I know it's one of your favourite places.'

When she came back out, she was glowing. 'Della's really up for it,' she told everyone, with Della's words – 'you done dat for *me*? She want to see me? When do I affe go?' – still ringing in her ears. It was part of the reason she didn't react to what Dan had to say the first time, so he repeated it, this time taking her to one side.

'Er, Chess, would this bastard of a boyfriend have a Nike Air tick shaved into his hair, by any chance?'

'Yes, why?' Her posture stiffened and a hot dread coursed up the back of her neck.

'Because he came looking for you here this morning.'

Chess drove the Golf at a blind panic through the busy streets to get to Clapham, veering recklessly up cycle routes she barely knew, and shouting at Vienna for directions from the *A to Z*.

'Why are we doing this?' the teenager asked without adding to the drama.

'Because Dan said someone was looking for me, and this man is dangerous. I don't trust him.'

'Who is *this man*?'

'Della's boyfriend. Ex, thanks to me.'

'Bear?'

'Yes.'

'And what does he want with you?'

'That's the bit I don't know.' But Chess could guess. He had been in the gallery, on her territory, there not by coincidence but design. He had infiltrated her world, turned up at the party uninvited like the bad fairy in a pantomime, a flash of acrid yellow smoke and an evil gold-capped tooth laugh.

Suddenly, nothing in her life had immunity from his risk. The fact that she had one of her children sitting in the back of the car now, singing along to *Joseph and the Technicolour Dreamcoat* was no comfort at all, because it merely meant the other one was alone.

Having neither child usually meant they were somewhere together and she had always believed there was safety in numbers. When she was young, she was never scared of anything if Judith was with her. She remembered a weekend three years ago when she, Nick and Kezia had flown to Germany for a weekend with friends and left Sam as a baby at home with Honor. She'd spent the whole break imagining the plane crashing, Sam being reared as an orphan, his entire family in pieces in the air.

He was still small, only five, and she knew he would go with anyone who waved chocolate in his face. School might be out before she got there, the teachers might be looking the other way when Bear waved his bag of sweets.

'Benson Place, Benson Place, where next? We need to head for Clapham or Streatham,' she bellowed at Vienna.

'Calm down, you'll crash the car. Go right, into Holmewood Avenue, then straight over to Marchmont Road, then we'll be on the north side of the Common. Try and tell me what kind of trouble you are in, Chess.'

'Self-induced. Oh God, I hate thinking of him in the gallery. Are you OK back there, Kez?' Chess asked, a light stranglehold on her voice.

'She's fine, she's got her headphones on. Why do you think he's out to get you?'

'Because I dared to stand up to him. I persuaded Della to leave him the other day for her own safety.'

'And now you think you've jeopardised your own?'

'I can't even think about it.'

Every parking space around the school was taken, and Chess remembered the Juniors Autumn Medley that afternoon. Kezia was supposed to have taken brown tights and a polo neck to be a squirrel.

'I should be in there, watching children scamper round collecting papier mâché nuts, not out here jumping dementedly from tree to tree trying to avoid the . . . the . . . whatever it is that eats squirrels.'

'I'm sure bears don't eat squirrels,' Vienna said calmly.

'Nike Air tick, look for a Nike Air tick.' Chess circuited the block, staring intently into the insides of cars.

'What are you looking for, Mummy?' Kezia asked, taking off her headphones.

'Her peace of mind?' Vienna answered.

'Anything with mirrored windows, or beat up, or maybe too flashy, anything, just look, and take the number.'

The less they saw, the more rational Chess became. A lollipop lady took up her post, nannies driving employers' cars rolled up and double parked in youthful audacity, mothers and pushchairs arrived. By the time the children came trotting out of the classroom door trailing coats and bags, Chess was almost thinking sanely again. Perhaps Bear had come to ask her to arbitrate between him and Della, or to do him another favour, or God forbid, to chat her up. Her paranoia was based on very little really.

'Why are you crushing me?' Sam asked as his mother's arms clamped round his small body in the playground.

'Just pleased to see you,' Chess said, picking him up.

'I can walk,' he protested, trying to wriggle to the ground.

'Sorry, I forgot,' his mother said, watching him march towards the gates without fear.

She apologised to Vienna on the way home too. 'Thanks for holding me together back there. I lost it for a bit, didn't I?'

'You could say that. I wish you'd tell Dad.'

'Do you?' The age gap between Chess and Vienna sometimes seemed the other way round.

'I just think it's more dangerous not to.'

Her wise words hung in the air between them until they got home. The house showed no signs of unwarranted attention.

Prospects of having to change locks, get British Telecom to put an intercept on their phone, get the property properly alarmed – all those desperate strategies that had spun in Chess's head during the treacherous race to rescue Sam – faded to almost embarrassingly silly overreaction. Maybe she was even beginning to get off on all this drama. Maybe she needed to keep up this level of tension for some reason. Maybe it was even all self-fulfilling. A twenty-pound note was still there in the fruit bowl where she had left it yesterday. That must surely mean there had been no intruders.

The fruit bowl was the first thing Minnie noticed too when she let herself back into her thoroughfare of a flat. Astonishing though it was, someone other than her had filled it with bananas, pears and a packet of dried apricots. Then something else unusual caught her eye. On the side was a cereal bowl full of pistachio nuts, and some of the empty shells had been painted with what looked like glitter nail varnish and were drying on a newspaper on the windowsill. It felt to the old woman like she had been gone a lifetime.

The reminder that Della's life was on the turn, that the girl still had enough time left to be that much of a mother to her children, made Minnie's optimistic blood start to flow again. It had become rather congealed, sitting in a depressed puddle in her tight smart patent shoes making her ankles swell for the last few hours as the train rattled up the lonely line from Portsmouth away from Reuben. Her heart then hadn't been up to pumping anything of any substance round her body. It was too busy crying into the little gold ring that sat on her breast at the end of a thin gold chain – parting presents from her love.

Reuben had wanted to drive her to her door, but she couldn't allow it. His plane back home to Jamaica left in the early hours of tomorrow morning and he needed the rest of his stay to say his goodbyes in Portsmouth too. So they had parted at the railway station, keeping themselves together over sugared tea in the platform buffet. He had trotted along beside the chugging train for as long as his age would allow before the train took her off and away. Even as a speck, she could tell his forlorn figure had slumped into a shared misery. Only God knew if they would meet again.

Not only was the fruit bowl full, but there was chicken in the fridge and money in the meter. Della had kept to her word then, about not going back to her bad man. Mercedes would be pleased – she didn't like her father any more than Minnie did, although what Tyrone thought nowadays was anyone's guess. Minnie feared for him at thirteen as much as she feared for Della now. Families, families, how had it all come to this?

And yet in one way, her family felt more solid to her today than it ever had done. All her precious time with Reuben, she had tingled with another warmth too. Snatches of the long 'confessional' she'd enjoyed with Della and Frankie before she'd left kept coming back to hug her. She had learnt things that afternoon after her West End shopping trip that she had never asked before and would never question again – and they in turn had learnt things about her. And she had gone to Weymouth not only understanding at last their desires, regrets, jealousies and fears, but also rejoicing in the fact that Reuben was no longer a secret. She could put his photograph on the mantelpiece now if she wanted to, drop him into the conversation, phone him when the flat was full instead of empty. And that, after so many years, was a miracle.

She pulled her suitcase along the corridor, abandoned it outside the bathroom, and for want of anything better to do, took up her familiar position in the plastic-wrapped chair in front of the television. It was time to catch up on her teatime soap.

But the characters seemed more false than ever and the storyline was ridiculous. 'People don't do that,' she tutted to herself, 'they don't act like that, it's silly, it's all so silly.' She lost her patience with it all together, flicked it over halfway through and then turned the television off with an exclamation of distaste.

'I got better t'ings to do!' she said to herself just as the flat filled with the noises of real life – a mother chiding her child, the grunting broken voice of a teenage boy, bags being dumped and a kettle being filled. 'Ah!'

Perhaps she would try harder to save for the automatic reclining chair after all, she decided as her arthritic knees protested with the effort of heaving herself up. Still, it was worth the pain to see them all again.

'I come back!' she said, looking at them round the door-frame. 'Did yuh miss me?' Their London skins looked under-nourished, their clothes were discoloured by wash and wear, but they were there – her family – and they were smiling. How she would like to show them the sea!

'Granny, I t'ink I got a job!'

As she and Della hugged, Reuben's ring – now tucked discreetly inside her acrylic jumper and nylon slip – pressed into her bosom. 'It is happenin',' she heard him say. 'We are gettin' our happy ending after all.'

Whether it was disbelief, shock or denial, the first time Nick tried to walk across the room after Chess had told him everything, he pitched and rolled just as if he were on a ship. His balance was barely intact as he reeled down the steep wooden stairs into their cellar to retrieve another very necessary bottle of wine. In the cool darkness, he had lingered a little. His world now felt more precarious than the rotten steps back up. God, what had she *done*? The first bit, about going to the Notting Hill Carnival and rekindling a relationship with her real family was almost a relief. It had been so good not to hear his wife say anything along the corny but dreaded lines of, 'I've met someone else,' that anything would have been more acceptable.

There was a sting of false memory though, from that August evening's barbecue with Kezia and her sore bottom, and Sam being so chivalrous, and them both curling up in their sleeping bags using laps for pillows while the wine was finished. He'd carried that balmy family scene around in his imaginary photo album ever since, cheered with the idea that a new house brought new snapshots, but he wouldn't be able to look at it again now, would he? He'd have to tear it up and pretend it never happened. It felt as if his wife had ransacked his understanding.

More hurtful though was the thought that she had considered him, her flexible tolerant husband, a problem area. For why? He had never expressed any view one way or another about her real family. It was an area way beyond their joint experience and he'd assumed that was where his wife had wanted it to stay. He had never labelled her, never pigeonholed her, never forced her to do or be anything for his benefit – only ever hers.

Even as he made this mitigation to himself down there in the chill bowels of their home, he realised it wasn't true. He *had* noticed Chess putting out her feelers again, but he had purposefully ignored them. And yet part of his defence mechanism to turn the other way could be justified – he'd seen trouble ahead, and now look.

The first few minutes of her bombshell might have been surprising, but they were nothing he felt would cause their lives to explode. But then she had taken the pin out of a hidden hand grenade and thrown it right into the centre of their camp. That's what he was finding it difficult to forgive her for, that was why he wished he could stay down here, with the wine and the freezer and his toolbox, safe from the urge to shake her and shout at her for being so damn fucking selfish. A confession of infidelity at that point would almost have been preferable.

At the very mention of a locked tin that belonged to a man called 'Bear' who sounded inhuman enough to be truly anthropomorphic, all sympathy had frozen inside him. He'd stopped paying lip service then. All the questions he would normally have asked in encouragement – How did she feel? What did she want to do next? Did she know he still loved her? – just dried right up. He'd sat there, staring in disbelief at the level of her stupidity. Delivering locked tins, police arrest, a day in the cells . . . *a search of their house*?

'Oh, come on Chess, you're having me on.'

'No, listen, please. I'm not. I block it, Nick, you should too.'

'Oh I should, should I?'

'I'm only telling you so there are no more secrets. I returned the tin to him the next day, and the two hundred pounds he gave me, and told him I couldn't be involved in anything like that any more.'

'You said that to his face, did you?'

'Well, no, I said it to Della, but then I went back the next day and that was when Della walked out.'

'Because you told her to?'

'Yes.'

Nick didn't speak again until she had finished. Bear standing naked in the bathroom door shouting threats, the flashback to the gorilla and big stick nightmare of her childhood, the two of them running from the flat and screaming, the morning's visit to the Pinegrove – and then Bear going to the gallery to find her. When she got to the bit about her berserk driving through London to get to Sam, she'd made the mistake of laughing. It had sounded so crazy, the way she'd told it.

'I can't believe you think it's funny,' he shouted.

'I don't, I'm sorry, I don't. I was terrified, really, I lost my head. I really thought Bear was out there to get me, or my children.'

'*Our* children. But what for?'

'For depriving him of his punchbag? I don't know! But what kind of a sister would I be if I stood by and watched that happen?'

She'd said the word *sister* totally unselfconsciously, but Nick heard it in italics as a deliberate point, stirring both pity and derision in his angry mind. What kind of mother? What kind of wife?

'The same kind of sister that couldn't find the time to go and visit her premature nephew in hospital?' he'd asked sarcastically and headed unsteadily for the cellar. It had only taken them half an hour to drink the first bottle, but that was not why he stumbled. The equilibrium in his life had gone.

While he was down there, Chess sat at the table pressing her fingertips into her closed eyelids and thinking she really had lost him. In that moment, it was almost as if he had already gone, and the prospect of a life without him frightened her so much she could hardly think of what to say or do next.

Her feet took her to the top of the cellar steps where she called his name feebly, but he was up and out of there in a surge of anger, hiding his rage and confusion behind practicalities. Chess wondered at first if he was trying to scare her even more than Bear had, for punishment.

'Have you checked your credit cards?' he barked, grabbing her handbag and pulling out her wallet, which he spun across the table towards her.

'Why?'

'Come on – if you tipped your bag out in this bloke's flat then you might have left something more than Kezia's spelling book. What other parts of our life does he have access to? Does he have our address? Our telephone number? Come on, think, THINK!'

He opened a low cupboard and dragged out a cardboard concertina file. 'Tomorrow, you'll have to cancel all your cards. Say you've lost them, and ask them to send you new ones. I want the locks changed on the house. I'll take the children to school, you stay here until it's done. Fuck it, we'll even put this place on the market.'

'Nick, it's a Saturday tomorrow.'

He was on overdrive.

'*Nick!*'

'What? You want to be safe, don't you? Wasn't that the number one priority when we came here? Wasn't that top of our list when we bought the house and chose the school?' He wasn't looking at her, but flicking madly through papers for helplines and locksmiths.

'We *are* safe. You're just doing what I did in the car after Dan told me he'd been at the gallery.'

He continued to search without answering.

'Nick, please, just stop and sit down with me. I love you, I'm sorry, I really, really am. I couldn't bear it if anything ruined this.'

'*If*?' he shouted. 'What do you mean, *if*?'

'It hasn't, has it? We'll be OK, we'll get over it.'

'Will we?' It wasn't reassurance he was after, it was reality.

She started sobbing, laying her head in her hands on Sam's Star Wars placemat, and waited for him to come over, to lift her head and kiss her better. But he didn't. He just carried on combing his files for PIN numbers and cheque guarantee cards.

'This is *exactly* why I've kept it from you,' she found herself shouting through her tears, even though she knew it would only make things worse. 'You're not helping. I didn't do any of this lightly – ask Dan.'

'Ask *Dan*? Don't tell me you were taking advice from Dan.'

'Please, Nick, can't we sit down and talk about this rationally? I really need–'

The phone next to her rang.

'Hello?' She heard breathing against background noise and, once she had slammed it back down, she thought she could remember a Jamaican voice say, 'She dere, man.'

'Who was that?' Nick asked.

'Kids,' she said. 'Wrong number.'

Chapter 20

Dan woke in the annexe of the mews house he shared with his parents and felt oddly deprived. His time with Vienna the day before had been cut short by Chess's hysterical departure from the gallery, and the pocket of air she had left empty had followed him round for the rest of the day.

When it was still there the next morning – a previously unheard-of turn in his romantic history – he decided to go for a quick fix, so he reached for the phone even before he got out of bed.

'What are you up to today?'

Her voice sounded sleepy, which caused a stir somewhere other than just in his groin. 'Taking Kezia and Sam to a circus thing on the Common.'

'You like a bit of trapeze, do you?'

'It could be performing hamsters for all I care, I just want to be out of the house for as long as possible.'

'Oh, what, it's a shit and fan situation there, is it?'

'Uh huh. I hate it when people take my advice.'

'Why?'

'Oh, because I told Chess after all that mad panic yesterday that I thought it was time to put Dad in the picture. I didn't mean the *whole* picture though.'

'Chess doesn't possess an editing facility, you should know that. It's either all or nothing with her.'

'I'm learning that. Anyway, you could cut it here this morning with a knife.'

'Mmmm, well, I could always come and walk the tightrope with you, if you like.'

'OK. Bring Todd.'

'Who?'

'Todd. Chess has got a HUGE mouth, Dan – and you should know *that*.'

'Oh, *Todd* . . . passing phase, passing phase. In fact, I can tell you that the phase has actually passed. It's history.'

'God-damn butterfly,' she teased, lying on her back on her bed, waving one of her crossed legs flirtatiously in the air. She could only do flirtatious over the phone. Her sense of cool kicked in at all other times.

'So . . . what else do you know about me?' he asked.

'You know Chess! All or nothing, isn't it?'

'And you're *still* prepared to spend time with me?'

'I'd never have had you down as humble, Dan.'

Good answer, he thought, wishing they were having this conversation in bed.

A small painted bus was parked in the middle of the green beyond a church that had already seen one wedding off that morning and was gearing up for another. Confetti swirled around the forecourt, and the Jacoby children, oblivious to the shades of mutual attraction passing between their escorts, picked up handfuls of the stuff mixed with autumn leaves and rammed them down each other's necks. It was a game other young flirting couples might have echoed, but not Dan and Vienna.

Their movements were poised and assured, and the signals they gave off were in collective opinions or shared jokes. They chose to play with each other through speech instead, which made their stroll towards the bus all the more absorbing, arousing even.

Dan knew now he was bored with relationships revolving around the physical, and his brief foray into homosexuality had made him feel like a trainee contortionist. See who can do this one! The more acrobatic the sex had become, the less he had been interested. As an experiment, it had ultimately failed. This time, he was going to get it right. If it took a long time for it to happen, it took a long time. In some ways, the longer it took, the more he would want her.

A small crowd had already gathered around the circus site to watch the warm-up antics. A performer in a striped bathing suit and flippers was constructing a semi-circle of stepped seats and shouting theatrically at other members of the troupe who got purposely in his way. Two large battered A-frames joined by a wire were being dragged from the bus by a slight woman with aubergine hair and a big bloke with no hair at all. They had to-ing and fro-ing off to a fine art.

Sam barged a thigh-high busy path through to the front, but Kezia hung back more cautiously until she saw him sit down at a ringside seat, put his elbows on his knees, his palms either side of his chin, and wait patiently for the action to begin. She was about to join him – brothers were useful for paving the way sometimes – when the bathing-suit man zoomed in, clambered cartoon-like up the boxed seating and settled next to Sam in a perfect imitation of the boy's patient position. Soon, the drama school graduate had launched into improvisation, scratching the child's head, untying his shoelaces, pressing his nose to see if it made a noise. As an ice-breaker, it worked well, and before the little boy could back off, he was up on his shoulders, upside down, through his legs and back on top again.

Sam's round cinnamon face remained expressionless at first, his brain still undecided which message to send to his mouth, but then he understood and relaxed enough to start smiling, at first shyly, and then without even being conscious that he was. Soon, he was shouting 'Whoooaahh!' and 'Aaaagghhhh!' at every acrobatic turn.

Kezia, proud, envious, worried and excited, hopped from foot to foot, and then turned to find a familiar grown-up to tell her everything was all right. But Vienna and Dan had walked away from the seating and round the back of the bus, where they were engrossed in watching the unpacking.

It was like a three-dimensional jigsaw. Unicycles hung from ladders suspended on rods that doubled as tent-poles, wooden stage flooring was stacked neatly into steps to reach the highest props rigged from the roof, and costumes dangled from fixed chicken wire around the sides.

'I'm in awe,' Vienna said to the big bloke with the shaved head.

'Logistical nightmare,' he smiled.

'I bet.'

'Stick around and you can help us put it all away again. We're always after cheap labour.'

Kezia found them just as she was starting to fret. 'Sam's on the clown! Sam's on the clown! Come and see!'

They ran, but when they reached the mini-amphitheatre with its circular wooden stage and scuffed painted star, Sam's show was over. He wasn't on the bathing-suit man's shoulders any more, nor back in his saved place. In fact, he was nowhere to be seen.

All three of them swivelled their heads and spun on the balls of their feet two or three times, fully expecting to pick him up on their radars. Then they moved to the outside of the crowd and back around the bus to do the same.

Sam was small and similar in appearance to at least twenty per cent of the other children his age, so it was a little like looking for a needle in a haystack.

'He had him last!' Kezia shouted, pointing to the clown, but when they approached him, he told them he thought the child had gone with his dad.

'His dad's not here!' Vienna told him, a panic in her voice rising to a cry that was swallowed by a clash of cymbals.

Dan held tightly on to Kezia's hand. 'Don't worry,' he said, although the Nike Air Tick man from yesterday had begun to squat like an evil troll in his mind.

'Sam? Sam? SAM?'

Kezia burst into tears. Why had Daddy been going on at breakfast about not talking to strangers and keeping close to your special adult, and what to do if anyone you didn't know tried to persuade you to go off with them? Why had he told them to shout 'NO! YOU'RE NOT MY DAD. GO AWAY!'

and if they got lost, to head for the nearest shop and speak to someone behind the till? Did he know Sam was going to get lost today?

'Where is he? What's happened to him?' she sobbed.

'We'll find him. He'll be on the swings, wondering what all the fuss is about.'

They combed the immediate area to no avail before splitting up and searching further afield. Without asking her permission, Dan ran Kezia back to the circus bus and handed her, still crying, over to the woman with the aubergine hair.

'Lost her little brother – can you just . . .?' He was out of breath.

'No, Dan, I want to come!'

'Yes, Kez, just for five minutes. I can run faster than you.'

'Shall we go and have a look inside the bus?' the woman smiled to Kezia.

Dan legged it up the park to hail a female cyclist and borrow her bike. As he tore up and down the grid of roads that crossed the Common, he tried to minimise the threat. How long had Sam been out of sight for? Five minutes? Maybe ten? Any abductor would have had to watch carefully to take advantage of that small window, and there had been no sign of Mr Nike Air Tick. A bloke like that wouldn't blend in with all this lot easily. But then – and the 'but' was getting bigger every minute that passed – he had been too busy studying Vienna and she had been too busy studying the bus to notice.

Vienna meanwhile was running in wide concentric circles, asking questions. 'Have you seen a little boy in a black puffa?' It wasn't specific enough.

'Have you seen a darkish-skinned little boy, mixed race, in a black puffa and sort of petrolly-blue trousers?' Vienna was too worried to think about political correctness. It still wasn't enough. People wanted to help, but they couldn't. They stared, tried to be useful, looked around with her, but then they apologised and went on their way.

'Sam? Sam? SAM?'

In her mind, she was already back at the house, telling Chess her son was missing. It didn't bear thinking about. Oh God, Bear. Bear. She should look for Bear.

'Have you seen a big black man with a little boy?'

More detail, more detail.

'Have you seen a big black man with a Nike Air tick shaved into the back of his hair with a little boy?'

But no one had registered him if they had.

Back in the once-calm family home, Nick felt like a human pressure-cooker. He'd been on the hob all night and the steam was now rising inside him to screaming pitch. It had started the final build-up at dawn, with the children running up and down the landing, making nests from bedclothes, running water in the bathroom – activities designed purely to winkle parents out of their shells and start the day. Chess had remained with her head under the spare room duvet pretending not to hear, and he had assumed she was avoiding him. Actually, she was avoiding herself.

He had never seen her in the state she had been in last night, and he still hadn't been able to comfort her. Usually, all she had to do was let a few tears escape and he'd be there apologising. Not this time. This time he instinctively knew they both had to hit the pits – the real pits – before deciding if it was worth trying to climb back up together or not. They'd never been in the real pits before, because he hadn't let things get that far. That was why today was different.

Neither of them had bothered to clear the kitchen table last night before going to their separate beds, which meant that Sugar Puffs and milk were slopped on the papers from the file, and toast was clumsily buttered in fat wedges by small hands with the smell of red wine still heavy in the air.

Two Silk Cut cigarette butts sat in a saucer. Chess had produced them without apology from an already-opened packet in her bag. He wasn't going to clear them away. He wanted them to sit and stare at her over her cereal and remind her that it wasn't just the odour of stale smoke she had brought into the house.

When she did eventually surface, they concentrated on the children or spoke through Vienna, but as soon as these three human shields had disappeared to the Common and the house had been empty, they were required at last to look each other in the eye.

'Please Nick, I'm sorry,' Chess pleaded.

'I don't want to discuss it,' was all he could muster as a reply.

Their conversation from then on stuck to the practical – locksmiths, credit cards, British Telecom. Nick was able to suffer it no more than twenty minutes before putting on his running shoes and escaping into the lighter air outside. At a point in their relationship not so long ago, he would have been able to see beyond the crisis. He would have seen a lost soul. Not today. Today, Chess was selfish, unthinking, and reckless. And worse than that, he wasn't sure if he could ever feel the same way about her again.

He jogged down the uniform streets wondering where it would all lead. If she removed the threat, that would be a start. If she would bring him in, include the children, that would be another. But separate lives? He couldn't even imagine it, until it occurred to him that, actually, they had already been leading them.

The convivial air on the Common was initially good to breathe. Secure human relationships, stable homes, happy safe protected children were everywhere. Maybe his two looked like just that to strangers too, sitting next to Vienna and Dan somewhere over there, by the painted van and trapeze wires, waiting for a performance to begin. He decided to run the perimeter of the middle section before going over to find them. He was proud of them, he wanted people to know they were his. If he convinced outsiders that everything was all right, then maybe he'd convince himself.

Dan returned the bike to its apprehensive owner and collected Kezia from the van with profound thanks. Then he found Vienna, still circling wildly and shouting Sam's name repeatedly. His heart sank when he saw her alone. He'd been keeping himself going imagining a luckier outcome.

'Why don't you and Kez start walking home in case he's set off on his own? If he's still not turned up here in fifteen minutes, I'll call you and then we'll call the police.'

Kezia let out a wail of alarm. 'I want my baby brother, I want Sam, my baby brother, where is he?' Her lament grew louder and people stared with detached concern.

'Don't cry. He's probably having a much better time than we are.' Vienna's lips were dry and white with fear.

'Hey,' Dan said, putting his arm around her shoulders and feeling the wiggled texture of her long-haired fleece which looked as if it came from a mad saffron sheep, 'this isn't a movie. It'll be OK.' It was the first time they had touched, but the moment was lost on them both.

She nodded but they could both see the straight and very empty pavement ahead. Sam wasn't on this road, and as soon as she turned the corner, the whole of the next one would stretch out before her and she knew he wouldn't be on that one either. There's no way the child knew his way home. It wouldn't even occur to him to try and find it.

She swung her little sister's arm to try and ease the terror and they marched briskly. Kezia's face was wet, she was sniffing, her lips were blubbering and she kept tripping over her laces to keep up, but by the time they got to the familiar black and white tiled path of home and started to unlock the green door, they had both fallen silent. There was always a chance, of course.

Chess heard the key being turned, stopped unloading the washing machine, and looked up to see the familiar taller and shorter silhouettes through the glass.

'Back already?' she shouted before the door was opened. She would try not to appear too broken. It wasn't the children's fault.

'Is Sam here?' Kezia screamed through the letterbox. 'Is he?'

A bird's-eye view of the scene might have been comical if it hadn't been so bloody horrifying too. The four adults converged like latterday Keystone Cops from different points to a central unpremeditated location. Chess, Vienna and Kezia ran along the residential roads, panting, explaining, listening, and panicking. Dan ran across the Common grass from east to west, thinking, planning and searching. And then there was Nick, running from the north, boiling, seething – and thank God, thank God, thank God – comforting.

Sam was in his arms, too big to carry, too small to run, and too upset at this moment to be told off for wandering. His father had spotted him by pure chance, being spun round and knocked over by an oblivious swarm of bigger boys in football strips, too far away from the circus and familiar faces to know what to do next. As the soccer team thinned and dispersed, Nick jogged past and saw a little lad with muddy knees and grit in his palms. Then he recognised the exact pitch of the crying.

Following the identical thought-process of the other three adults in that morning's drama, he swooped in to rescue his son from the sure danger of a lurking child-snatcher. In the invention of his mind, there had been only minutes to spare.

When the six of them all but collided on the paving outside the church, Nick's pressure cooker finally and noisily let off its blast of scorching hot steam. He was too busy firing off at all of them to notice that his wife and daughters were all crying. Dan wasn't far off losing it either.

'What the FUCK did you think you were doing? You were supposed to be looking after them! Where were you? Do you realise what the consequences might have been?'

But no sooner were the words out than they evaporated into the air, just like the hot mist rising from the polystyrene coffee cups and the fog of smoke from the beefburgers being sold from the nearby van. Everyone knew Nick's anger wasn't really aimed at Vienna or Dan. He clung to Sam, held his tiny head wet with tears against his shoulder and turned on Chess.

'This is YOUR doing! YOUR doing! We can't even feel safe about our kids playing in the bloody park any more. Your selfish reckless plans . . . what do you think it does to Kezia, eh, to see us like this? Or Sam? All this grief heaped on a five-year-old kid for just wandering off and going to watch some football, for God's sake!'

There was a silence. It had taken Nick a lifetime to launch an offensive like this and to see the fallout amount to so little was frustrating. Kezia stared, waiting for the next blast. Sam wept gently into his father's clothes and Vienna and Dan made moves to slope off. It was the sight of Dan sliding his hand protectively into his eldest daughter's, as if to keep her strong against the enemy, that brought him round.

'No, don't go.' Nick's voice suddenly dropped a few decibels and his damp form drooped with fatigue. 'I'm sorry, I'm sorry kids, I was as scared as the rest of you, that's all.'

No one moved or spoke, although Kezia nodded.

'London takes some getting used to,' he said feebly. 'I'm sorry.'

He by-passed Chess with his words and his eyes, but she understood. His skin and clothes were clammy with the sweat of panic and exertion, and she was shaking with the after-effects of shock. Together they made a sorry sight. At risk of almost certain rejection, she moved forward to clasp his hand.

'You're always apologising,' she said quietly. He didn't withdraw but instead squeezed it tightly back until it almost hurt. It wasn't quite a message of love and forgiveness. She could feel his heart still churning through his fingers. 'But I'm sorry too,' she added. *Sorry for antagonising Bear, that is. Sorry for putting other people at risk. Sorry for creating a gap in our marriage.* But she still couldn't be sorry for the other stuff, for forging her way back to Minnie or for rescuing Della. 'I think we're scaring ourselves unnecessarily. We don't know enough about him to do this. We're being silly.'

'OK, kids? Show over?' Nick said, unclasping his hand from Chess and clapping once in encouragement. His wife missed his grasp and the hole appeared in her heart again. Kezia and Sam nodded.

'Hug?' Chess asked. It was a family thing, and the four of them pulled together, little arms, big arms, white arms, black ones, all folded round jackets, jumpers, scarves and gloves. 'Do you forgive me?' she whispered in her husband's ear. *For what?* she asked herself. *I still don't know what it is I think I've done wrong*. But she asked again anyway. 'Please forgive me.'

Nick just increased the pressure of his embrace and exhaled slowly and heavily. 'We'll talk later,' he said.

'Who wants you? Is dat Frankie?' Minnie was hovering by the phone in her hall, trying to pick up the threads of the unlikely conversation her granddaughter seemed to be having. Della had one foot on a skateboard and was pushing it up and down and occasionally into the textured wallpaper just above the skirting board as she spoke.

Minnie bent down, slapped her shin in reproach just as she would to a child, and pulled the board away. 'Look what you done!'

The new hole made no difference really, since it blended invisibly into all the other scrapes and rips from pedals and wheels over the years, but it gave the older woman a reason to be there, to listen to the soft reassurance and sympathy and other tilts of the voice she wasn't used to hearing when Della spoke. It was pretty music to her ageing ears.

'Was dat Frankie?' she asked again when the conversation ended.

'Yeh, but she don't answer to Frankie, Granny. She answer to Chess, innit? Call her dat, or you'll confuse us all.'

'And since when do I answer to Granny, eh? Not since you a chile.'

'You bin a Granny all yuh life!' Della teased. 'No, but listen. Chess t'ink Bear is out to get her. I try tellin' her he jus' want to scare her, punish her for interferin' and dat, but she really t'ink he might do somet'ing real bad, to her or her family. He might do somet'ing, I don't know, I t'ink he won't. My feelin' here is dat he's gone, y'nah?'

'If he dare try it, I . . .' Minnie was walking back down the dim hallway to take up her post in the kitchen again. It was stew day, for a change.

'But her baby boy got lost today in de park and her man . . .'

'Husbaand,' Minnie said. 'Her man is a husbaand, an' he has a name, Nick. An' de boy is Sam.'

'Whatever, but he – Nick – t'ink for one minute dat Sam bin kidnapped by Bear an' he's gone apeshit an'–'

'Della! Wash yuh mouth!'

'Listen – he's gonna change all de locks an–'

'Yuh not tellin' me de boy is gone?'

'No, no, he jus' got lost an he's safe now, but you missin' de point, Granny. Chess has lost her head, y'nah? She was beggin' me jus' den to ask Bear to leave her alone. I told her he probably ain't even t'inkin' 'bout her no more, dat she's small fry now, an' he will soon forget 'bout her altogether an' dat, but she jus' din't wan' to listen. I tell her dat 'cos I really t'ink it's de truth, but y'nah, she knows wha' he does, an' . . .'

'She done not'ing, not'ing.'

'But she's so frightened, she don't know how she gonna deal wid it.'

As Minnie pulled and pushed the fat away from the meat and the meat away from the bone, Della gave her every detail – Bear's trip to the gallery, his threats, Nick's fear.

'Choh! It's not right she suffer for him. You goin' affe put dis right.'

'How den? If I tell him wha' she wan' me to say, dat she's frightened an' she wants him to leave her alone, he jus' gonna carry on, innit? If I say not'ing, he will forget.'

Minnie was thinking, nodding her head slowly up and down, recognising her granddaughter's logic.

'But I need to do somet'ing, jus' for Chess an' her own peace. She's so frightened, Granny.' Della stopped talking for a moment and then, staring out of the kitchen window into the grimy distance, she said quietly as if her mind was already made up, 'I gonna affe go back to Bear.'

Minnie whimpered. 'No,' she said, starting to shake her head.

'But dat's wha' he want, Granny. If he t'inks he won, he won't trouble her no more.'

'Dat's not wah' yuh sistah wants!'

Minnie looked at Della and saw again the transformation that had crept up on her granddaughter in the last few weeks.

She was dressed in clothes – tracksuit bottoms and a faded hooped sweatshirt – that she had forgotten she still had. Her previously split-site living meant there had always been enough of her things at Minnie's for her to survive happily for days without returning to Bear's, but they were mainly items she could live without – leggings, jumpers that had gone bobbly, skirts that had lost their shape. Now, they were all she had. She looked more innocent somehow.

'Yuh an' me got to talk, darlin',' Minnie said. 'Bring de Guinness punch, eh?'

A few weeks ago, they could never have talked like they did then, but there was a new honesty between them, a softer, needier intimacy which meant they could open up their whole lives and see them for what they were.

'I need to tell you some t'ings about me, an' you got to promise not to cry, eh?'

'You hurtin'?'

'Not any more, chile, not any more.'

When Minnie talked about Gladstone, her nostrils flared. When she spoke of Reuben, her head tilted and her eyes were soft. 'I should have left yuh Grandaddy de first time he raise his hand to me but I was young an' scared, jus' like you now. You got years ahead, darlin', years and years. You don't let Bear steal dem from you, eh?'

'But I caan't let him steal from Chess either, can I? Not when she done so much for me. If I go back to him, he gonna t'ink he won de day and den, when he forget Chess and dat, I can leave him again, f'real . . . y'get me?'

'If you still alive by den.'

'So wha'? You t'ink it's a good idea to let her worry like dat, when she's tryin' so hard to help me? How else to get rid o' him?'

'Hist'ry repeatin',' Minnie tutted. 'Hist'ry repeatin'.' The years that she had put up with Gladstone sloshed around her ankles like a stagnant puddle. If she had had the courage to leave him at that first slap, she would have been looking back on a different life. She wasn't sure she wanted that for herself now because what was done was done, but she sure wanted it for Della.

'Y'know, Grandad still t'ink he own you,' Della said truthfully. 'He still t'ink he got a right to you.'

'Dat's de trick, darlin', dat's de trick. Dese big stupid men, you let dem t'ink dey *need* to get rid of yuh! Yuh affe become somet'ing he have no use for, see? Yuh affe become *in de way*. Den he goin' a see you as not'ing he has use for. Bear like his women dotin', eh? Find him a dotin' woman. Den tell him he caan't have her, dat he has to have you.'

'I c'n t'ink of one already. She bin waitin' in de wings for always.'

'Who?'

'Kim. You seen her around.'

'She got hair like dis?' Minnie pulled her hair off her forehead and Della laughed.

'Dat's her!'

'Den you mus' catch him wid her – and, Della?'

'Yeh, Granny?'

'Be very, very cross when you do.'

Chapter 21

Judith looked at the green neon Exit sign glaring over the swing doors in the semi-darkness of this twenty-four-hour ward and decided there was something very figurative about crossing thresholds. It was only six-thirty in the morning, but she was already dressed. Her small suitcase was sitting neatly outside the door of the middle birthing-in room with its floral wallpaper and clashing curtains that had been her home on and off for the last four weeks. She had managed the occasional night away, but not often, and now it was time to make space for someone else.

The only other mother on the unit had been there all night, fixated by the monitor, still mentally paralysed by the shock of premature labour. The rings under her eyes were the same colour as her red Chinese Dragon dressing-gown and she belonged to a world where exit signs or clock times meant nothing to her. Her baby, a two-pound girl, was still in intensive care and at the moment she lay under a perspex saffron hood, like a hi-tec facial tanning lamp. Jaundice, Judith diagnosed correctly. Amongst other problems, no doubt.

Will had progressed to nursery three where he was now sleeping peacefully, tired out from his new daily routine of looking for food and putting on weight. The further away from the serious machines you got, the better you were. Judith remembered how she'd once looked so enviously in at the 'nursery three mothers', feeding their growing progeny competently through a tangle of wires while they swapped stories of growth retardation and food intolerance. At that time, she hadn't been able to imagine that her day would ever come.

Will had been wheeled or carried through seven entrances on the unit since he'd been born, in and out, in and out, in out and in. Today, he could notch up the eighth. The ninth would take them out into the big wide world.

Thresholds, she thought. They aren't always easy to pass through, either on the way in or the way out. Sometimes they are golden gates, and other times they might be the doors of hell. Very often, you never know until you lock up behind you. It only takes a step or two to move from house to pavement, hospital ward to visitor lift, highrise flat to concrete balcony, street to church, but it can feel like you are taking the biggest stride of your life.

In a few hours' time, she would be crossing the one she looked at now for the last time. In her arms, there would be a baby, one who could breathe on his own, digest the same fluids that other babies digested, and cry for the Olympics. He would go home in his bucket seat, the one they had used for Kate and that Tim had got down from the attic two days ago. Maybe tonight he would sleep in the wicker crib that the other three had slept in, and herself before that.

Some special friendships had been forged this side of the Exit sign, ones that would never even have come about on the other – there's nothing quite like being in the same boat for creating a bond. And yet most of her fellow mothers didn't envy her entirely today. Life at home with their baby was what they were all working towards, and at the same time it was what many of them were shying away from too. The effects of institutionalisation were never greater than on a neo-natal unit, as the Anthropology Research Department at Judith's own university could confirm.

She found herself thinking about Honor, drifting almost idly into the thought rather than it coming uninvited to grab her by her heels as before. That was a miracle in itself. Her mother, wherever she was, would be pleased to see the cradle used for a fifth time. Babies had always been her thing.

A regular bleep sounded somewhere in another room, and she craned her neck to peer into Will's cot. He'd fought the pain and won – his pain, hers, and her mum's. His foot flinched. Maybe he was having a football dream.

'We're going home today, little one,' she whispered. 'It's a bit noisier than this place and a lot messier but you'll like it there. It's fun.'

Della was planning to cross a threshold for the last time that day too. The bundles she would carry away in her arms – a heap of clothes and a few CDs – would be considerably less precious, but the future would be just as hopeful if her plans all worked out. It had taken some clever orchestration just to get to the portals. Once Minnie's wickedly clear-eyed wisdom had sunk in – that Della should set Bear up with another woman and then play the spurned hag – it had been simple.

Kim was pretty much the obvious answer. She was a tall slinky girl who wore fur-trimmed everything, from coats to underwear, and would do anything – *anything* – to gain position with Bear. So far, the only trust she had with him was over the selling of drugs, and at this she was good. He always paid her in powder, which ensured her continuing enthusiasm, and Bear liked that. Women who came running were exactly his type.

Kim had ambition. She wanted to be powerful and influential, she wanted people to be scared of her, she wanted to be able to click her fingers and get things done. But the ladder she wanted to climb had a strict hierarchy and she had long ago realised that the quick route to the top rung was to become some bad man's girl. Her problem was that behind every bad man, there was usually an even scarier woman. The latest dirt had been music to her ears.

'Bear's entertainin' again.'

'His girl is on de streets, he jus' t'rew her out.'

'Nah, man, she jus' walk out.'

The next time she'd seen Della walking with Mercedes along the road from the Tube, she'd seen it as a heaven-sent opportunity to wheedle for the truth. Her hipbones moved first and her feet, in platform boots, cut a catwalk line to their side.

It didn't occur to her that Della had seen her first, and had stopped to check her purse only to make a little more time.

'Is it true? Are you an' Bear finished?'

'What's it to you?'

'I jus' thought you were f'keeps.'

'Well, he say he don' wan' me any more.'

'Shall I try an' talk to him for you?'

There was a time when Della could have slapped Kim for her blatant conniving, but now she could almost kiss her for it. The girl was obviously ripe for a break, so Della looked back with such convincing wide and grateful eyes that her adversary – or her ally – thought she had got away with the proposal.

'Me 'fraid I lost him Kim, y'nah?'

'I'll go an' see him, report back.'

Della dropped clues like a paper trail. 'If you do, try an' get him around noon. His day never start before dat, an' I'm tellin' you, he's a pussy cat for his first half-hour.'

'I c'n try.'

'I can t'ink of one way to persuade him, but dere's no way I c'n even t'ink of employin' dat tactic wid him jus' now.'

The smile playing on Kim's glossy lips when she walked away confirmed she thought a gift had just fallen from the gods, but in terms of cunning, her plan was nothing compared to her rival's. Not that it mattered. They were both after the same result anyway.

Della waited in her neighbour's flat across the block and watched the front door. Mr and Mrs Amos – she never used their first names – hadn't minded her using their kitchen table as an observatory at all. They had prayed for the girl more than once with Minnie at church, for her inner and outer healing, for her heart and soul, her split lip and cracked head. If Della knew what she was doing – and her grandmother Minnie had told them at the market this morning that it finally seemed as if she did – then they were pleased to be in a position to help. It was a fine position too – a better vantage point you couldn't wish for.

They were keeping watch with her when Kim, in high suede

boots, a black mini-skirt and a long thin coat with fluffy cuffs and collar, sashayed her predictable way to the flat. They were still fixated when Bear, dressed only to the waist, let her in.

'Dere she blows!' Mr Amos said, almost enjoying himself.

'Told you!' Della smiled.

'Now you be careful.'

'De danger's long gone, Mrs Amos, but t'anks.'

'We prayin' for you,' the elderly childless couple said into the air together, but Della was on a mission, and she was already walking purposefully out of their home.

After a calculated gap loitering around the back with the dustbins, she made her ascent. Sitting still in the Amos's flat had contained her nervousness and she needed to give vent to it now, so she swung herself round the stairwells, using the cold metal rails to heave herself up three steps at a time. She had a game plan all worked out. Bear liked her to look smart, so she looked drab. He liked her hair back, so she wore it loose. He liked his women compliant, so she would be difficult. Her voice should be angry, not scared. She had to play needy and nagging, like a spurned wife.

Della opened the door carefully and quietly, suppressing her puffs by taking deep breaths through her nose. It wasn't just the physical exertion that took her air away. She had forgotten in the space of a few days just how much she had hated living here. Padding in her old grubby trainers that she had left at Minnie's a year ago and never reclaimed, she made her way down the grey-pink carpet of the hall. Two steps from the door, she heard the rattle of Bear's leather belt as he took it off in the sitting room.

Not so long ago, such a noise would have forewarned her to brace herself for a whipping and she curled her lips at the memory. Now though, it was a clue that things were going the way she planned, a cue for her to emerge from the passageway and 'style it out' as she'd promised Minnie she was going to do. Her grandmother's words of advice to 'be very, very cross' rang through her head as she came through the door. She called his name sweetly. The anger had to come later.

Kim was a quick worker. She was on her knees in front of a for-once disarmed Bear, who was standing in the middle of the room with his trousers around his ankles. His expression of groaning pleasure – his head was swaying and his eyes were rolling around looking up to the ceiling – changed to agitation when he heard her voice.

Della found herself wanting to laugh. He looked so suddenly pathetic, like a child on the lavatory. She put a hand up to cover her mouth, pressing it hard against her lips to kill the urge as Kim carried on with the job in hand, but Bear was no longer lost in the moment, and he struggled to bend over to retrieve a more dignified position.

Della knew her fury had to be immediate, so she raised her voice to a penetrating shriek, hoping that she would sound as if she meant it.

'Wha' de bomba claat you a' doin?'

It was like opening a floodgate. The moment the words left her lips, she found a torrent of hatred had been building up behind them all the time. The banks she had created to contain it all – the years of being hit, verbally assaulted, drugged up and fucked up and being made to feel worthless, when once upon a time she'd been Minnie's little choirgirl – broke now all over the sitting room. So he thought he'd knocked all her natural resource out of her, did he? He might have stripped her of her finery and forced her into rags but he couldn't disrobe her that easily! She might as well have worn a ball and fucking chain all those years. Bastard, bastard, bastard!

She hurled the props she was carrying – a bottle of wine, a chicken and some vegetables – on the sofa, not that she had ever had any intention of cooking them for him.

'I *was* comin' to say I was sorry, but it looks like I'm too late.'

Bear pushed Kim's head to one side and pulled his pants up. He looked as defenceless as she'd once been.

'It's jus' cash me a deal wid her, y'nah?'

'Wha? She takin' money for it now, is she?' Della screamed.

Kim stood up, almost as tall as Bear in her platform boots. She smoothed her skirt and pushed her long fingernails either side of her head to scrape any hairs that might have strayed from her tight ponytail. This was her moment, and she wasn't going to let the petulance of a jilted witch like Della get in her way.

'I do no such t'ing. Honey, where's de bathroom?' she drawled passively.

Minnie's words came to Della again – *Dese big stupid men, you let dem t'ink dey need to get rid of yuh!* The trick was in the contrast. Kim was doing sophisticated, so she should opt for coarse. She spat at the girl's disappearing back and grabbed her own breasts, giving them an aggressive and lewd jiggle in Kim's direction.

'So wha' kinda fuckery's you call dis?' she screeched.

'It's not what yuh t'ink,' Bear protested.

'So what do I t'ink, wid yuh pants dropped to your boot?'

'Hey, you no say you goin' a come back, babes.' He wasn't sure if he wanted her now or not. It was better to have the choice though.

Della didn't like his conciliatory tone. She had expected him to roar at her to get out, or demand she remove her belongings while she was here, or even throw something at her. She was there only to provoke him into making the final decision, so he could feel king of his own castle again. It was a bit worrying, this repentance. A burden, that's what she needed to be now, a millstone round his fat sweaty neck.

'Well, y'din't ask, did yuh? Dis a' my house too, y'nah? And *she* . . .' Della jabbed at the air towards the bathroom '. . . can get de fuck out.'

'Ey! Yuh don' tell me what to do.'

That was better. He was getting annoyed, he didn't like being told what to do. She should stick with being the cross he had to bear. Her voice dropped from anger to whine.

'Minnie say she caan't 'ave Mercedes an' Tyrone livin' dere no more. I ain't got nowhere, man. You gonna affi be a father to dem now, for de first time in yuh life.'

'No, me caan't bother wid dis, Della.'

Kim came out of the bathroom and took up her place by

Bear. Her voice was slow and sexy. 'I mus' go, star.' She was conducting herself as if she had never even met Della before, let alone offered to help her in the street yesterday.

'No, stay,' Bear said, putting a hand on her forearm. The girl hadn't finished what she had started yet, and besides, it might be useful to her future if she witnessed him in his hour of glory. No woman left him and then thought she could come back.

'Della, take yuh t'ings an' go.'

'Why? 'Cos dis one here make a better fuck dan me?'

'Not'ing to do wid fuck, Della. To do wid respect.'

'T'ink say me need yuh?' she cried, entirely through exhilaration. 'T'ink say me need yuh?' She ran into the bedroom, knocking over a lava lamp with her right hand as she passed by, and started to throw her favourite clothes into a leather bag. The rest he could burn, for all she cared. Swiping her make-up off the windowsill and letting it fall loose on to her clothes in the bag with a single move of her hand, she allowed herself a smirk. Grabbing the bag handles, she glanced around the room with its unmade bed and mirrored ceiling and punched her fist into the stale air before running out.

Bear took Kim's hand and guided it to his groin. 'Me finished wid dat one,' he said. 'And when she gone, you can finish wid me.'

Judith knew the pinboard of photographs Tim was reading almost by heart. The little boy on his bicycle was Jordan Cox, born at twenty-six weeks and weighing two pounds on 17 July 1996. The Girl Guide was Rachel Hughes, born at twenty-nine weeks and weighing two pounds and eight ounces on 12 March 1988. The twins with their birthday cake were Aaron and Tyler Hurst, born at thirty weeks on 25 September 1994 and weighing under five pounds between them. Their proud, relieved, grateful parents kept the photos and the cheques coming, which meant the nurses could pin the former up for inspiration and bank the latter for hope. As wall displays go, it was powerful stuff. It had certainly kept Judith's demons at bay.

The doctor had checked Will for the last time, the medicines and prescriptions were in a small plastic bag in Judith's suitcase, and the bucket seat was ready, handle down, clasps undone. It was time to go. All they were waiting for was someone to see them off the premises.

In Judith's imagination, the consultants were dressed as trumpeters and the nurses were waving flags to send the three of them on their brave new way. In reality, everyone was too busy connecting intra-venous infusions, saturation monitors and ECG leads to make too much fuss of one healthy baby leaving. After all, goodbyes happened on a daily basis for the staff. At last, the sister came towards them with the familiar flip and flop of her comfortable cushion-soled shoes. Will was in her arms, dressed in his white and powder blue going-home outfit. None of Judith's other children had worn such predictable colours, but when you were as small as Will you wore what fitted, simple as that. Even the newborn sizes still swamped him.

'We'll expect you to provide us with the same,' the staff nurse smiled to Tim, who was still studying the pinboard. 'A picture every birthday, please.'

'We'll do our best to remember,' he replied, putting his arm around Judith's shoulder and looking down at Will being settled into his seat. Would his head ever reach the head cushion?

'As if we could forget,' Judith said, touching her son's nose lightly with her forefinger and breathing in to begin the longest thank-you of her life.

Chess stood with her back to the stable door of Honor's cottage and leant over the ancient leather sofa as Nick stoked the fire. He'd lit it for a visual comfort more than anything else, since the central heating had dealt quickly and efficiently with the slightly fusty air they'd breathed in on first entering. The orange glow through the cast-iron and blackened glass doors had helped them both find a little inner warmth, or at least thaw the edge off the ice that had been sitting in the pit of their stomachs since the chaos of Sam in the park.

They were at that point in their crisis where everything had been said but nothing had been resolved, so they were covering the same ground again and again, combing for clues that they might have missed first time, something that might just make sense of it all.

'Just to take the chill off,' Nick said unnecessarily, closing the wood-burner doors and rubbing his hands.

What chill? The cottage felt exactly as it had always done to Chess, or rather it had reverted to type. In the last few weeks of Honor's life, the sitting room in particular had been turned into something akin to a private hospice with a commode, a walking frame, and a whole table full of drugs propped against the antiques, but now the bed had gone (Judith had burnt it) and there wasn't a hint of its recent past.

I understand this place, Chess thought as she walked round the sofa and let herself flop over its arm. I don't have to question it. I know that Dad did the painting of sea clouds above the desk, that the glass-fronted cabinet was made by Mum's uncle who died in the war, that my old school books are in the bottom drawer of that chest on the landing and my old Brownie uniform is with Judith's in the spare room stripped pine wardrobe that used to be blue.

'Maybe I do know who I am after all,' she said out loud, because Nick had left the room, and then realised that what she meant was that she only knew who she *used* to be.

The cottage was now hers and Judith's to share, not that either of them would ever force a sale. Judith had initially tried to encourage them both to use it together as the perfect bolt-hole for them all, but with six children, four adults and only three bedrooms (let alone the fact that Tim and Chess in the same house was never a good combination) she had been out on a limb with the idea. There had then evolved an unspoken agreement that the two families would use it separately with given notice, although 'bolt-hole' was about right just now. Nick and Chess had certainly bolted from something. Good old Vienna, just to repeat a well-worn phrase. It had been her idea for them to get away.

Their twelve years together had been sporadically punctuated by snatched weekends from the children or work. In better days, they hadn't wasted a minute, doing only those things that can be done without children – making love, reading, eating in bed – but this one had a different agenda. They had come here to see if they could manage another twelve, although it had been mostly charge and counter-charge to date. Nick kept coming back to the same question.

'*Why* didn't you tell me?'

'You put up so many barriers.'

'Like how?'

'Making me feel selfish, ungrateful for what I had. You didn't ever seem to understand that I might be missing something.'

'You never really let it show.'

'I tried. I'm sorry. I know it's all my fault, all this upheaval and everything, but I really need you to understand why.'

'Then explain it Chess, *explain* it.'

She tried, but still his questions kept coming.

'Where do the children fit into all this? Where do *I*?'

'You haven't even told me if you *want* to first.'

The telephone on the small table next to the sofa still had a sticker with the district nurse's mobile number on it, which seemed to Chess an unnecessary reminder of illness, so she picked it off and rubbed at the remaining glue with her thumb until she got it down to a grey smear. Her fingernail would have scraped off the rest, if only it hadn't been bitten to the quick over the last two days.

Judith had sounded fantastic during their phone call just now. Normal again, or maybe even completely different. She hadn't wanted to know the precise profile of their visit, why they were there, what was wrong, or who was looking after the children, like she usually did. She hadn't forced a family meeting or a conversation about Honor. She had just chatted effortlessly about Will's first night at home and how he was feeding like a pig every two hours and how when they'd taken him to Kate's nativity play he'd stayed awake for the whole thing. It was as if she had breathed fresh air down the mouthpiece and into Chess's own lungs.

'I'm longing to see him,' Chess had said. 'Why don't you come over?'

'What, and interrupt a dirty weekend? I wouldn't dream of it.'

'It's OK, it's not even remotely grubby. Oh please, go on.'

'OK, I'll do my best.'

'Did you tell her anything about the last few days?' Nick had asked edgily afterwards.

'No. I didn't think she needed to know.'

He felt pleased about that. It diluted their trouble somehow.

'I can definitely see Dad in him,' Chess murmured quietly.

The two sisters were lying on top of the only aired double bed in one of the cottage bedrooms, facing each other. Judith lay on her left side with her shirt undone, her bra unzipped and Will attached to her breast. Chess lay next to Will, with her dark hand resting lightly on the baby's head, still in its pale blue cotton hat. It was dark outside and Judith had phoned home to say she was here for the night. For the first time in an age, the two of them were both completely relaxed.

'He's too tiny to see anyone in him yet.'

'What about around the eyes?' Chess gave him another close inspection. 'Actually, I think he looks a bit like me.'

'Now you come to mention it.'

They swapped smiles.

'This is cosy,' Chess said, pulling the patchwork quilt she'd known almost all her life around her.

'Well, it would be if I hadn't leaked all over the place,' Judith replied, pulling her top away from her heavy-duty zip-up bra.

'Miss Wet T-Shirt.'

'I can't run anywhere any more for fear of being hit or squirted in the eye.'

'Very attractive.'

'They're bigger than yours now.'

'OK then, we'll compare again next year.'

'By which time mine will be empty sacks once more and yours will still point to bloody heaven.'

Chess squawked too loudly and Will pulled his lips off his mother's nipple in a start. 'Ooh, sorry, baby.'

'Don't worry, he's used to sudden surprises.'

'That's useful, living with us lot.'

'Yeah.'

A stumpy table-lamp that had begun life twenty years ago as one of a pair before Chess had knocked its twin off Honor's bedside cabinet during a trampolining session in 1978, cast a cone of yellow on to the sloping ceiling and both girls unknowingly traced the shape with their eyes. They had shared five thousand similar experiences. Bedtimes, night-lights, whispered talks.

Will was doing a sleepy rhythmic nibble now, so Judith popped her finger in his mouth to release herself and he let out a tiny sigh.

'Is he asleep?'

'Yes.'

'So can we do grown-up talk now?'

'We could give it a go, I suppose. There's always a first time for everything.'

'Listen, Jude, I want to say I'm sorry. I feel like I've really treated everyone badly lately, really badly. I did want to come and see you in hospital, I thought about you loads, it's just that . . .'

'Stop there a minute, Chess.'

'No, I should apologise, I–'

'Don't. There's no need. Would it make you feel any better if I told you I'm glad you didn't? You see, saying that makes me feel bad too, but the truth is I really *didn't* want to see you. I didn't want to see anyone other than Tim and the children.' She hesitated there, wondering how Chess would react to such treason.

'Didn't you?'

'No. It was so weird, Chess. I felt as if I had to strip every detail of my life right down to the basics if I was going to help

Will get through. I couldn't take on board anything, not Mum's death, not you and whatever it was you were going through – and I knew it was something.'

'It was.'

'I want to hear it, I'll be able to hear it all now, honestly, right down to the last awful detail. I tell you, I feel like I've escaped from some kind of prison.'

'I was very nearly in a *real* prison.'

'Is that true, or is that a Chess-ism?' Judith asked without fear.

'Well, maybe somewhere between the two,' her sister admitted. 'But I do feel as if I've escaped from something too.'

'Tell me,' Judith said. 'It's really important. I want us to know each other again, like we used to – you know, everything. But without the need. Do you know what I mean?'

'I do.'

'Well, go on then. Hit me with it.'

When Nick looked in half an hour later, his trouble was diluted even further. He understood everything he saw. His wife, her sister, his new nephew. He knew the kind of things they talked about, the sorts of things they liked doing together, he knew their *history*. But what of the other sister out there, and the other history that he had no knowledge of? Would he ever be able to share that part of his wife too? Did she really want him to? He went into another bedroom and took both feather eiderdowns off the two single beds. Then he laid them on top of the sleeping sisters and kissed Chess's cheek.

'I'll be downstairs if you want me,' he said.

'Do you mean that?' came the murmured reply.

'Yes,' he said, and walked away quickly. If *she* wanted him, then they could make a start.

'Nick. Wait.' She was behind him, on the corner stair. 'I do want you,' she said. It was the complete truth, and delivered as such.

'Then let's talk.'

'Can we talk afterwards?'

'No, before. Then we'll know if we both really mean it.'

For once, Chess could see the point in taking the less exciting option. She followed him into the sitting room and sat on the sofa. He didn't join her but took up the armchair opposite. 'Complete honesty,' he said. 'I just can't guess at things any more.'

'I promise. And you.'

'I promise too.'

They sat for a moment, wondering where to begin, until Nick spoke first.

'Do you really *really* believe we've got what it takes? I mean, is it really *me* you love, or is it the fact that I'm the father of your children, or the one that pulls in the money, or the one you thought you loved enough to marry once? Sometimes I just wonder if we're together out of habit.'

'Not habit,' Chess said strongly. 'Commitment. We're together because we made decisions, didn't we? To have children, to share our lives.'

'But do you love me? Me, Nick Jacoby, boring bastard of this parish? Tell me the truth, because at the moment I'm not sure whether I'd be surprised one way or the other.'

'Yes. I really do,' Chess nodded. 'I really do.'

'What about all those barriers you said I put up?'

'They're down now.'

'You accept that? Really?'

'I really do. I know now that it was me, my imagination, my confusion.'

'OK then, do you *fancy* me?'

She laughed, partly to disguise her slight hesitation and partly because, to her, it was such a minor detail. 'We have great sex, don't we?'

'Do we? Remind me.'

'What, now?'

'No, *tell* me. Do we have great sex? Or do you wish I was someone else?'

Chess fell completely silent and stared at the pattern of the rug. How honest did he want her to be? How much did it matter?

'No, I never wish you were someone else. When I make love, I make love to Nick Jacoby.'

He continued to look at her, because he could hear the underlying qualification. 'Except?'

'Except I sometimes pretend he's black,' she said.

'Is that all? Is that the only adjustment you'd make?' he asked, with the gentle lift to his voice that she hadn't heard for weeks.

'Yeah.'

'Really?'

'Yeah, really.'

There was a movement upstairs. Judith was stirring. They could hear her standing up and walking across the floor. Their time was almost up.

'God, I quite like that idea,' Nick said quickly.

'Do you?' Desire shivered in both their bodies.

'Yeah. I'd like to hear more about it sometime.'

'I'd enjoy telling you,' Chess replied, a split second before Judith and Will appeared at the foot of the stairs.

'I just feel the need to say that this is a big moment for me,' Judith announced lightly. 'Look at me. I'm in Mum's house, and I'm happy.'

The orange glow from the fire seemed to fill the whole room then, washing the walls, warming the air and shining the wood, the glass, the brass and their faces.

'It feels like we've done a lot of clearing up this weekend,' Chess said as Nick shovelled the ashes on to a wide spade the next day. A mini-dustcloud formed in the air as he brushed the remainder into a dustpan and put that in the bucket too.

'The trick is not to let it get too bad in the first place,' he answered, raising his eyebrows and looking hopeful.

'It's OK, I understand that now.'

She looked around for a final check. Heating off, fridge empty, windows shut. As joint owner, she was the keeper of the keys, so it was her job to lock both the stable door and the door to the porch.

'So,' she said when her task was complete and they were standing on the roadside with their overnight bags. 'Where do we go from here?'

'How about Minnie's?' Nick suggested. It felt to both of them like his finest hour.

Chapter 22

My beloved Reuben,

Are you feelin well today? Tell me those pains in your fine chest you speak of in your last letter were jus the heartache of goodbye. I think I have some myself but I will not tell you that incase you won't see a doctor if they still troublin you. Do that you promise me?

I been readin my book on Weymouth again about the King who swam in the sea as a cure for all his ills and I am thinkin some of that salty magic must have crept into my lungs too jus so I could breathe it out all over my family and cure their ills too. You know, since I come home (it is a strange home without you) people been mendin themselves all round me. Della is a diffrent girl and I could dance for joy. They all swimmin in our sea of happiness!.

The way she finally wash that man out of her life is secretly down to me and some old womanly wisdom Reuben but I don't want you to hear me boast! I say to her she needs to find him a new mistress and make out she still want to be the old one! It work! You never seen anyone run so fast (save Gladstone when he think responsibility comin his way of course). We can laugh now but it never is that funny at the time.

She is a good mother to her children at last. Mercedes go everywhere with her even to her work with the art project I wrote about last time and I have to find my own companionship with the church and my day club. The flat is full and empty at the same time! What would you say if

I told you I no longer so sure of the reason I am so far away from you? Would you run a mile like Gladstone? I joke Reuben. I know, I know.

Della gone paint crazy! She keep saying she going to do me a Caribbean scene all over my table. I don't see what she means but she has an idea in her head and the way she is at the moment, that mean she going to do it. I tell her she can do anything to it she want but I have to still work on it. Work? she say. Granny, it is time for you to stop work and start to play.

An who goin to cook you your dinner I ask? And she just grin at me like she used to as a chile. All these words, and still I haven't told you the other lucky news (I tell you, it is the magic sea air or the Lord, one or the other, that leads me to this happy place).

I have seen my great grandchildren! Frankie (everyone say I have to get use to call her Chess but to you, she can remain as she is in my heart) well she bring them to me at last a week ago, and they both so sweet, so like her! She bring her shy nice man back too for me to meet a second time and he talks so gentle to the children and he got respect written all over him. It make my old eyes quite wet just to listen to him speak. I tell her she have a good man there and then her eyes get wet too! It must be the cold. I enclose a photo of us all that day. I have a big bundle here of the same so you not depriving me in any way!

I am back to my Weymouth book now to look at the old pictures and imagine us walking along the harbour like those people in their Sunday Best too. One is taken in 1950 – it could have been us but for the colour of their skin! What do I mean it could have been us? It was us, just eight weeks ago.

The book say here the King liked Weymouth for the general tranquillity of the bay, the clearness of the water and the softness of the shore. If you still feeling poorly in the summer, I will take you there and make you swim in the sea.

Forever your cure all my darling.
Your loving Minnie.

Reuben counted the kisses as he sat on the edge of a hard wooden chair against a plain whitewashed wall, looking at her curious curvy handwriting. It must have taken her some wrist effort to cover nine sides of the wispy blue paper, but her energy burst through the misspellings and the ink nonetheless. It was reassuring to hear her so at peace with her family and he started reading it again, until a shrill voice stopped him at page three.

'Mr Fisher? Mr Fisher!'

The nurse, or at least a receptionist in a white uniform, chivvied him with every part of her body. Her foot tapped, her hand beckoned, her head nodded. Choh! He wouldn't like to end his days with her!

Reuben folded the letter neatly, put it carefully in the soft lining of his cotton jacket pocket and patted it for reassurance as if it were Minnie herself. See? He was doing what she asked and consulting a doctor. As he walked through the rickety door into the surgery, he took a laboured breath. How he hated these places. Still, his clean bill of health would make a nice birthday gift for her. She would be seventy-three at the weekend.

Minnie sat at the kitchen table pretending she wasn't waiting to hear the flap of the letterbox. The morning post was later than usual, but she justified it with the reminder that it wouldn't be the first time her birthday had hailed the start of the great Christmas card race.

She had dispatched her own festive airmail greetings already, sending a special one to Reuben with a monochrome photograph of a beach in winter on the front. Mercedes had turned her nose up at it and asked her if she would like her to add some glitter, but Della had said it was beautiful. Her granddaughter knew about beautiful things now she was a proper artist.

'Don' call me dat, Granny,' Della kept telling her shyly. 'I'm not an artist.'

'You workin for de Arts Project, aren't yuh? I seen it in big letters on de chapel.'

'Yeah, but I jus'–'

'You jus' not'ing! You an artist, and you let yuh old proud grandmother tell her friends about it if she want!'

The letter folded inside Reuben's card was probably the longest Minnie had ever written – the stamp had certainly cost more than usual and her arm had more than ached by the time she had placed the final kiss – but then there had been so much news in such a short space of time. Where was it now? Under his pillow, by his chair, in his jacket pocket? Or was it still caught up in a sorting office somewhere, causing him to wonder, just like she was this morning, when he would hear from his sweetheart again?

Imagining she'd heard the spring of metal from the letterbox, she waddled from the kitchen expectantly, but the hall carpet in front of the door was still bare. Perhaps there was a postal strike overseas. Perhaps there would be a second delivery later. Perhaps she was kidding herself. Her instinctive misgivings were hardly ever proved right and yet something really strong told her nothing from Reuben would arrive today. It didn't matter as long as he was all right. He would never forget her, she knew that.

She checked her seventy-three-year-old face in the mosaic tiled mirror Della had made at work the other day. Half of her, no, three-quarters of her felt at least seventy-three. The other quarter still felt nineteen. '*Windrush* nineteen', as one of Reuben's love poems had once said.

So far, her birthday hadn't brought anyone or anything, apart from a brief exchange with the family early on. When Della had taken her in a cup of tea first thing and told her she was taking Mercedes to the Pinegrove as she had done for the last three Saturdays, Minnie had been amazed to learn that Tyrone was going with them. Nothing could normally shift him from Saturday morning television, but his mother had apparently been able to encourage him with the promise of drums. Steel, Minnie assumed.

That was a birthday present in itself, to see her granddaughter and her family blossom in the way they had over the last few weeks. It wasn't just Della's new job, or the fact that she had left Bear, or her warm developing friendship with Chess, but rather it was the sum of all those parts and a little sprinkling of something the girl had found all by herself. When Minnie looked at Della lately, she saw in her face the same hopeful expression the child used to wear at ten, the way she was before adversity had lowered her expectations. That was a gift, a real gift.

She checked the clock on the kitchen cooker. It would be five in the morning in Jamaica. Reuben would be sleeping. What a marvel it was that so late in life she could suddenly conjure him like that, based no longer on imagination but recent memory. To be able to conceive how his brow shed its furrows, the lips that parted slightly as he breathed so regularly, the skin that was always so deliciously warm. She envisaged him opening his eyes and seeing her next to him. 'Happy Birthday, Mrs Fisher,' he would say. That was surely a gift too. The Lord was good.

Minnie smiled bravely, clapped her hands softly together as if in a split-second prayer and went back into the hall to pick her coat off its peg. Maybe a slow walk down Portobello Road would be in order, a peep around the Pinegrove doors to see Tyrone on those drums, and then by the time she got back Reuben might be awake and she could break their one-phone-call-a-month rule. A little gift to herself from herself, if you like.

A circle of assorted children sat cross-legged and expectant in a corner of the chapel hall as Della walked around them with theatrical steps. At arm's length she carried a crown, an elaborate affair made of padded velvet, stick-on jewels and cardboard, on a plump cushion. The crown had been left by a touring theatre workshop and discovered under heaps of scrap material too long after their departure to feel guilty about not returning it, so 'circle time' had been invented.

'Who's it gonna be dis time?' she whispered. 'Is it gonna be Sharna? No! Is it gonna be Ayeesha? No! Is it gonna be Gabriel? *Yes!*'

Gabriel, a soft-looking boy with shy eyes, sat regally still as Della placed the crown on his tight curls.

'De King can speak!'

Triumphant was how she felt nowadays, particularly as she was no longer a mere volunteer at the Pinegrove. When the part-time post of Assistant for the After School Club for under-elevens had come up, the co-ordinator, Jo Storey, had persuaded her she was up to the job. Now from three-thirty to seven during the week and from eight-thirty to one on Saturdays, working parents relied on a pre-arranged taxi to ferry their children from various school gates to the chapel where, for a not unreasonable fee, Della and her colleagues would keep them safe and creative at the same time.

There wasn't a television, video machine or computer in the place, but plenty of glue, fabric, paint, cardboard, wood and paper if they wanted to make their own. This Saturday, Della was creating giant bamboo and greaseproof-paper lanterns on sticks to carry head-high through the streets around the Grove on Christmas Eve.

The Procession of Lights was a new community ritual only in its second year, but as the posters round the neighbourhood said, traditions have to start somewhere. If the heavens poured, the PVA glue and water mix that stiffened the paper and tightened it around the wooden structures would undoubtedly make things a little sticky, but Della was optimistic. 'Ah, de sun gonna shine, I know it!' she kept reassuring Jo Storey, who recognised exactly her new recruit's particular brand of newfound positivity. In the fanciful gloss of the Pinegrove, split lips and cracked heads seemed a lifetime ago to them both.

The lanterns were drying and circle time was coming to an end, but there was still a great deal to do. When Della's shift ended at lunchtime today, she had no intention of going home.

Her main project was already going on without her and the deadline to have everything ready was three o'clock.

'Good, Gabriel. Very interestin' stuff. I t'ink in answer to yuh question dat tower blocks *do* have chimneys, but I don't t'ink in answer to yuh udder one dat Father Christmas would fit a real spaceship down one anyway. A toy one maybe, uh? Now, who want to help me fix up a surprise party?'

In the other room, Kezia, Sam and Mercedes were not helping at all, according to Tyrone. He was struggling with trestle tables, setting them up in a row against the solid wooden shelving on the far wall, and putting folded sheets on top of each one as instructed. The three younger cousins were taking advantage of the open floorspace by running and skidding along on their knees. It was the first time the Jacoby children had been left at the Pinegrove without either parent, but they had shown no signs of reluctance and, anyway, Vienna and Dan had been drafted in to assist too. Neither of them minded too much what they did on Saturdays as long as it was together. Strangely, spending the day in bed together was still not an alternative.

Nick and Chess were on their way to pick up Minnie's hastily arranged birthday present and there wasn't enough room in the car for that *and* the children. Traffic chaos in town wasn't helping their tight timetable, but Nick was resolutely confident in the face of his wife's growing agitation. He clasped her right knee and smiled. 'Relax, we'll get there.'

The gloom cloud that had been sitting over their lives ever since they came to London, the one he'd kept looking up at, wondering when it was going to shed its load and not stop raining until it had flooded them all, had been blown away by a fresh wind. There *had* been a temporary downpour, a deluge of a day or two that had all but drowned them before the turning point at Honor's cottage, but happily the two of them had found enough material between them to build an ark.

This party idea came like the little twig of olive tree in the dove's beak. It had been Della's idea, but Nick had been there when it was first discussed, and that small trust had been the first sign for him that not only was there dry land ahead but that it was a land they could all inhabit together. And Chess so wanted him and the children to explore it with her, he knew that now.

'Thank God for new weather fronts,' he said happily, tapping the steering wheel in time to The Beautiful South.

Chess agreed, even though she had no idea what she was agreeing with. She was too busy thinking about the easy way he had kissed Della goodbye at the Pinegrove just now and how he had pretended not to notice how her sister had flinched at such an unfamiliar throwaway display of male affection. How could it all seem so incredibly normal, Nick kissing Della; Kezia and Sam playing with their cousins; them all in on a secret that Minnie would never forget? It was a dream, surely.

'It'll be good for her knees,' she said as the traffic began to move. 'I noticed the other day how much pain they give her.'

Minnie's knees *were* aching, but not as much as her heart, which was as heavy as it had been on the train back from Portsmouth. Even her red coat and black hat weren't lifting her spirits this morning, but then the weight of disappointment was a heavy load. As she walked, she looked out for a friendly face. Dora Martin perhaps, or Mrs Amos, or anyone from the day club, but she only saw strangers. Never mind, her family were just around the corner now. She had no idea that most of her friends were with them too, buzzing around, joking tipsily on nothing more than tea and tension. If there was one thing at which Minnie's community surpassed all others, it was celebration. Even the preparation of a party was a party.

Tyrone was getting irritated by his little sister showing off to her new and adoring fans. 'Dey in de way, Mom!'

'Don' worry boy, 'cos here come de reinforcements!'

Mrs Amos and three other ladies from church bustled in, carrying biscuit tins and trays from Mr Amos's neat little car outside.

'Out de way, out de way!'

They bore their gifts like the wise men, solemnly delivering them to the open hatch to the kitchen at the back, where Jo was receiving all donated goodies. So far, there looked to be enough to feed the five thousand without a miracle.

'Cup of tea, ladies?'

'Certainly!'

Jo was wiping the hired glasses with a tea towel, then dipping their rims in a beaten egg mixture and dunking them in a saucer of sugar.

'Oooh!' Mercedes enthused, sliding up to the hatch. 'Tastes like Frosties. What you goin' a fill dese wid? Guinness punch?'

'I'll give you Guinness punch! We've got sparkling wine for these.'

'Yes!'

'You havin' grape juice,' Tyrone glowered at his sister. He was still cross with her for calling his palm tree 'a big bog-brush'.

He was proud of his tree. He'd found it in the storeroom, ten feet high, dusty and crumpled, but a palm tree nevertheless. Dan had helped him drag it out. The trunk was real wood, the leaves were stretchy green nylon sewn on to wire frames and it sat, more or less upright, in a sand-filled bucket. The best bit, he thought, were the bananas – 'de finishin' touch' – four clumps of them bought with his own money from the grocers next to the underground and now resting in the MDF branches.

The Saturday Club children had turned their attention to blowing the balloons and batting them in the air, losing points for every time one hit the floor. Vienna was keeping score. Della was busy pushing an old armchair on castors from the storeroom. It was draped with silk banners from past workshops which she thought she might tack across the shelves to hide the paint pots, brushes, hammers and nails.

'Granny could do wid dat!' Tyrone said. 'She always goin' on about her chair bein' so bad for her knees.'

'She won' have no use for it soon.'

'Why?'

'Secret!' Della winked. 'But she can sit on it for today if she like.'

'Go and get the circle-time crown,' Jo said. 'We'll queen her on her throne, shall we?'

'Intruder alert, intruder alert!' Kezia ran in breathless from the courtyard outside.

'Wha' you sayin?' her aunt asked, not yet used to the rural tones in her niece's voice. It was a mutual difficulty. Kezia could hardly understand anything that was said to her either, but somehow they managed. Lack of reserve was the thing.

'Great-Granny's coming. I've just seen her in the road. She's coming this way.'

'Who – Minnie? True? You not jokin' me?'

'She tellin' de truth,' Mercedes hollered, bolting in and grabbing Kezia by the arm to spin her round in excited alarm. 'Hide, everybody!'

Della dashed out just in time to catch Minnie pottering up the steps.

'Hello, Granny,' she said calmly, changing her sprint to a saunter and putting her left hand on the doorframe at shoulder level with her right foot as wide across the entrance as it would reach. 'What you doin' here?'

'I jus' felt like takin' de air.'

'You not at de seaside now!'

Minnie hadn't noticed Mr Amos's car parked just below her, nor its driver with his head bowed, trying to look inconspicuous.

'Am I comin' in?' she asked.

'Ah, dey got a mime workshop goin' on in dere. I bin creepin' around all mornin'.'

'So what 'appen wid Tyrone's drums?'

'Uh?'

'Dat's what you tell me dis mornin'. Tyrone comin' here to play de drums.'

'Yeah, dat's right. Er, oh, de . . . er . . . de drum man is comin' dis afternoon. His car, his van broke down.'

'Dere's a pity,' said Minnie.

'Yeah, pity,' agreed her granddaughter, with her fingers crossed behind her back.

'You comin' home for a meal?'

''Bout two o'clock, I should t'ink. Will you be in?'

'I don' have not'ing else to do.' The way Minnie thrust her hands into her tweed coat pockets and turned forlornly back towards the way she came made Della call after her, 'Don' go makin' any plans den!'

But there *was* something the old woman intended to do. She was going to speak to Reuben as soon as she got home, and the promise put enough spring in her step to make the return journey enjoyable.

'All we need now is de birthday girl!' Mrs Amos said, patting her beads with satisfaction as she took a step back to look at the spread of food.

The trestle tables were covered in old bedsheets dyed pink, not that you could see much cloth between the plates of sausage, tandoori chicken, samosas, coconut biscuits and chocolate fudge cake. The old armchair was at the bottom end by the door, draped in one of the green parachute silks with the excess material bunched like washed-up seaweed around its base. Tyrone had pushed his palm tree next to it, so it looked for all the world like the Queen of the South's throne.

'Turn it round, Tyrone, so it face de room. She don' wan a be de only one sittin' at de table!'

Hot water sat in the giant urn, rows and rows of cups and saucers stood by. Thirty friends, neighbours and relatives from Minnie's church, tower block and family milled around in their party clothes. The men wore hats, the women wore brooches and the children had left their trainers at home, even Tyrone.

'Let's go den,' Della said to Mr Amos, checking her watch. 'Let's go.'

'00 1 809 . . .' Minnie pressed the buttons on her portable telephone carefully, saying each number out loud as she read it from her little book. Her heart was thumping in anticipation of hearing his voice. It would now be breakfast-time and she tried to imagine Reuben outside, feeding his chickens or tending to his herb garden and listening for the kettle to whistle inside. She could usually create the scenes easily, but her dreams weren't working today. She just wasn't receiving him. His yard and his house were empty.

'Yuh no clairvoyant, Minnie George,' she puffed at her anxiety as the ringing tone came quickly down the line, long monotone beeps in a different rhythm to her own. He would maybe guess it was her. How close was he now to picking it up? Two more rings? Three?

After twenty, she put it down and sat quietly on the arm of her chair. If she sat in it properly, she might never find the strength to hoist herself back up. He couldn't still be in bed because it would have woken him. She had got the time difference wrong the very first time she had ever called him, thinking he was five hours ahead, not behind. He had answered it within two rings because it was next to his bed. 'What's dis, a dawn chorus?' he'd teased. Mind you, he'd been eight years younger then.

Perhaps she had misdialled. She went through the process again, saying the numbers in her head this time, but still the phone rang and rang. Exactly how bad *were* those pains in his chest?

Minnie left her front door on the latch and walked the ten steps along the concrete balcony to her neighbour's door, but Mrs Chanderpaul was out and her reclusive daughter didn't know if the first and second posts had arrived at their usual times or not.

This is just being silly, she told herself, going back inside. He could be staying at his son's, he could be out in the fields, he could have moved the phone away from the bed. Just because she hadn't received a birthday card from him was no reason to torture herself with images of . . . she couldn't even bring herself to go any further with the thought.

'00 1 801 . . .' This time her unsteady fingers were dialling Reuben's son, a number given to her in case of emergency. I mus' be in some panic to do this, she thought. Someone picked it up quickly.

'Curtis Fisher.'

'Curtis, it is Minnie George. I'm phonin' from London to speak wid yuh father. Is he dere?'

'No, you have dialled my home. His number is–'

'Yes, yes, but I caan't get a reply dere an' I t'ink he could be wid you.'

'No, he's not. I don't t'ink we're expectin' him.'

'Have you seen him?'

'Today? No. Yesterday, yes.'

'Was he well?'

'I t'ink, yes. A little tired but he's an ol' man. Are you concerned for a reason? Has he spoken of somet'ing?'

'He's gettin' pains in his chest.'

'I t'ink he's seen a doctor. He say somet'ing to my wife.'

'Lissen, I goin' a try his home again later an' if dere is still no reply, you min' if I call you again?'

'Certainly you can. Would you like fe me to go check?'

'T'ank you, Curtis.'

'No problem.'

'Is de sun shinin' dere today?'

'Of course, Mrs George!'

'You so lucky, eh? Bye bye.'

'Goodbye, Mrs George. Don' worry now.'

Stop it, Minnie, she told herself again. Stop it. Curtis had sounded contrite, like he should have had better answers to her questions, but she knew what sons and daughters could be like. She reached for the open pages of one of Mercedes' Disney comics and started to finish a wordsearch. Ah! She found Cinderella straight away but she didn't circle it. Her mind wasn't really on the job. It was wandering through the wards of a Jamaican hospital, looking at all the faces on the pillows for one that might be waiting for her to come and kiss it better.

'Aw, Granny, I feel dat bad,' Della said when she burst into the flat. 'It's yuh birthday, innit? I din't remember dis mornin'. Have you bin here all alone?'

'Choh! Birthdays don't mean a t'ing to old ladies! No worries.'

'Still, I c'n make it up to you now.' Della wondered if the trick had gone too far when she saw the void in her grandmother's face. She must have had a terrible morning thinking no one loved her.

'Della, I caan't reach Reuben. I gettin' a bad feelin all mornin'. I'll be fine once I speak wid him.'

'You worryin' 'bout him?'

'A little.'

'C'mon, we'll try him later. For now, we gonna go shoppin' an' choose you a present.'

'Wha' wid, darlin'? Buttons?'

'You forgettin'? I earnin' now, see? Take dat apron off! No, take it all off, and put on yuh Sunday dress. It's a special day.'

Good girl, Minnie thought now, sitting on her throne under the shade of Tyrone's palm tree, wiping her eyes and trying to believe everything she took in. It wouldn't have been right for her to turn up here wearing her old brown woollen skirt and blue cardigan that she had knitted herself. Not when all her friends looked so lovely. And look at the children! She felt as if she were at her own wedding reception, save for the absence of a groom. Still, she could tell Reuben all about it later, like the acting skills Della had displayed earlier for starters.

'You not cryin' again are you, Granny?' Mercedes asked, leaning over the back of the green silk armchair and letting her legs flail in the air behind her.

'No, course not. I mus' have got somet'ing in my eye when yuh mudder put de blindfold on me, eh?'

'You *are* cryin'!' Mercedes teased. 'Look, yuh cheeks are wet!'

'Nah, it's jus' the fizzy stuff's gettin' to you,' Della said, coming up to check her. She looked lovely, Minnie thought, in her red crushed velvet dress that swung above her knees and a black feather boa that she said she'd found in a cupboard. Were they tap shoes on her feet? It was important to remember these details, so she could relate them all to Reuben later on, when he'd returned from wherever he'd been this morning. And how he would wonder at it all!

Her breathing was deliberately deep and slow. She was trying to catch up after all that dancing – and there was still a whole line of hopeful partners left to get through. Someone had a fine collection of big band and calypso music, just what she liked, and the rhythm came easy, arthritis or not. She'd already obliged Mr Amos, then Stanley from the market, and Mercedes and Kezia together, and she'd been all but out of breath when Tyrone had slipped something else into the cassette machine.

'Wha's dis tight-arm bit?' she'd laughed as people around her stopped moving in their familiar loose-limbed way and started doing something like the Highland Fling or the Sailor's Hornpipe or Morris Dancing. Whatever it was, she couldn't dance to it for sure.

'Riverdance, Granny. C'mon!'

Luckily, Mr Amos had been right behind her when she started to fall, and the only casualty had been her discretion.

'Now ev'ryone know what colour you wear, Granny!' Della had called, clapping her hands.

The last time Minnie had celebrated her birthday with a party like this was at eighteen, in a church hall near a beach the year before she'd made the silliest decision of her life. No, she thought, sitting on her throne now, she couldn't say silly exactly, could she? It hadn't been a bad life here really, because if it wasn't for Gladstone there would have been no Christine, and without Christine there would have been no Della and no Frankie.

'Where *is* Frankie?' she asked Della.

'Gettin' your present, so hush yuh face!'

A wave of belonging engulfed her as she watched Della grab Tyrone and try to get him moving. Her other great-grand-children were holding hands in a circle with the two other people Frankie had brought into her life. Mrs Chanderpaul's retarded adult son lumbered around with them, oblivious of the discrepancy in age and height. She hardly knew Dan or Vienna but she liked them already, since Kezia and Sam obviously did – and anyway, they were young and they had *still* given up their entire day to help. They were falling in love, she could tell by the way their eyes locked.

'About us,' Vienna whispered to Dan as they swung round. 'About sex, I mean, or the lack of it. I'm a bit confused.'

'*You're* confused?' he laughed gently into her ear. 'I'm completely bloody lost.'

'Why?'

'Because for the first time in my entire life, I'm prepared to wait.'

'You think I'm not ready?'

'No, I think I'm not.' And with that, he picked up Sam and threw him in the air so his screams filled the hall. 'I don't want to let this one drop,' he shouted to Vienna as he clamped his hands firmly around the boy's descending form.

'Nor do I,' she shouted back.

Minnie's face wavered as she caught the splashes of excitement between the two of them and her thoughts returned to Reuben again. For something to do, she checked through the pile of coloured envelopes at the end of the table. If one of them had a Jamaican stamp – well, she would recognise his writing anyway.

Della came up waving her mobile phone. 'Chess is on her way. She jus' phoned.'

'You got a phone, do you?'

'You not still t'inkin' 'bout Reuben?'

'It's jus' a little strange . . .'

'So look, how 'bout I call him for you? We caan't have you frettin' like dis on yuh birthday!' Della started pressing buttons.

'Oh, so you know his number by heart, do you?' Her granddaughter pretended not to hear.

'You mustn't tease me like dis. You wait till you an old lady in love.'

'Who say I'm teasin'? Hello, I mus' speak wid Mr Fisher, please.'

Minnie shook her head in disapproval, but kept a small smile on her face. Now was not the time for chastisement. The girl was only trying to have some fun.

'Mr Fisher? Dis is Della George here. Hold on, I got someone who wants to speak wid you.' Della handed the phone to Minnie.

'It's cruel to tease me like dis.'

'She's not teasin' you, my sweet,' said a man's voice through the crackles.

'Reuben? Is dat you?'

'Who else calls you his sweet, eh?'

Minnie was back to her half-laugh half-cry again. Her whole life had been like that, mixed blessings all the way. 'Where you bin? I bin tryin' to reach you. Oh, no worries now, no worries now. How she call you jus' like dat? Where are you?'

'You got me jus' where you want me, as always.'

His voice was in a strange stereo. It came crackling down the line, across the seas and over the land that separated them like distant music from a far-off country. She could almost have taken the phone on to the dance-floor, and held it to her cheek while he whispered in her ear. She held the receiver close, her hands trembling with relief that, of course, he was alive and well. Then his sound came from somewhere else too, from living memory, drifting over her shoulder, surrounding her, hugging her, just as if he was in the room with her.

'Not so,' she said. 'I want you here, Reuben.'

'You do?'

'Yes, at dis party, takin' me round de floor, dancin cheek to cheek.'

'Den you got me!' He put his head around the corner of her chair. 'Happy Birthday, Mrs Fisher! An' don't be havin' a heart attack on me, 'cos you not dreamin', see?'

She couldn't speak for a long time, but she held his hand and squeezed and squeezed and squeezed as the tears rolled down her face.

'Now I know you my queen,' he whispered in her ear as he pulled her up from her throne.

An' dis a me kingdom,' she whispered back. 'Dis a me kingdom.'

And if anywhere really was her kingdom, then the Lord had surely built it there in that very hall. As she and Reuben took to the floor, she felt as if she were on a merry-go-round, catching the familiar faces in the watching crowd as she was reeled round and round.

There was Frankie, kind of laughing and kind of crying in a mix of emotions she entirely understood. If that is your genetic inheritance, then God help you, darlin'. But it's not so bad! I have Reuben and you have Nick. He was a good husband, Minnie could see, the way he was smiling, stroking her hair and wiping her cheeks.

'It worked,' he was saying to Chess. 'It was worth it, wasn't it? You pulled it off and it worked.'

He might have meant the party or he might have meant her journey there, but Chess didn't need to know. She was so, so happy.

'I'd like to think Mum and Dad were . . .' she choked, tears rolling.

'They will be,' he squeezed.

'Yeah, yeah, I think they will.'

And there was Della, hugging Tyrone around his waist, who for once was not struggling to get away.

'Dis a me boy! Dis a me boy! Give yuh mudder a kiss!'

Then Minnie saw Mercedes and her other two great-grandchildren, Kezia and Sam, the ones she had not so long ago believed would only ever exist for her in a photograph. The three of them were skidding and clapping and tugging at each other in excitement.

She looked at her man, the love of her entire adult life, and she let out a loud laugh. Reuben slid his hand down to touch the birthday card he had for her in his pocket. In the card was an open ticket to Jamaica, bought by one granddaughter with the blessing of the other. Two packed suitcases sat in the hallway of her flat. He *had* thought he was going to take her home at last, but maybe she was already home. It was something they should talk about, but there was no rush – they had the rest of their lives ahead of them.

So did they all. Chess, Della, Nick – and even, two hundred miles away, Judith and Will. Kingdoms and futures, posterity and pasts. All these things float in invisible seeds in the air above us all the time, and every now and again a grain of a truth drops and beds itself in the touch or the words of another person – the kiss of a lover, the hug of a sister, the hand of a child or the milky nibble of a baby's suck. From that seed, family trees and all their renewable and intricate branches grow, whether we want them to or not.